the ORDINARILY Extraordinary LiFE of BRIONY

PURBECK WINTOUR

This book is dedicated to Dick Teague.
The most inspirational English teacher
there ever was. Sorry it took me so long.
RIP.

MARCH

SUBJECT: FW: RE: RE: RE: NEW HOUSE

James! Pls see forwarded emails from your mother. We are up to our necks in it at the mo, but that appears to have gone over her head as per. She's YOUR mother so please DEAL WITH HER and make sure she understands it's bloody inconvenient to just 'pop over' at the moment.

Briony xx

MONDAY 9TH MARCH

SUBJECT: NEW HOUSE

Dear Margaret

Thank you for the 'New Home' card which we received today—along with a pile of mail addressed to the old householder who has not left a forwarding address (unsurprisingly, as most of the mail looked to be from bailiff and loan companies). I am sure James will let you know as soon as we are settled, and you can come over one afternoon and see the house and the boys. At the moment we are horribly busy with sorting the boxes out and getting bedrooms in a fit state to sleep in. The boys' bedrooms need to be decorated first as they have so much 'stuff' there is no point in putting it all in their rooms just to be cleared again in a few weeks to paint. Poor James has had to do something to his car as well—there was a problem with the exhaust—and so we have barely had a minute to relax. I seem to spend all my time up a ladder putting things in the loft or stripping wallpaper.

Anyway, must get back to the chaos!

Love Briony

WEDNESDAY 11TH MARCH
SUBJECT: RE: NEW HOUSE
Dear Briony

Yes, it would be lovely to come over and see the new house and the boys. I can do Wednesday afternoon next week or Sunday, whichever is more convenient to you. Are we not calling it a 'cottage' anymore? I do think 'cottage' sums up images of quaint little thatches, and yours is neither quaint nor thatched. I do hope James hasn't taken on too much financially—it's such a drain when only one member of the household is actually contributing financially, isn't it?

The glorious weather this week has seen Arthur and I

pottering about in the garden. In fact, I wondered if James might like to come over at the weekend and help Arthur take down the pine that was damaged in the storm? You could all come over for the day and the boys could help me with the weeding and planting. We always need an extra person for tea making duties, so you won't be left out, Briony.

Shall we say 1–ish on Sunday then?

Love Margaret

THURSDAY *12TH MARCH*
SUBJECT: BIRCH COTTAGE
Hi Margaret

I'm afraid next weekend would not be good for us. As I said we are in the thick of it at the moment so would be best to leave it a couple of weeks. I'm not sure if you have spoken to James yet but it's unlikely he will have the spare time to help out presently. Maybe a tree surgeon might be a better option as that pine is rather large and in frightening proximity to the summer house . . . or maybe Sarah and George could help if they are visiting from Devon soon?

Yes, the house is still called Birch Cottage. Cottages come in all shapes and sizes and it's been called that for about 200 years, which is probably how old the birch in the garden is. It was originally thatched, but as you may have noticed, many people replace their thatch with slate or tile roofs and, in my opinion, it does little to change

the character of the property when done sympathetically—also lowers the insurance premiums.

Enjoy pottering in the garden.

Love Briony

THURSDAY 12TH MARCH
SUBJECT: RE: BIRCH COTTAGE
Dear Briony

Maybe you could change its name to 'Birch House'. I
have a sneaking suspicion the laundry room and office extension are not 200 years old. I suppose the lack of thatch
will save James money in the long run.

Love Margaret

THURSDAY 12TH MARCH
SUBJECT: CHAOS AND MAYHEM?
Hi Melissa

Well, we are finally in, although far from organised. All
in all we did quite well, with the movers managing to break
just two large picture frames and a large stone plant pot.
I'm not sure the cheese plant will ever recover though, but
that could be more to do with my emptying out the bathroom cleaner bottle into the pot during a panic attack on
moving day.

James couldn't work out how to light the ancient range
cooker, so the frozen fish pie I'd packed for moving day

supper stayed that way. Thankfully, it would appear that although we may have changed postcodes, we're still in the delivery zone for pizza—albeit barely warm and slightly soggy pizza. After getting the over excited boys to bed (on air mattresses as their beds have not yet been re assembled since 'someone' lost the screws) the gods looked down kindly upon us and sent our new neighbour around with a bottle of rather nice Merlot! Turns out Cosmo Jones, who owns the cottage to the left of us, is in the wine business (hallelujah!) and thought we could probably do with a drink after the stressful day we'd had (must have heard us hissing and swearing at each other over the garden wall—eek!) Seems like a pretty nice guy actually, with the added bonus of a plentiful supply of good quality wine at his disposal.

So anyway, now begins the real hard work—organising builders, fending off the in-laws, getting the kitchen done, fending off the in-laws, finding out which supermarkets deliver to this area, fending off the in-laws . . .

How are things with you? Still in lust? Or has it gone all serious and moved onto 'lurve'?

Love Bri x

TEXT MESSAGE RECEIVED SATURDAY 14TH MARCH 9.43AM
Arthur and I at John Lewis so thought might pop over to see new house and have spot of lunch since we are passing. See you 1–ish? Margaret x

Margaret, I'm sorry, we're terribly busy—did James not phone you?—another time maybe x

SUNDAY 15TH MARCH (9.52PM)
SUBJECT: HOME SAFELY?
Dear Briony

Just a quick one to let you know we arrived home safely. It was lovely to see you all at Birch House yesterday. The area is indeed much quieter, and that charming new neighbour is certainly of a higher calibre than you are used to. Do thank him again for the delicious Pinot Noir he sent us home with—so terribly generous of him. Anyway, I'm sure you all enjoyed the excuse of a break from decorating and sorting all those boxes out—and didn't time fly? Isn't it fortunate that you have a Waitrose so close by so you could go off and get things for lunch for us all? And supper. You know how Arthur gets if he misses a meal and by that time it would have been far too late had we driven home for supper.

I don't recall what day James said he could come over to help with the tree? I suppose it would be better if it were Saturday then he can always come back on Sunday if there is a lot of clearing up to do. These mature pines do tend to take a lot of work, but at least we shall have plenty of firewood for next winter once James has chopped it all up.

Sarah, George and the children are off skiing again at the end of this week so I've said I will go down and help with

6

the children for a couple of days from Tuesday as Sarah has a bit of a cold and doesn't want to wear herself out before the holiday. I'll leave early in the morning as I can often make the journey in less than four hours without traffic.

Apologies for not being able to baby-sit for you on the 26th but I don't like to miss my senior ladies line dancing class and by the time I have travelled back from Devon to Dorset on Thursday I am going to be too late for that session so can't miss another in the same month—got to keep trim, Briony! I had intended upon leaving Sarah's by lunchtime but she wants to go shopping for last minute holiday clothes with a friend in Exeter that day so I won't be leaving until late afternoon now.

Bye for now
Margaret x

MONDAY 16TH MARCH
SUBJECT: RE: HOME SAFELY? (DRAFT)
Hi Margaret

So glad you managed to drive the 30 minutes home safely and without incident on Saturday evening. Yes, wasn't it lucky about the 'local' Waitrose? We had just planned to eat the pizza and leftovers I had in the fridge that weekend so as we could crack on with the house, but, of course, it's always nice to make unnecessary trips to a supermarket 10 miles away on a busy Saturday for food we would never normally eat. What a shame Arthur doesn't eat anything 'continental,' although, I have to say I don't really think of pizza as an exotic foreign delicacy. I'm sure we will find some use for the extra tins of corned beef you insisted I buy—maybe put them away as emergency rations in case of an apocalypse or something. Also a shame that Arthur didn't want it for supper as well, as then I would not have had to go to Waitrose again in the torrential rain for more 'non continental' food, and, as I had pointed out to you, although you do seem to forget, the boys would not eat corned beef as we are vegetarian and even though, admittedly, tinned corned beef resembles no meat known to mankind, at the end of the day, corned beef is meat and there was no fooling them, or I, of that fact.

I am sure we will find someone else to baby-sit on the 26th. After all, you are right not to want to miss your senior line dancing class, and driving 21 miles to baby-sit for us would be far too much to ask just a week after you have done an 8 hour 300 mile trip down to Devon and back to look after snotty Sarah's insufferable children whilst she shops with friends. Whatever was I thinking of?! Oh yes, that's right! You had offered to baby-sit for us after we told you the reason we didn't go out much as a couple was because paying a babysitter, even if you could find a trusted one that was available, was often more expensive than the night out itself. But, never mind. We shall just do as we had said we couldn't afford to do in the first place, and pay a babysitter £10 an hour plus taxi fare home.

On a more positive note, it would seem Sarah's cold is

not too bad if she is planning a shopping trip for Thursday. Heaven forbid she has a runny nose on the slopes of Val d'Isere!

Unfortunately, as stated on numerous occasions now but for reasons you are just not quite comprehending, James is unable to spend a whole weekend helping you chop up an old tree, and although it may be hard to believe, I have better things to do than spend a weekend making you and Arthur bloody tea—after all I may bring the wrong type of biscuit or heaven forbid some continental delicacy such as pain au chocolate! If you really need so much help with the garden maybe it's time to pay a gardener or even consider a move to a house with slightly less acreage than your current abode.

Fondest regards from your dearest, although not altogether most obedient daughter in law,

Briony x

MONDAY 16TH MARCH
SUBJECT: RE: HOME SAFELY! (SENT)
Dear Margaret

It was indeed lovely to see Arthur and yourself at the weekend. Unfortunately, James will be unable to come over to help with the garden this weekend as we have to finish the decorating of the boys' rooms that we were unable to complete during your lovely surprise visit on Saturday.

Do pass on my best regards to Sarah and the family and

let's hope she gets over that cold before they fly out to France.

Briony

P.S. It's staying as Birch Cottage, regardless of slate roof and 20th century extensions.

TUESDAY 17TH MARCH
SUBJECT: SNOW BOOTS-URGENT
Hi Briony

As mum may have told you, we are off skiing on Friday and I have just discovered Barnaby has outgrown his snow boots. Could you post me Zac's as I am sure you won't need them in the next two weeks and I don't want to buy new as he will have probably grown out of those by next year. I tried to call you but no one answered? Is your line working? Best to send them Next Day or Special Delivery so as we get them in time to pack. Actually, might be a good idea for you to include Zac's snow jacket and salopettes as well—just so as I have spares.

Thanks
Sarah x

P.S. Mum emailed pics of the cottage. Lovely. Is it classed as a proper cottage without thatch though?

WEDNESDAY 18TH MARCH
SUBJECT: RE: SNOW BOOTS—URGENT
Hi Sarah

The boys' skiing gear is packed in a box somewhere—probably in the loft with all the other 'misc' boxes or possibly lost in storage. We are up to our eyes in boxes and decorating at the moment so not really able to rifle through all the boxes to find those items in time for you. Sorry.

Briony

P.S. Yes, Sarah. It is a proper cottage.

THURSDAY 19TH MARCH
SUBJECT: RE: SNOW BOOTS—URGENT
Hi Briony

Bugger. Didn't think to check my email yesterday and assumed I would be getting a parcel today. Okay. Can you send direct to the ski chalet? I think Airsure would get them there in 48 hours?

Thanks
Sarah

FRIDAY 20TH MARCH
SUBJECT: RE: SNOW BOOTS—URGENT
Hi Sarah

Sorry, but as I said, I have no idea where they are and am not able to go through all 30 boxes of miscellaneous stuff stacked in the loft and garage. In fact, I think I may have eBayed them knowing the boys would have outgrown them before our next ski trip. Surely you can get something in the town when you get there?

Have a nice holiday.

Briony

VOICEMAIL MESSAGE RECEIVED SUNDAY 11.35AM

"Hello, Briony? Are you there? Can you hear me?

It's Margaret . . .

I've just had a call from Sarah about the skiing stuff you promised to send. She hasn't received it yet and wants to know that you definitely sent it Priority Airsure 48 or something like that? She's rather concerned as Barnaby hasn't been able to go skiing yet and has spent two days in the kids club so isn't very happy . . . as you can imagine . . .

So anyway, she has internet access and says could you email her the tracking number so as she can follow it up.

Anyway . . . speak to you soon. Love to the boys.'

Sunday 22nd March
SUBJECT: RE: SNOW BOOTS—URGENT (SENT)
Hi Sarah

I had a voicemail message from your mother. I did reply to your email saying I was unable to send the ski stuff. Am sure you can get what you need there.

Have fun.

Briony

VOICEMAIL MESSAGE RECEIVED SUNDAY 22ND MARCH

'Mummy, it's Sarah. Got an email from Briony saying she hasn't even sent the skiing stuff she promised! Apparently she sent me an email saying she was too busy or something before we left. Now I have to miss the slopes tomorrow morning to take a trip into the town to buy Barnaby everything he needs. I'm rather annoyed to be honest as I gave her plenty of time to find the clothes and options to send the stuff straight here so it's not like I asked her to do it the same day.

Anyway, other than that we are all having a super time—apart from poor Barnaby of course who has not been happy to go to the kids club instead of joining his sister with the children's ski school.

So, don't worry too much about us . . . Oh! Has James felled that tree yet? If so, can he put aside some logs for us? Make sure he chops them up enough so they can go straight in the wood shed and you can bring as many down with you as you can fit in the boot when you next visit. Bye for now.'

WEDNESDAY 25TH MARCH
SUBJECT: HELLO

Dear James

I hope this finds you well and getting more settled into your new home. By all accounts it appears you have all been terribly overwhelmed with the move. As you may be aware, Briony was apparently unable to send Sarah a few items by post that she needed rather urgently for her holiday—but it's all sorted now. Unfortunately, they do rather bump prices up in these ski resorts so it has cost Sarah a small fortune to get the items Briony didn't send. Such a shame to have to spend money unnecessarily. But anyhow, as I said, it's all sorted now, so don't worry Briony too much about it all.

I was wondering when you would be free to come and help us fell this wretched pine that's threatening to take out the summer house at the next slightest breeze. Sarah wants some of the wood from it, so we need it all chopped and ready to go for them. Might you be passing their way anytime soon? I'm sure you could fit more logs in the boot of your car than I, so might be a thought? Maybe you could borrow a trailer from someone?

Dad decided you needed a better house sign as it's far too easy to miss along that overgrown frontage of yours, so he had a fantastic idea and has made you a 'Birch House' sign out of some things he had lying around the garage. It's terribly charming and quaint and I know Briony will love it. You can collect it when you come to chop the pine down if we don't pop over first.

Love to all
Mum x

P.S. Please do pass our thanks to your charming new neighbour, Cosmo, for the Pinot Noir which Arthur and I thoroughly enjoyed with our roast chicken, last night.

TEXT MESSAGE RECEIVED 9.32AM

Where WERE you this morn Bri?! Virginia Coldstone aka The Cold Virgin is after cakes and volunteers for cake stall this Fri—you have been warned!—*Lucy x*

TEXT MESSAGE SENT 9.35AM

LOL at Cold Virgin! Bugger. Don't have time to bake and still getting to grips with this ancient cooker! Maybe I'll give her some M&S brownies sprinkled with cocoa to look home baked?!

WEDNESDAY 25TH MARCH
WHATSAPP MESSAGE

MELISSA: Hey Bri. Sounds like the move hasn't jaded you too much. Have the out-laws descended on you yet? Be thankful you only have one set to fend off—your parents must have been in France over a year now? Any plans to visit them? I jest, of course!

BRIONY: Yeah, parents have been in France just about a year and thankfully due to their complete technophobia we're limited to occasional phone calls and letters—and that does me just fine!

MELISSA: Bet James hates this charming neighbour of yours.

BRIONY: Yeah, course he does! Cosmo brought over a couple of bottles of Shiraz Friday evening when James was still busy, but I felt it would be rude not to, so I shared a

15

bottle with him whilst James banged and huffed about.

MELISSA: What was James busy with on a Fri night?! Is work still hectic for him? He's lucky the company is doing so well, all things considered, although tough on you not having him around as much.

BRIONY: I don't know, he's such a grump it's a better atmosphere when he's not around. When he is here he's preoccupied in the study. I'm gagging for a shag but no chance of that with Mr Workaholic so last night I decided to console myself with a plate of brownies and watching repeats of Most Haunted on my laptop in bed. Well, no one will want to shag me anyway once the fat content of that hits my thighs.

MELISSA: Christ, Bri that really is shit.

BRIONY: Tell me about it. I'm so sexually frustrated I'm eyeing up the surfers when power walking along the beach in a most unsavoury way.

MELISSA: No, I meant watching Most Haunted.

BRIONY: 😶

MONDAY 30TH MARCH
SUBJECT: HELLO
Dear Briony

Doesn't time fly! I can't believe you have been in your new house for almost a month already. How is everything coming along?

I have been thinking about Sarah's 40th in July. I thought it would be nice for me to arrange a surprise party for her and invite all the family and friends. As her birthday falls on a Saturday this year it makes it so much easier—so pencil in 18th July as I am going to book a cottage for us all just outside the village so we can all be there without her knowing and getting suspicious! I have asked George to invite all the village people and I will sort the family out. I thought we could have a celebration barbecue starting at lunchtime. Any ideas to make it extra special would be much appreciated, so, thinking cap on, Briony!

I spoke to James last week and he said you have men in to do the kitchen, making it so much easier for you all. It's a shame James is still too busy to help his father with the pine tree so we've had to enrol the help of Richard from up the road—at number 52—so hopefully it will all be sorted soon.

Love Margaret x

P.S. Did James mention if he'd thanked that charming neighbour of yours for the wine? Arthur and I enjoyed it so much we were thinking of ordering a case.

PPS—Did you get the lovely rustic house sign Arthur made for you? He was terribly proud having used bits and pieces from around the garage, and we very much look forward to seeing it outside the house when we next visit.

SUBJECT: RE: HELLO

Dear Margaret

I didn't actually realise Sarah was 40 this year. I thought that was last year as she threw that big party for herself? In fact, did she not throw a big party for herself the year before that also? If memory serves me well, she does appear to throw big parties for herself every year, however, I'll give it some thought when I have five mins but to be honest I can't think of anything that would top having the Village People attend your party. Will they be doing the old classics, YMCA and In The Navy?

I did thank our neighbour, Cosmo, on your behalf, but as his company imports and sells wine to top restaurants and hotels, as opposed to flogging a few knock-off bottles on eBay, I don't think he takes orders himself. Neither is it exclusive to him, so I'm sure you could pick up a few bottles at the supermarket next time you are there?

Love Briony

P.S. Isn't Richard from number 52 in a wheelchair?
P.P.S—Yes, we did indeed receive the 'rustic' house sign. So glad Arthur's error of originally engraving 'Bitch House' didn't cause him to abandon the project and start anew, and although I'm sure no one would notice his error of the 't' crossed out with permanent marker and arrow pointing to 'r' above it, the house is, as previously discussed, a cottage and not a house. The post office has it listed as

'Birch Cottage' so we really can't go changing it to 'house' and neither do we want to. We also rather like the grey Welsh slate sign we already have, and although a sign made from the varnished fibreboard of an old drawer bottom and innovatively 'engraved' using a blunt knife and tippex is certainly unique, we feel it is not really in keeping with the rest of the house. But thanks anyway.

APRIL

THURSDAY 2ND APRIL

SUBJECT: RE: HELLO

Dear Briony

No, Sarah is definitely 40 this year—although, I confess I had a senior moment and had to check after reading your email. The party she had last year was for her 39th. She does enjoy having parties so we shall have to make this party one to remember!

Now, do you think we should bring the caterers in or can we manage ourselves? I shall have to ask George how many of the village people will be coming nearer the time. I'm not sure I am familiar with the songs you mentioned but I think some of them sang carols in the village pantomime last Christmas. Do you really think we should ask them to sing?

What house number is your charming neighbour or does he also go by house name? I wanted to pop a thank you card in the post. Arthur looked for the wine in the supermarket but couldn't find it. Maybe I shall pop over for a quick chat with him next time I'm over seeing you all?

Yes, Richard from number 52 does still use a wheel-chair. He never did regain full use of his knees again after the pirate incident, but Arthur thinks that shouldn't be too much of a problem and Richard has always insisted he is not an invalid and doesn't like to be treated differently, so it will be good for him.

As I write, Arthur is busy beavering away making you a new house sign. He does like to keep busy, and, I like him to keep busy. He'd just be under my feet all day if he weren't busy and we couldn't have that, could we Briony.

Love Margaret x

P.S. I've popped a card in the post for James' birthday so if it arrives early please put it aside until the day. There's a £20 DIY gift voucher inside so he can treat himself to something really nice.

THURSDAY 2ND APRIL
WHATSAPP MESSAGE

KATE: Hey Bri! Guess who won the PR account for Sexy-HoneyLove?! Moi, of course! What a bonus! Terribly excit-ed—and not just for the obvious reasons. Of course, it goes without saying I shall be passing on my good fortune to my closest friends, so expect a parcel of goodies to land on your doorstep anytime soon . . . and tell James, his pleasure is all my pleasure. Err, eugh, no, that doesn't sound right.

But you know what I mean.

BRIONY: Wow, that's great. However, it has to be said I am more than just a little anxious at what exactly is going to be arriving on my doorstep?!? I'm not sure Little Mistford's postman is ready for vibrating packages on his rounds—and please tell me it's all 'discreetly packaged'?!? Anyway, James is rather distracted with work at the mo, so I might be SexyHoneyLoving by myself . . .

KATE: Oh, he won't be able to resist what I'm sending you 😊

SATURDAY 4TH APRIL
SUBJECT: RE: HELLO

Dear Margaret

I was joking about the Village People. I didn't mean the villagers, I meant, the Village People . . . oh, it doesn't matter.

Do you not think that as Sarah arranges her own party every year she might cotton on to the fact something is amiss if she is not allowed to do so this year? Especially as it's the big 4-0? Although I would never in a million years suggest she has control issues, she does tend to like to take control of these things . . . birthday things . . . well, all things actually, so maybe a strategy is needed? Anyway, you still have three to four months to think about it, so I don't think there is any hurry.

I'm sure our 'charming neighbour' who we like to call by his given name, Cosmo, doesn't expect a thank you card for a bottle of wine but, if you insist, it's 'Willow Cottage'. I shall mention it to him next time I see him and find out which retailers sell the wine you have become so fond of. It must be quite a vintage as I thought you were virtually teetotal other than the occasional medicinal g&t?

I have to say I'm a bit concerned about this tree business. Isn't there a tree surgeon that lives just outside the village who took down that horse chestnut for your neighbours last year after Richard's pirate incident? I'm really not sure enrolling his help is a good idea no matter how eager he is. Invalid or not, he is considerably limited in his mobility, Margaret.

Briony

SATURDAY 4TH APRIL
WHATSAPP MESSAGE

BRIONY: I've had James' mother on at me about his sister's 40th in July. JULY! I have a house that looks like a tornado has hit it and only half a kitchen and she is asking me if 'we' should get caterers in or can 'we' manage all the food 'ourselves'?! This is a woman who considers supermarket bought flans nouvelle cuisine and once decided to teach me how to make gravy . . . by the dark art of adding gravy granules to a jug of boiling water! And she even messed that up. She intends to rent a cottage near Sarah's village for ALL of us *gulp* and this is the day after school breaks up! Sarah arranges a huge party for herself every year regardless, so I don't see why she can't leave her to do that and just invite family to come along as well. Oh, Christ. She will want ideas for some elaborate present that will mean us going without a holiday this year to pay for it!

MELISSA: Why doesn't James deal with her? It's always left to you.

BRIONY: Because he's a man, Melissa. Talking of which. How's Dan? Did you discover him in bed with another man? I did warn you the chances of him being a handbag designer and straight were virtually non-existent . . .

MELISSA: He's not a handbag designer, Briony.

BRIONY: But he is gay . . . ? I knew it. It's usually just the Greeks that try and do that to you on a first date.

MELISSA: No, he is not gay! And he designs all types of bags—not just handbags. And what experience have you had with Greeks, anyway?

BRIONY: I spent some time in Greece after Uni olive picking in the Peloponnese, remember? Let's just say it was a summer of discovery in more ways than one, and we will not allude to this fact in front of James. Ever.

MELISSA: Ahh so this is why the Peloponnese is otherwise referred to as the PurplePenis

BRIONY: 😃

SATURDAY 4TH APRIL
SUBJECT: SPUNKYLOVEJUICE
Hi Kate

Got your text re: SpunkyLoveJuice—what fab news!

24

Had a quick look at their website and was suitably . . . err . . . well gobsmacked, really. Those 'love eggs' looked . . . interesting? And the sweetie love rings—do they go on what I think they go on? You'd get more than you bargained for if you chomped down on those—like a trip to A&E to re-attach a sugar coated cock! And the hard core stuff—OMG the hard core stuff. Seriously, who wants a Donald Trump butt plug?! Hmm, probably Donald Trump, actually.

Have you spoken to Bri lately? She's a bit down—has she said anything to you? She's not getting any, and you know how she gets when she's not getting any. Send her a sweetie cock ring. If she still doesn't get any she can at least eat it.

Speak soon
Melissa x

MONDAY 6TH APRIL
SUBJECT: RE: SPUNKYLOVEJUICE
It's SexyHoneyLove! SpunkyLoveJuice is for fetishists, darling, and anyway, don't pretend that's the first time you've looked at that website—remember I saw the fluffy handcuffs on your bed that time . . .

Yeah, great client, but I'm rushed off my feet. Spoke to Bri at the weekend, albeit briefly as she was walking on some cliff top with the boys and the signal kept going. From what I gather, James is just really preoccupied with work so she's feeling a bit neglected aka not getting any, so you're right. By the sounds of it she's been spending the evenings sampling the contents of her neighbour's wine cellar which can't be all bad. I said I'd bung some Sexy-HoneyLove goodies in the post for her to tempt him with. Think a David Cameron butt plug is more James' style . . . if he were into that . . . which I don't think he is . . . eww, now I have images in my head I cannot unsee . . . Eeewwwwwww!

How's you anyway? We must catch up for a drink and chat soon. Are you free any eve this week?

Kate x

PS—parcel headed your way. You're welcome

MONDAY 6TH APRIL
SUBJECT: PARTY
Dear Briony

I've been giving Sarah's surprise party some more thought. What do you think about a circus act performing on the day? Well, I say circus act; they are really more an acrobatics act that dress up like circus acts and perform at functions in their large marquee. I think Sarah and George's garden would be more than big enough for the llamas and trapeze. It's just a question of whether they could get their lorry to the village—those roads are terribly narrow and overgrown in parts and a blockage could have frightful ramifications for the whole village.

You're right about some of the village people not being

villagers. Some were not born in the parish and for some their village home is not their main home, but, will people think ostracising them from Sarah's party a tad harsh, Briony?

Unfortunately, Jonty (the tree surgeon you mentioned) left the village last summer after he was found 'planting his potatoes in another man's patch,' if you get my meaning. Dreadful business. Anyway, Richard is very eager, so we just await a few days of fair weather as the lawn is a little too soft for his wheelchair at the moment and we don't want him getting stuck and causing problems for Arthur's back. Plus we've spent a lot of money on that lawn and wheelchair tyre marks would ruin it.

Hope all is going well with the house. We must have a day out with you and the boys soon. Easter hols would suit.

Love Margaret x

THURSDAY 9TH APRIL
SUBJECT: EASTER HOLIDAYS
Margaret, I'm really not sure about the performing clowns. Although, I can't quite put into words why . . .

Briony

P.S
Easter hols— Fri 24th is good for us.
PPS—Planting his potatoes in another man's patch?? So Jonty the tree surgeon was gay? Surely that's no reason to

banish him from the village in this day and age?! Homo-
sexuality isn't illegal anymore you know. I hear some even
hold down jobs, vote, and shop in John Lewis. People born
outside the parish and calling themselves villagers however
is another matter entirely . . .

SATURDAY 11TH APRIL
SUBJECT: MY 40TH!
Hi Briony

Just a quick one to let you know to keep the weekend of
the 18th July free as I'm just throwing some ideas around
for my 40th birthday celebrations! 40! Can you even believe that I will be 40?! I think it will come as quite a shock
to the village ladies and the PTA who always compliment
me on my rested complexion.

Now don't fret about my present. I've decided to make
it easy for everyone and will do a list from Liberty or Har-
rods so as you can order online and get it sent direct to me.
Clever, huh?

Love Sarah

P.S. You'll be pleased to hear Barnaby has finally forgiven
you for the ski gear problems. Bless him. He's such a sweet
child.

SUBJECT: SARAH

Dear Margaret

Please find attached an email I received from Sarah yesterday.

I really don't think she can be outwitted on the party front. Maybe compromise and join forces . . . ?

Briony

WHATSAPP GROUP MESSAGE

BRIONY: Losing the will to live arghhhhhhhhh!!!!!!!!!!!!!!

MELISSA: You always get tetchy like this when you're not getting any.

KATE: Didn't my parcel of samples arrive yet? Fuck. What's your address again?

BRIONY: It's not that. Well, it's not *just* that although *that* is certainly not helping.

KATE: Ahh the out-laws.

BRIONY: Now I have James' mother and sister emailing me about Sarah's birthday. I'm not sure I can deal with this for the next three months. I wonder if so much effort will be put into my 40th birthday?!? I doubt it somehow—probably just end up with another acrylic polo neck ('you need to keep your chest warm, Briony and I thought this was just the thing!') and a fake silver necklace that leaves a green mark all around my neck, making it look like I don't wash.

MELISSA: You should have moved farther away from them.

BRIONY: Well, funnily enough, I was collecting the drowned, drunk slugs from yoghurt pots full of continental lager on Saturday

KATE: You've got so posh you even kill your slugs with posh beer . . .

BRIONY: It was all we had. I couldn't be arsed to find a supermarket selling the cheap stuff. Don't tell James.

MELISSA: Do they die of alcohol poisoning first or just drown before they've drunk it?

BRIONY: ANYWAY, I'm in the garden and whose not-so-dulcet tones came wafting over the garden wall? Only Margaret's! The woman can't drive 30 mins to baby-sit once a bloody year, but turns up out of the blue to hand deliver a thank you card to my neighbour for the bottle of wine he gave her and Arthur weeks ago! I swear she has a 'thing' for him—what with all the gushing and arm patting and, 'Oh really, Cosmo, do call me Margaret; "Mrs Denley" makes me sound so senior.' Titter titter. Err, well, you are senior to him, Margaret! He's young enough to be your son. It's really quite obscene, Melissa. Thank goodness James wasn't here to witness his mother making a complete fool of herself. Of course, Cosmo was charming and heroically tolerant of her, but that's his way. He's heroically tolerant of James and his snarky remarks as well. He's going to think I married into a family of loons. Oh, it made me shudder, although maybe I shouldn't complain. In fact, it almost brightens the mundaneness of everyday life.

KATE: Let's plan a trip! Crazy weekend away. When was the last time you did something really daring and exciting?

BRIONY: Well, this morning I threw caution to the wind and put two sachets of laundry GloWhite in with the 400 thread count Egyptian bedding when they strictly recommend just one 😄

KATE: You're such a rebel.

BRIONY: I may think about doing some charity work—helping an old person, or even getting a proper little job.

MELISSA: It won't be the first time someone has signed up to Help the Aged to keep their mind off sex, I'm sure.

BRIONY: I'm serious.

KATE: That's what's worrying me. You're not good with old people, Briony. You don't have any patience and you have an uncannily heightened sense of smell.

BRIONY: Well, a job then. The boys don't need me as much and I never wanted to be one of those women who give up a successful career to raise kids, and then once they are more independent ends up getting a puppy as a substitute baby and pouring herself a large wine with a vodka chaser just to get her through an afternoon of daytime TV. I've seen those shows and believe me, if ever my life became so empty I found myself calling the studio every day in the misguided belief anyone there actually cared for my opinion on Katie Price's latest baby's name then the next step would be shoving my head in the oven and knowing my luck it would be an electric fan-assisted so I'd just end up with a very slow, bad blow dry.

31

KATE: Would you go back into PR?

MELISSA: *Could* she go back into PR?!

BRIONY: Have I been blackballed?

KATE: Possibly . . .

MELISSA: Meaning, quite probably . . . 😕

KATE: 😃

BRIONY: So, Melissa, does Dan make rucksacks and those holdalls on wheels as well then?

MELISSA: No. Just posh day bags really. Quite exclusive ones. You know, to put your keys, purse, phone and lipgloss in.

BRIONY: So that's handbags then.

MELISSA: Shut up.

KATE: Were you feeling a bit jealous of Margaret getting Cosmo's attention?

BRIONY: What? No! What an odd thing to say! Why would you say that?!

KATE: Christ, you're tetchy. Sod James and go and give yourself a little 'treat.' After all, it's what the suffragettes fought for.

MELISSA: Kate, I'm pretty confident Emmeline Pankhurst didn't go on hunger strike just to give women the right to wank . . .

BRIONY HAS LEFT THE GROUP.

KATE: Hahahahahahaha

MELISSA: Oh . . .

SUBJECT: RE: SARAH

Dear Briony

Arthur and I went away for a couple of days so I had no idea of Sarah's murmurings about a party! I phoned George as soon as I got your email and he has assured me he will do everything to put her off the scent. Isn't it exciting? Just like an undercover operation! George has suggested that we let her think she is organising her own party when in fact we are doing it all!

As I said, Arthur and I went away to visit our old friends Celia and John in Norfolk. You remember Celia and John from my 60th? Celia got tipsy on Tia Maria and was dancing with the neighbour's teenage son in the garden. Anyway, we decided to get the train which turned out to be an almighty mistake. No direct line from here, so we ended up going via Coventry with a two hour wait for the connection. I'm sure that's not right, you know Briony, there must be a more direct route? But it was lovely to catch up with Celia and John. I have to say, I think dear Celia is having a bit of a late mid-life crisis. When we arrived the weather was so lovely and Arthur and I were in dire need of fresh air after so long on the trains that Celia suggested we have drinks in the garden. My goodness! You should have seen the variety of undergarments on the washing line! Now, I may be drawing my pension but I'm young enough to know that tasselled corsets are not the underwear of choice for our generation. Especially not with all those sequins and glitter—a nightmare to iron, I'm sure. Well, it pepped Arthur up no end. He had certainly been wilting after seven hours of travel but, seeing Celia's suspender belts blowing in the breeze put a smile back on his face. I can't tell you how flustered Celia and John were!

So sorry I didn't have time to stop at the weekend. I was just passing when I remembered I had that 'Thank You' for Cosmo in my bag. I never have a book of stamps on me, and cards and letters tend to get lost at the bottom of my bag, so very glad he was in when I called. Thank goodness for email otherwise I would never get to communicate with you, Briony, as you never answer your phone. Do you think there is problem with the line? Maybe look at getting it sorted, then we can have a lovely long chatter just as Sarah and I enjoy.

Briony—did I mention the fire jugglers? A smaller troupe than the acrobats and they just travel in a small van, so Devon country roads shouldn't be a problem for them. Do give me your thoughts.

Love to all
Margaret x

PS—No, Jonty isn't a homosexual. When I said he was 'planting his potatoes in another man's patch' I was trying to be delicate. The other man's 'patch,' as so to speak, was his wife.

PPS—Does Cosmo have an email address, would you know . . . ?

WEDNESDAY 15TH APRIL
SUBJECT: RE: SARAH
Dear Margaret

Are you sure it wouldn't just be easier to let Sarah arrange her own party? You could just organise something as a surprise for the day—like the fire jugglers—or maybe just a cake? Seems like a much simpler option.

Glad you had fun at your friends. The image of Celia dressed in tasselled basques and suspenders is something that shall now be imprinted on my mind forever more. Thank you.

So Jonty was having an affair with a married woman and helping her with her vegetable patch?

Yes, I am sure Cosmo has an email address but I really wouldn't know what it is . . . is there something else you need to thank him for already? And yes, what luck for email!

Briony

THURSDAY 16TH APRIL
SUBJECT: RE: MY 40TH?
Dear Sarah

Gosh. Doesn't time fly! The past year has positively flown by. You will be emailing me about your 50th before you know it! Of course we will pencil the 18th July in but there is the smallest possibility we will be flying off to Greece that weekend—got to grab the bargain flights when you can—but I'll keep you posted.

I have to say you seem to be taking your approaching 50th in your stride and good on you! No point in wallowing in self-pity along with the increasing wrinkle count and loss of elasticity in the vital areas. It's great to embrace middle age with open arms; and I hope that is what I do when I am your age.

So glad Barnaby has found it in himself to forgive me. We just need me to forgive him now for trying to drown Zac last summer. I jest, of course.

Good luck with the party plans.

Love Briony

Thursday 16th April
SUBJECT: RE: MY 40TH!
Oops! Didn't check that before I hit send. Obviously a Freudian slip with the 50th/40th.

Briony x

Friday 17th April
SUBJECT: RE: MY 40TH!
Dear Briony

I must insist you fly out to Greece after my party! It simply would not be the same without you, James and the boys. Besides, Barnaby and Ella are so looking forward to seeing their cousins. I know you were terribly upset about the swimming pool incident, but I assure you Barnaby didn't mean to hurt Zac last summer. He just misjudged the jump and yes, I admit it was unfortunate he landed on Zac's head but it was an accident nonetheless.

Will try and call you sometime soon. It's been an age since I spoke to you and that not so little brother of mine!

Love Sarah x

SUNDAY 19TH APRIL
WHATSAPP GROUP MESSAGE

BRIONY: Melissa—What do you wear in bed?

MELISSA: I'm sorry, but I refuse to give you fodder for your spank bank.

KATE: Are you into fantasising about women now then, Briony? It's very common. You'd be surprised how many hetero women get off on lesbian porn but have no desire to actually indulge themselves. I have to confess, the lesbian section of PornTube is my go-to of choice, and I've never been with a woman and don't really desire to

BRIONY: Err, no, Kate. I was asking as I can't sleep wearing anything in bed and James keeps telling me I'll have to nip that one in the bud as soon as the boys start puberty.

MELISSA: Really?!?

BRIONY: Oedipus syndrome and all that.

MELISSA: No, I meant, REALLY, Kate?!?

KATE: Err *blush*

BRIONY: You mean you've never accidently been sent

links to Kate's porn clips of choice?

MELISSA:?

BRIONY: Why do they even have a 'share link' button on those sites anyway?

KATE: It happened once, Briony. I dropped my phone and it accidently shared the link to the last person I'd text.

MELISSA: Imagine if you'd shared to FB. Comedy gold.

BRIONY: Anyway, the reason I asked is that I've recently been nursing a penchant to buy a long white cotton Victorianesque 'nightie'. Not worn a 'nightie' past puberty and the word makes me shudder even more than 'gusset' or 'seatee'. Hmm . . . Radio Four and long white nighties; is this the beginning of the end?

MELISSA: The beginning of an early menopause more like.

KATE: Look on the positive side—at least you yearn for long white cotton nighties and not those god awful poly-cotton nightshirts emblazoned with Disney characters some women seem to favour.

BRIONY: And I'm only 37 which is far too young for the menopause. Isn't it??

MELISSA: How moist are you these days anyway? Drying up down below is a sure sign changes are imminent. Along with the mood swings and hot flushes, of course.

KATE: She's got the mood swings covered.

BRIONY: Thanks, Melissa, but I am very moist. Of that I can assure you. And I don't have mood swings, Kate, it's part of my dynamic personality.

KATE: You're about as stable as nitro-glycerine.

BRIONY: Are a dry foof and hot flushes all I have to look forward to for the next 10 years?! Shit. Wonder if I can get a good deal on job lots of Replens from eBay?

MELISSA: Please tell me you don't really call it a 'foof'?! In my line of work I've heard it called a lot of things, but 'foof'?!

KATE: Does James call it a foof? Christ. Actually, don't answer that. That's a whole window into your life I really don't want to know about.

THURSDAY 23RD APRIL
SUBJECT: FRIDAY
Hi Margaret

Got your voicemail. Just to confirm that 10.30am tomorrow is fine. It makes more sense for the boys and I to meet you there if that's okay—saves you going out of your way to come here first, and I believe Cosmo is away on business in London, so you wouldn't be able to introduce Celia to him anyway, as you suggested.

Of course I don't mind Celia joining us. As you said on the phone yesterday, it will keep her mind off things. Probably best she doesn't talk about it in front of the boys though, as although I personally don't have an issue with cross-dressing, it could be a confusing issue for the boys to take in—especially in her, . . . I imagine, 'emotional' state. It's nice that she has a friend like you to confide in—although, as you said yesterday, it has come as a shock to you and I can understand not being able to look at her husband,

John, in the same way. No wonder John looked so flustered when you saw the stuff on the washing line—although, as you said, the last thing you would have expected was that it was John who was wearing the tasselled basques. Does Celia dress up as well or have you not gone into that much detail? I would have thought that as she has supported his 'quirk,' as you put it, all these years, she can't find it that upsetting—so maybe there is more to her suddenly turning up to stay with you than she is letting on?

Anyway, the boys are looking forward to the castle visit tomorrow, so see you at the gates.

Briony

Thursday 23rd April
WHATSAPP MESSAGE
BRIONY: Gayle, I'm a bit worried about Cliff Richard. He hurt his foot a few days ago which I thought would heal on its own but it appears he has now chewed his toes off—which as you can imagine is a bit distressing for all concerned (!) Any advice?

GAYLE: Have you been reading the Daily Mail online again, Briony? I'm pretty sure a man of Cliff's age wouldn't be supple enough to chew his own toes off.

BRIONY: The hamster, Gayle. Cliff Richard is the hamster's name—remember?!

GAYLE: Why can't you give a hamster a normal name like Hammy or Fluffy?

BRIONY: It amuses me to hear James complain, 'Bloody Cliff Richard has kicked all his shit onto my laptop again.'

GAYLE: Hmm. How did he hurt his foot? Was it roller skating to 'Wired for Sound'? Arf arf 😉 I'll pop over on my way home from work later and take a look anyway. Did you power walk today? How is your blister?

BRIONY: Blister not healing at all so I didn't power walk today. However, rest assured I have no intention of chewing my own foot off . . .

SATURDAY 25TH APRIL
SUBJECT: PHONE
Hi Melissa

Sorry I couldn't talk for long yesterday. The boys and I were on a day trip with James' mother and her friend, Celia, and not only was the signal crap but I was trying to keep Celia from divulging too much about her husband's 'quirk' in front of the boys.

To cut a long story short, Celia turned up on Margaret and Arthur's doorstep a few days ago in a complete state sobbing that she couldn't take it any longer and she needed to confide in someone before she had a breakdown. It transpires that her husband has a penchant for wearing women's underwear. Christ, Melissa, the man is in his sixties and used to be something high up in the army. I can't imagine he was wearing stockings and suspenders under his fatigues on the assault course back then!

Anyway, unbeknown to us (initially) Celia had a hip

41

flask full of Crofts Original tucked away in her handbag (I thought she kept turning away filled with emotional angst while fighting back the tears, when in fact she was taking the opportunity to have a 'medicinal' swig!). As you can imagine, by lunchtime she was half-cut and hell-bent on giving us all the juicy details of her husband's kinky ways. Margaret and I desperately tried to get some hummus and grated carrot sandwiches into her to mop up the sherry but it was a lost cause. The most shocking part of all this—for me at least—was the revelation that John buys his underwear from Agent Provocateur! I asked Celia what size he bought as I didn't think they catered for larger sizes. James bought me some a few years back and I was devastated I could barely squeeze into a 12, which I swear was more like a 6. So anyway, thankfully, the hot afternoon sun mixed with sherry on an empty stomach do not mix, so we were able to leave Celia asleep and snoring under a tree while the boys explored the rest of the castle. Margaret says she will hide the rest of the Crofts Original for the duration of Celia's visit and is hoping she returns to John early next week. I don't think it's so much the cross-dressing that Celia is upset about as it's been going on for years. I think she's more worried that John is going to take part in some fly on the wall reality show revealing all—although I did remind her they are hardly the Kardashian's of Norfolk.

Thankfully, Celia's inebriated state meant that Margaret had to drive them straight home at the end of the day as she had been threatening to come back with us to show

Celia the house—well that was her guise anyway. I am sure she really just wanted to come back on the off chance Cosmo was back from London—which would have been tricky as he was never in London anyway. I had told her he was away to stop her from coming to the house that morning and pestering him before we left. It's really quite an embarrassment, Melissa—the woman is one step away from being his official stalker!

She'd be green with envy if she knew that while James is away in Scotland this weekend, this evening Cosmo is going to educate me on 'Old World' wines. Apparently, it's all to do with the valleys and the altitude where the grapes are grown—fascinating stuff.

Bx

MONDAY 27TH APRIL
SUBJECT: RE: MY 40TH?
Dear Sarah

Sorry I missed your call yesterday.

Of course, we will try our best to arrange our holiday around your 40th birthday party, but you know how the cheap flights get booked up so far in advance and it would be foolish to opt for a flight five times the price just to fly a couple of days later.

Sorry I didn't get Ella a present from your online list for her fifth birthday, but I saw the doll with curly lilac hair, crop top and purple lipstick and just knew she would love it. You know how frightfully bad I am at getting presents for girls. It was either that or a mini inflatable lap dancing pole I saw online—but I thought I'd save that for Christmas . . .

Of course I know Barnaby didn't mean to jump on Zac's head in the pool. It was more the fact that he continued to wrap his legs around Zac's neck and force his head under the water like an anaconda drowning its prey, that I took issue with.

Anyway, hopefully catch up very soon.

Briony

MONDAY 27TH APRIL
WHATSAPP MESSAGE

BRIONY: Kate, I tried calling you but only got your voicemail. Maybe you are avoiding my call since you sent a substantial parcel of toys to cater for all sexual perversions to my neighbour!!! We are 'Birch Cottage,' it is my forty something, unmarried, male neighbour who lives at 'Willow Cottage' and quite what he would do with Thai love beads and a David Cameron butt plug (really?!?) I simply do not want to dwell on.

KATE: OMG Bri, I am so sorry! God, how stupid of me! Shit. I knew the cottage was the name of a tree and I could have sworn it was 'Willow'? Who do I know who lives at Willow Cottage then . . . ? Odd.

BRIONY: Kate, your parents live at 'Willow House' . . .

You remember your parents, don't you?

KATE: Oh, yes! My parents! Sorry again. I really am. Was he okay about it? Why did he open it if it was your name on the parcel anyway? Oh, that's so funny . . . he's going to think you're a right vixen with a kink for David Cameron—haha. Could have been worse—imagine if it had been a Jeremy Corbyn butt plug—you'd be snubbed then.

BRIONY: It wasn't even addressed with my name, Kate! Just to 'Willow Cottage, Little Mistford.'

KATE: Oh, whoops. Will James be getting a 'treat' from my parcel tonight?

BRIONY: It was only on Saturday evening when Cosmo was educating me on Chilean wines and I happened to mention I had a friend who worked in PR who had recently been given the account for a saucy internet company that he clicked the parcel was meant for me. It was so embarrassing, Kate. One minute I was learning about how humidity affects grapes in the Limari Valley and the next I had a pile of love beads, nipple clips and strawberry lube on my lap. Oh and the butt plug! Just what did you think I was going to do with a David Cameron butt plug anyway?!?

KATE: It's kinda self-explanatory, Bri . . .

BRIONY: Well, anyway, after we had moved onto sampling the Elqui Valley, another from the Coquimbo Region, I was pissed enough to laugh about it . . . but I am still crippled with embarrassment every time I think about it.

KATE: Hot bachelor gets sexually frustrated neighbour

pissed and brings over box of sex toys . . . that's kind of a prelude to a film I once saw . . .

BRIONY: Amateur porn on the internet doesn't count as a film, Kate.

KATE: Oh, don't be such a movie snob.

BRIONY: And, no, James isn't getting a 'treat' tonight as he is still away in Scotland. In fact, if he finds out Cosmo got the package first by mistake he will not be impressed. He has no sense of humour these days . . .

KATE: I think James would be a lot less impressed by the fact his neighbour is getting his wife pissed on fine wines whilst he is away on business to be honest, Bri.

WEDNESDAY 29TH APRIL
SUBJECT: CELIA
Dear Briony

I am writing this having just seen Celia off—finally!

Although, it is of course, always quite wonderful to see one's old friends, I hope you don't think me uncharitable in my relief at Celia's departure. It was, to say the least, a somewhat stressful and revelation-filled week.

According to Celia, the last straw came when she was putting some washing away one day and realised how pathetic and sorry her collection of greying and baggy M&S undies were compared to John's exotic and hugely expensive collection. Well, it's a fair point as I told her; no wife wants to be comparing the flamboyance of their undergarments with her husband's, for goodness sake. However, as the week progressed (and the Crofts Original steadily depleted—that women can sniff out sherry like no one else I know) Celia seemed to cheer up and took herself off to town for an afternoon. Arthur and I were somewhat concerned for her mental well-being, but on her return she was weighted down with all variety of bags, as well as sporting a new hair style and manicure. She announced she would be leaving in the morning. I didn't dare ask her to share with me what she had bought and she didn't offer. The mind boggles, Briony.

I do hope the boys had a lovely time last Friday and were not too perturbed by Celia's behaviour?

Sarah tells me you may be missing her party as you can only afford cheap flights to Greece? I presumed this was a rouse to throw her off the scent? You don't really need to fly cheaply, do you? Is everything going alright for James and the business? I have told him I worry this move has put him under unnecessary financial strain while you are still only a one-income family.

I shall sign off now as I have to change the bedding in the spare room and air the house out. There is a distinct smell of stale sherry that I am hoping will lift now Celia has gone.

Love to all my little boys

Margaret xxx

WHATSAPP MESSAGE

GAYLE: Hey Bri—how's little Cliff's foot since I last saw him?

BRIONY: Oh god, Gayle, I forgot to tell you! A couple of days after you saw little Cliff the situation worsened so I took him to the vets in the village who sadly confirmed my fears and advised he be put to sleep. Oh, it was devastating—he was so happy and alert in himself—bar the fact he was limping around with a stump of a hind leg that kept catching on things and the bone made a tapping noise when he was on his wheel—but other than that he was just sweet little Cliff Richard. I burst into floods of tears as I took him out his cage, vet must have thought me unhinged—do you get many grown women sobbing over their kids' hamsters, Gayle? So anyway, she did the deed and I took his lifeless body, wrapped in paper towel shroud, to reception to pay (really think it's somewhat sadistic to make us pay for the privilege of euthanising our children's beloved pets, you know). Woman waiting to be seen with her cat asked if I was okay (puffy swollen eyes, blotchy red face, snot city, always a giveaway) cue more uncontrollable sobs, cat woman hugs me, another woman with small dog joins in (hugging, not sobbing) elderly gent with rabbit starts telling me what a lovely life Cliff must have had with such a caring owner, which made it worse and I started hyperventilating and started to feel faint. The receptionist got paper bag and I was told to breathe into that and put my head between my legs—and through all this she still managed to get me to tap in my PIN number and pay. Stealthy!

GAYLE: Oh Bri, really sorry to hear that. How did the boys take it? So Cliff Richard is buried in your garden?

BRIONY: We had a mix and match funeral—they've been learning about Egyptians and Buddhism at school. So Cliff was laid to rest with his favourite things beside him—a shreddie, a sultana, and toilet roll tube. We did try to squeeze him into the toilet roll as a sort of shroud/coffin but rigor mortis had set in and I didn't want anything snapping off, so he was just wrapped in kitchen roll and we planted an evergreen shrub on top of him. I'm just hoping the hole was deep enough—can't face finding bits of his body scattered around the garden if the foxes dig him up. We did bury him in a large terracotta pot so as we can take him with us if we move again. I don't think the foxes will bother with that, will they?

So anyway, kids being kids, we were at the pet shop the next day looking for a replacement and have welcomed 'Bear Grylls' into the fold . . .

GAYLE: Sweet. What's he look like?

BRIONY: She. Didn't realise until we got it home, but Bear Grylls is distinctly lacking in the balls department.

GAYLE: That won't be the first time someone has said that . . .

49

SUBJECT: RE: CELIA

Dear Margaret

So glad to hear Celia has gone back to John. It's for the best I am sure—after all they have been together for donkey's years so I am sure it will take more than an Agent Provocateur 'Nikita' garter belt to come between them.

Of course the boys had a wonderful day out, and other than a slightly bewildered Zac asking me why, if it was illegal to spank a child how come Celia spanked John, they seemed generally quite none the worse for Celia's indiscretions.

Actually, yes, there is a small possibility of us flying off the day of Sarah's party and it depends on the price of flights. Everything is going just fine for James and he shoulders the burden of being the breadwinner supporting his wife and young children just fine, but I am not prepared to fork out a silly price for seats if we can get them a lot cheaper a day or two earlier.

Have you given any more thought to the fire jugglers? I thought Celia had a good point regarding the safety and insurance. It would only take one errant spark and someone's dress could be turned into a fireworks display of its own. At worst, Sarah's summerhouse will be charcoal. Of course, it was the sherry talking when she started on about fire jugglers belonging to the occult, putting spells on the guests with their rhythmic drumming and slaughtering chickens. I think she was confusing it with voodoo; which is easily done I suppose.

Do let me know when you hear anything more from Celia.

Briony

WHATSAPP MESSAGE

BRIONY: James, just to let you know I am going out next Tues with Melissa. Put it in your diary as I'll need you home for the boys before I leave.

JAMES: I've got a meeting that could go on until late next Tuesday. Can you see if my mother can come over and look after the boys?

BRIONY: No, James. Meetings that end up in a pub don't count as proper meetings.

I'll be leaving 6.45 prompt.

JAMES: Umm. Okay.

BRIONY: Got nice Chilean Sauvignon to go with dinner that Cosmo gave us.

BRIONY: Don't roll your eyes like that, James. It's very generous of him.

MAY

THURSDAY 7TH MAY
WHATSAPP MESSAGE

BRIONY: OMG Melissa—carnage on a school night! Great to see you though and inevitable we would overdo it once you told me your wedding news!

MELISSA: I know! I could hardly wait to tell you.

BRIONY: James had to take the boys to school as I lay in bed trying to unstick my tongue from the roof of my mouth with a cup of tea. They've already had enough sick days due to hung over mummy being too ill to get out of bed, let alone drive, so thank god he was here for once.

MELISSA: Was he shirty about the noise we made when we got in?

BRIONY: No, he was still awake in the study working, re-member . . . 🙁

MELISSA: No, don't remember much after the fifth mojito . . .

BRIONY: Now, obviously I am flattered to have been asked

52

to be maid of honour but don't really know if this entails any duties as such? When are you asking Kate to be bridesmaid? I don't want to ruin your surprise by opening my mouth before you have got to her. Any idea on dates yet?

MELISSA: We've decided on 31st December THIS YEAR for the wedding and think the church in Dan's home village would be just the perfect venue—especially if it snows—soooo romantic!

BRIONY: 31st December as in New Year's Eve . . . ?!

MELISSA: Yes! Isn't it a brilliant idea?! A New Year's Eve wedding and party all rolled into one!

BRIONY: Oh Yes. Being snowed in for days in a remote northern village. Very romantic, Melissa. I anticipated a summer break in Yorkshire, not winter. Don't the roads close and snow gates shut around there?

MELISSA: That's Scotland. And anyway, there will be alcohol and food if we all get snowed in.

BRIONY: Well, that's okay then . . .

MELISSA: Just my mother to bring round to the idea of it not being in Dorset and the venue she's had earmarked for her only daughter's nuptials for the past 37 years . . .

BRIONY: I'm sure your mother will come round in the end. After all, surely at your age she is just relieved you are finally getting married.

MELISSA: Thanks.

SUBJECT: MELISSA & DAN

Hi Kate—I know you said to email as the boss has his eye on you, but are you sure he can't check your emails??

Anyway . . . the wedding of the year . . . what do we think?! Will be great fun I am sure, although, I hope not too much is expected of me/us in our roles as bridesmaids. I'm going to feel like Dame Edna Everage's oldest bridesmaid in town. Hope the dresses are flattering . . . Melissa wouldn't put us in anything awful, would she . . . ?

I'm feeling rather ropey today after a record two nights on the mojitos last week. How did we ever manage it almost every night 'back in the day'?! I felt so hung over after Melissa's surprise announcement, I had no choice but go the hair of the dog route the following night for the monthly Mojitos and SingStar night with the girls. I think Lucy may be regretting showing us the anniversary gift her husband bought her—a 'Randy Rabbit' of all things! I mean, seriously, is that an acceptable ten year wedding anniversary gift?! She was pretty hacked off to put it mildly (not least because the old scrooge had got her the older and cheaper model with only one speed setting) so after a few drinks the vitriol came spilling out to such an extent that when she took us upstairs to show us this piece of vibrating silicone, she gesticulated so wildly with it in her hand as she ranted that the bloody thing went flying out the window, landed on her neighbour, Reverend McGregor's flat extension roof, and sat there vibrating away in its full, pink (single-speed) and sparkly glory. Actually, it looked rather beautiful in the early evening sun to our alcohol-infused vision, and we all paused for a moment to take it in. Ever the daredevil, my fuzzy mojito brain saw this as the ideal opportunity to live out my 'Charlie's Angels' fantasy. So, without a moment's hesitation I deftly climbed out the bedroom window, forward-rolled all 'Mission Impossible' stylie over the extension roofs, retrieved the offending item and returned to the bedroom window only to discover it's a lot harder to climb back up into a window from a flat roof than it is to jump out. Mild panic set in when it became apparent we would need to get a ladder, followed by slightly less mild verging-on-mass-hysteria, when Lucy realised we would need to ask to borrow a ladder from the vicar. Is this how a woman on the cusp of her forties should be behaving?

Needless to say, the vicar's face was a picture as I climbed down his ladder clutching a sparkly pink dildo.

Speak soon,

Briony x

(Maybe we should use code when emailing so your boss doesn't get suspicious? I could pretend to be a prospective client?)

MONDAY 11TH MAY
SUBJECT: DANCE TROUPE AND COTTAGE BOOKED?
Dear Briony

I thought it best to grab the bull by the horns and book

the dance troupe act in case they got booked up. I did have a link to their website but can't find it now so you will just have to trust me that they really do look rather good! A vibrant group of young ladies in shiny red and black costumes and extravagant head pieces—very Folies Bergère—or so I imagine, having never been to Paris myself. They are going to be terribly good and get changed in their van so no suspicion will be aroused with unknown guests wandering around. All we need do is prepare an area of the garden that they will use as their 'stage' and at the arranged time we will gather everyone together for speeches or cake cutting or some other excuse and the ladies will enter through the garden gate and perform! Isn't it all terribly exciting, Briony?

Now, I have booked a lovely cottage in the next village for us all. It was a little pricey, but I thought that as this is a very special family occasion we could justify splashing out. I've attached the internet link for you.

Did you find out Cosmo's email address yet, Briony? I was rather hoping he might be able to supply us with the wine for Sarah's birthday. I may pop over at the weekend to see you all and catch him in then? I could also collect the cheque for the cottage from you then.

Much love,
Margaret x

SUBJECT: RE: DANCE TROOP AND COTTAGE BOOKED?

Dear Margaret

I've looked at the link to the cottage and have to say I am not sure if it is a little extravagant? Do we really need seven bedrooms? I know there will be six of us, and crazy as it sounds, James and usually share a bedroom—as would the boys on this occasion. Also, why three nights when surely we only need to be there for one or two at most? Have you already paid the deposit? I did mention we were not 100% sure we wouldn't be in Greece and the cost of this cottage would cover the whole holiday in Greece!

Briony

SUBJECT: RE: DANCE TROUPE AND COTTAGE BOOKED?

Dear Briony

Yes, I know seven bedrooms does seem a little surplus to requirements, but Celia and John will probably be joining us and the smaller holiday cottages were rather too cosy for my liking. Celia thought we should make a long weekend of it whilst we were there, hence the three-night booking. I've spoken to James regarding Greece and he has assured me you can get later flights at not much more expense; so one less worry for you there.

Do you have Cosmo's phone number?

Regards Margaret x

WHATSAPP MESSAGE

BRIONY: James. I have your mother emailing me regarding this bloody party of your sister's and the seven-bedroom, £1500 'cottage' she has booked for us all to stay at. Apparently, you told her we would definitely be able to make it as we were booking later flights to Greece?!? I thought we were still to discuss this when you were home between business trips for longer than five minutes? Not only has she booked this blasted mansion cottage, but she expects us to pay a share for the privilege of spending three days with them and their friends, Celia and John! Really, James, I should not have to tell you that paying for the privilege of spending 3 days with your parents and their friends is hardly my idea of fun . . .

JAMES: Sorry, Briony, I did mean to mention it to you. It will be more trouble than it's worth to not go to Sarah's party so I just went along with her plans. I'm not paying a grand for the privilege though, so just say we only plan to stay for a night as we need to get back to pack for Greece or something.

Shouldn't be too late back tonight.

BRIONY: You say that every night . . .

SUBJECT: RE: DANCE TROUPE AND COTTAGE BOOKED?

Dear Margaret

I've spoken to James and he has said, we will absolutely

only be staying one night as will need to get back to prepare for the holiday. Probably best to find another cottage for yourselves and we will stay in a B&B—after all, don't want that sort of expense just before a holiday. I'm sure you understand.

Love Briony

PS. No, I don't have Cosmo's phone number. As he only lives next door I've never really needed it.

TUESDAY 12TH MAY
SUBJECT: HOLT COTTAGE
Dear Celia

I am sorry to inform you that we may have to abandon our plans for a long weekend of luxury at Holt Cottage. Briony has informed me that she, James and the children only plan on staying one night as they need to take cheap flights to Greece soon after Sarah's birthday. I have to say, I really don't see what the rush is all about, after all they have six weeks summer holidays, and if James' business is really doing so badly that they have to fly with the lower end of the airlines, and then complain about the cost of accommodation, gift and entertainment cost for Sarah's very special party, maybe they should not be taking a summer holiday at all this year? Poor James seems to be working himself into an early grave, while Briony is just concerned about flying off to exotic countries. Stop me if I am being unkind, Celia, but one might have thought she would be

59

too busy helping to do up that new house of theirs this summer instead of hiring in professional tradespeople at every opportunity and at further expense to my poor son.

I shall try and find us other suitable accommodation, but at this short notice we may be forced to consider properties aimed at less discerning persons. Celia, would you consider a property without a dishwasher and only one bathroom? I know it's rather going back to basics and I apologise for my daughter-in-law's selfishness, but maybe we could get a local woman in to wash up and clean for the three days we are there?

Best Regards
Margaret

PS I do hope all has settled down with yourself and John and the little issue now?

TUESDAY 12TH MAY
SUBJECT: RE: HOLT COTTAGE
Dear Margaret

Although, I do appreciate your dilemma, and I agree that Briony is being a little precious regarding her summer holiday, I really don't think you would enjoy sharing a bathroom with John. There are habits a wife gets used to during a marriage, but to force her husband's habits upon her friends would, I fear, be putting the friendship in great peril.

I say no more.

Sincere Regards
Celia

SUBJECT: AFFORDABLE PROPERTY
Dear Briony

You will notice I have changed the subject title of my email as I have regrettably had to cancel the cottage booking after your recent revelations that yourself, James and children would not be joining us for the lovely long, family break we had planned. Celia is most disappointed which is a terrible shame, as she really could have done with something to look forward to considering recent events, and the swimming pool, hot tub and tennis courts really did make Holt Cottage a splendid choice.

However, I have now found a property which may be more affordable for you (please see link). Briefly, it compromises just four bedrooms; of which just one is en-suite. I have had to book it for a week as that was the minimum requirement, but I shall just ask you for one seventh of the total cost plus cleaning services charge, which I hope will not adversely affect your budget break to Greece.

If you could confirm this is acceptable to yourself as soon as possible I would be greatly appreciative.

Bests Margaret

WEDNESDAY 13TH MAY
SUBJECT: RE: AFFORDABLE PROPERTY
Dear Margaret

I think Greenacre Cottage is a lovely and far more suitable choice. I am sure Celia, John and yourselves will have a lovely extended break there, and anyway, I thought you couldn't play tennis since you strained the ligament in your arm wheeling Richard from number 52 to the mobile library?

Briony

WEDNESDAY 13TH MAY
SUBJECT: RE: AFFORDABLE PROPERTY
Dear Briony

I am so glad you like my second choice. As you can see from the website, we will all be lowering our standards somewhat compared to Holt Cottage, but are more than happy to do that to accommodate your budget.

Fondests
Margaret

PS—I shall inform Celia she can have the en-suite bedroom as apparently John has some unsavoury bathroom habits.

SUBJECT: BIRTHDAY LIST
Hi Briony

Just to let you know, I've got a birthday wishlist online at

Liberty, which you can use to order my present. It makes it so much easier for everyone—I don't know why everyone doesn't do it? If you are really unsure of what to choose, I'll just hint that I am particularly fond of the 'wardrobe book' in navy calfskin ... mum discreetly mentioned your money problems so it should also be within your budget.

Love, Sarah

THURSDAY 14TH MAY
SUBJECT: WINE
Dear Cosmo

I hope you don't think me terribly rude by contacting you in this manner, but, I am finding Briony rather unreliable with messages at the moment. As you may be aware, it is my daughter's 40th birthday in July (I married very young) for which we are arranging a party and I thought I might order the wine from yourself—if that isn't a huge inconvenience to you? It's always such a trial to know which wines to get to please all palates and therefore would hugely appreciate your expert guidance. I shall be visiting James and Briony at the weekend, and maybe if you are free I could pop in and discuss our requirements more fully with you.

Best regards,
Margaret Denley

SUBJECT: RE: WINE
Dear Mrs Denley

It would be my absolute pleasure to supply the wine for your daughter's birthday. I have no firm plans on Sunday and will therefore look forward to your visit.

Yours,
Cosmo Huntington Jones

FRIDAY 15TH MAY
WHATSAPP MESSAGE:
BRIONY: James, I have had a call from your mother informing me she will be paying us a brief visit on Sunday while she is discussing business with Cosmo(!) Apparently, he is supplying the wine for your sister's birthday extravaganza. You do realise that we will probably be footing half the bill for this, along with the entertainment and catering? If you still have the £20 DIY voucher she got you for your birthday, you could put it towards a cheap BBQ and we could take that down with us to sizzle sausages on and save a few quid?!

JAMES: Who the hell gave her that idea? I'm sure she will backtrack once she realises just how much decent wine actually costs once someone has added his profit on top. Or is he supplying her wholesale prices? Somehow, I think not. You don't go around buying Aston Martin DBE's selling a few bottles of plonk to little old ladies for birthday parties—no matter how excessive the mark-up.

BRIONY: Your mother is hardly a helpless 'little old lady' and as I said, she will—for reasons only justified by herself—be expecting us to foot half the bill for this whole 'event' unless you make it quite clear otherwise . . .

JAMES: Hmm. How are we fixed for hosting a little supper for Ralph and his wife next week?

BRIONY: How are 'we' fixed? Well, I don't know about you, but I am rather busy. However, if you would like to clean the house, cook a gourmet meal on par with a top Michelin starred London restaurant, entertain dull, money obsessed business colleague and equally dull cosmetically-enhanced, designer label-obsessed wife, with intelligent yet witty repartees all night whilst running between kitchen and dining room with the illusion of effortless ease, then please, do invite them. In return, I shall try terribly hard not to stare at Eloise's amazing immobile forehead and smile politely when she claims her youthful demeanour is all down to healthy living. What fun it shall be.

JAMES: Great. Shall we say Friday next week then?

BRIONY: No. We'll say Thursday in the hope that they won't stay too late with work the next day.

MONDAY 18TH MAY
WHATSAPP GROUP MESSAGE

KARA: Anyone fancy a surf lesson next week? Got discount offer on. Shortie wetsuits provided if you don't have your own.

GAYLE: I look awful in a shortie—I have fat knees

LUCY: I've never noticed your fat knees, Gayle?

GAYLE: Wetsuit squishes all the fat together around there.

KARA: Fat knees?! Shit excuse.

BRIONY: I'm up for it. My knees look great in a shortie

KARA: I'll book. How was your weekend? Did the outlaws visit go relatively painlessly?

BRIONY: Painfully cringeworthy. Margaret arrived minus Arthur at lunchtime, dressed in what I can only describe as a crinoline kaftan in oranges, reds and golds and make up to match. Poor James initially didn't even recognise his mother as he casually glanced out of the bedroom window and snidely told me of the 'wanton hussy' floating around after Cosmo in his garden. Imagine his mortification when the penny dropped (and much to my unabashed amusement) he realised that the flame enrobed hussy was in fact his sexagenarian mother coquettishly flirting with our neighbour amongst the wisteria. Ha! I tell you, I have never seen the colour drain from a man as quickly as it did James. I might have felt sorry for him were it not for the fact he took an almost instant and unfathomable dislike to Cosmo and uses every opportunity to have a dig, when as far as I can see Cosmo has done nothing but be incredibly hospitable and made us feel really welcome ever since we moved in. So anyway, after a stiff espresso and (homemade) shortbread finger, James ventured over to Cosmo's to retrieve his mother. It's really not a pretty sight when your OAP mother-in-law develops a girlish crush on the neighbour, believe me. James is convinced Cosmo is going to take advantage of his mother—financially—with regard to the wine for Sarah's party—although appears oblivious to the fact his mother is constantly taking advantage of us in order to finance her luxurious weekend breaks with friends and fund her daughter's totally over-the-top 40th birthday party!

KARA: Why are men such bloody hard work?! Sometimes I think it's easier being a single mum in some respects, not having a husband to deal with.

BRIONY: He's never at home as always at the office. We communicate mostly via texts these days, and he's rarely home before 10pm as entertaining clients or 'networking' (ie in the pub?!) after work.

KARA: Well, maybe a lesson with the hot surfers will cheer you up 😉

MONDAY 18TH MAY
SUBJECT: SUNDAY
Dear Briony

It was lovely to see you all at the weekend—albeit briefly. It was such a shame I had to hurry back to Arthur so soon after my meeting with Cosmo, but as you know, we had Richard over to help with the tree, and my goodness it was a jolly good thing that I was there, Briony, otherwise I fear they both would have ended up at A&E.

Anyway, the budget cottage is all booked and paid for

and Cosmo is going to have the wine delivered there the day we arrive, so we don't have to worry ourselves with transporting it all the way to Devon. He really has been so helpful, Briony, and has such abundant pelargoniums this early in the year!

Have you chosen a gift from Sarah's list yet? Wasn't that just such a clever idea of hers? And she does have such refined taste it makes it all so much easier for us all.

I will call James for a little chat soon as he seemed rather stressed and flustered on Sunday and not like himself at all. Do you think he's taken on too much, Briony? Maybe there is something you could do to ease his stress as he is always away on business and it can't be much fun all alone in strange hotel rooms and eating from the room service menus every night while you are tucked up with the boys in your lovely new house. I'm sure the inequality of it all must get him down.

Much Love
Margaret x

P.S. Almost forgot to mention the caterers! I took the liberty of going for the 'deluxe' plan as that included waiting staff and wine waiters. After all, we will certainly need wine waiters to serve Cosmo's splendid wines.

SUBJECT: RE: SUNDAY
Margaret—who ended up in A&E?!

I can assure you James is fine. The hotels he stays in are not exactly budget dives and he eats with business associates in top restaurants every night; so he is far from lonely. In fact, he never has time to skype or phone the boys as he's busy having so much fun, whilst I, on the other hand, am on the hamster wheel of school runs, after school clubs, cooking, cleaning, house renovating . . . I know who I think is getting the better deal . . .

Briony

SUBJECT: RE: SUNDAY
Dear Briony

Please don't fret! It's a minor soft tissue injury and Richard is laughing about it now. Well, I say laughing . . . more trying not to laugh really, as it's still too sore. But Arthur and I have assured him he will be laughing by the time his outpatient's appointment comes through. Fortunately, his wheelchair is insured—unlike our summerhouse which is still under threat from being smashed by the half dead tree in the next slightest breeze. I dare not ask Richard for help again before he has been given the all clear by the consultant and you know how they do seem to drag these things out. It's such a worry. All my geraniums have been

69

over-wintered in the summerhouse and I didn't want to bring them out for another couple of weeks.

I never saw my role as a wife and mother as in any way tedious or repetitive and enjoyed every moment. Maybe a visit to the doctor might be an idea and see if you can't get yourself a little tonic to pep you up? Some of us are born to be great wives and mothers, and some of us struggle. Nothing to be ashamed about, dear.

These things do so come to try us, don't they Briony?

Chin up,
Margaret x

TUESDAY 19TH MAY
WHATSAPP MESSAGE

KATE: OMG, you will never guess who I bumped into yesterday?! Only Piers bloody Hartley! He's working in our 'Noo Yoik' office and is over for a few days mixing business with pleasure. He's not changed too much since you and he were an item all those years ago, and of course he asked about you. I'm meeting him for dinner tomorrow night for a proper catch up before he flies back. Small world, huh?

BRIONY: No way! Wow. That's going back a fair bit. How old were we? Eighteen? Nineteen? So he's in PR now? That's a step up from dressing up as 'Snappy the Shark' at the Ocean Life Aquarium.

What did you say about me? And exactly where is 'Noo Yoik'?

KATE: 'New York', Briony. It's how they say it over there. You know that and I know that you are being pedantic.

BRIONY: Nooooooo, Piers was 'Terry the Turtle'! Snappy was that weird middle aged guy who made odd noises inside his costume.

KATE: I just told him you were married with a couple of kids and living in the country. Nothing too incriminating.

BRIONY: Oh, gee thanks, you make my life sound beyond exhilarating! You could have 'excited' it up a bit!

KATE: You're married with kids and live in the country, Bri—excitement left long ago.

BRIONY: Thanks again, Kate. Actually, Piers started off as Terry the Turtle, but when the manager discovered what it was that Snappy was doing to cause all the odd noises, he got the boot and Piers got promoted to Snappy. I definitely only started seeing him after he got promoted to Snappy. I would never have been attracted to a boy in a turtle costume—give me some credit! I wonder how many other people who used to have summer jobs dressed as marine creatures for the Ocean Life Aquarium are working in the same company as you, now? Must be a natural progression . . .

KATE: What exactly was Snappy doing in his costume that warranted dismissal, Briony?!

BRIONY: Well, the weird noises and heavy breathing weren't because he was asthmatic, Kate. And that costume had to be professionally cleaned before Piers could use it.

KATE: Eugh. I really had no idea about that. I was obviously too young and naïve and to be aware of such things.

BRIONY: When you say 'he hasn't changed much', do you mean he still has all his own hair?

KATE: Umm, yeah he still has his hair—pretty much. He's looking good, Bri. And he's not married or even divorced—which surprised me.

BRIONY: So he's gay? He went gay after me?!

KATE: No he's not gay! Why did you guys split up anyway? I can't remember.

BRIONY: It was a very long time ago . . . let's not go there.

KATE: Still raw, huh? 😉

BRIONY: Far from it. Anyway, did I tell you that Margaret has booked waitresses and wine waiters for Sarah's party?! Apparently, we need them now Cosmo is providing the wine. She sent me an email going on and on about 'poor James' working too hard and being holed up in lonely hotels away from home. She has no bloody idea, does she? Yes, he does work hard but he also plays very hard as well and while he away drinking fine wines and eating gourmet meals under the guise of 'business' I am the one left holding the fort here. Do I get any praise or even acknowledgment from everything I do? Not bloody likely! It's as if she has forgotten how hard it actually is to run a household and look after two small children. I gave up a successful career in PR of my own don't forget, and now my life is looking after a family twenty-four-seven. She even suggested I needed a 'tonic' from the doctor as I'm obviously not a natural mother! The only tonic I needed after reading that was to accompany the large Shiraz I poured to stop myself emailing back something altogether less polite.

KATE: Fgs Briony, it's the 21st century and you don't need a man for sexual satisfaction, so just go give the budgie tongue a little tweak yourself. You know, go flick the bean? Polish the pearl? Buff the bead?

BRIONY: Tweaking the budgie tongue? I had a budgie as a child and that just conjures up a very wrong image.

KATE: I'll send you a little something from SHL to help you on your way 😉

BRIONY: I don't need you to send me anything—got everything I need in my filthy imagination.

KATE: So get frotting!

BRIONY: Sometimes a girl just needs a big, hard cock.

KATE: And plastic really ain't so fantastic ☹

BRIONY: James is always either away on business, or when home he's working late or holed up in the study on his laptop. I am sick of waiting for him to come to bed. We used to nip upstairs for a bit of fun when they boys were watching a film at the weekend, but these days he's more likely to use the time to 'catch up on some work.' Honestly, I'm starting to wonder if I should be worried . . . .

KATE: OMG you think he's got a drug problem? It's becoming more widespread amongst the middle aged middle classes—I read an online article. Maybe he picked up the habit when on business in the Far East? Shit, Briony, what are you going to do? Plan an intervention? Bit of tough love?

BRIONY: Err, no, Kate, actually I was referring (albeit

73

light-heartedly) to him having an affair. But thanks for now adding potential class A drug habit to the mix. And we are not middle aged!!

KATE: Oh. An affair. Well, yes I guess that would be better than a mieow mieow habit. Who is he having an affair with then? Bastard! You've given him two sons and heirs. Absolute bastard! Wait til I see him! I'll give him tough love! How dare he lie and cheat to you for all these years. Is it years, do you think? Maybe it's just since the boredom and repetitiveness of married life kicked in? And you are on the cusp on being middle aged. Sorry to break it to you.

BRIONY: He's not really, actually, having an affair, Kate—calm down! Well, at least I didn't think he was. I was just kind of feeling sorry for myself, as they do say if a husband no longer wants sex with you then he's having sex with someone else. You don't seriously think he's having an affair, do you? I'd know if he was, I'm sure I would know!

KATE: Nooooo, of course he's not having an affair.

BRIONY: 😀

KATE: Much more likely to be onset of erectile dysfunction—another symptom of middle age. Finger up the bum apparently sorts it.

BRIONY: Okay, I'm ignoring you now, Kate. Go away.

WEDNESDAY 20TH MAY
WHATSAPP MESSAGE

BRIONY: Could you email me the recipe for that chilli bean stew? I have James' dull business colleague and his deplorable wife coming for dinner on Thursday. Can't be bothered with fannying around too much, so thought I could make this and add chicken or something for them?

Well, I'm guessing you don't care to impress them much if you're just going to give them chilli bean stew?!

KARA: I'm going on a peaceful march in aid of the Tibet issue next week so can't make lunch on Tues. Any chance of postponing? If not, count me out and I'll make sure I'm there next time.

Link to recipe attached. You do know how to cooka chicken, don't you?

BRIONY: Don't be absurd! I'm not going to cook the chicken. I'm just going to buy some ready cooked bits and chuck them in at the end.

KARA: Ha. I admire and deplore your 'couldn't give a shit' attitude in equal amounts.

BRIONY: As far as James' business associates go—zero fucks given. I'll come with you on the Tibet march, if you like? What time are we leaving and I'll arrange for the boys to go to a friend.

KARA: You really want to come on the Tibet march? I mean, I know you had a 'Free Tibet' patch on your jeans and you've watched 'Kundun' but I thought that's as far as it went? Anyway, I'm driving up early in the morning and hope to be back around 8pm.

BRIONY: Let's make a night of it! It's half term so I'll see if Margaret wants to have the boys or get Lucy to have them for a night and we can go out, stay in a nice hotel and do a little shopping the next day? I deserve it!

KARA: Yeah, Bri. Maybe we should scrap the march and go straight to Covent Garden.

BRIONY: Great idea. So I'll book a hotel. My treat.

KARA: Briony, I was joking. I'm not missing the march. We meet everyone at Hyde Park at 11am so plenty of time to shop afterwards. And you hate shopping so I'm only humouring you as I know after an hour you'll be desperate to find a brasserie for a drink, and I'll be desperate to replenish your fading sugar levels before The Rage kicks in.

BRIONY: How rude! I don't get 'The Rage.' Maybe a little snippy. But not The Rage.

KARA: Somerset 2014. four miles into a day-long hike in the countryside. Another five miles to the nearest village. Tears, tantrums and a sit down strike in the middle of a field. T'was only the fact you unknowingly staged your sit-down strop in a field full of bullocks that got you moving again once they started coming your way . . . Well, that and the crushed, melted, half a KitKat Lucy found in her rucksack, of course. Not the first time a sticky finger has pepped you up again, I'm sure . . . 😉

THURSDAY 21ST MAY
SUBJECT: HALF TERM
Dear Margaret

The boys have said they would love to come and stay with you for a night in the half term holiday, so I wondered if the Tues would be any good as I have to go to London early and will be away the night. If it's not possible don't worry as they can go to their friends for a night.

Re: the tree. James said he had spoken to you and advised you to get it done professionally. I have a friend who uses someone local to us who also covers your area. Would you like me to pass on your number? I have to say I do agree with James' concern. Richard was lucky to only suffer minor injuries. If he had not been strapped into his wheelchair when the rope got caught, hoisting him up alongside the tree, he may have been a lot more seriously injured and even fatally so.

In regards to the waiting staff for Sarah's party, I am not sure we do need them as it may create rather too formal an atmosphere and Cosmo did tell me he specifically choose wines with an 'easy nature and ambling palate' in order to appeal to the majority of the guests. Will help cut the costs also, of course, which I feel are spiralling just a little out of control.

Briony x

THURSDAY 21ST MAY
SUBJECT: RE: HALF TERM
Dear Briony

Although I do appreciate your concern, I think we shall keep to the original plan for the deluxe service. I really don't think the atmosphere we want will be created by people helping themselves to wine in plastic cups spread

77

out on a trestle table amongst soggy sausage rolls. After all, it is a very special occasion and deserves to be treated as such. If finances are concerning you I'm sure it's not too late to cancel your bargain break to Greece and have a 'staycation' this year instead.

I shall check my diary for next Tuesday and get back to you.

Much Love
Margaret

THURSDAY 21ST MAY
WHATSAPP MESSAGE

BRIONY: Just wanted to see if you might be able to have the boys on Tuesday and overnight for me, Luce? I'm hoping to go to London with Kara for a Tibet march and a bit of R&R and Margaret has informed me she will 'check her diary' which usually means she is hoping to be invited to the opening of an envelope rather than spend time with her grandsons and help me out that day.

LUCY: Hey, Bri. That would be fine. I have to take Algernon to the homeopath that afternoon but other than that I have the day free.

BRIONY: Thanks, Luce. Actually, I think Margaret is rather irked as I dared suggest we didn't need the wine waiters for Sarah's birthday party, which she interpreted as me expecting people to serve themselves soggy defrosted vol-au-vents, and drink from polystyrene cups or something!

LUCY: I would let James' mother have her silver service or whatever it is, but make it clear it's her daughter and you are not sure why she feels you are under an obligation to pay for the bloody thing! It's just odd, Bri. Why would James be expected to pay for his sister's birthday party?!? It's not as if his parents are hard up pensioners, is it now? They're loaded! He should be telling her this, not leaving it up to you!

BRIONY: Yes, but that would involve James growing a pair and we both know that's never going to happen when it comes to his bloody parents.

LUCY: Are you staying with Kate in London? How very unique to integrate a peace march with shopping! Would love a shopping trip myself, but can't leave Algey overnight.

BRIONY: What's wrong with Algey? Is he still getting stressed and growly when people cross their arms in his presence?

LUCY: No, Algey is fine with arm crossing now. He seems to have transferred his anxiety to people with their hands in their pockets and apparently that needs another remedy. I know it can look alarming when he's baring his teeth and barking manically, but really he's all bark and no bite. However, I have a lovely canine therapist coming this afternoon who does the most amazing deep muscle massages with essential oils and that always helps. Don't tell Tom. You know what he's like about Algey's little problems. He just doesn't understand that dogs are as individual as people, and god knows we all have our little 'issues' don't we?

BRIONY: Oh yes, Lucy. I needed weeks of therapy to stop me growling at anyone with their hands in their pockets, and James just can't kick that little habit of his of dragging his bum along the carpet . . .

LUCY: It cost you five times the cost of your hamster to have it euthanized, Briony, so don't pretend you don't care about our fluffy friends.

BRIONY: The hamsters don't cost more in medical care than my kids though Lucy! No, not staying with Kate as she's got something on apparently. Was about to book a hotel but then Cosmo came over earlier with some wine for tonight (entertaining James' business colleague and wife—yawn) and said he was in London on business next week and we could stay with him. Did I mention he has a little Pied-à-terre in Chelsea? He's offered to take us out as well as he has loads of connections around town. Really looking forward to it. It's been an age since I went away for the night—well, other than the night in A&E when Sam fell out of bed and we thought he had a broken arm . . . but fluorescent lighting, the smell of Dettol and weak vending machine coffee never really do it for me . . .

LUCY: Oh really, how convenient. And James is okay with that, is he?

BRIONY: Thing is, I might not mention Cosmo's offer to James in case he gets a bit . . . you know . . . I mean, he's probably unlikely to even ask me as he'll assume we're staying with Kate anyway, so it's not like I'm lying anyway.

LUCY: No, Briony, not like you're lying at all. Just being mildly deceptive . . .

WHATSAPP MESSAGE

BRIONY: Hey, Kara guess what? Cosmo (my neighbour, Cosmo, remember him?) has offered to put us up at his place in Chelsea, Tues night. How does that sound? He's also offered to take us out that evening if we don't have any plans—which we don't, really, do we?

KARA: Of course I know who Cosmo is, not a week goes by without you mentioning him, so it will be interesting to meet him, finally. Do I sense a teeny mid-life crisis crush?

BRIONY: Don't be absurd. How could I have a mid-life crisis crush when I am nowhere near mid-life. Although admittedly, my life is in crisis. Cosmo and I get on very well and he is the perfect gentleman—attentive, charming . . .

KARA: Everything that James isn't then . . .

BRIONY: James has his moments. Few and far between, admittedly. What are you wearing for the demo thing? I'm thinking urban casual with a shot of ethnic chic thrown in? I'm not sure what to pack for the evening and might have a look around the shops on Sat for something a bit special. I'm really quite excited!

KARA: I wasn't really looking at the march as a fashion event . . . but now you've asked I think urban chic tribal whatever sounds good—just so long as that includes sensible footwear.

BRIONY: Sensible footwear?! Damn. Well, that blows out my wedge heel boots, I guess.

KARA: Seriously, Bri, maybe you need to get out more if

you're getting this over excited about a Free Tibet march in London. Is everything okay with you guys?

BRIONY: James is just busy. You know how it is. He's away a lot of the time and I'm left holding the fort with little or no recognition for everything I do around here that keeps it all together and ticking over smoothly. I guess sometimes I just feel taken for granted.

KARA: You need a hobby.

BRIONY: Funnily enough, Cosmo has rather stirred an interest in wine in me, and apparently he says I have a very acute palate, so who knows where that might lead?

KARA: Fuck me, hell yeah, where could an acute palate lead you?!

BRIONY: We had James' business colleague and wife over last night which was pretty dire. The woman is obsessed with designer labels and has a serious addiction to botox. She arrived wearing six-inch razor sharp Louboutins which meant I spent most of the evening surreptitiously trying to arrange rugs and runners in her path so as her spikes wouldn't dent the oak flooring. Honestly, Kara, both James and I were visibly cringing every time the woman got up from the table (which she did to excess, I must say and made me wonder if she was bulimic). At one point she deviated from my anticipated route and stood looking out the bi-fold doors at the garden causing me to panic and pretend to spill something just so as I could edge a rug closer to her heels. Of course, while I was on all fours the silly cow had to go and step back and trip over me as she turned around, which led her to fall flat bang on her 100% fat free, scrawny arse and scrape a Louboutin across the floor in the process. I was beyond mortified, Kara. I could have fallen to the floor myself and wept had it not been for the fact that the woman was sat sobbing making a sound not dissimilar to a dying duck (and yet still her face did not even twitch a muscle—truly bizarre and somewhat unnerving.) I am not sure even her husband could tell if she was actually crying, laughing, or having some sort of fit, and for a moment we all just knelt there staring at her in the hope one errant un-paralysed nerve might give away the true meaning of her strangulated gasps. All the noise and commotion woke Sam up who came running downstairs and upon being confronted with this odd sight exclaimed 'Oh, Mummy! Look at the horrible big scrape on the floor!' Swiftly followed by, 'What is wrong with that lady's face, mummy?" I'm not surprised the poor child was afraid to go back to bed after seeing that bride of Frankenstein, and he'll probably have nightmares for weeks. On the upside, at least it cut the evening short.

KARA: Every cloud and all that!

FRIDAY 22ND MAY
WHATSAPP MESSAGE

LUCY: Hey Kara, what's all this about a demo you're taking Briony on?! We've had to postpone our lunch now—but for the best really as Gayle has the dentist that morning and could end up dribbling all over her croque monsieur if her mouth is still numb.

KARA: To be honest, I think Briony is more interested in the opportunity to shop for something nice to wear for the glitzy night out we're apparently being taken on by Cosmo (who seems far too keen to impress her if you ask me?) Hmm, maybe I am just cynical but with James away so much this Cosmo seems to take every opportunity to spend an evening sampling his vintage delights at Briony's. Apparently he's 'stirred an interest in wine' in her which did make me wonder of that's all he's stirred. Well, at least I will be accompanying her and keeping her out of harms way—although I'm already starting to feel like a gooseberry . . .

LUCY: Oh Kara, I have met Cosmo and he really is the most charming man—charming, knowledgeable, well-read, well-travelled and wealthy—so I am sure he has absolutely no designs on Briony.

KARA: Hmm, maybe you're right. How is Reverend McGregor after the unfortunate incident—or should I not ask?

LUCY: Reverend McGregor would probably be fine by now had it not been for the other small incident of him receiving a mail order sex toy catalogue through his letterbox sent by Briony's friend, Kate, which he kindly got his wife to drop round to me—along with a leaflet about how the church can help cure the 'sins of the flesh.' I think we may now have to move house, Kara.

SUBJECT: TIRESOME

Dear Celia

I do hope this email finds you well. I was going to phone you but remembered that your son and his family are staying this weekend and didn't like to intrude. I find email so convenient in that respect, as one can choose if and when to reply to correspondence without it interfering in other matters.

'Tiresome', Celia. That is the subject of my email and that is how I am finding Briony. You know how I hate to say anything negative about anyone, and how I always look for the good in people, but really, I am finding it quite a struggle to find anything positive to say about Briony at the moment. As you will recall, she has been frightfully difficult regarding Sarah's surprise party plans and has been of little help, but I have just had to bite my tongue and soldier on with the arrangements myself, and that is just fine. Poor James is so terribly over-worked, and I think I mentioned when I spoke to you on the phone last that he seemed terribly stressed and flustered the Sunday I was visiting their charming neighbour, Cosmo, about wine for the party. Since then, I have voiced my concerns with Briony, who seems completely oblivious to the strain James is under—being away from home all the time in lonely hotels eating room service club sandwiches—I mean really, Celia, what kind of a life is that? One cannot live on club sandwiches alone—no matter how many fillings they manage

85

to fit between two slices of bread; it is still essentially just a sandwich and by its nature therefore a 'snack' and not a wholesome home cooked meal. I don't know though, Celia, maybe that is better than the alternative Briony prepares for my son at home. I can't ever imagine tofu and quinoa being a satisfying meal for a hard working grown man, let alone growing boys—although, I never comment, Celia, it is not in my nature to interfere, as you know.

And now, just as I was looking forward to the half term holiday and the chance to see my delightful grandsons, Briony informs me she is gallivanting—yes, gallivanting, Celia, for there is no other word for it—off to London for a couple of days R&R! R&R?!? All the girl does is float around that lovely big house all day, so, just why she needs time away for rest and relaxation when my son is working all the hours God sends to pay the mortgage, I shall never know. She did ask if I could have the boys for a night while she is away, and of course, I jumped at the chance, Celia, you know how I adore all my grandchildren, and as those two poor boys are still being 'educated' (I use the term loosely) at a state school, I feel it's so terribly important to keep regular contact to make sure they are not being too influenced by the more 'socially diverse' classes, if you get my meaning, Celia. Of course, I did need to check a few things with Catherine at the WIs as I was aware we may have had a special visitor coming some time that week. The lady who does that Channel Four programme is doing a piece on WI's and how they have had to adapt in order to keep up with the times. She had requested coming to one of our meetings, so, of course, being one of the longest serving members, it would only be expected for me to have been there. However, by the time I had rearranged my diary to suit Briony, she informs me she has made alternative plans for the boys and they would be staying with a friend. A friend, Celia! A friend over a family member; their own flesh and blood! And friend whose children also attend the state school no doubt! As you can imagine, I was quite devastated to have sacrificed my chance to be interviewed by the Channel Four lady, and more than a little upset 'a friend' was given precedence to look after my grandchildren when their own grandmother was more than willing and able to help her out—even after the trouble she has caused me. So, once again, Celia, I feel I have gone above and beyond the call of duty in order to help Briony out and once again my efforts and enthusiasm have been trampled upon.

I do hope your daughter-in-law is more considerate than mine. I can't imagine treating my own mother-in-law with such disrespect. It just would never have happened in our day would it, Celia? And goodness knows my mother-in-law was not an easy woman. In fact, I would go as far to say that never have I known a woman be so obsessed and deluded regarding their own adult son and so over indulgent of their daughter, that one truly wondered if the girl had angel's wings growing from her shoulders. If ever there was a case of apron strings that needed to be cut, my mother-in-law could have done with a mighty sharp pair, Celia. I shan't be so uncharitable as to say it was a relief when she died . . . but it did alleviate a lot of the pressure I felt as a wife and mother. Of course, Briony would know little about pressure. Lesbians have solved all that for her.

Do enjoy the rest of your weekend, Celia, and please don't bother yourself with replying to my little diatribe if you are too busy

Bests,
Margaret

SUNDAY 24TH MAY
SUBJECT: RE: TIRESOME
Dear Margaret

How could I not reply? It sounds as though you are having a beastly time, my dear friend, and as you say, all you do is put yourself out for that girl. I shall telephone you as soon as Patrick and Melanie have left—which I am hoping will be very soon. Some people seem to be oblivious to when they have overstayed their welcome. I've been eBaying on my laptop for the past hour and they still haven't taken the hint.

Yours, Celia

PS. I'm not sure I understand how the lesbians have helped Briony, dear? Do you mean feminists?

SUBJECT: RE: TIRESOME
Dear Celia

Are not feminists and lesbians one and the same? Neither have any time for men and both embrace an abundance of body hair.

What on earth are you doing on eBay, Celia? Surely, what John Lewis does not stock, one has no use for in life?

Yours, Margaret

SUBJECT: RE: TIRESOME
Dear Margaret

I think you will find that these days both feminists and lesbians alike are avid fans of the 'Brazilian'.

Unfortunately, as far as I am aware, John Lewis does not yet have a transvestite department—hence the eBaying.

Melanie has just offered to make a 'light tea' so I fear they are here for another couple of hours, yet. God knows what a 'light tea' might entail, but I fear hummus and brioche will be making an appearance. What's so wrong with fish paste sandwiches and fruit cake for Sunday tea I'll never know.

Yours, Celia

PS—I thought a quinoa was a small Australian mammal? Do vegetarians turn a blind eye to eating small Australian mammals these days?

SUBJECT: RE: TIRESOME

Dear Celia

I had no idea lesbians and feminists had such a fondness for Latin Americans. I suppose it's the tan, which despite the health warnings, always makes one look more attractive.

What a dutiful wife you are, Celia, to be purchasing your husband's 'special requirements' for him. Have you thought about doing a presentation on women with husbands such as yourself for the WI one week? I think we have a gap next month since Edna Squint has passed over.

At least your daughter-in-law prepares proper food, Celia. With Briony it's all this vegetarian, clean eating nonsense. I once tried to hide some ham in the cheese sandwiches I had made for lunch, but she was on to it immediately. What harm could it have done, Celia? It's not as if a whole pig had to die for a few slices of wafer thin honey roast, is it?

Bests, Margaret

PS You are confusing quinoa with quokka, I think, dear. I bought some once and added it to a casserole. Once tasted, never forgotten. That was a waste of a casserole, I can tell you.

SUBJECT: RE: TIRESOME

Dear Margaret

I fear you have become somewhat confused. It's not Latin Americans that lesbians and feminists have a fondness for. Have you never had a quick flick through 'Cosmopolitan' or 'Red' whilst in the doctors' waiting room, Margaret? It is an education, I can tell you. While waiting for my flu jab I was somewhat surprised to discover I had never had a G-Spot orgasm. Women these days get to choose from a multitude of orgasms and if they are not experiencing them all, they can Google instructions on how to achieve the one they are lacking.

As for John's 'ways' as you so delicately put it; he's a six-foot-two-inch grown man with a fondness for wearing women's underwear, and you don't get much more specialised than that, my dear! However, although I am tolerant of my husband's 'ways' I would rather not discuss the complexities of our marriage to the rest of the WI if it's all the same to you. In fact, we could end up with a lot less members were I to too start discussing such matters with women who consider the use of a food processor in cake making, the height of vulgarity.

Melanie may not be a vegetarian but she is a 'carnivore with a conscience,' which, simply put, means we have to pay three times the price for organically reared, hand massaged, corn-and-real-ale-fed meat that comes with some absurd authentication certifying they have lived and died happy! Have you heard of anything quite so ridiculous, Margaret? If they don't leave in the next hour I may get distracted by the baby and forget to place a last minute 'sniper' bid on the red satin ruffled French knickers John has expressed an interest in.

Yours, Celia

PS—I shall look out for a nice bit of quokka when next in town. Always good to try new things.

WEDNESDAY 27TH MAY
WHATSAPP MESSAGE

BRIONY: Sorry I didn't get to see you when I was in town, Melissa. Had a fantastic night out though, and think I should take time out for myself more often. Cosmo has said I am welcome to use his place as a crash pad anytime I want and has even offered to get me some keys cut. I appreciate the offer of a bed at yours but Cosmo's place is so much more conveniently located so saves on cab fares. I didn't get to see Kate either as she had prior plans she couldn't get out of, but as I said, it was so much fun! I have to admit, I was a little worried that Kara's arrest was going to put a dampener on things, but Cosmo helped me drown my worries in champagne cocktails and insisted his own solicitor went down to the station to take on her case. To be honest, I'm not really sure how it all happened, but my feet were killing me after walking a mile in my new wedge heel boots and I know Kara was getting slightly snappy with me

92

about keeping up the pace, however, I am certain she never meant to throw my boot at the policeman. Admittedly, it was an extraordinary accurate shot to knock his helmet off, but I stand by my statement that she was just trying to shake a small stone out of the boot for me that was causing us to lag behind. It's amazing how easily a riot is started isn't it? I said it was just mass hysteria but the solicitor said it all amounted to a riot and that was unfortunately why Kara was arrested as the instigator, having aimed the first throw that apparently started it all. Cosmo said I was lucky not to have been arrested for aiding and abetting, as it was my boot that was used, but luckily the TV cameraman had caught it all on film. Well . . . maybe not so luckily for Kara, I guess. Anyway, my boot is being held as evidence so goodness knows when or even if I'll ever see that again. Apparently pics were all over Twitter and Facebook! Fame at last!

MELISSA: Fuck, Briony, how is Kara?!

BRIONY: She was a bit miffed that I still went out for dinner that night, but what was I supposed to do? I could hardly sit at the police station all night drinking weak tea waiting for her to be bailed—and after all she did have a top solicitor there so really there was very little else I could have done. Besides, I was starving and wanted to thank Cosmo for his help and not let him down when he had a table booked at The Ivy for us. I've never been to The Ivy, and James considers a bar meal at the local a treat as far as I am concerned, so I thought I deserved it. My phone was honestly switched on all night waiting for a call to say she had been released, so it was unfortunate that when she they did release her at 6am I was soundly sleeping off the effects of far too much champagne and Michelin starred food, so regrettably didn't hear my mobile. With hindsight, it would probably have been prudent to have given her Cosmo's address beforehand so as she could have got a cab straight there and no, it wasn't very wise for her to drive straight back to Dorset having spent the night with no sleep in the cells.

MELISSA: Christ on a bike, Bri! With friends like you . . .

BRIONY: Let's not forget I had to sit in that police station with only one boot on for over an hour until Cosmo arrived, after her initial arrest, and you should have seen the state of my socks—it was humiliating to say the least. Anyway, I'm sure once the court case is over we will all laugh about it.

MELISSA: Court case?!?

BRIONY: The solicitor says she has nothing to worry about and we can use temporary hormonal insanity due to HRT or something like that, if we really have to. Kara is not thrilled, but I say who cares if we use her early menopause as an excuse, so long as it's her get out of jail free card.

MELISSA: Oh my god, Briony! What has James said about all this? In fact, what does James say to you being wined and dined by your hot, charming neighbour? You were quite pissed when I spoke to you on the phone last night and that wasn't even very late.

BRIONY: I'd hardly eaten all day being on that march and then waiting around in the bloody police station! I was drinking on an empty stomach.

MELISSA: And why were you wearing wedge heeled boots on a march?!? I suppose it's crossed your mind that Kara wouldn't be in this mess had you not chosen fashion over practicality?

BRIONY: They were practical! Ish . . . Anyway, how are the wedding plans coming along?

MELISSA: Well, the church is all booked, although, Dan and I still have to attend a couple of pre-wedding sessions with the vicar where he talks to us about the sanctity of marriage or some such nonsense. It's a royal pain in the posterior as it means we have to stay with Dan's parents for a night when we go up for the weekend and I have to survive on a diet of cheese bloody sandwiches and chocolate digestives. You would have thought the concept of vegetarianism might have filtered through to our northern countrymen by now, but apparently not—or at least not to Dan's family. If I had known I was marrying into a stereotype I may have had second thoughts—it's all pie and mash, faggots, and chips with gravy. I get a little bowl of grated cheddar cheese with every meal—even a roast dinner—in lieu of a meat substitute. For lunch one Saturday I had chips in gravy with grated cheddar and for dinner, mash with gravy and grated cheddar! Once I managed to get hold of a packet of Linda McCartney veggie sausages from the local supermarket and his mother took them from me like they were radioactive! Then when she did cook a couple for me at dinner time, she, his dad, brother and sister stared at them on my plate with such suspicion and disgust you would have thought I was about to eat the flesh of a freshly slaughtered virgin in front on them. They even poke and prodded them with their forks asking what they were made from and kept repeating, 'But NO meat . . . really? How do they do that, then?' until finally I asked if they wanted to try a bit, they all stabbed up all my sausages with their forks, masticated like Neanderthals and promptly spat the lot back out into the bin leaving me with just my bloody grated cheddar again. It's not fun and I know I wanted to lose a few pounds before the wedding but with the amount of treacle thick, strong tea I am force fed, I am going to need my teeth whitened as well. Oh, Christ, and Dan's mum suggested meeting up with my parents before the wedding!!! The colour visibly drained from my face and I later blamed the fainting fit on too much caffeine making me dizzy. But needless to say, Briony, they can't possibly meet before the wedding. I mean, if I had my way, they wouldn't even meet at the wedding, and as it is, strategic planning will need to take place ensuring my mother is never left alone with any of Dan's family members for more than a millisecond.

BRIONY: If you're parents meet his, there will be no wedding.

MELISSA: Exactly, so here's a pic of the dresses I am getting for you and Kate. You are going to need to give me your measurements and once they are made you are absolutely forbidden to gain or lose so much as a pound in weight. Oh, and don't worry as I have already booked rooms for you and Kate and a few others. I'm not paying for them—obviously—but they've been preliminarily booked under my name and credit card and when you decide what kind of room you want you just have to call them, mention my name and take over the booking. Simples! So, thoughts on the bridesmaid dresses . . . ?

BRIONY: Hmm, well, they look like something a seven-year-old might wear. Maybe something with a lower neckline and more fitted? What did Kate think? Has she seen the pictures yet? Also, shouldn't the maid of honour's dress be slightly more . . . well, different? Otherwise people will just mistake me for a bog standard run of the mill bridesmaid.

MELISSA ADDED KATE TO THE GROUP

MELISSA: Why do you want something with a low neckline? I don't want the vicar or best man being distracted by my bridesmaid's cleavage? Nor, the groom for that matter. The Maid of Honour is just the name for the chief bridesmaid, and not so as you could have a better dress. But now you have worried me and I will have to consult my pile of Weddings and Bride magazines to check that the MOH doesn't need to necessarily be wearing a different dress to the bridesmaid.

KATE: Yet, saw your Tibet march riot pics on FB! Riot-tastic! Hahaha. There's one of Kara looking confused and bewildered trending on Twitter which is hilarious. Did you get your boot back?

BRIONY: Fuck, really? Kara's going to kill me. Does privacy mean nothing these days?

MELISSA: Kate, I've left countless message on your phone and I know you're probably too busy being all loved up with Piers to bother replying to me about something as unimportant and petty as the dress you will wear on the most important day of my life, but I need your input—I'm not sure I trust Briony's.

BRIONY: Err, thanks

MELISSA: No offence.

BRIONY: And calm down. I just wanted a slightly lower neckline

KATE: Polo necks make her claustrophobic

MELISSA: WTF?!

KATE: Post traumatic stress from a bondage incident.

BRIONY: It wasn't a bondage incident, Kate

KATE: I'd call being tied up and blindfolded with your polo neck bondage

MELISSA: Really?!?

BRIONY: It wasn't bondage. It was just a bit of fun.

KATE: Bondage is fun.

MELISSA: Which resulted in you having a phobia of polo necks?

BRIONY: It's not a phobia

KATE: If you can't wear polo necks because they make you hyperventilate due to flashbacks from when bondage went wrong, that's a phobia

BRIONY: Ffs!

MELISSA: Jesus

BRIONY: Anyway, who is this Piers? I didn't know you were seeing anyone, Kate! You're a dark horse 😉

KATE: Don't change the subject

MELISSA: Who's Piers? Well, you should know, Briony, you used to date him!

BRIONY: Piers Hartley?!? Snappy the Shark, Piers Hartley?! You're dating Snappy? I know you bumped into him recently but you didn't tell me you'd started seeing him!

KATE: Not really dating. Just been to dinner etc a few times when he's over from New York. But, I really like him, Briony. You don't mind, do you?

BRIONY: OMG why would I mind you going out with a man who used to dress up in a latex shark costume that I had a summer fling with when I was eighteen? Have you harboured a secret desire for him all these years? Did you fancy him when he was Terry the Turtle or was it only after he got his promotion to Snappy? I guess that shell was never particularly flattering, but a man who can rock a foam sharks fin . . .

MELISSA: *Snurk*

KATE: This is possibly why I didn't tell you, Briony.

MELISSA: So, back to my wedding . . .

KATE: Actually, I can't wear high necks either, Melissa; they make me itch. If I itch I need antihistamine pills. If I take anti-histamine I get pissed too quickly.

BRIONY: And if she gets too pissed her vagina gets overly friendly.

KATE: And I end up shagging anything with a pulse, which, in turn leads to me getting an itchy vagina and needing to take anti-histamines. It's a vicious circle for me.

MELISSA HAS LEFT THE GROUP

Thursday 28th May

SUBJECT: ON THE TELEVISION!

Dear Briony

You will no doubt be pleased to hear that I was able to re-arrange my appointments after your last minute cancellation of the boys' sleepover, and will now be appearing on next week's local news programme in their continuing, 'How Times Have Changed' series. I was interviewed at length regarding the village WI—which is one of the longest running WI's in the country—and I have to say, I think Judy was rather impressed with my varied knowledge of local history, cake baking, and how our WI has adapted and changed over the years. I am preparing myself in become something of a local celebrity, Briony!

Now, onto Sarah's party, which I feel we have neglected somewhat recently. The catering company asked if we had a theme—and goodness me, we don't! So, thinking caps on, Briony, as time is creeping up on us. I was thinking along the lines of something like 'years gone by'—maybe the roaring 20s as then the waiting staff would come dressed as flapper girls and everyone would look terribly smart.

Arthur has taken the liberty of passing your phone number onto Dickie Dwyer at the village art club. They are in desperate need of new models and I know you're not busy on a Monday so it would give you something useful to do of a morning—we've got to keep you out of trouble after your recent 'escapade,' which James told me made the evening news! Anyway, you'll be paid ten pounds for your trouble with as many free cups of tea and biscuits as you desire. Dickie said he will give you a call quite soon-ish so best book a trip to the hairdressers asap.

Much Love
Margaret x

THURSDAY 28TH MAY
SUBJECT: RE: ON THE TELEVISION?
Hi Margaret

How exciting for you. I shall certainly try and remember to watch next week. Do try not to let fame change you—you hear such terrible stories of normal people becoming complete self-absorbed narcissists once the fickle hand of fame has touched them.

Gosh, yes. Haven't we just been neglecting Sarah's party arrangements! I'm not sure I see the point of a specific theme as I thought the fact it was her 40th birthday was a theme in itself? However, if we must, 'vicars and tarts' is always a popular choice isn't it?

I do hope James didn't give you the wrong impression of

my 'escapades' in London. It was all an unfortunate misunderstanding between my friend, Kara, and the policeman, and we are confident the charges will be dropped. It was a shame Kara had to miss out on Cosmo's hospitality that evening. However, I have promised her we will be doing it all again very soon (minus the night in the cells, of course).

It was very thoughtful of you to pass on my details to Arthur's art club friend, but I am actually rather busy during the week as have enrolled myself on a short wine tasting course which meets on Monday evenings at the local college, so think I would find it a bit of a squash to fit everything in that day. Maybe the group should advertise locally for art models to draw?

Briony

Friday 29th May
SUBJECT: RE: ON THE TELEVISION?
Dear Briony

I'm not sure 'vicars and tarts' is quite the theme we are looking for—no matter how popular a choice it may appear to be. I have spoken to the catering company and they think something along the lines of 'Hollywood Glamour' would be easy for everyone to join in. Ladies always love an excuse to dress up glamorously and the men folk just need to come in black tie—what could be easier?! Sarah always makes the most of her appearance and unlike some would die rather than be seen out of the house with no make-up or unkempt hair, so we can rest assured she will be the belle of her ball!

James didn't mention you were in London with Cosmo. I had quite forgotten he also has a residence in the city. Is the wine tasting course his idea as well? I was rather thinking I might like to do something along those lines since Cosmo renewed my interest with his delicious wines and fascinating knowledge into their production. I shall contact the college and see if they have any places left.

Dickie has advertised locally but unfortunately no suitable applicants came forth. There are, apparently, only so many ways one can sketch wrinkles and beards, so they were rather hoping to entice a young, female model—although Dickie says you will be fine for now. It will only be for two consecutive mornings initially, so I am sure you can re-arrange things to help out. Often members will be happy to give you their works, so you might even gain some unique artworks of yourself.

Much love
Margaret x

SATURDAY 30TH MAY
WHATSAPP GROUP MESSAGE
MELISSA: Attached are the new designs for bridesmaid dresses with adapted necklines to take into account bondage phobias and friendly vagina problems. As you can see from the designs, Briony's dress will feature a cerise sash

around the hemline to complement the cerise bouquet I will be holding and also identify her as the maid of honour. Monique thinks it would be prudent for us all to have a meeting with the hair stylist to discuss styles for the day so please can you both give me dates for when you would be able to meet. Bri, I am sure you won't mind coming to London again and I thought we could also use this time for the three of us to go for a meal out and catch up while discussing wedding plans.

BRIONY: Who is Monique, exactly?

MELISSA: Monique is my wedding planner—did I not mention before? My mother hired her and although, admittedly, I was less than enthusiastic about the idea, she is proving to be worth her weight in gold (which is probably about what my mother is paying for her).

BRIONY: Dresses look fine. When did you have in mind for meetings about hair. If I can't make it then I am sure it will be fine as the wedding is more about you than the bridesmaids and our hair.

Will call you tonight when I get back from the college. Got to rush to art club now.

MELISSA: Art club? I had no idea you were taking up painting?

BRIONY: I haven't . . .

MELISSA: And of course the wedding is about me but it's highly critical that our hair is coordinated and it's imperative you make it to the meetings.

JUNE

WHATSAPP MESSAGE

GAYLE: Guess who got back in contact with Dudley recently? Jeffrey Salter! You do remember Jeffrey from school, don't you? Jezza emailed him through Facebook and they've corresponded a bit. He looks well—have attached a screenshot from his FB—he hasn't aged a bit!

BRIONY: Wow, Gayle, yeah, Jezza certainly looks like he found the magical elixir of youth. Bit of a surprise that he came out though—although when I mentioned it to James he said he wasn't surprised as he was always a bit of a pretty boy and never had a girlfriend that anyone can recall. I just think it's a shame he didn't come out sooner—imagine living all those years pretending to be someone you're not? At least he's found love now and looks really happy.

GAYLE: Jeffrey is gay?!? Wow. I had no idea. I wonder if his wife knows?! Actually, I s'pose he's bi then. Maybe she does know and is cool with it. No reason why she shouldn't

105

be. I just had no idea he swung both ways.

BRIONY: Jeffrey got married?!? Oh, so yeah, I guess he was actually bi-sexual all along then? I think it's called 'sexually fluid' these days, actually. I quite like the sound of it. Makes you sound quite enigmatic, if not a little . . . sticky? Has he been married long? What's his wife like? I suppose she must know then . . . . ?

GAYLE: Briony, the photo I screenshot for you was of Jeffrey at his own wedding—his wife was the one on the far right with the tousled dark hair.

BRIONY: Oh. I assumed the photo was Jeffrey at a gay wedding as all the men around him looked . . . well . . . very handsome, well-groomed and particularly smart? Is he not gay then? I'm going to presume not then as he married a woman—albeit a woman with lank hair who looks a bit like an effeminate man. Maybe he's sexually fluid but hasn't found his fluidity yet? Either way, how awful to a bride who's mistaken for a gay man in your wedding photos . . . 🙁

GAYLE: Oh Christ, Briony. I think you need to remember that there are some heterosexual men who can look handsome and well-groomed as well—although granted it's a rarity....

BRIONY: Will Kara be at coffee Thurs? Did she say if the police will post my boot back? I'm a bit loathe to ask her myself if she's still a bit touchy about the whole thing.

GAYLE: Saw Kara yesterday. I wouldn't so much say she's relieved at having the charges dropped—more still fuming about the whole incident, tbh. She did mention that your boot has now been released as it's no longer needed as evidence—so there's a bit of luck.

BRIONY: Yes, what luck :o/

GAYLE: So, what's this about art classes Lucy was telling me about?

BRIONY: Oh, I went to James' father's art group yesterday to sit as a 'model' for them. Needless to say, sitting motionless and prostrate in a hard backed wooden chair for two-hours while a bunch of octogenarians sketch every blemish and wrinkle is hardly my idea of fun, but it was Margaret's idea to 'keep me out of trouble', as she put it. Apparently, I have far too much spare time on my hands—highlighted by my bringing the Denley name into disrepute during the Tibet march recently. Margaret had tried to entice me with promises that the amateur artists often hand over the fruits of their two hour creative endeavour to the model. However, it would seem a Dead Sea mud mask, eight hours sleep and forty five minutes of contorting facial exercises on the drive to the village hall and I still get painted as a sixty year old fish wife. It really was quite astounding, Gayle. Dickie did warn me explain that each member would interpret my face in their own unique way—and let's just say that there were some very unique interpretations indeed. In fact, I appear to resemble the bastard love-child of Camilla Parker Bowles & Margaret Thatcher. Never has botox howled my name louder . . .

GAYLE: Oh, I want to see the paintings! Are you taking

107

the boys to see Terrance Dere at the bookshop on Saturday? I'm thinking it's going to get busy so best queue early if you are going. I would say we should save each other places, but you know how territorial people get about their place in the queue—you could end up starting another riot and as we all know; to start one riot is unfortunate, but, to start two is just plain stupid 😀

BRIONY: Yeah, was planning on spending Sat morning queuing to get books signed by Terence Dere. Can't possibly get out of it, as boys adore his books and are very excited. My mother-in-law phoned to say she would like to join us since she saw a piece in the local paper about his book signing visit—so that will be . . . 'fun' for me :o/

GAYLE: Well, she's got a point about keeping you out of trouble . . .

WEDNESDAY 3RD JUNE
WHATSAPP MESSAGE
BRIONY: Hey, Kate, have you heard any more about 'Monique' the wedding coordinator? She sounds scary! Melissa said that her mother said that Monique said (take breath) that once the styles for our hair have been decided upon, we cannot go changing our current style in a manner that would mean it would not accommodate the wedding day styles! That's a bit strict isn't it? I thought Melissa was going to be pretty chilled about it all but I think her mother has well and truly got to her. Have you booked your room? I called the hotel where Melissa had provisional-

ly booked rooms and have taken two double rooms with adjoining door. I figured that way James and I would get more chance of a lie-in the morning after if the boys are in the next room yet if I work out a way to lock their door from the inside, they won't be able to escape without going through our room first. Cunning, eh? Although the way things are going between James and I at the moment, I may leave him behind, anyway.

So, how are things going with Piers? Does he wear his Snappy the Shark costume for you on special occasions? Will he be your plus one at the wedding? Will you be rugby tackling everyone out the way to catch the bouquet so as you and Piers can have a sea life themed wedding? If so, bagsy I get to come as an angel fish 😉

KATE: An angel fish? I see you more as a blue ringed octopus—intriguing when spotted for the first time, yet armed with a deadly sting.

BRIONY: Intriguing yet deadly. I'll take that 😃

KATE: Something tells me this wedding is going to be an exercise in diplomacy. The revised dresses are better, I guess, although you can see Melissa's mother has had the presiding hand over them and doesn't want to risk us upstaging her daughter in any way, shape or form. I strongly suspect we shall be wearing ballet pumps and have hairstyles that make us look dowdy and dull yet inoffensive to the viewing public and unobtrusive for the wedding photographs. You have to bring James as he will need to provide the trusty medicinal hip flask for us, as no doubt we will be standing around a freezing churchyard for hours getting the 'right shot'.

BRIONY: So? How are things with Sharkboy?

KATE: Things with Piers are going very well . . . I think. He is such a gentleman—which is a nice change . . . for now . . .

BRIONY: What do you mean by 'gentleman'? Does he lay down his coat over puddles for you?

KATE: Yes, Briony, exactly that. Anyway, it's far too early to be thinking about if I will be bringing him along to the wedding, although, I'll make sure he is wearing his shark outfit just for you . . .

BRIONY: A gentleman shark. How very . . . modern!

KATE: Anyway, what has James done to irk you so much?

BRIONY: He's not really irked me over anything specific. It's just he's never here, and when he is, he may as well not be here for all the attention he pays me.

KATE: Things not improved then?

BRIONY: I know that makes me sound needy and trite

KATE: No, it doesn't. It wouldn't kill him to give you more kudos for everything you do.

BRIONY: And he never listens to me or takes any notice of anything I do. I feel like an extension to the business—here just to entertain business colleagues, play the dutiful wife and to make sure the 'family' element ticks over nicely in his absence, but other than that I am redundant as a person in my own right. Everything revolves around him, and everything and everybody takes second place. I know he is busy and I know I should be grateful to have a lovely home and a successful husband—and I am—it's just that we don't seem to be working as a couple anymore. When I got back from London he didn't see any humour in what had been a surreal and absurd situation with Kara being arrested; he was more concerned about it making the news and people recognising me as his wife. He's turned into a boring old dullard.

KATE: Much as I love James, he was never the life and soul of the party, Briony.

BRIONY: So he was always a dullard?

KATE: I didn't say that . . .

BRIONY: Anyway, I'm doing this wine course at the local college one evening a week which so far I am really enjoying it. Cosmo has opened my eyes to the world of wine and he's taught me a lot but I thought if I go on a proper course I will be able to regale James' business colleagues with my knowledge when we entertain and lever myself up from being 'just' the wife. Cosmo has even suggested I might like to accompany him when he next takes a trip to one of the vineyards he does business with in Europe. How fab would that be?

KATE: Sounds like a bit of a mid-life crisis—or 'mid-life disillusionment.' I don't think James sees you as anything but his equal but I guess he needs to show his appreciation for everything you do a little more. You're not 'just' a wife and you should feel you have to lever yourself up from being 'just' that. I think the wine course is a great idea but does that mean we will be banned from quaffing cheap plonk in your presence?!

BRIONY: Maybe I am going through a bit of mid-life disillusionment (I Googled it!). I gave up a lot to stay at home and be a mother to the boys, and I don't regret that, but I just feel something is missing now. Ah well, I'm sure it will sort itself out. I'm probably just a bit pre-menstrual.

KATE: Forgot to mention, I'm coming down this weekend to see the folks. Are you free Saturday night? I could pop over with a bottle of mid-range Merlot and see the new house in real life, which, I am sure is quite different to the numerous Facebook photos and skype tour I had?

BRIONY: Saturday would be great. Is Piers coming with you? How does it work with him in New York, anyway?

KATE: Piers is over in London for a few months setting up the new department. I'm not thinking about when he goes back to the States and just enjoying it for now. Don't tell Melissa I'm coming down—she may try and wrangle a trip to her folks and use it as an excuse to get us all together for this wedding briefing! The longer we manage to postpone that the better, in my opinion. I wonder if Dan will make us little clutch bags to match the dresses?

How does 7ish suit for Sat?

BRIONY: 7ish sounds great. I'll sort out something to eat.

KATE: Crisps in a bowl—The Briony special.

BRIONY: I might really push the boat out and mix different flavours in the same bowl.

KATE: You spoil me! See you Sat.

TO: VIRGINA COLDSTONE CHAIR TO PTA
FROM: BRIONY DENLEY
THURSDAY 4TH JUNE
SUBJECT: ORGANIC FREE RANGE EGGS

Dear Virginia

I refer to the letter set out by the PTA on Tuesday, regarding the provision of props and refreshments for the upcoming school sports day. I have to confess I find it rather puzzling and slightly hypocritical of the PTA to insist that cakes baked for the refreshment tent should be made using 'organic free range eggs in line with the schools healthy eating policy,' yet, on the next paragraph you request the donation of boxes of eggs for the egg and spoon race and distinctly state 'economy eggs will be perfectly acceptable'. Well, Virginia, I am afraid I have to disagree with you there. When is it ever acceptable to play party to the abuse and exploitation of innocent battery hens whose every waking hour is spent torturously pecking out the eyes of its neighbour while being fed upon a diet of hormone fortified low-rate grain in the knowledge its free range cousin clucks happily on its diet of organic corn whilst roaming green and luscious pastures?

I urge the PTA to give this issue serious reconsideration.

Best Regards
Briony Denley

(Mother to Sam and Zac Denley)

TO: BRIONY DENLEY
FROM: VIRGINA COLDSTONE CHAIR TO PTA
FRIDAY 5TH JUNE
SUBJECT: RE: ORGANIC FREE RANGE EGGS

Dear Briony

Thank you for raising you concerns regarding the use of eggs at the forthcoming Festival of Sports (please note the correct term for this event, discussed and decided upon at the last PTA meeting which you would be aware of had you attended). The decision to request the use of free range eggs in cakes donated for the refreshment tent was indeed based upon the schools 'healthy food for all' policy. However, as we anticipated the majority of eggs used in the egg and spoon races would be smashed and never used for consumption, we decided that it would be unjust to insist upon donations of the more expensive free range eggs for this purpose.

If you have any further concerns or would like to participate more fully with the substantial organisation involved with the school's Festival of Sports, you are very welcome to attend our next meeting, held in the staffroom on June 22nd at 7.30pm. As you know we are always eager to welcome our friends into the fold and if memory serves me well, we have not welcomed you at a meeting since your eldest son started in Reception Year when you made such an impression assisting us with the cake auction at the Christmas Fayre—and what an amazing set of lungs for such a petite lady as yourself, if I may say so.

Best Regards
Virginia Coldstone
Chair to the PTA

TO: VIRGINA COLDSTONE CHAIR TO PTA
FROM: BRIONY DENLEY
THURSDAY 4TH JUNE
SUBJECT: RE: ORGANIC FREE RANGE EGGS
(DRAFTS/UNSENT)

Dear Virginia

Thanks for your prompt reply. I am sure the battery hens will suffer happily in the knowledge their eggs are not being consumed in scrumptious cakes and only smashed to the ground during the primary school children's sports day. Maybe the PTA should invest some of its funds in purchasing some plastic eggs for such events instead of squandering it away on self-congratulatory meals out for the core PTA team and kitting the secretary out with a funky new printer in the guise she needs it for flyers, when we all know your husband owns a printing company who prints all the flyers and letters out . . . then invoices his costs to the PTA. Hmm, quite a racket you've got going there, Ginny.

Sadly, I am unable to participate more with the PTA as, unlike you and your coven, I have a life, and I seldom enjoy spending my precious evenings with a bunch of cliquey, smug, fat-bottomed women, stuffing my face with short-bread fingers and gossiping about who was wearing last season's Boden 'flirty ruffle dress' in the playground. Thank you for your acknowledgement to my lungs. I certainly had to bellow during the cake auction to be heard over the cackle of PTA members knocking back the mulled wine.

Yours, Briony Denley

THURSDAY 4TH JUNE
WHATSAPP GROUP MESSAGE
2.05PM

BRIONY: I got a reply from Virginia about the eggs! I am a marked woman. It's all your fault!

BRIONY: I SAID—I GOT A REPLY FROM VIRGINIA! Ffs where are you all?!?

BRIONY: I drafted a reply but should prob hold back until I'm feeling less...hormonal . . .

BRIONY: Gotta do the school run now . . . oh, which means I'll see Virginia . . . .

4.11PM

GAYLE: Gosh, never would have guessed you're pre-menstrual. Sorry, was busy castrating a cat.

BRIONY: Tbh angsty appears to be my default setting some months 😉

KARA: You need a bloody good seeing too before you kill someone.

BRIONY: Tell me about it . . .

LUCY: Was driving. Just arrived home.

KARA: That reply is hilarious, although you're fucked now!

BRIONY: I wish 😬

KARA: Oh, and you'll be happy to hear I enquired about your boot and apparently they will send it on to you and yes, I'm sure we will all laugh about this in the future, but, for the sake of our friendship, just don't ask to come with me to anymore demos or marches. By the sounds of it, you obviously had an enjoyable evening with Cosmo whilst I was incarcerated . . .

GAYLE: Have you thought about going away with James for a weekend without the boys? It might be just what you need. I know you tend to joke about things as a way of distraction but you're obviously quite unhappy at the moment and if James is so wrapped up in work then I doubt he's even noticed just how unhappy you are.

KARA: You know what men are like.

GAYLE: And as your friend I have to say I'm not sure it's wise to distract yourself having meals out with your neighbour who obviously has a soft spot for you . . .

KARA: Because as we all know, it's only a matter of time before a soft spot becomes hard 😃

BRIONY: Kara 😃

GAYLE: Book a nice hotel for a weekend and farm the boys out to someone. I'm happy to have them—It would be the perfect way to regain some intimacy and talk about all those things that have been building up.

BRIONY: Do I use humour as a distraction?

KARA: Yes.

GAYLE: Yeah!

LUCY: Yes.

BRIONY: Oh. I'd never really thought about it to be honest. Do you really think Cosmo has a soft spot for me?

KARA: Well, durrrrr.

BRIONY: I think he is just being kind, after all why would he be interested in a married mother of two when he's quite the eligible bachelor?? I obviously moaned for far too long last week and I have made it sound a lot worse than it is . . . so don't worry about me! Once I get my other boot back I shall be happy!

KARA: Using humour as a distraction technique . . .

LUCY: Just told Abbie about you and the school caretaker. She's here for Algey's massage session. Can't stop laughing . . . 😊

GAYLE: So what's this I'm hearing from the playground about you and the caretaker?? The kids were babbling something when I got them from after school club.

Briony: Ahh yes, rather embarrassing. After my PMT fuelled bravado of the email, I turned in to a complete wuss when I spotted Virginia at the gates accosting people for promises of help at the summer fayre (or should that be 'Festival of Summertime?!). Sooooo . . . I thought it would be a good idea nip around the back of the school via the staff car park to enter the playground from behind—as you do. Unfortunately, the security gates were locked, sabotaging my cunning plan, but, thinking back to my stealthy retrieval of Lucy's 'Raging Rabbit' from the vicar's roof, I decided to scale the gates—a mere six foot at most, and with large foot sized holes in the steel fencing it was a doddle . . . until the caretaker spotted me, skirt wrapped nappy-esque style around my bum, one leg over the top of the fence, the other Birkenstock clad foot dangling at an unflattering angle as I tried to balance the slipping Birky on my big toe and stop it falling back down and my bag strap caught around my neck about to asphyxiate me. It was not a good look, Kara, and not least because my exposed twisted and dangling legs are still a whiter shade of pale and stubbly—who the fuck shaves their legs before June anyway?! Tried to concoct a story about how I suffered occasional and sudden bouts of extreme shyness and this had occurred without warning just as I parked my car down the road from the school, causing me to desperately seek out a way of entering the playground without having to see too many people. Not convinced the caretaker bought it, but, not wanting to mess with an obviously deranged mother at school pick up time, he kindly helped me back down and opened the gate for me. I was simply dying inside, and with retrospect, I think facing up to Virginia would have been preferable.

GAYLE: Hahahahahahahahaha—Too funny! Let's hope no one saw you on the CCTV in the office! I wouldn't put it past those school admin assistants to post it on YouTube. My god, Briony, you could go viral!

BRIONY CCTV? YOUTUBE?!? GO VIRAL?!?! Faaaaaaarrrrkkkkkk!!!!

SUBJECT: TERENCE DEARE

Dear Celia

I do hope this finds you well? I had rather an exciting weekend by all accounts which started on Saturday when Briony and I took the boys to a book signing in the town. Have you heard of Terence Deare, Celia? Are your grandchildren fans? His books are rather intense and littered with scientific and historical facts, so may be rather advanced for yours at the moment. But anyway, Sam and Zac are great readers for their age and huge fans of Terence's blockbusters, so they were terribly excited to meet him. I had the foresight to arrive early, having anticipated his visit would draw in the crowds from the surrounding towns and villages—and I was right! By the time the book shop opened its doors, fans were queuing all down to the bottom of the high street. The local newspaper and a lady from the local TV news were there to record the early-comers as we entered the shop, and although we were not first in the queue outside, excitement seemed to get the better of the family in front as they tripped over each other by the crime fiction and fell into such an embarrassing bundle on the floor, it was kinder for us to pretend we hadn't noticed, step over them and continue to make our way to Terence and the eager film crew. Oh, Celia! We had a number of photos taken next to Terence and then the local news people interviewed us. It was quite something! I'm on a quite a run at the moment what with my WI interview with Judy and now this. I wouldn't be surprised if people started asking for my autograph soon.

After excitement of Saturday, the weekend was topped off by Sarah informing me that their house is going to be featured in one of the top 'Homes' magazines in July/September, so of course I have already put my order in with the local newsagent. I suspect a number of my friends will be eager to see the spread so I made sure Mr Pringle knew I would be requiring a number of copies and the reason why. I shall of course keep one aside to send to you.

Now, Celia, are we all ready for the big event, do you think? Sarah thinks only a few close friends will be joining a small family gathering on the day itself, which I have to admit, she seemed rather unimpressed by . . . oh, she does so love a party though, so it will be quite a welcome surprise for her to discover so many of her nearest and dearest have come to help her celebrate.

That reminds me, thank you for your cheque, Celia—I am still yet to get the remaining monies owed from Briony. No point asking poor James as he is so busy with the business. I also need to confirm the final cost of the wine from Cosmo—although as we are such good friends I am expecting a substantial discount. I don't like to accept 'favours' such as this from friends usually, but I know Cosmo would be insulted if I insisted on paying the full retail price—such a gentleman.

Yours
Margaret

Monday 8th June
SUBJECT: RE: TERENCE DEARE
Dear Margaret

How quickly you forget! My eldest grandson, Joshua, has been recognised as being gifted and has a reading age at least five years above his actual age, so please be assured he finds few books or authors too advanced. If memory serves me well, I do believe he had read most of Terence Deare's books by the time he was six and moved onto more complex plots with a more challenging vocabulary.

Now, Margaret, I did mean to ring you about our cottaging holiday. As James and Briony will not being staying for the full week, would it be terribly cheeky of me to ask if Angela and Gerry could join us? You remember Angela and Gerry from my 60th don't you? As I recall, Arthur and yourself got along like a house on fire with them, so I did rather think it might be fun to have them join us? Do tell me if you think I am being rude in asking.

Yours, Celia

Tuesday 9th June
WHATSAPP GROUP MESSAGE
BRIONY: So, Melissa, Kate and I were just wondering if Dan is going to be making clutch bags or something to match our dresses? Thought it would be a nice touch and we will need somewhere to put our lip gloss and phones, won't we?

KATE: Briony was wondering more than me.

BRIONY: We were both wondering in equal amounts.

KATE: You were definitely more concerned about it then I, Briony.

BRIONY: You were the one who brought it up first, actually, Kate.

KATE: But then you showed far more concern about it al than I, Briony, I think you will find.

BRIONY: Anyway, check out this link to the local paper as there is a good photo of the boys and Terence Deare . . . . ..and Margaret, of course, from Saturday's book signing. She had insisted we go early to get a place near the front of the queue which meant standing around with two very bored boys for two hours whilst she wafted off to have a full English with copious amounts of Earl Grey in a local café that opens at 7am. We were fortunate to be second in the queue behind a lovely family who had just pipped us to the post, but as soon as the book shop opened its doors, Margaret turned into a raving groupie! The woman barged into the store right on the heels of the other family, and I swear to you Melissa, I am sure she purposely tripped the little girl up which in turn caused her brother and mum to trip over each other, as Margaret—with psychotic, manic grin and eyes still glued to her quarry, like a hyena sighting an injured baby gazelle—ungraciously stepped over the pile of bodies on the floor and arrived at the book signing table to a somewhat bemused and slightly scared looking Terence Deare! As I was left to apologise profusely to the family—who by this point had a sobbing child and a mum with a suspected sprained ankle—Margaret was interviewed by the local TV news and had numerous photos taken with Terence and the boys. By the time I got to them, Margaret had managed to prize a kiss from the poor man as an aghast Zac trilled 'Grandma! Why are you licking him?!' Honestly, Melissa, every time that woman comes out with us lately my poor children are witness to some sort of disturbing scene no child of their age should be privy too—think back to the sherry sodden Celia and her tales of a spanking cross-dressing John!

KATE: OMFG Pensioners spanking!!! That sentence should come with a health warning, Briony!

BRIONY: Where is Melissa, anyway?

KATE: Oh, probably delivering a baby. You know how tiresome it is when work gets in the way of chatting . . .

BRIONY: Anyway, I've booked James and I into a little hotel in the Cotswolds the weekend after next which he doesn't know about yet. The boys are going to friends for the weekend so it will be nice to 'reconnect' with my husband—as Kara so eloquently puts it . . . Personally, I'm just looking forward to a weekend of uninterrupted shagging—fuck the Cotswold rambles and quaint pubs, as far as I'm concerned pre- and post-coital snacks will be taken in our room, and if I'm not sporting a 'shagged to within an inch of my life' glow on the Monday school-run, then something is very amiss!

KATE: Ohh good luck with that. I'll be thinking about you

BRIONY: Umm, Please don't.

KATE: Err, no, no, eww . . . wrong.

TUESDAY 9TH JUNE
SUBJECT: COTTAGING

Dear Celia

You may have noticed I have changed the title of this email. I do find it helps to change the subject title if one has moved on from the original subject matter. Just a tip for future reference, Celia, dear.

Of course I don't think you rude in asking if Angela and Gerry Fothergill can join us! What a marvellous idea. You're right; Arthur and I found them great fun at your 60th and it would be a shame to waste the extra bedroom. I'll work out their share of the cost and you can tell them to send a cheque and then I can reimburse you in part. What fun cottaging with new friends and old will be!

Silly me! I had forgotten all about your grandson, Joshua. I thought by 'gifted' you had meant he had one of these special disabilities that seem to be so popular with parents nowadays. One is always reading about some new affliction doctors are labelling difficult and odd children with. Of course, we didn't have that luxury when we were young mothers; if your child was odd or badly behaved you just got on with it—and you particularly did a sterling job in that respect, Celia.

Yours, Margaret

SUBJECT: RE: COTTAGING

Dear Margaret

I can assure you Joshua is neither badly behaved nor 'odd'. He is simply exceptionally well-read and articulate for his age.

I have now told Angela and Gerry they are welcome to join our cottaging break, and they are most excited saying how nice it will be to spend time with people who have the same interests as themselves. You certainly appear to have made quite an impression on them at my party. What day will James and Briony be leaving? Angela mentioned they would quite like to join us on the Sunday as Gerry thinks the traffic will be good for travelling early morning. They're terribly eager!

Yours Celia

PS—What do you mean I did a sterling job? Neither of my children were odd or badly behaved, Margaret.

WEDNESDAY 10TH JUNE
SUBJECT: RE: COTTAGING

Dear Celia

I didn't mean to cause offence regarding your own children, or your special grandson—I was simply commenting on all the new excuses mothers seem to have these days for their child's bad behaviour. I am sure Joshua is remarkably well behaved and quite normal acting—just like all the other bog standard grandsons around the country who read age-appropriate books, such as mine. I do think it should be remembered, Celia, that there is a reason Stephen King is not found next to Horrid Henry . . . and it's nothing to do with the Dewey Decimal system.

I shall contact Briony and ask what time she thinks they will be leaving. I'm sure it won't be a problem. I think cottaging with friends is something we should do more often.

Yours, Margaret.

WEDNESDAY 10TH JUNE
SUBJECT: MY GRANDSON, JOSHUA, IS GIFTED.
Dear Margaret

Thank you for the tip regarding subject titles, which as you can see, I have taken on board.

I think calling a child 'special' is a politically correct term used to describe a child with a disability, Margaret. Joshua is gifted, but not remotely special, and I can assure you he is not tucked up in bed reading inappropriate books of an evening.

Now, the cottage. Are we getting shopping delivered and how shall we go about this so as everyone has the items they require? You mentioned Briony and James are struggling financially, but I really cannot abide economy label cornflakes.

Yours, Celia

WEDNESDAY 10TH JUNE

SUBJECT: STILL COTTAGING

Dear Celia

Thank you for taking the time to enlighten me as to the politically correct terms in current usage. Of course, when I was at school, I too was quite the book worm, but no one felt the need to attach a label to me or hand out extra funding simply because I had reached the end of 'Janet and John's adventures' before my peers.

With regards to the shopping—I have already started an order to be delivered so if you have any special requests please let me know and I will add them. I use the term 'special' in this instance to denote items you particularly favour and not in a politically correct term.

I will let you know the cost of your share—and Angela and Gerry—when it is complete.

Yours, Margaret

THURSDAY 11TH JUNE

WHATSAPP MESSAGE

KATE: Thanks for a great night the other Saturday! It's amazing how much fun two woman can have with a few cans of ready-made mojito and bowls of crisps.

BRIONY: Thank fuck for cocktails in a can, eh? Whoever invented those deserves a Noble Peace Prize. I fear cycling to the village shop and stuffing our rucksacks with as many cans as we could carry has left me with an unfair reputation in the village though . . .

KATE: Like you don't have a reputation already 😉 Have you told James about the weekend mini break yet? I bet he's going to be thrilled with you—I'm sure it's just what he needs to relax with you and forget about the business for a couple of days.

BRIONY: Yeah, told James about the mini break last night, and I have to say I feel quite pissed off with him. He was not exactly overwhelmed by my gesture and more concerned that he was going to have to reschedule any meetings he had on Monday as he wouldn't have time to prepare at the weekend—unless I allowed him to take his laptop with us! Christ on a bike, Kate! Can you believe he even suggested taking his laptop away with us for a romantic weekend, and when I said no, he said, well, at least he'd have his phone. Feel quite deflated about the whole break now and if it wasn't for the fact I feel I might spontaneously combust if I don't get a good porking soon, I'd cancel it and sulk.

KATE: Ohhhhh, Bri! What a twat! It's a good job I didn't see James before I left as I may have given him a sizeable piece of my mind. What is he playing at? Most men would be thrilled that their wife had the thoughtfulness to book a weekend away to help them de-stress. Don't be deflated. Try and be positive as I'm sure it's just the stress talking. Once he and you drive off on Friday night I am sure all his stress and worry will melt away and you will have a fantastic break.

BRIONY: Maybe I'll take a good book just in case . . . 😃

KATE: I have to say, it was good to meet Cosmo the other night. Melissa had said something about him which had made me draw conclusions as to his intentions towards you. Nothing sinister. Just that with James away a lot I think some people may have thought he was being a bit lecherous by always popping over with wine and that, but now I have met him I can see he's a really decent chap and obviously not interested in you in that way at all.

BRIONY: WTF?! Why wouldn't Cosmo be interested in me? What's wrong with me? Kara said she thought he had a soft spot for me, actually. I'm pretty sure that it's only the fact that he IS a really decent chap and I AM a married woman that's stopped him making a move, actually.

KATE: Oh, yeah, totes. If it weren't for all that, I don't doubt he'd be trying to take you from behind in the utility room every time he popped round.

BRIONY: Humpth.

SCHOOL NEWSLETTER THURSDAY 11TH JUNE

Please may we remind all parents that for the safety of the children, the main school gates are the only entrance that should be used to collect your children from school. In the interest of the security of the school and its pupils, it is unacceptable for parents to take alternative routes around the back of the school, and our school health and safety policy deems it unwise to attempt to climb the locked car park gates. Our school likes to lead by example and this is not the good example we expect of our parents. Thank you.

WHATSAPP MESSAGE

MELISSA: Briony, what do you mean by 'we will need somewhere to put our lip-gloss and phones'?! Who exactly do you think you will be texting whilst I am getting married?!? Phones are not allowed, Briony. The ushers will be asking guests to make sure their phones are turned off before they are seated, so you and Kate certainly will not need a bag for yours! And I certainly will not be expecting anyone to be taking selfies to post on Facebook before the end of the ceremony. I'm beginning to worry that you might not be taking your position as matron of honour as seriously as you should be?

BRIONY: No live tweeting of the wedding?

MELISSA: Absofuckinglutely not!

BRIONY: Everyone puts the wedding pics on FB. It's expected.

MELISSA: I want editorial control.

KATE: And I want clitorial control. I don't want pics of me totally mashed on FB with body parts on show. Unless I look hot. Mashed and hot, fine.

BRIONY: When have you ever flashed your clit on FB?!

KATE: A camera flash reveals a lot more than you realise, Briony.

BRIONY: Eww.

MELISSA: So, I've been at Dan's parents for the past few days. We've had the obligatory meetings with the vicar which included couple's counselling. I had no idea we had

131

to be counselled before we got married; but apparently we do. So, the vicar asked 'when' we have children, will we be taking on the traditional roles of mother staying at home to bring up the child whilst father brings home the bacon (or words to that effect). Well, for a start I thought it rather presumptuous of him to assume we were even decided on if we were going to have children, let alone expecting us to discuss who was going to do the child rearing, but, just as I was getting over my mild to moderate surprise at such an audacious query, and telling myself that he was a man of the cloth who was essentially interviewing us before he agreed to marry us in his picturesque little church, Dan rendered me smack bang speechless with his response! Apparently, I will be taking an extended career break to bring up our three children, only returning to work on a part time basis—in order to fit in with the school day—once our youngest child is settled at primary school. It was at this point that I choked on the vicar's wife's cucumber sand-wiches and Dan had to administer a half-hearted attempt at the Heinrich manoeuvre. Never quite regaining my composure, we left shortly afterwards and spent the jour-ney back to London in icy silence only broken by the occa-sional sharp intake of breaths and sighs at each other. I had no idea Dan had all these ideas and opinions. Why would he even assume I even wanted children, let alone want to give up my career to become a down trodden housewife and mother? Not happy.

BRIONY: It may have escaped your notice but I gave up

my career to become a 'downtrodden housewife and mother', Melissa. Thanks for that!

KATE: Seriously, maybe the fact you deliver babies for a living made him come to the outlandish conclusion that you might one day actually want to have children yourself? Just a thought . . . ?

BRIONY: And I can assure you I am taking my responsibilities as Matron of Honour super seriously . . . however, I still need a bag to hold my lip-gloss and tissues. Of course, I would be happy to provide my own bag but it might not be in keeping with your 'theme.'

MELISSA: Do you think you might cry? Aww, that's so sweet, Briony 🙂

BRIONY: No. It's winter. I'm bound to have a cold.

KATE: Fuck yeah, better stock up on flu remedies 💊

BRIONY: Oh, by the way—Kate thinks Cosmo would never be interested in me . . .

KATE: I didn't say that.

BRIONY: I thought we had quite a rapport. I mean, obviously I couldn't be interested in that way, but I would be interested to have someone be interested in me in that way. If you see what I mean? What do you think? Kara thinks he has a soft spot for me. Do you think he might have a soft spot for me?

MELISSA: He's gay, Briony.

BRIONY: He's not!

MELISSA: My gaydar is well tuned, Briony. He's gay.

SATURDAY 13TH JUNE
SUBJECT: INVOICE
Dear Margaret

Please find attached my invoice for wine supplied to you for your daughter's forthcoming birthday party. The order is now complete and awaiting despatch to the address in Devon you specified.

May I take this opportunity to wish you an enjoyable event, and if I can be of any further assistance please do not hesitate to contact me or my staff who will be happy to deal with any queries.

Yours sincerely
Cosmo Huntington Jones

SUNDAY 14TH JUNE
SUBJECT: DISILLUSIONED
Dear Celia

As you can see from my subject line, I am feeling some-what disillusioned. This morning I received an email from James and Briony's neighbour, Cosmo, invoicing me for the wine he recommended I purchase for Sarah's party. The cost is, shall we say, a little higher than I had anticipated and there appears to be no mention of a discount applied to the order. Although, to be truthful, even if a discount was offered it would seem I stand little chance of getting much change from one thousand pounds. Yes, you heard correctly, Celia, ONE THOUSAND POUNDS. I trusted

Mr Huntington Jones to guide me in recommendations for wines to suit the discerning palates of Sarah's friends. I did not expect to be presented with a bill worthy of the Ambassador's Ball. What would you advise? Should I contact Mr Huntington Jones with my concerns, or would that seem . . . churlish?

Yours,
Margaret

SUNDAY 14TH JUNE
SUBJECT: FLABBERGASTED?
Dear Margaret

Oh, my goodness! I have to admit to being rather stunned at the cost involved (as outlined in my subject title, thanks again for your little tip). However, maybe it would have been prudent to have given Cosmo an idea as to your budget? I am sure he only had your best interests at heart and didn't want you embarrassed in front of the guests with inferior wines.

I have attached a list of food items to be added to the shopping. Gerry and Angela are being terribly easy and have said they have no specific requirements other than the champers. I have the grandchildren here again today while their parents gallivant around some organic farmers' market or something. I did ask Patrick and Melanie why the children couldn't go with them but they seemed to think it was an ideal opportunity for us to spend time with our grandchildren! Really, Margaret, sometimes I think they assume we don't have lives of our own and have nothing better to do but child-mind for them. As it is, I have cleared out the loft and am listing items to sell on EBay, of which Joshua is helping by taking photographs and measurements. I suspect Melanie will be complaining that doesn't count as spending 'quality time' with my grandson. I overfed the baby, gave it a 'forbidden' dummy dipped in honey, and have put it to sleep in the sweltering back bedroom in the hope it doesn't wake before they return. Just what sort of quality time can one have with a baby anyway? At least Joshua (being gifted, of course) can make himself useful weighing and working out the postage costs.

Yours,
Celia

MONDAY 15TH JUNE
SUBJECT: MONIES
Dear Briony

I do hope you and James had a lovely break away and the children were not too distressed by the upheaval. I was watching a documentary recently that explored the high rate of deviant behaviour in children who had an unsettled and insecure childhood. Apparently, that homosexual German cannibal had parents who would regularly leave him with neighbours while they holidayed around the country. It's always a worry, isn't it?

I have attached the invoice sent to me by Cosmo regarding the wine. As you can see he truly went above and beyond the call of duty in sourcing only the finest wines for our guests. If you could send me a cheque for your share of the bill along with the balance owed on the cottage I would be most grateful. I am sure the monies owed on the cottage had just slipped your mind as you've been terribly busy organising your trip to London and the mini break. I don't recall if I have already mentioned it, but friends of Celia and John's—Angela and Gerry—whom we became very friendly with at Celia's 60th, are going to be arriving early on the Sunday morning, so just wanted to make sure you all plan to make an early start that day? Could I also request you bring your own bed linen so as Angela and Gerry can use the clean bedding provided on their arrival.

Much Love,
Margaret x

TUESDAY 16TH JUNE
WHATSAPP MESSAGE
BRIONY: James, I received an email from your mother this morning requesting the best part of one thousand pounds for one night in the cottage they decided to rent, and 'our' share of your sister's party costs which includes an extortionate amount on wine supplied by Cosmo (at your mother's request). I did have grave concerns regarding your mother's eagerness to apparently impress Cosmo with her laissez-faire attitude to cost when choosing the wine. I am not sure if she was more intent on impressing Cosmo him-

self, or the guests attending the party?! But either way, I do feel you need to speak up here before it gets even more out of hand. I am still to purchase a gift for insufferable Sarah that will not involve re-mortgaging the house and unless you want your children to go hungry or live off the gourmet doggy bag remains of the party feast (for even buffets of the highest standard do not cost as much as this is costing per head!) I suggest you call your mother tonight and let her know that you do not consider it appropriate to be expected to cover party costs for your own sister—especially when those party costs have escalated to such great heights as these. I do think it would work out more cost effective to fly everyone to London and have high tea at the Ritz!

JAMES: Why are we being charged a cleaning fee when we are only staying one night?

BRIONY: The cleaning fee is the least part of the problem, James!

JAMES: I'll have a word with Cosmo. Can't believe he is trying to fleece my mother. No, actually I can.

BRIONY: Cosmo is not trying to fleece your mother! Your mother was trying to impress him with her extravagant nature and it's come back to bite her on the bum. Have you not noticed the way she dresses up like something from 'Abigail's Party' in vibrant crinoline kaftans and elaborate matching head scarves every time she comes to visit? It's not for our benefit, James. Why she thinks someone like Cosmo would be interested in her I do not know?! Does your father have no say in the matter?

So it's baked beans for dinner.

JAMES: Really? Beans?

BRIONY: Yes beans. Really, beans. We can't afford luxuries like eating decent meals any more when there are more important things to pour our hard earned cash into—such as your sister's birthday party . . .

JAMES: Not even a rasher of bacon to go with it?

BRIONY: You had far too much meat during our weekend break. Unlike me.

TUESDAY 16TH JUNE

WHATSAPP MESSAGE

KATE: Hey, Bri. So how was the shagfest? Tried to call you last night but just keep getting your voicemail. Maybe l'amour is continuing into the week . . . .?

BRIONY: Sorry, you wouldn't have wanted to speak to me in the mood I was in last night.

KATE: Oh?

BRIONY: The weekend was fine, I suppose. It was a lovely boutique hotel with a couple of nice restaurants in the area and the traffic wasn't too bad either way.

KATE: 'It was fine and the traffic wasn't too bad'?!? Well, I'm no Jessica Fletcher, but I sense something's amiss?! You went away with your husband for a dirty weekend, and when asked you say it was 'fine' and comment on the traffic?! Come on and offload on me—as obviously James didn't offload on you 😉

BRIONY: It's not just that. James' mother is holding a

grudge about the fact the boys went to stay with a friend rather than her (although it was her fuss about having them that caused me to look for alternative arrangements). She emailed me to insinuate that letting them have a sleepover at their friends once in a while was going to turn them into Russian cannibals. Yesterday I got an invoice from her for the best part of a grand for our 'share' of hosting James' sister's party, and I'm on the verge of telling her that if she chooses to organise a party for her daughter and include fire juggling, vintage wines and waiter service, then her son should not really be expected to foot half the bill. This whole saga has caused a huge ruckus with James and I as he is blaming Cosmo for 'fleecing' his mother for the wine and lacks the balls to tell his mother straight that we will not be footing the bill. She has even charged us a cleaning fee for staying in the cottage for one night! And we have to take our own bedding as they have friends arriving on the Sunday who will want to use the cottage ben linen!

KATE: He shouldn't leave you to deal with his bloody parents!

BRIONY: Anyway, sorry to vent. How are things with you and Piers.

KATE: Actually, I think I need to talk to you about Piers. It feels a bit weird, what with the fact you used to go out with him, and all that; but we've been seeing each other for ages now and things haven't moved on and it's getting rather frustrating. And it is a bit odd, isn't it? Any suggestions?

BRIONY: Look, we dated for one summer twenty odd

years ago—I was paying my uni overdraft off by teaching French exchange students and he was entertaining the masses dressed in a rubber shark costume. It was hardly the romance of the century, Kate, so I don't know what's to feel weird about.

KATE: I know, but . . .

BRIONY: What do you mean by, 'things have not moved on' . . . exactly? He hasn't declared his undying love to you? Presented you with Tiffany jewellery? Demanded you fly back to New York with him where you will set up home in an apartment overlooking Central Park and never have to work another day in your life?

KATE: Not exactly . . .

BRIONY: What then?!?

KATE: Okay, Okay. So, we've not got past the kissing and hand holding stage.

BRIONY: You HAD a kissing and handholding stage?

KATE: I can be restrained.

BRIONY: Only when handcuffs are in use, Kate.

KATE: So anyway, it was nice at first and I thought he must really like and respect me by not trying to shag me after the second date. But it's just getting beyond a joke now and I feel like a teenager who spends ages snogging after a date only to be left hot and bothered as he makes his excuses and leaves. I've spent a fortune on batteries and my flat mate is always complaining about interference on the TV.

BRIONY: I hear ya sista! But, I think you will find teen-

141

agers these days are probably doing a lot more than just snogging;—however, I get your point.

KATE: So what do I do??

BRIONY: Just tie him and up so he can't escape and seduce him 😉

KATE: I wish . . .

BRIONY: I don't know?! Maybe he is a born again Christian or something? Have you asked?

KATE: Do you really think it's a fetish thing then? He needs a kink to get him off and he's not built up to telling me yet?

BRIONY: I don't know what Piers is into! I was barely 19 for god's sake and light bondage was not something in my sexual repertoire at that sweet age! Anyway, I really don't think I'm the one to be asking for seduction techniques at the moment. I can't even arouse my own husband's interest.

KATE: You've been with James yonks so you must have been doing something right during that time. It's not your fault the crack has made him impotent.

BRIONY: James is not impotent through drug use, Kate! We live in a sleepy Dorset village not Primrose Hill. There's no wife swapping, drug fuelled sex parties or toyboys in bondage here.

KATE: Oh, sleepy villages are the worst for it. I bet your neighbour is hosting bondage parties every month. He's probably a gimp every other weekend. Do you know what a gimp is, Briony?

BRIONY: Yes, I know what a gimp is, thank you, Kate, and no, I am pretty sure Cosmo is not one. Nor is he hosting bondage parties. I would have noticed an increase in bottles in the recycling bin and the PVC clad couples parking on his drive.

THURSDAY 18TH JUNE
SUBJECT: BIRTHDAY COUNTDOWN?
Hi Briony,

Well, I'm on the final countdown to turning the big '4-0'! It's all very exciting and I am looking forward to seeing you all for my little family get-together. Of course, as you know, George and I usually like to have a big party for my birthday, but mum has convinced me a family affair with just a few close friends would be more intimate and fitting for such a landmark celebration. I fully intend to make the most of my remaining few weeks as a thirty something so we have a few friends coming over the weekend before for a 'Farewell to the Thirties' party which I am really looking forward to.

I was going through my birthday wish-list online and noticed James and yourself have yet to purchase from it. Mum has mentioned that you might be having financial problems so I thought I would add a few more items more in keeping with your budget. After all—it's the thought that counts, isn't it?

You may have heard that Barnaby was recently made head prefect of his year at school. I do think that giving children these responsibilities at such a young age is so good for their confidence and very morale building, don't you? It's such a shame state schools don't seem to take the same approach, although I suppose that is why we are paying such an extortionate amount on school fees every year and you are so lucky to get it for free. Mustn't grumble, though. How are Sam and Zac getting on in their school? Mum says it is one of the better state schools in the area so that must be a relief for you? It's such a lottery these days, isn't it? I'm not sure I could cope with it the way you do, Briony, you're so very stoical. I suppose if you had not given up your career then you would be able to afford private education, but, the boys have you at home this way, so sacrifices had to be made one way or another. In my darker moments I often wonder what I would have done in your situation, but thankfully George's executive position allows us the luxury of both private education and a mother at home for her children. I count myself as very fortunate, Briony.

Anyway, I must leave it there as I have a ton of baking to do for the school fete this Saturday. Does the boys' school have a school fete? Ours is terribly popular and is open to all, so we get a lot of the local children coming along with their parents. I have to admit I find it a bit sad when you see the awe in some of the state-schooled children's eyes once they have seen the facilities we have and our lovely grounds. Still, we let them come and play us at rugby so they get a bit of practice on a decent pitch.

Bye for now
Sarah x

SUBJECT: RE: BIRTHDAY COUNTDOWN!
Hi Sarah

My goodness! You really are taking your approaching step into official middle-age terribly well! I suppose you have had time to get used to it though. I still chuckle to myself when I recall the faux pas five or six years or so ago when a number of your close friends from the village arrived with a bunch of helium filled 'Happy 40th Birthday' balloons for your party. We had fun with the helium though so they didn't go to waste, and you were so very stoical about it all then. Of course, I've always been cursed with looking years younger than my actual age, which has caused me numerous problems—people think I must have been a very young mum when I had the boys.

Thank you for updating me on Barnaby's achievements. I can understand your pride, especially considering the trouble he has caused you in the past. Did the parents of the little school friend whose arm he broke see the funny side in the end? And how is your cleaner? Did she agree to come back and clean for you after the cupboard/poo incident? Claustrophobia's certainly no joke, is it? And certainly not helped when you're locked in a cupboard with a stinky poo. Did the child psychologist ever get to the bottom (no pun intended) of why he would never shit in a toilet for the first six years of his life and preferred cupboards, drawers and gardens?

You will be pleased to hear that James and I have purchased your birthday gift, although it's not anything from your official list, it was something I saw that just had your name written all over it.

Although it's terribly sweet to know Margaret is so concerned about the private matter of our bank balance, rest assured we are not on the bread line just yet.

Anyway, must rush as have to pick the boys up from their state-funded school, and it takes an age to put the bullet proof vest on and fight my way through the baying crowd of parents.

Briony

MONDAY 22ND JUNE
WHATSAPP MESSAGE
BRIONY: How are the wedding plans going? Have you resolved the issue regarding Dan's outrageous presumption that you might have some desire to bear his children?

MELISSA: Not all of us have uteruses aching with the desire to carry babies. The world is overpopulated enough.

BRIONY: Do you spout that line out at your parentcraft classes 😄 Anyway, was just wondering if you know what the signs of dementia are?

MELISSA: I'm a midwife, Briony; not a mental health specialist.

BRIONY: I've Googled, but that just freaked me out completely as I appeared to have most of the symptoms myself!

MELISSA: Is this about James?

BRIONY: It's actually James' mother. I think she is getting very forgetful and confused. We came back from visiting friends on Saturday to find her leaving Cosmo's cottage. She was terribly flustered and confused and when James apologised for us not being in, saying she hadn't told us she was planning on coming, she became terribly flustered and incoherent and babbled nonsensically until Cosmo appeared and explained Margaret had apparently been discussing food and menus to complement the wines he was supplying for Sarah's birthday.

MELISSA: She didn't want you finding out she was going to be spending more money on his insufferable sister's party.

BRIONY: She really did look so confused, Melissa. In fact, I have never seen that odd expression and panicky look in her eyes ever before. She was quite flushed as well. I would say menopausal hot flush were it not for the fact that ship sailed long ago.

MELISSA: Symptoms can go on for years post-menopause, actually.

BRIONY: James, of course, appeared oblivious other than saying he hoped Cosmo wasn't charging his mother for his advice. I do hope she is not becoming mentally unstable, as I am sure Sarah would try and insist her mother came to live with us and I really could not ever, ever, even begin to imagine the nightmare that would be . . .

MELISSA: Get James to have a word with his dad and make a doctor's apt?

BRIONY: James is useless, you know that.

MELISSA: Then forget about it and focus on your marriage, Briony. Marriage is sanctity, and all that shit you know.

BRIONY: It's just shit, actually.

MELISSA: Anyway, on to matters of far more importance. You really need to find a date when you and Kate can both come and meet Monique for discussions. I will feel much happier when I know the styling is coming together. My mother is obsessing about her 'mother of the bride' outfit and doesn't want to be outdone by Dan's mother (seriously, that is never going to happen considering Dan's mother considers Primark haute couture). But you know what she's like and wants me to find out exactly what the woman is going to be wearing on the day. That's the least of my worries as at the moment I am more concerned about Dan's sister who apparently has a habit of showing people her nipple piercing after a few Chardonnays, and her boyfriend who has an even more intimate piercing.

BRIONY: Actually, I'd be quite intrigued about the todger piercing. You'll have to point him out to me.

MELISSA: He won't be hard to spot, he'll be the only guest with a tattoo of a spider covering his cheek. So, dates?

BRIONY: Umm, okay, will look at my diary, but I am pretty busy until after summer hols.

MELISSA: Busy? Busy with what exactly?

BRIONY: Busy with my LIFE, Melissa—kids, house, and

stuff! You're in for a shock if you ever do have kids with Dan—then you will know what hard work really is.

MELISSA: Okay, calm down. I'm not about to start arguing with my maid of honour. Have you any idea just how much you NOT turning up to the wedding would mess up the styling?

TUESDAY 23ND JUNE
WHATSAPP MESSAGE

KARA: Got your voicemail message—well, from what I could decipher from the hysterical laughter. Can't talk at mo as in hairdressers having colours done. So, what has happened with Zac and your knickers, exactly?

BRIONY: Oh Christ, Kara, I am DYING!

KARA: Is this something I really want to know?

BRIONY: I was getting dressed after yoga and realised I had Zac's PE shorts in my yoga bag . . . . meaning that I must have inadvertently put my knickers in his PE bag that morning(!)

KARA: As you do . . .

BRIONY: So, realising it would cause him immense embarrassment if he were to pull my red lacy knicks out of his bag whilst getting changed for PE, I called the school and asked to speak to Zac—to pre-warn him of my error.

KARA: How do you even have that conversation with your child?!

BRIONY: Anyway, the dragon of a school receptionist who is already iffy with me since seeing me on the CCTV scaling the security gates that time, well, she got really narky about getting Zac out of lessons to speak to me. She kept saying she could take a message but I insisted I needed to speak to my son and it was a 'private family matter.' Eventually she got him on the phone and I whispered the situation to Zac (whispered, as I was sure the dragon and her minions were trying to listen in). I thought I had expressed how important it was that Zac must not tell the office staff what I had said, and he was just to say that mummy said it was private.

KARA: Oh gawd . . .

BRIONY: So anyway, I thought I had got away with it until I arrived to pick the boys up that afternoon and Lucy with a massive grin on her face and told me she had been in the office making an appointment to see the deputy head, when Zac was on the phone. She said all she and the office dragon could hear were his disconnected replies to me...'but, mummy, it's wrong to tell lies . . . so you don't have any knickers on now?'

KARA: You must be on social services' radar by now

BRIONY: As soon as he hung up he turned to the office dragons who were waiting in hushed silence and announced 'Mummy says I'm not to tell you why I've got her knickers as it's a family secret.'!!!!!

KARA: Cringing for you!

BRIONY: I know, right! Mortified.

WHATSAPP MESSAGE

KATE: Why didn't you warn me, Briony?!? Why?!?!?!?

BRIONY: Erm . . . so what exactly did you expect me to warn you about?!

KATE: Finally got past first base with Piers last night . . .

BRIONY: And this came as a shock to you? You do know which bits go where, no?

KATE: Yes, I know which bits go where, but, said 'bits' were, shall we say, not as anticipated. Considerably less than anticipated. Miniscule, in fact. You knew this and you didn't warn me?! Jesus, Briony, it was mortifying. Oh gaaaawwwd, what am I going to do?

BRIONY: Ahhhhhhh. Yeeeeeesss. That.

KATE: 'Ahhhh yeeeeeeeeesssss' it was not! My travel vibrator is bigger than his cock.

BRIONY: Travel vibrator? You have a travel vibrator? Really?! Why? In case you need relief inbetween tube stations?!

KATE: I thought everyone had a vibrator for holidays.

BRIONY: Really?!

KATE: You've got to pack light these days.

BRIONY: I'm sooo outta the loop.

KATE: But what am I going to do, Briony?

BRIONY: Well, try restraining from masturbation whilst on holiday or just use your . . .

KATE: About Piers!

BRIONY: Oh. Well, I thought you were really loved up? He's a nice guy, great job, treats you with respect. He just happens to have a micro-dick. You can get pills and con-traptions for that these days. Just check your spambox. Did you manage to hide your disappointment? Poor man.

KATE: I tried to hide my disappointment, Briony, but I have a feeling he heard me talking to Jemima, as he left shortly afterwards and I haven't heard from him today.

BRIONY: You told your FLATMATE?!? While he was still in your BED?!?

KATE: I was in shock, Bri! I was acting irrationally. Don't judge me—you dumped him after all! And now I know why . . .

BRIONY: I dumped him as I was at uni 200 miles away, Kate. Not because he had a micro-dick.

KATE: Please stop saying micro-dick

BRIONY: Oh so now you're all Ms Sensitive?

KATE: You didn't dump him because of his dick?

BRIONY: I didn't actually sleep with him, Kate. It was more just ardent fumbling in the back of his Capri after a few Scrumpy's on a Saturday night. But yes, I was sort of aware of his . . . situation.

KATE: What should I do?

BRIONY: I think you should call him. I feel sorry for him. For goodness sake, Kate, you had the sex toy contract and they sold penis extension thingies with bobbles on, so it's not the end of the world. We all know size isn't everything, and it's more what they do with it that counts.

KATE: True . . . to a point . . .

BRIONY: Think of it from his point of view—must have

felt like chucking a chipolata up the middle of Fifth Avenue. Maybe you should consider a snatch-plasty or whatever they call it—tighten yourself up for him, you heartless hussy.

KATE: Snort at 'snatch-plasty!' I'm not surgically messing with my minge for any man. He'd probably be a tosser if he had a normal sized cock anyway . . .

SATURDAY 27TH JUNE
SUBJECT: COTTAGING QUERIES
Dear Celia

Thank you for being so prompt in sending me you and your friends shopping requirements. However, I have to confess to being somewhat taken aback at Angela and Gerry's very specific and often (I feel) extravagant needs. Although I am not about to deny them the Malaysian langoustines at £27.99 a kilo or indeed suggest they suffer inferior brands of champagne, I am sure you appreciate that Sarah's party is causing a considerable dent in our bank balance as things are, so I am going to ask if you think it terribly rude of me to request each couple pays their own share of the shopping bill. To be honest, Celia, I do intend to keep a number of the bottles of wine back for myself anyway, so feel Angela and Gerry's bottles of vintage port is excessive to myself and Arthur's needs. I did also notice that some amendments had been made to the original list I emailed to you—namely bathroom tissue. Do you think we might be able to sacrifice the 'triple quilted velour feel' for regular 'softest luxury' just for a few days? I'm not usually one to scrimp, Celia, and you of all people know how I do like my household luxuries, but on this occasion I don't think it would hurt if we all lowered our considerably high standards for the short duration we will be at the cottage.

Your friend,
Margaret.

SATURDAY 27TH JUNE
SUBJECT: RE: COTTAGING QUERIES
Dear Margaret

I do see your point regarding the extravagance of Angela and Gerry's requirements. However, maybe we should 'go with the flow' on this occasion, as need I remind you, they are close acquaintances of Lord and Lady Montgomery, and we really wouldn't want to be spoken of in anything other than a favourable manner when they are next invited to dinner at Montgomery Hall . . . .?

Fondests
Celia

PS Did you not manage to mention your surprise at the cost of the wine to Cosmo? I thought that is what you planned to do?

SUNDAY 28TH JUNE
SUBJECT: RE: COTTAGING QUERIES
Dear Celia

I had no idea Angela and Gerry held such esteemed company. Well, of course, that changes everything. Do you think the cottage will be up to their standards, Celia? I feel all of a dither now I know we will be holidaying with friends of the Royal Family.

Fondests,
Margaret

MONDAY 29TH JUNE
SUBJECT: RE: COTTAGING QUERIES
Dearest Margaret

I can assure you there is no need to be 'all of a dither.' Angela and Gerry are very down to earth, as you know, and hardly ever mention their esteemed acquaintances (of which they have many). And besides, I don't think Lord and Lady Montgomery are related to the Royal Family— although they do go skiing at Klosters . . .

TUESDAY 30TH JUNE
SUBJECT: COTTAGING AMENDMENT
Dear Briony

I am afraid I have to make some minor amendments to the accommodation arrangements for Sarah's party. Since we are now being joined by Celia and John's close friends who happen to be related to the Royal Family, I feel it would be inappropriate to have members of the public and their children staying the night before their arrival—mainly for security purposes, but also due to the smell of small children (the royal bloodline is unused to such things, as I am sure you can understand). Therefore, I would suggest you book yourselves a B&B for the night. I am sure this will be of no bother to you, particularly as I had still not received your payment for the cottage.

Fondest Regards,
Margaret

JULY

WHATSAPP MESSAGE

BRIONY: James. We have been dumped from the 'lovely family weekend break' in favour of Celia's blue-blooded friends (who, knowing your mother's habit of embellishing the truth, are probably no more than the descendants of Queen Victoria's footman.) Although I am relieved not to have to deal with this whole issue, I am somewhat put out that the woman thinks it's acceptable to erase us from the equation at such a late date and insinuate our children's (HER grandchildren) smell would cause offence to her friends delicate constitutions! Please tell me why we didn't just book our holiday to clash with this event, to start with?! Does your mother know what 'cottaging' actually is?!

JAMES: Sorry, Briony, but you've got to laugh, haven't you? She's probably telling all her friends she and dad are going cottaging!

SUBJECT: RE: COTTAGING AMENDMENT
Dear Margaret

No problem at all. In fact, you may recall a B&B had been my initial plan way back when you first started planning Sarah's party. Do hope you enjoy your time with the minor Royals—although I am not quite sure I understand how the smell of my children might upset them—are they related to the child catcher in Chitty Chitty Bang Bang?

WHATSAPP MESSAGE
MELISSA: Here are the pics of hairstyles suggested by Monique that I mentioned on the phone the other night. I've already booked a hairdresser in the next village to where the ceremony is who was recommended by Dan's sister. I'll admit, I was a little wary of booking a salon recommended by a woman who sports tri-colour wedges of colour in her over processed hair, but I looked at their website and they seem really good. Anyway, I was a little stuck for choice as the next nearest hairdressers is 17 miles away and only opens twice a week for pensioners.

BRIONY: Melissa, my hair is not long enough for any of those styles—unless you were thinking of using hair pieces—which can look awfully tacky . . . what did Kate think? She changes her hairstyle more often than I change my bedding, so think you need a few more options that will be flexible depending on Kate's current hair style in December.

MELISSA: The wedding is over five months away, Briony, you have time to grow it! That's why I've sent the pictures to you now. I'm having a word with Kate about her hair when she and Piers come over for dinner on Saturday.

BRIONY: Umm, what if I don't want to grow my hair?

MELISSA: It's my wedding, Briony, of course you'll want to grow your hair for my wedding. And anyway, that messy grown-out bob of yours—that's not even a proper hair style.

BRIONY: It's my signature look.

MELISSA: Hmm. So, how is Zac after the clingfilm incident? Is he still having nightmares? You know that's how men's fetishes start, don't you? A small boy walks in on his mummy slathered in shea butter and wrapped in cling film, and twenty years later he's on anti-depressants after his wife leaves him, unable to keep up with his perverted demands and the spiralling cost of cling film. Maybe time to put a lock on the bathroom door?

BRIONY: Thanks for your reassurances. We already have a lock on the bathroom door, but it was as I was walking from the bathroom to the bedroom, wrapped from head to foot in the cling film that he suddenly appeared. And anyway, I swear my skin looks so smooth and supple now— you should try it.

MELISSA: So it's actually a thing then?

BRIONY: Yes, it's actually a *thing*! I didn't make it up, you know. I read about it online. I think Kate Middleton does it.

MELISSA: I highly doubt that. Briony, Oh yeah, I think I've knocked the baby thing on the head as far is Dan is concerned—I left him with a 'Modern Midwifery' training DVD while I was at work one evening and made sure I came home and discussed all the gory details of the home birth I attended when I got in. Starting a family is well on the back burner as far as he is concerned for now!

TEXT MESSAGE SENT THURSDAY 2ND JULY 2.47PM
Hey Gayle—are you power walking tomorrow? I can pick you up if you want? Bri.

TEXT MESSAGE SENT THURSDAY 2ND JULY 2.53PM
No can do. Toenails too long. G.

TEXT MESSAGE SENT THURSDAY 2ND JULY 2.55PM
Toenails too long?!?!? Really? That's scraping the bottom of the barrel for excuses.

SATURDAY 4TH JULY
WHATSAPP MESSAGE
    LUCY: Christ, I'm at Tom's bloody parents again in bloody deepest, darkest bloody Cornwall.

    BRIONY: Not that deep or dark if you've got 4G

    LUCY: If there wasn't 4G I wouldn't even come.

    BRIONY: #FirstWorldProblems

    LUCY: We got here at lunchtime and honestly, Briony, you just couldn't make it up. As we pulled into the drive

I noticed the garage doors were open and there was Peggy, lying on a sunbed IN the garage wearing nothing but her girdle! Well, that's a sight no one should see, least of all her son and grandchildren. Even the dog was so shocked he wouldn't get out the car and wee'd over my cashmere picnic blanket. As soon as we parked Peggy jumped up and came waddling over to greet us just as Wilf appeared wearing Speedos and slathered in baby oil. Oh, god, Bri, I didn't know where to look and not least because there was something resembling an eighty-year-old dehydrated saveloy escaping from Wilf's Speedos as he approached to hug me. The sensation of my father-in-law's decrepit dick rubbing against my hip is something I will unfortunately never forget.

BRIONY: Oh god, Lucy! You almost make my in-laws sound like sane, reasonable human beings!

So, why were they sunbathing IN the garage?! Surely that defeats the object? Or does the garage have a roof that opens??

LUCY: They think that by sunbathing in the garage—which is at the bottom of a steep drive allowing the sun to come in at an angle between certain hours—they get the sun's beneficial effects i.e. vit D but avoid the ageing effects (!?!) They are octogenarians for god's sake!

BRIONY: 😃.

LUCY: So, here I am, sat on the post-war hessian covered sofa, on my phone whilst my mother-in-law pegs out my now tie-dye effect shrunken cashmere blanket (having washed it on 60 degrees with 'a splash of bleach' to get the dog wee smell out), my father-in-law (still wearing Speedos although with saveloy now thankfully tucked back into place) teaching my nine-year-old daughter to play poker, and my husband desperately searching through the recycle bin for takeaway delivery places to spare us from his mother's 'speciality' tongue and kidney pie ('why have steak when tongue is so less wasteful' is her motto!—does she seriously think they use the tongue and kidneys of the same animal?!) I must have been a very bad person in a previous life . . .

BRIONY: How long are you staying?

LUCY: Thankfully, we leave tomorrow lunchtime—well, before lunch if I can help it as Peggy's got homemade cauliflower and leek soup planned and I've seen the state of the cauliflower which is resembling a putrefying grey brain in the larder at present. If all goes quiet you will know the tongue or jellified cauli got me . . . or my battery ran out (forgot the charger!)

TEXT MESSAGE RECEIVED 2.37PM

Do you want to come with me to 'Weighty Issues' on Mon? Could do with the support . . . Gx

TEXT MESSAGE RECEIVED 2.43PM

Do you think I NEED to come with you to a slimming club?!?

I think you need to support your fat friend ...?

I don't have a fat friend and anyway, isn't the idea to go to a slimming club to gain support? You're not meant to need to take a friend for support, surely? Sorry, busy Monday but let me know how you get on.

MONDAY 6TH JULY
SUBJECT: HOLIDAYS ARE COMING!!
As suspected, my bloody phone battery went so had to survive the rest of the day in the weird twilight zone world of Peggy and Wilf. Thank god for small mercies though in that it clouded over in the afternoon so Wilf finally put some clothes on. Seriously, Briony, it's not right seeing your eighty-year-old father-in-law's bulging crotch sat across from you during lunch. Well, I say lunch but more like a kid's party from the seventies as her 'spread' included fish paste sandwiches, cocktail sausages and cheese and pineapple on sticks finished off with blancmange. I'll never be able to face a cocktail sausage again ...

TUESDAY 7TH JULY
WHATSAPP MESSAGE
GAYLE: Only got a few mins before I start castrating, but had to tell you about my Weighty Issues meeting yesterday.
BRIONY: Ohhhhh do tell! Still can't believe you're going

though. You're a size 12 ffs. They must all hate you there.

GAYLE: I'm 5'1" Briony. There's not enough of me to carry any extra weight.

BRIONY: You may be a little person but you're lucky you have a strong, sturdy frame, so you can carry weight better than me with my fragile, delicate frame.

GAYLE: You're making me sound like a midget farm girl, now, Briony.

BRIONY: But you're surprisingly supple and bendy with it.

GAYLE: Who left the farm to join a travelling acrobatics troupe . . .

BRIONY: Sorry. Go on.

GAYLE: Well, Weighty Issues isn't a support club for slimmers, it's a surreal parallel universe. Our leader goes by the name of Belinda Bacon

BRIONY: Nooooo!

GAYLE: I kid you not. Who, incidentally, has no humour regarding the irony of her name whatsoever. She weighs each member in turn with a steely glare to the backdrop of a life size cardboard cut-out of herself (when she was slimmer of the year—and either that picture is airbrushed or she's piled it back on a fair bit now!) During the meeting, we learnt that fellow Weighty Issues member Jennifer, had been struggling to lose weight, even though she sticks religiously to her diet sheet. The mystery was apparently solved this week by Jennifer's husband, who found his *sleepwalking* wife at 3am, head in the fridge and stuffing

164

her face with everything she could get her hands on—cold roast potatoes, fudge cake, salami. Jennifer is mortified and sobbed as she told us all of her shame. It was raised eyebrows all round, Bri, I can tell you. I LOVED IT!

BRIONY: I betcha did! Wish I'd come to support you now.

GAYLE: I'm hoping to lose a stone, so going to keep going for now—the fear of Belinda Bacon's shameful glare if you don't lose, or heaven forbid, gain weight each week is enough to keep me out the biscuit tin. Anyway, testicles all prepped and awaiting the chop so got to dash.

WEDNESDAY 8TH JULY
WHATSAPP MESSAGE

KATE: Bridezilla has instructed me that I must grow my hair and keep it a neutral shade of brown until after her wedding! Oh, and neither of us is allowed to gain or lose more than 3Ilbs in weight—did you know that?!?

BRIONY: Yes . . . I have been briefed/threatened 😬

KATE: The cut of the dresses doesn't allow for a severe drop or weight gain apparently. I've half a mind to get pregnant, Briony, I really have—and have huge hair extensions in deep auburn. For God's sake, it's getting beyond a joke. While she was making coffee she grabbed me as I went to the loo and had a 'quiet word' where she explained Piers was welcome to accompany me to the wedding but she hoped I understood that if we split up any new boyfriends would have to meet with her approval beforehand as she didn't want to risk any situations occurring. What the hell does she mean by that?!? Is she planning on mix and matching partners so as there are no clashes on the 'theme?'

BRIONY: Fuck knows, Kate. And I tell you what, when people moan about the fact I ran off to get married secretly with no fuss and nonsense, this is why! I should be thanked for my consideration, but berated!

KATE: You know, I don't even like Dan all that much? I think he's a bit of a chauvinist to be honest and he's got the whole working-class-chip-on-his-shoulder thing going on. Or maybe that's just a northern thing? The north/south divide? I don't know, but it amounts to the same thing. He's a twunt.

BRIONY: I know! I know, Kate! But what can we do?!

KATE: You know he calls us the posh totty just because of our accents.

BRIONY: But we don't have accents.

KATE: I know we don't have accents, Briony,

BRIONY: We just talk normally . . .

KATE: But he thinks the fact we don't have accents means we have sticks up are arses.

BRIONY: Well, to be fair, we do, sometimes. But that's just our humour.

KATE: He doesn't get our humour.

BRIONY: Few do . . .

KATE: What does Melissa even see in him?! What are we going to do?!

BRIONY: I suppose we could set a honeytrap and make

sure Melissa catches him in the act? Or hire a hitman to frighten him off? I think that would cost a bomb though and I'm mortgaged up to the hilt at the mo.

KATE: Yeah, but where do we find a hitman? Can't Google it or GCHQ will be on to us and we'll never get away with it then.

BRIONY: Umm, I was joking, Kate!

KATE: I wasn't.

BRIONY: We just have to sit it for now and just maybe try and talk her out of her most absurd ideas and expectations. Are you at work? Can you talk?

KATE: No, can't talk. Got hauled into see the Big Boss about my internet usage. Apparently, I spend too many hours a week on Facebook and not enough doing the work I am paid to do—YAWN! I'm in PR! I'm social media-ing darling—that's work!

BRIONY: Look on the bright side—at least we all have somewhere to go for New Year's Eve this year.

KATE: I always have somewhere to go on NYE and usually it's somewhere far more exciting than a bloody three star hotel in Yorkshire. Christ, I hope we can change into something of our own in time for the evening 'do'.

BRIONY: Actually, talking of which, I need something to wear to James' sister's birthday party. I need to look stunning yet understated—like I haven't really tried very hard and just always look that good. Any ideas?

KATE: There's a place online that sells designer dresses at a fraction of cost. I'll find the link and send it to you. Make sure you get a decent uplift bra if you're going for cleavage, and laser-cut flesh coloured thong if going for high slashed thigh, but just remember the old adage: baps or vag out but never the two.

BRIONY: I've never got my vag out at a public event, Kate.

KATE: Koh Samui, aged 19, wet t-shirt competition that went a little too far.

BRIONY: That was an accident and I won first prize.

KATE: The photos are probably still up in that bar.

BRIONY: Best I never get famous and have my skeletons pulled kicking and screaming out the closet then.

THURSDAY 9TH JULY
SUBJECT: B&B
Dear Briony

Well, time is flying and the countdown has started! Mum has told me she is staying in a cottage locally with some friends and you were looking for a B&B for the night of my little family gathering, so I have taken the liberty of booking you into a friend of mine's farmhouse B&B just a mile or so from our house, so very convenient for you. What a shame you can't make a proper break of it and stay longer. Mum said you are flying out to Greece which I am sure the boys will love, so you mustn't feel guilty about it all as children their age have no real standards and are just happy to holiday anywhere, aren't they? I have to say, sometimes Ella and Barnaby seem so nonchalant about our annual family skiing holidays and summers in Tuscany that a little part of me often wants to give them a bit of a shock and take them somewhere like Greece, or even, heaven forbid, Spain one year in order to show them what other families have to put up with—what a mean mummy you must think I am!

I left a message on James' voicemail at the weekend but he has not returned my call as yet—is he away on business again? You're a very trusting wife, Briony, I'm not sure I'd be happy if George were away so often—not that I ever have anything to worry about with George, of course; he never so much as looks at another woman. I'm a very lucky lady, Briony. Devoted husbands are not as easy to find as you'd think.

How are the boys getting on at their school? I suppose with James working so hard you might be able to stretch the pennies and take them out of the state system in the next couple of years? What a relief that would be to you, I'm sure. Of course, there's always boarding school—more pricey but would allow you to go back to work and contribute towards it.

Much love, Sarah

Thursday 9th July
SUBJECT: RE: B&B
Dear Sarah

Thank you for thinking of us, but we are already booked into a B&B which we are very happy with. Yes, isn't it a shame we can't stay longer? However, we had to take the Monday flight as they were the cheapest we could find, otherwise, it would have meant compromising on the accommodation and James and I insist upon nothing smaller than a 42-foot yacht to sail around the Greek Islands. Anything smaller would be simply unthinkable, don't you agree?

The boys are very happy at their school and seem to mix rather well with the other children of varying social backgrounds—some even have parents still in the lower tax bracket, if you can imagine such a thing?! In fact, just the other week, a friend was telling me how her son's hamster came back from being looked after by a school friend for the half term with its cage lined with a tabloid newspaper! How that hamster slept with shredded celebrity gossip for bedding we shall never know.

Anyway, must dash—got to get the boys to their Mandarin lesson after school. So important for children to be fluent in the oriental languages these days, what with China being an emerging economic super-power, don't you think? Which are Barnaby and Ella learning?

Zai jian, Briony

SUBJECT: RE: B&B

Dear Briony

I'm not sure I can cancel your booking at Verity's farm-house without incurring a cancellation fee, so maybe have a re-think on that one unless you don't mind paying the extra charge?

Barnaby and Ella have been taking private French and Italian lessons since they were tiny as we felt it was so important they could converse with the locals in Tuscany or the chalet girl when we are skiing. Unless one is buying property in China I really don't see the point in Mandarin? You're not upping sticks and leaving us for the Orient, are you, Briony?

I am currently on a strict detoxifying diet after the last few weeks pre-birthday celebrations have riddled my body with toxins. I have the most divine little dress to wear that night which is too unforgiving and cost the equivalent of some people's annual holidays, but you only celebrate your 40th once, so why not splash out, I thought to myself? I take it you will be making an extra special effort that night? I've always admired your au natural style, Briony, but sometimes it is nice too throw away the natural fibres for a night and bask in sparkles—and I am sure James would appreciate it. Too many women seem to let themselves go once settled in a marriage with children and a house to look after, and then they seem surprised when their husband gets distracted by the attractive little office girl or waitress in their favourite little restaurant while on business trips.

So, I'll tell Verity to expect you sometime on Saturday then?

Much love,
Sarah x

SATURDAY 11TH JULY
SUBJECT: RE: B&B
Dear Sarah

As previously stated, I had already booked and paid for accommodation for us so please cancel the booking you made with your friend. I am sure your *friend* will not charge you a cancellation fee for *your* booking.

No, we are not moving to China. Property is so much more reasonable in Mongolia, and Ulaanbaatar is much less smoggy than Beijing.

Good luck with your detox. As you know, I was blessed with a naturally slender figure which at times is a curse. If I forget to eat breakfast the pounds simply drop off and before I know it my size 8s are literally hanging off me. I shouldn't worry yourself too much though, Sarah, as all that hockey playing you used to do has given you such robust thighs, and muscle doesn't wobble like flab so best to just concentrate on the problems areas like your tummy and underarms for now. After all, there's nothing worse than seeing bingo wings like an African elephant's ears flapping about in a strapless Karen Millen, is there?

See you Saturday
Briony

WHATSAPP MESSAGE

BRIONY: Wow Kate, thanks for the link—got myself a stunning dress for Sat. I'm away on hols for two weeks after the 19th but why not come down and visit for a weekend when we get back and bring Piers?

KATE: I'm sure you will knock 'em dead at Sarah's party. Don't forget to tell me all about it before you go away— deep breaths now Briony, and take plenty of herbal stress pills. It would be great to come and stay for a weekend .. . are you sure about bringing Piers? Would that be weird for you?

BRIONY: Only weird if he turns up in his shark costume. I'll pencil you in for the weekend after we get back.

TUESDAY 14TH JULY
SUBJECT: MONGOLIA?!
Hi Mum

Have you heard that James and Briony are thinking about moving to Mongolia? Apparently, property is very reasonable there and the boys already speak fluent Mandarin—although I am somewhat vexed by that as didn't know Mongolians spoke Mandarin?

You didn't tell me they were holidaying on a yacht, either, Mother. You said they were doing Greece on the cheap? Is it owned by a business associate of James'? Of course, George and I have dallied with a sailing holiday but Barnaby isn't so good on the water—which is strange as he has been swimming like a fish since he was a baby.

Looking forward to my special day on Sat.

Love, Sarah x

TUESDAY 14TH JULY
WHATSAPP MESSAGE
JAMES: Briony, why am I getting texts and voicemails from my mother and sister asking me why I didn't inform them we were planning on moving to Ulaanbaatar? Apparently, my mother is very concerned about not being able to see her grandchildren grow up as she doesn't think her health will deal with the altitude, not to mention the fact she won't be able to communicate with them if they develop a 'strange accent', and Sarah is demanding our property agent details in case she and George want to invest in a place there . . .

BRIONY: Oopsy! She winds me up, James. And anyway, I didn't say we were moving to Mongolia . . . I just mentioned something about property investment...

JAMES: Did you get Sarah a present in the end and did we need a bank loan to buy it?

BRIONY: Yes, present bought and wrapped and no bank

174

loan needed. My innovativeness in present buying is one reason you married me, no? Now what were the other reasons . . . 😉

JAMES: Your 'innovativeness' when buying my sister a present, worries me, Briony. Debt and bankruptcy is preferable to the wrath of my sister's displeasure, you should know that by now. I don't know what the other reasons were and I don't have time to play games, Briony. I need to get things wrapped up at work as I can't be guaranteed to get a signal in parts of Greece we'll be sailing around.

BRIONY: Ffs James, you're not even thinking about trying to work when in Greece?!

JAMES: I can't be incommunicado for that length of time, Briony.

WEDNESDAY 15TH JULY
SUBJECT: FWD: INCREASE YOUR SEXUAL PROWESS FOR JUST $29.98!
Dear Margaret

I felt it was only polite to forward you this email I have received from Arthur's email address, waxing lyrical about the wonder of 'natural Viagra for just $29.98.' Apparently, he has the libido of a nineteen year old . . . which must be exhausting for you. In the highly likely event that Arthur has not in fact discovered the magical elixir of renewed sexual prowess and has, in fact, had his email account hacked by unscrupulous South East Asian fraudsters , I thought it only prudent to inform you before his boasts concerning your 'marital privacies' get sent to less liberal and open-minded contacts than myself.

RE: your voicemail regarding the party—yes, James and I will be suitably attired, although, you know my feelings on dressing young children up in outfits neither practical nor comfortable for them, so the boys will be more smart/casual than 'red carpet'. I can also ensure you that my 'Oscars' dress is neither too tight, too low or a made of red sequins—you appear to have confused me for Jessica Rabbit.

Love, Briony

WEDNESDAY 15TH JULY
SUBJECT: RE: INCREASE YOUR SEXUAL PROWESS FOR JUST $29.98!
Dear Arthur

Although John and I have been friends with you for many years now, I'm not sure this is information you should be sharing with me. Have you become involved with one of these pyramid selling schemes? I know Julian from next door was very keen a few years ago and enlisted most of the cul-de-sac into his enterprise (although that was miracle kitchen cleaning products so a slightly different target market). It all went rather wrong for him though with quite a few people out of pocket and it was at least a year before anyone would even include him in the cul-de-sac summer drinks party. Still, we've not had to buy oven cleaner for years now . . .

Please tell Margaret I shall give her a ring later to confirm the arrangements for the weekend. I do hope you won't be trying to enlist The Fothergills into your selling scheme, Arthur. I am sure people of their standing have no need to be part of a money-making scheme of this smutty nature and it could cause embarrassment all round. Besides, the blue-bloods only fornicate to procreate, and The Fothergills already have an heir.

Fondests
Celia

P.S. John will have no interest, either, since he got his fingers burnt with Julian's scheme, and I can assure you he has no need for such 'improved performance' potions—natural or not.

THURSDAY 16TH JULY

SUBJECT: RE: FWD: INCREASE YOUR SEXUAL PROWESS FOR JUST $29.98!

Dear Briony

Oh dear! I really am quite stunned and shaken at the lengths gone to by these unscrupulous heathens! As you know, Arthur rarely uses email, so I dread to think the damage that has been done before he has had a chance to log-on again. In fact, I am not even sure he knows his password so just how these fraudsters got it, is beyond me, Briony! Whatever should we do? Do you think we are being watched? Maybe our identities have been stolen? Are they travelling on our passports already? Will we need new identities? Oh, what a mess! And so close to Sarah's party when I have so much to organise already.

I've taken the liberty of buying Sam and Zac lovely little party suits that came with adorable top hats and I know they will simply love them! I assure you they won't be uncomfortable at all and I simply won't take no for answer. Let's just call it an early Christmas present to them; they have more than enough Lego anyway. I shall pop round tomorrow with them and I can have a quick look at your dress as well. I'm sure your outfit is lovely, Briony, but it doesn't hurt to get a second opinion now, does it?

Much Love
Margaret x

FRIDAY 17TH JULY
WHATSAPP MESSAGE
KARA: Are you dropping Sergei off or shall I collect?

BRIONY: Sorry, Kara, Lucy has my spare house keys so if you could collect from her and then collect Sergei that would be fab. He needs cleaning out once a week and I've left a bag of everything he needs next to his cage.

KARA: Do your kids know you've named their hamster after a hot male ballet dancer you fancy? Seriously, have a great holiday. I have a feeling you are going to need it after this party! What did you get Sarah as a present in the end anyway . . . .?

BRIONY: Just got back from coffee with Lucy to find my mother-in-law has left me two penguin suits she has bought for the boys to wear to Sarah's party. I am fuming. I told her I didn't think it fair to expect children (especially boys for goodness sake!) to be expected to wear such restrictive outfits to a party just to fit in with the 'theme.' It's bad enough we are all expected to dress up like we're Oscar nominees for a bloody birthday party, but I refuse to cause my sons discomfort and embarrassment just for the sake of showing off. Can you believe she wanted to check my dress before the event?! Seriously! Probably concerned I will outshine her precious daughter. Well, at least I missed her so now she can't have me running around the shops at the eleventh hour searching for a more 'suitable' i.e. less flattering, dress! I got a designer bargain from an online store Kate told me about and think I look pretty damn hot in this little number, even if I do say so myself. Hope James notices . . . 😬

KARA: I hope James notices as well :/ Maybe this holiday will give you guys a chance to relight that spark.

BRIONY: So do I as that spark is in danger of being snuffed out forever, truth be told Kara . . . 😊

KARA: Well, you've nothing to worry about with Sergei.

BRIONY: Thanks again for hamster sitting. Take care of the fluffy little guy, we all love him and I'm not sure I could take the emotional distress of losing another one so soon after Cliff's demise. Did I mention he likes his cage lined with the gardening supplements of the weekend papers before you add the wood shavings. Reminds him of the outdoors I think.

KARA: He's from the Syrian desert, Briony. There are no F&B painted pergolas or azure-glazed pots filled with agapanthus there.

WHATSAPP GROUP MESSAGE
BRIONY: Surreal twenty-four hours. So hung over I can't even . . .

KARA: Try! I've been waiting for this!

GAYLE: Let me get my coffee . . . I want to enjoy this . . .

BRIONY: So, arrived at B&B late due to the usual caravans maxing 40 on the drive down to Devon. Boys refused point black to wear the ridiculous top hat and tails Margaret had bought for them. I knew they would, didn't blame them and didn't have time or energy to argue with them. I did point out this was Grandma's early Christmas present in lieu of Lego, but they said they'd sell the outfits on eBay and buy themselves a present with the proceeds—fair dos, I say. Finally got to Sarah's two hours late, and a 'butler' (drama student taking role frighteningly earnestly) answered the door and took us through to the garden where about a hundred 'close friends and family' where standing around looking cringingly uncomfortable in cocktail dresses and black ties sipping champagne whilst 'Oscar' waiters, painted head to foot in gold body paint and wearing gold lurex loin clothes (I kid you not!) sauntered around offering top-ups and nibbles. Margaret stood by the temporary 'stage' where a geriatric band played and a Sinatra wan-

nabe crooned away. Margaret appeared to be swathed in
a number stolen straight from Liz Taylor's 'podgy period,'
with excessive fake gold and ruby costume jewellery and
lips so pursed I thought nothing could penetrate them . . .
until she spotted me—at which point she audibly gasped,
inhaling her just sipped champagne and started choking,
whereupon Sarah appeared beside her firmly slapping her
back until she looked across to spot me . . . wearing the
SAME BLOODY DRESS! Have to admit, at this point, my
first thought was 'I bet she was going to pretend she paid
full price for that from some exclusive French boutique,'
shortly followed by a feeling of supreme smugness when I
realised I looked (and I hate to be immodest and mean, but
this is 'Insufferable Sarah' we are talking about here) well,
I really did look *so* much better in it. Some of you saw
the dress didn't you? It's a very fine, clingy, unforgiving silk
which showed off her wobbly thighs to perfection while
the off the shoulder bodice accentuated her bingo wings
quite supremely. I swear you could see every dimple of
cellulite on her backside as she turned and wobbled away
from me, hissing at Margaret as she followed. At this point
I was aware of the hushed silence that had fallen upon the
gathering as all eyes appeared to be glued to me awaiting
my response to Sarah's flounce. Call it wild abandon or call
it a death wish, but I just exclaimed 'Don't you just hate it
when that happens?!' to the stunned guests, laughed loudly, grabbed a glass of champers from a passing golden waiter, and with a shrug of my shoulders sauntered off to place

181

our gift on the present table (yes, the present table! This woman has no shame!). Champagne always goes straight to my head, so by the time I realised I had Margaret by my side trying to emotionally blackmail me into changing my dress, as, after all, Sarah was the 'birthday girl', I was already quite tiddly and in no mood to start changing frocks. Eventually, Sarah returned to her guests with a face like thunder having made it clear it was not she who should change, so instead, tried to cover me up with an oversized wax jacket which I quickly 'lost' with the help of a nearby leafy shrub.

As for the Oscar statue waiters—their body paint was far from colourfast and was rubbing off onto anything they came into contact with, be it garden furniture, Sarah's Farrow and Ball 'antique white' walls, or Mr Beaver, the deputy head of the exclusive private school Sarah's kids attend. Evidently, it would appear by the amount of gold paint decorating 'happily married', Mr Beaver's groin area, and the twinkle in the eyes of one particular 'Oscar', Mr Beaver is, shall we say, Beaver by name but almost certainly not by nature.

KATE: Having brunch in Covent Garden and laughing out loud at this—getting odd looks

BRIONY: As you know, Margaret did not scrimp on the alcohol (don't think we ever did give her our 'share' of the bill.) In fact, this was a godsend of sorts as at least everyone could get plastered. However, unbeknown to me, Bratty Barnaby and my darling sons had ensconced themselves behind the makeshift (gold, of course!) bar and were merrily concocting cocktails for the guests. Now, it's a well-known fact that children of this age have little understanding of a standard spirit measure, so it was of little surprise that the level of intoxication amongst the guests hit nuclear proportions and, may have had something to do with Mr Beaver reappearing after a brief absence with gold paint smudged all around his mouth . . . did Oscar have a gold todger? Well, possibly so, until Mr Beaver got hold of it . . .

GAYLE: OMFG.

KARA: You couldn't make this shit up.

BRIONY: Just when I thought all the fun was over, Barbara (middle-aged villager who talks in nervous whispers and has an unfortunate twitchy eye that makes it look like she's winking at you) came to alert me that there were some 'oddly dressed men claiming to be the entertainment waiting at the back gates'. Realising this must be the dance troupe Margaret had hired, I informed Babs (for mojitos cause me to become terribly over-familiar with complete strangers and all that winking had certainly made me feel quite over-familiar with twitchy-eyed Babs) not to worry and to just tell them to take their cue from me when the Frank Sinatra impersonator had stopped singing 'New York, New York' for the umpteenth time. Babs tottered off to the back gate just as I spied Margaret tucking bottles of Chateau de Ripoff into boxes and hiding them around the house and garden (having obviously decided the guests were taking liberties by actually drinking all the wine she had provided and were too pissed on cocktails to appreciate the vintage!) I told her the dance troupe were awaiting their cue, so after stuffing the box of wine under a shrub (I dread to think what else was hidden in shrubs that day) she hurried to the stage where Frank and his band were quickly ejected as she summoned the guests for their attention. Once everyone had surrounded the stage with eager anticipation of what Margaret termed 'an extra special and highly exclusive performance by a group of phenomenally talented artistes,' a hushed silence fell and the dance troupe made their entrance . . . and what an entrance that was! Through the back gate, along the Cotswold stone path and onto the red and gold stage assembled a group of seven dancers dressed in crimson satin basques, black fishnet stockings, six-inch stilettoes and thigh high boots . . . and all with a serious case of five o'clock shadow! Yes, the 'exclusive and phenomenally talented' dance troupe Margaret had hired to impress the friends and acquaintances-in-high-places of her daughter, were a transvestite burlesque cabaret act! Fricking priceless! As the music played, a decidedly muscular 'Liza Minnelli' with an Adam's apple the size of a Golden Delicious, belted out hits from 'Cabaret' whilst surrounded by gyrating g-strings and thrusting frilly French knickers, whilst a shaky Margaret clutched my arm, stammering, "Briony, Briony, they're a bit . . . well, Briony....do you think . . . they might be . . . ?"

"Men dressed in women's underwear?" I replied, barely stifling my delight. "I think you might be on to something

184

there, Margaret."

I cannot even begin to explain to you the looks on the guests' faces . . . but, I can show you, as Barnaby was running around like a gerbil on speed filming everything in sight with Mr Beaver's phone (which I suspect he acquired by blackmail after spying the poor man during his fumblings with the gold waiter). I have cunningly managed to get him to email me a copy which I will forward to you all in a separate message.

LUCY: Brilliant!

BRIONY: Now, the fun/hilarity/mortification—delete as appropriate, didn't stop there. Celia's husband, John, having ill-advisedly consumed the children's 100% proof cocktails during the course of the party, took this opportunity to showcase his own Agent Provocateurs, and having thrown his outerwear into (yet another!) shrub, he jumped on stage to join the act in all his 'Tali' silk with lace trim high-legs glory.' I have to say, for a sexagenarian, the man has great thighs and a mighty lean, toned stomach! Celia, bless her, turned to a group of guests and cool as a cucumber announced, "Don't go thinking I paid full price for that—£9.99, eBay. Snippered on the matching camisole though . . . "

There's more, of course, but I'll regale you with that when I'm back—just arrived at airport parking so gotta go . . .

KARA: I'm speechless.

LUCY: Who would buy used Agent Provocateur underwear on eBay? Euck!

MELISSA: I do think you should have changed your dress, actually, Briony. Imagine if someone came in the same dress as me to my wedding? I don't blame her for being upset.

BRIONY: In all the history of the world, I sincerely doubt anyone has turned up to a wedding wearing the same dress as the bride, Melissa! Does Monique not offer counselling services to irrational and paranoid brides-to-be?

MELISSA: I'm not being irrational or paranoid. Why would you say that? Has someone said something to you? Who was it? Was it Kate? You have no idea how stressful arranging a wedding is—not made any easier by my bridemaid's reluctance to actually meet with the bride to discuss plans!

MONDAY 20TH JULY

BRIONY: Villa amazing. Shame we're not here for long but looking forward to the sailing. Okay, so anyway, still not heard anything from the out-laws. Their silence instils fear into my heart, although, I guess Margaret at least is busy having fun with her friends for the next few days. The village won't know what's hit them with those saga-louts on the loose 😉

KATE: And what about John? Poor Celia!

BRIONY: John did leave the stage eventually—but not until after he had truly outdone himself with all the shimmying, thrusting and feather teasing dance. The man's missed his vocation, I can tell you, and I wasn't the only one heartily applauding him—although Lucy, I was more surprised that he was wearing those garments under formal suit at a garden birthday party to be honest. I had presumed it was something he did in the privacy of his own home while Celia was at the OAP aerobics class. By the way, I noticed a few other women nodded and 'hmmed' resignedly to themselves. I got the distinct impression it was something they were not unfamiliar with. I shall certainly be checking my knicker drawer for illicit disturbance in future . . .

GAYLE: Hmm . . . I wish Dudley would wear my knickers—at least he'd stretch them a bit and I'd feel less fat. Didn't lose anything at the weigh-in this week. Belinda Bacon was not happy with me at all and made me stand on stage with secret-midnight-eater, Mary, to make examples of us. I'm living off dust this week. Dust and hot water with lemon. I might go for a sauna to see if that helps shed a few pounds.

KATE: Can't check Whatsapp at work much. Phones on verge of being banned during work hours. How's the weather? Are you de-stressing and getting lots of 'holiday delight'?

WEDNESDAY 22ND JULY

BRIONY: 'Holiday delight'?!? If you're talking about sex, Kate, the answer is no. The boys are up with us until late and then James is up with the larks getting some swimming in before breakfast. I'm determined to get some 'holiday delight' in at some point though. If it wasn't for your parcel of pleasure, (or 'jiffy bag of jizz', as James rather snidely referred to it) I would be like a dog on heat, humping anything in sight!

GAYLE: Get the kids to bed earlier one night and get the old pulsating phallus of fun out to surprise James 😃

BRIONY: 'Pulsating phallus of fun?!' Seriously? What has got into you?!

KATE: Snoooooort!

GAYLE: More a case of what's NOT got into you 😉

KATE: Snoooooort!

BRIONY: Well, not that giant pulsating phallus of fun, that's for sure.

KATE: Snooooooooooort!!

BRIONY: Enough of the snorting, Kate!

KATE: Sorry, all I can do with boss in the office.

BRIONY: I didn't bring it anyway. Would you want that in your luggage with all the baggage security checks that take place these days? And to be quite honest, if James found me sat in bed holding a glittery rubber dildo he'd be on the next plane home. He's never been one for any of 'that.' In fact, I once blindfolded him and cuffed him with Sam's toy handcuffs and he had a panic attack. I thought all the heavy breathing and gulping was sexual excitement when in fact he was hyperventilating. Shame. I was having quite a nice time before he passed out, but felt it verged on sexual deviance to carry on . . .

LUCY: Sam's toy handcuffs?! So wrong, Briony!

BRIONY: From a policeman set Margaret got him.

LUCY: You indulged in mild bondage with your son's toy handcuff set bought by your husband's mother?!

GAYLE: 😱

KATE: Snoooooooooooooooooort!!!!!

KARA: So, how's it going in the land of Ouzo and olives? And what about the Greek men? I used to have a Greek boyfriend—did I ever tell you about him? It was when I travelled Europe after uni. Yannis was his name—all curly black hair, liquid brown eyes and tanned torso. We explored the Peloponnesus on the back of his motorbike and he introduced me to olives and salami—oh, it was a whole new world, Bri! Are you going anywhere near Porto Heli? Look out for him if you do.

BRIONY: Olives and salami? Is salami of Greek origin or was that a metaphor for something else resembling a stinky pink sausage?

KARA: No, that resembled something altogether more girthsome and meaty.

BRIONY: Eww.

KATE: 🥒

KARA: Close, Kate 😏

BRIONY: Eww. And ouch! Anyway, I don't know if we're going near Porto Heli. I'd have to ask the skipper who James has gone off to meet today when he checks the boat over and signs the papers etc. I hope he's nice as I don't fancy spending a week on board with some Metaxa breath, sweaty old Captain Birdseye. But rest assured, if we do dock in the port of your lost stinky sausage love, I shall

189

indeed send my regards—after all, there can't be that many Greeks named Yannis, around(!!!)

LUCY: Don't dirty the name of Captain Birdseye!

BRIONY: Had you really not tasted olives until you were 22, Kara? Didn't they have deli's in London back then . . . ?

KARA: Bri. I didn't have aubergine until I was 25. I thought fish paste sandwich spread was exotic and only rich people had chocolate biscuits wrapped in foil with marshmallow in.

KATE: Incredible . . .

KARA: If you do stop there, he's got a brother, Takis, who used to chase people off the beach with a speargun. Probably still does.

BRIONY: Riiiiiigght . . .

KARA: Ah well. Have fun sailing and don't worry about the gerbil—she's fine and dandy.

BRIONY: HE is a HAMSTER, Kara. Did the short, stubby tail not give you a clue?

KARA: Oh. I thought its tail just hadn't grown yet . . . or you'd had it docked 😉

WEDNESDAY 29TH JULY

BRIONY: Ahoy there me landlubber mateys! Tis Salty Sea Dog Bri, here, with tales of my ocean-faring adventures!

KARA HAS LEFT THE GROUP

LUCY HAS LEFT THE GROUP

MELISSA HAS LEFT THE GROUP

GAYLE HAS LEFT THE GROUP

KATE: Well, that went down well 😀
BRIONY ADDED KARA TO THE GROUP
BRIONY ADDED LUCY TO THE GROUP
BRIONY ADDED MELISSA TO THE GROUP
BRIONY ADDED GAYLE TO THE GROUP

LUCY: No fecking pirate talk or I'm blocking you.

BRIONY: Actually, you're lucky I am even able to message you. Our 'skipper' got sea sick on day one of the sail and had to disembark at the next island. I might have been sympathetic (unlikely, yet vague possibility, none the less) had we set sail in stormy seas, but it was flat calm with no wind so we had to use the engine to motor into port. We suspect Metaxa was the true cause so after furious phone calls to the yacht charter company, who didn't have a re-placement for us, it was agreed that we could continue with the yacht and skipper it ourselves at no extra cost on the insurance. Feeling pissed off and very gung-ho about it all, I foolishly agreed to this . . . and regretted that decision precisely 57 minutes later when James almost ripped the whole pontoon off with him when we cast off again. By the time he had negotiated his way out of the marina, I was a nervous wreck and he had shed a stone in pure sweat alone.

GAYLE: Damn you and your accidental weight loss!

BRIONY: I won't say it was plain sailing to Agistri, as James has a habit of screaming orders at me like I am some skivvy whenever we are on a boat. The boys seemed to enjoy it whilst James and I sat on deck chewing our nails and occa-sionally glaring at each other. Apparently, my helming skills are 'amateur,' and so James now has a new love in his life; the auto pilot he has lovingly named, 'Annabel.' Of course, the boys find much amusement each time James changes Annabel's course with an adoring look in his eye, and she responds appropriately and with no argument or rolling of the eyes. Just a shame she can't make tea or relieve me of other mundane marital duties.

LUCY: So where are you now?

BRIONY: Moored up just off Aegina and very pleasant and peaceful it is too—apart from the disconcerting sound of a lady on the mooring next to us, squealing, 'Norman! Stop licking that! Oh Norman, you are a naughty boy, now get off me at once.' And the particularly worrying, 'Norman! Don't nibble me there, it's too salty.'

KARA: Which bit was too salty?!

BRIONY: I dread to think, Kara. Anyway, it transpired later that day that Norman is not in fact a seafaring gimp, but rather a giant white poodle that was taken in the couple's dingy to the beach for walkies.

KATE: That's really not that much better . . .

KARA: I still want to know what was the saltiest bit.

BRIONY: James is enjoying himself so much we are staying an extra week! I almost choked on my spanakopita when he announced that one on us! Even the boys were stunned speechless for a moment. I think it's being skipper of the boat that's done it and I'm not complaining. Especially as the yacht charter company have agreed a nominal fee for the extra week based on the fact the skipper let us down.

The only crux in these plans is the fact that James wants to set sail and do another two islands when I would be happy staying here. Not sure our marriage can survive any more weak tacks or jammed sails. At least when we're moored up it's like a proper holiday though . . .

KARA: So I've got to entertain Sergei for another week??

BRIONY: Umm, yes, but i didn't think hamsters needed entertaining as such . . . ? Hope all is good and well with everyone in blighty!

MELISSA: No, everything is not good and well, Briony! I've scheduled in a meeting with you and Kate to meet with Monique next Tuesday, so you can't stay an extra bloody week in Greece! Seriously, this is getting beyond a joke. I'm up to my eyeballs in table plans, menus, dress designs, and where is my best friend—my maid of honour no less—when I need her to meet with my planner to discuss matters of utmost importance? It's hard enough pinning Kate down these days now she's all loved up over Piers (no offence, Kate) and now you decided to stay on holiday an extra week without even discussing it with me first? If you don't want to be part of my special day then just say so and I'll get Kate to step in as Matron of Honour, and I have plenty of other friends who would jump at the chance of being my bridesmaid. I can't take much more, Briony, I'm sorry but I just can't.

BRIONY: Umm . . . How can you be doing the table plans already when you haven't even sent the invites out yet and don't know who will be coming? If you would prefer Kate as matron of honour, that's fine with me

KATE HAS LEFT THE GROUP

MELISSA: What do you mean I won't know who will be coming? The invites are merely a formality. Surely everyone will be coming? It's my wedding and it's on New Year's Eve. What better plans could anyone have?!

MELISSA ADDED KATE TO THE GROUP

BRIONY: Although she'd be more of a Matron of Dishonour 😉

KATE HAS LEFT THE GROUP

MELISSA: Don't call me bridezilla. I am not anything like those women on those god awful trashy TV shows. My wedding is going to be classy and refined and calm and wonderful—or at least it would be if my friends would stop forcing me to change plans and start co-operating with me. I am not stressed at all, I am merely pointing out that you are being selfish, self-centred and unreasonable to be on holiday when I am trying to organise a meeting which is essentially for your benefit.

MELISSA ADDED KATE TO THE GROUP

MELISSA: Stay there Kate!

KATE: Matron of dishonour! Snooooooort!

MELISSA: Now, if you are going to insist on staying away, please give me a definite date when you will be back and I shall re-arrange the meeting—although I fear Monique will not be happy. She has been very prickly with me lately and rather jumpy in general.

BRIONY: Umm, just how is this meeting to *my* benefit?

194

BRIONY: I'll probably almost definitely be free last week in August.

MELISSA: How is it to your benefit?! How else are you going to know what to do and what underwear to wear? I don't want bra straps peeking out from under the dresses ruining the photos and if Kate changes her hair colour again she risks clashing with the flowers (no offence, Kate). You have no idea how stressful all this is, Briony. Let us not forget how you were selfish enough to secretly elope, not giving any of your dearest friends or family the chance to come and participate in your special day. Remember, I, your oldest friend, only discovered you'd got married when you changed your name on Facebook. I still get upset about it, you know, I'd dreamed of being your bridesmaid since we were seven and used to play pretend weddings in the garden during the summer holidays.

KATE: Sorry, not free last week in August

BRIONY: We secretly eloped for the very reason that I knew it would be too stressful to organise a wedding knowing full well that both our families together in one room was not conducive of a happy relaxing day.

MELISSA: What do you mean you're not free the last week in August, Kate?!?!

BRIONY: And, if it's any consolation, I never would have had any bridesmaids anyway; I'm far too tight to buy the dresses.

MELISSA: Kate! Why are you not free the last week in August?!?

BRIONY: Now I'm going snorkelling before I get the shark fear again 😃

KATE HAS LEFT THE GROUP

MELISSA: 😳

FRIDAY 31ST JULY

SUBJECT: THE GARDEN

Dear Celia

I do hope you are well and your journey back from Devon was not too tiring or congested. Arthur decided to take a short cut to avoid the M5 which he was sure would be gridlocked on a Saturday, but unfortunately sewage works on the B roads meant it took us seven hours to get home instead of the usual three. It was lucky we had packed some of the leftover food as we were able to have a picnic on the way which broke the journey up nicely (although added an extra hour after Arthur got stung by a wasp causing his lip to swell quite dramatically, meaning we had to unpack all the bags to find the antihistamine tablets).

The garden is looking lovely and we have enlisted the help of Richard from number 52 to come and help us clean the pond up before we purchase some fish to add some life to it. We used to have fish many years ago, if you remember, but there was the unfortunate incident with Mrs Tinks' son and the vegetarian piranha which turned out not to be vegetarian after all.

I do hope your friends, the Fothergills, got home safely. Unfortunately, I discovered that Arthur mistakenly packed a duck-egg blue pashmina which I believe belongs to Angela, so I shall either post that back to you or give it to you when we next see each other, as, under the circumstances, it is highly unlikely I shall be seeing your friends again.

Love to John,
Margaret

AUGUST

SUBJECT: RE: THE GARDEN

Dear Margaret

Our journey was indeed congestion-free, and we even managed a leisurely lunch and a spot of shopping in one of the market towns en-route.

I shall forward you the Fothergills' address so as you can send the pashmina directly back to Angela if you are sure it is hers? I don't recall her wearing a duck-egg blue pashmina during our stay at the cottage, so are you sure it doesn't belong to one of the other couples they invited over?

I do indeed remember the piranha incident; and what a messy incident it was. To this day, I always get 'what is the name of the vegetarian species of piranha' correct during games of Trivial Pursuit or pub quizzes, so some good came of it. I can still envisage Mrs Tinks running around the garden screaming, 'but the man told us it was a Pacu, Mrs Denley!' as you were dispatching the wretched fish with a cricket bat on the lawn. How we can laugh about it now; just as we shall surely laugh about the Fothergill incident in years to some.

Well, maybe, anyway.

Yours
Celia

SATURDAY 1ST AUGUST
SUBJECT: RE: THE GARDEN
Dear Celia

Thank you for forwarding the Fothergills' address to me. I shall send the pashmina off when I have a spare jiffy bag. Forgive me for being uncharitable, but after the excessive amount of my wine and champagne they and their 'friends' consumed during our break, I do not feel inclined to go to the trouble of purchasing a new jiffy bag just for their benefit. And yes, I am sure it is Angela's pashmina; the image is branded into my memory for evermore, Celia.

Rest assured, we will be purchasing our fish from a reputable garden aquatics company, and not agreeing to re-home 'vegetarian piranhas' which have grown too large for their tanks. In fact, I have spoken to Cosmo regarding the matter—he has a delightful pond in his cottage garden. He is going to put me in touch with the company who supplied his pond life.

Bests, Margaret

SUNDAY 2ND AUGUST

SUBJECT: RE: THE GARDEN

Dear Margaret

Do I take it Cosmo is back in favour with you, then? Do be sure to get a free quote before purchasing anything this time, Margaret. Have James and Briony returned from their holidays yet? They must have had a lovely time, and perfect timing for them to avoid the aftermath of Sarah's party—speaking of which; has Sarah forgiven you yet? In your defence, I still think everyone had a super time and it will indeed be the talk of the village for many years to come.

Yours, Celia

PS—I'm sure that pashmina belonged to the stout woman Gerry and Angela invited over. She was wearing a dress in the same shade.

MONDAY 3RD AUGUST

SUBJECT: RE: THE GARDEN

Celia! Cosmo was never out of favour; I really don't know where you get these ideas from. I was simply a little taken aback at the high quality of the wines he supplied for me, which were, of course, understandably, reflected in the price. I am also still more than a little taken aback with the Fothergills' for taking the remaining bottles with them when they left the cottage.

It is very kind of you to say everyone had a lovely time

at the party. Sadly, Sarah is not convinced and claims the faux pas with the dancing group has tarnished her reputation. However, it is next month that her house features in the glossy homes magazine, 'Village Life', so I am rather hoping that shifts her focus in a more positive direction.

Bests, Margaret

P.S. Yes, I really am quite certain the pashmina belongs to Angela. The image of her draped in it and nothing else as she sauntered out of our bedroom refuses to leave my mind; no matter how hard I try and erase it. In fact, there are many moments of that week I have tried to vaporize from my memory to no avail. I wake in the early hours with images and scenarios going around and around in my head. Arthur tells me 'their' sort prey on people like us, and Cosmo tells me there are even special clubs where such people go to meet others of that persuasion. But not us, Celia, surely, those sort of people are not people like us, so how could we have been mistaken for 'their sort'?

TUESDAY 4TH AUGUST
SUBJECT: THE FOTHERGILL INCIDENT
Dear Margaret

What can I say? I, too, have been waking in the early hours, haunted by the events at the cottage, and I, of course, have the added onus of having introduced you to them and encouraged you to include them in our cottaging holiday. You all got on so well at my sixtieth and never in my most depraved of dreams would I ever have thought their intentions were anything other than entirely honourable. John has suggested to me that we should be flattered by their attentions, although, after seeing the odd couple they invited back on that last night, I don't think they were particularly picky as to who they selected for their games.

I have to say, Margaret, maybe you and I are particularly naïve? I shudder to think about the goings on at such clubs, and Margaret, was it wise to discuss this with Cosmo? I thought we agreed to discuss with no one? We both have high standing reputations and neither of us could be doing with having our reputations tarnished at this stage on our lives.

Where were the signs, Margaret? This is the question I ask myself over and over again? Where were the signs and why didn't we spot them? If this is how the blue-bloods behave, it's no wonder the country is in the state it's in.

Your friend,
Celia

TUESDAY 4TH AUGUST
SUBJECT: RE: THE FOTHERGILL INCIDENT
Oh, Celia

Hindsight is a wonderful thing and we must not beat ourselves up questioning where our own goodwill was taken for anything other than goodwill and a kind heart. For that is what we are, Celia; not naïve, but kind-hearted.

Having said that, I have a sneaking suspicion The Fothergills' title may be bought rather than inherited.

Please do not distress yourself over exactly what I have divulged to Cosmo. He is a man of the world, Celia, whose travels have brought him into contact with people from many socially diverse areas of life. I did not need to say much for him to realise something was amiss. He tells me 'swinging' as it is known in those circles, is surprisingly popular with the upper middle classes, so at least our social class was not in question, if not our morals.

Although I am reluctant to bring it up, and am in no way making accusations towards you, Celia, do you think John's 'display' at Sarah's party may have encouraged them into assuming we were all far more liberal than we are. I don't know where they met the couples they kept bringing back to join us, but I fear word of John's performance was doing the rounds of the South Hams.

Yours,
Margaret

Wednesday 5th August
SUBJECT: RE: THE FOTHERGILL INCIDENT
Dear Margaret

Although you say you mean no offence, I do feel rather insulted that you are hinting that John's private little hobby was in some way responsible for the Fothergill incident. Although gossip is indeed rife around the South Hams, may I politely remind you that it was you who was the first to jump in the hot tub at Gerry's suggestion, and while admittedly, it can't be argued you looked somewhat taken aback when he followed suit minus his trunks, I can't help but feel this was the catalyst for what was to come. After all, Margaret, it was into you and Arthur's bed that Angela crept that night, not mine and Johns. She must have got a sense of something—some unspoken understanding, between yourselves, which she did not with John and I.

How is the pond coming along? Have you got the bill for the fish yet?

All Bests,
Celia

SUBJECT: RE: THE FOTHERGILL INCIDENT
Dear Celia

It may have been into my bedroom that Angela crept (although one can hardly 'creep' when wearing six inch stilettos) but I can assure you she was in no way encouraged by myself or Arthur, who, for your information, is on medication for hypertension and therefore needs to avoid any excitement of that manner. In fact, poor Arthur became terribly befuddled by the whole incident and being the caring man he is, was so concerned for Angela, whom he thought may have been sleepwalking, insisted upon escorting her back to her room before she caught a chill or tripped in those ridiculous shoes. It must have been praying on his mind all night, as the poor man was exhausted the next day and looked like he's hardly slept a wink. Luckily for me I have always been a good sleeper and nodded off immediately—not even stirring when Arthur returned to bed.

The pond is taking more time than anticipated as Richard finds it hard to get a grip on the weeds from his wheelchair. It takes Arthur and I some time and considerable effort to manoeuvre him into the right position out of his wheelchair and onto a cushioned gardening pad, and then of course, with no back support he tends to roll over if he loses his balance tugging on a particularly tough weed. I thought we'd lost him yesterday when I'd gone inside to make a pot of tea and he plain disappeared from sight. Arthur had been emptying a bucket on the compost heap and it took us quite a few minutes before eventually spotting Richard stuck between the fatsia japonica and wheelbarrow, having roly-polied down the grassy bank. I can't tell you the trouble we had trying to roll him back up the bank to his wheelchair. In fact, it was such a job we had to have a halfway break—wedging a large lounger cushion under him to stop him rolling down again whilst we had a refreshing cup of tea. My back is still suffering.

The fish and aquatic life are being carefully selected for us and I foresee no problem with the cost of such a personalised service, so please do not concern yourself, Celia.

Yours,
Margaret

P.S. I'm not quite so sure you can claim John's hobby is a private matter since most of the South Hams watched him perform at the party. Did he ever take the dance troupe up on their offer of a place in the group? It's certainly one way to top up your pensions.

THURSDAY 6TH AUGUST
SUBJECT: RE: THE FOTHERGILL INCIDENT
Dear Margaret

Yes, how kind of Arthur to escort Angela back to her room, and equally fortunate you are such a deep sleeper. Sadly, the same cannot be said for myself, since I was kept awake most of that night by the animalistic noises emanating from the Fothergills' room. Such a cacophony at times, it certainly sounded like there were more than just the two of them at it!

Thank you for asking but no, John declined Bernard's kind offer to join 'TransTastic,' although the lure of free satin underwear almost proved too much. I must ask, Margaret, did the name of the dance troupe not alert you to the possibility all may not be as it seemed?

Poor Richard. He does seem to have quite a few scrapes in your garden. Have you thought of hiring a professional to do the pond? I have images of dead heavy-set, bearded men floating face down amongst the duckweed. You know, death by misadventure in your own garden reduces the house value considerably.

Bests,
Celia

SUBJECT: RE: THE FOTHERGILL INCIDENT
Please don't fret, Celia, safety is always paramount at the Denleys', and we have found an old foam pad to tape around Richard's torso for buoyancy, should he start ro-ly-polying off again. I do hope he puts some welly into it though as Arthur and I are always picking up the slack and I was hoping to have the fish in by next week.

With regards to the name 'TransTastic,' I feel quite fool-ish to confess now that I assumed the 'Trans' referred to their international status. You know, like 'Trans-atlantic.' I am now just glad I didn't book, 'Golden Rain' as Cosmo tells me there is an alternative and highly unsavoury defi-nition, and I fear there may have been more than just gold tinsel and sequins to that act.

Yours,
Margaret

SUBJECT: VILLAGE LIFE
Dear Briony
    Now you are finally back from your holiday, I thought

I would let you know that we feature in this month's 'Village Life' which goes on sale on Monday. I am sure you are just as excited as we are and it will be lovely to finally see the results of the photo shoot. I can barely recall from which angle many of the rooms were photographed, and some will come as a complete surprise, as I was, of course, being interviewed by the features editor whilst their photographer took many of the pictures.

I must thank you for the delightful tea-towels you so kindly gave me for my birthday. We must have quite similar taste, as if I am not very much mistaken, they are uncannily similar to the set I gave you last Christmas . . . as is the Victoriana style egg basket.

I do hope you enjoyed your extended break. I must confess I wish I could have gone away for a while after my party. Although it was a lovely idea of mother to surprise me, there are some surprises that are not altogether welcomed—and a group of cross-dressing men taking centre stage in my lavishly landscaped garden, is one of them. Mother tells me you encouraged her in this idea having poo-pooed most of her other suggestions. Briony, please may I remind you that not all of us have led such a 'diverse' lifestyle as yourself, and I for one managed to pay off my university overdraft helping out at the stables in the holidays, as opposed to your more 'cutting edge' employment during that time.

I have tried to telephone James to thank him for my tea-towels and egg basket, but it always goes through to voicemail. I suspect he is terribly busy working overtime to pay off that extended holiday of yours. Do give him my love.

Sarah

SUBJECT: RE: VILLAGE LIFE
Dear Sarah

Firstly, you are welcome. I know how much you love your kitchen (and thank you for the breakdown of costs spreadsheet you forwarded to us at the time, it's always useful to know how much someone pays for a granite island and solid teak cabinets). I noticed you had accidentally omitted any kitchen items from your birthday list, so took the liberty of righting that for you. How funny that I chose items so similar to the ones you gave us last Christmas! That must be my subconscious working overtime and would explain why I turned up wearing the same dress as you to your party! Just how uncanny was that? I do hope you were not too disgruntled that I chose not to wear the jacket you provided, but I did think that as we are such different shapes and sizes, the dresses did, in actual fact, look like completely different designs. In fact, that lovely lady who owns the flower shop in the village commented that I was the only woman at the party with a figure capable of showing off that style of dress. So you see? She, for one, hadn't noticed that they were identical and I am sure that

209

was the case for most of the other guests.

I think we can both be fairly confident that any attention paid to us was short-lived once TransTastic got on stage. And oh my! What a show that was! Incidentally, I don't think I can be accused of encouraging Margaret in her choice of party act. I had virtually no input in the matter other than warning her that a fire juggling circus act might cause damage not covered by your home insurance.

We are all very excited by your feature in Village Life, which I purchased today. The photographer obviously took time to gauge the best time of day for lighting each room, and you certainly arranged all your little knick-knacks to give us a fine impression of the lifestyle you lead and the person you are. Incidentally, my friend Lucy was particularly impressed with your fertility phallus. Is it sculpted from clay or carved in wood we wondered? It was very life-like.

Love, Briony

PS—There was very little 'cutting edge' about my post uni 'holiday job.' Kiss-o-grams were all the rage back then and prancing around in my underwear meant paying off my uni debts in triple quick time, allowing me to travel Asia and Australia. Occasionally, I would whip my baps out for an extra tenner—after all, if you've got it, flaunt it, eh? 😉

SUBJECT: RE: VILLAGE LIFE
Dear Briony

I think you may be looking at the wrong feature. I can assure you my holiday finds have never led me to purchase a 'fertility phallus,' wood, clay, or otherwise. Unfortunately, my copy of Village Life is yet to drop through my letter box. The postal strike is causing untold suffering across the villages. If it doesn't arrive by today, I shall have to drive into town and get a copy—the village shop will have none left as I know all my friends were eager to see the feature. In the meantime, I am curbing my excitement by creating online Christmas lists for the children. Friends and family will be able to click on the gift idea that suits them best and a link will take them to the relevant online store, add it to their basket with pre-chosen gift wrap of my choice, in order for the present to be delivered directly to us by independent courier. I refuse to let this dratted postal service adversely impact upon my Christmas.

Love Sarah

TUESDAY 11TH AUGUST
SUBJECT: RE: VILLAGE LIFE
No, it's definitely your house, Sarah. I recognise the towels in the en-suite bathroom.

If it's not an African fertility phallus, whatever can it be? A novelty loo roll holder??

TUESDAY 11TH AUGUST
SUBJECT: RE: VILLAGE LIFE

The en-suite? I wasn't aware the en-suite was photo-graphed. Either way, we don't have any phallic shaped fertility phahfbusabfjabjclnc3hjndsniwqj2ihniu7856r6tgh-n^%$^%$%$*I&*

TUESDAY 11TH AUGUST
SUBJECT: RE: VILLAGE LIFE

Sarah? Did the cat jump on the keyboard? Whatever has happened?!

FRIDAY 14TH AUGUST
WHATSAPP MESSAGE

LUCY: I'll pick you up Monday just after 9am for the test drive. Really appreciate you coming with me, Briony. I'm terrible at asking the right questions and bartering and the like. We're going to the showroom just off the main road first if that's okay? Is your mother-in-law still coming to look after the boys? Do you think we might squeeze lunch in as long as she's happy to stick around for a bit?

BRIONY: Lunch should be fine. Margaret is usually in no hurry to leave. Does a salesman accompany us or do we get to drive off in a new car Thelma and Louise stylie?

LUCY: I hope he doesn't accompany us as that will make me nervous. Have you told your sister-in-law about her vi-brator on full view in the windowsill of the photo yet? The feature's online now, so you can email the pic to anyone who might not have seen it and even pop it on your Face-book page >snurk<

BRIONY: I didn't actually tell my sister-in-law directly about the vibrator. I let her work it out herself. Much more fun that way.

SATURDAY 15TH AUGUST
SUBJECT: INVITE
Dear Celia

Arthur and I are terribly excited as the pond springs into life this weekend! As I type, I have two men taking various samples and testing the water in anticipation of introducing the fish and aquatic life. Would John and yourself care to stay next weekend once the fish have settled in and we can enjoy a few drinks and a barbeque whilst admiring my new aquatic feature. Richard will whizz over to see the fruits of his labour, but other than that, I thought I'd keep it an exclusive event as we're still a little drained from the Fothergill incident.

Yours, Margaret

SUNDAY 16TH AUGUST
SUBJECT: RE: INVITE
Dear Margaret

How kind of you to think of us at this time. As you know, John has always taken a keen interest in pond life so we would be delighted to come and inspect yours. I have the grandchildren here again today as their parents once more go gallivanting around retail parks for new sofas and the like. Honestly, Margaret, if I'd wanted to spend my Sundays' with toddlers at my time of life, I would have released the equity from the house and paid for some unscrupulous pseudo obstetrician to impregnate me. I'm really going to have to say something to them soon.

Oh, I finally got my copy of 'Village Life' and have to say, they did a fine job on Sarah's house. Do they use special lighting or filters on the lenses? It looked so much less grey, than in real life. You would have thought she would have popped a few loo rolls on that holder in the en-suite though wouldn't you? It looks a little crude standing empty and just sticking up like that on the windowsill. Still, I expect she was busy fluffing cushions ready for the next shot, wasn't she?

See you Saturday. We'll aim for lunchtime, traffic permitting.

Bests as always,
Celia

PS I'm really not sure Richard should be whizzing anywhere in that chair of his, Margaret. He does seem a little accident prone . . .
P.P.S. What was the final bill for the fish—just out of interest?

SUBJECT: RE: INVITE

Dear Celia

The cost of the expertise involved in selecting and providing suitable aquatic life with follow up advice for my pond was very reasonable; and with that, the matter is closed, my dear friend. I think you will see why on Saturday. There is nothing lovelier than watching beautifully hued fish swimming hypnotically in a well-tended, lusciously planted pond. You simply cannot put a price on that, Celia.

It's funny you should mention the lavatory roll holder as I said the same thing to Sarah myself and she completely exploded. Maybe she is still touchy about the party. I merely mentioned the fact she is usually so well stocked on triple cushioned comfort in a shade to match the whichever bathroom's décor and she started bitterly lamenting the fact of why no one could focus on the positive aspects of her featuring in such a nationally renowned glossy homes magazine, and how everyone was joking at her expense— including the photographer and his team to have done such a thing. She says she is thinking of suing, Celia! Suing over a lavatory roll holder of all things! I know items such as these are not as popular these days, and some may even say to have one is old fashioned, but I thought hers looked much nicer than the ballerina doll style holders popular in our time. Regardless of her displeasure at such a minor faux pas, I took copies of the magazine to my WI meeting and I shall be doing the same at my aerobics class this week, as I for one am very proud of my daughter's lovely home; depleted lavatory roll holder or not!

I am hurrying off to look after the boys for Briony in a minute, so Arthur and I look forward to seeing you on Saturday.

Yours, as always,
Margaret

P.S. I know what you mean about Richard. Arthur and I were having second thoughts about letting him mow the lawn later this week. But he does seem to so enjoy the fun of being pulled around the garden whilst tied to the mower, and his chair is stable enough to make sure he only goes in straight lines. Of course, we have to watch out for the trees. It's quite astounding the momentum that can build up from a petrol powered mower, and Richard doesn't always gage the stopping distance as accurately as we would like.

WEDNESDAY 19TH AUGUST
WHATSAPP MESSAGE
BRIONY: Hi Lucy. Attached are scans of my insurance and driving licence details as requested. Sorry it took me a while to hunt them out. As I explained to the car salesman, I used to always carry my licence, but once I changed it for a photo-card I got worried about identity theft so took it out my bag in case it got stolen. Also, as you can see from

the scanned pic, it's really not the best photo of me—in fact, James says it looks like a mug shot for a hooker; all big hair and lip gloss.

So, anyway, James has contacted our lawyer and I have to tell you that his preliminary opinion is that I was acting in your best interests and the best interests of the car showroom by showing sensible initiative in taking over the driving from you, since you were essentially, well . . . pissed. I know you said the antibiotics you are on caused the alcohol to have that effect, and you had only had the one glass of wine, and Lucy, you were drooling over the front of your dress and leering at the waiter in a most unsavoury fashion. I, for one, really didn't feel happy about you driving us back to the showroom, and what about poor Algernon in the back? The salesman wasn't thrilled that you turned up with him and insisted upon taking him for the test drive as it was. I know you weren't to know the poor man was allergic to dogs, but it was the fact the salesman then wasn't able to accompany us on the drive that started this whole chain of events. I knew we were pushing it by stopping for lunch. The test drive is meant to be just that; a short drive to test the car It's not so as the potential buyer can park up outside a brasserie to see how the car looks while they are sat inside eating bruschetta and goats cheese tart, Lucy.

BRIONY: Lucy?

BRIONY: Lucy? You are still speaking to me aren't you?

BRIONY: So, what has Tom said about all this? Is he cross? My mother-in-law is having a field day! This is the second time I've had dealings with the police in the last few months, what with the Kara furore in London. She's going to start telling people I'm an unfit mother—well, she probably does already to be fair . . .

BRIONY: . . . It really wasn't my fault, Lucy . . .

WHATSAPP MESSAGE

KATE: Hey Bri—Looking forward to our weekend at Bitch Cottage. Piers and I are going to leave London a bit early to avoid the Friday-get-the-hell-outta-Dodge-traffic. Shall we bring anything special?

BRIONY: *Birch* Kate. Although, with the way I'm feeling . . . 🙁 Don't worry about bringing anything—I've got it all covered. Will be a relief to chill with friends this weekend after the week I am having.

KATE: Ffs is James still being a workaholic bore?

BRIONY: No. Well, yes, but that's not what I meant.

KATE: Are you sure he's not having an affair Bri? You need to protect your assets before he gives it all away to some Thai chick he's met online.

BRIONY: Thanks, Kate. Very reassuring.

KATE: Have you checked his phone for messages or does he have a passcode? We can try and hack it this weekend. We'll YouTube how to do it—there's bound to be a video on it.

BRIONY: He's not having an affair. He doesn't have time for an affair.

BRIONY: Does he?

218

KATE: Best get your fanny swabbed. My friend Donna only found out her husband was having an affair when a chlamydia swab came back positive.

BRIONY: Right. Thanks again . . .

KATE: Sorry, so what's the prob if it's not James?

BRIONY: Well, I very kindly agreed to go with Lucy to test drive a couple of new cars on Monday, and now as a result I might be up in court for reckless driving and driving without insurance! Basically, Lucy brought her bloody dog along for the ride (leaving her kids at home to be baby-sat by the dog walker!) The salesman had a dog allergy and as under no circumstances was Lucy leaving her beloved Algey in the showroom, we were given the keys and off we went—like Thelma and Louise with a hound in the back. As we were late anyway (Margaret was late arriving to look after the boys) and the salesman had got her back up by assuming we were a lesbian couple (I was slightly offended by the filthy look Lucy gave me as she replied, 'She's not my partner! As if I'd go for her!'). Lucy decided we would stop off for a quick bite at a brasserie en-route. She had the set lunch, 'Lite Bite,' that included a glass of house wine which reacted to the antibiotics she is on. I decided it would be prudent for me to drive us back with a semi-conscious and dribbling Lucy in the back with the dog. Well, Algey spotted another dog looking out the back window of a car we were behind at the lights so just as I pulled off he launched himself in to the front, barking like a thing possessed, scaring the bejesus out of me and causing me to

219

go into the back of the car. Of course, I wasn't officially the named test driver and the named driver was intoxicated, so it's all got a bit 'complicated' now the police are involved.

KATE: Extraordinary!

BRIONY: Ordinarily extraordinary, but just another day in my life, it would seem . . . 😬

KATE: Quite! Why did the salesman even think you were a couple? Have you been wearing your 'Dip Me in Honey and Throw Me to the Lesbians' top again?

BRIONY: Ha. No, whilst going through the sales spiel he happened to innocently ask if Lucy and I were 'partners.' He meant business partners, of course. Christ she was so touchy about it. I'm quite of I always thought I'd be quite a good catch if I ever changed track . . . I couldn't muff dive myself, but I reckon I could happily be the recipient.

KATE: You'd be a lazy lesbian lover. All take and no give— who would have you? Stick to cock, Briony. You know where you are with cock.

BRIONY: I'm not getting any of that either.

KATE: Check his internet history.

BRIONY: Hmm . . .

BRIONY: But seriously, Lucy needs to get a grip where that dog of hers is concerned. I know some people substitute children for dogs, but Lucy has children who seem to come second best to the mutt. He even has his own aromatherapist and masseuse for goodness sake.

KATE: Algey does?! Well, if she's nuts enough to pay someone to do that for her dog . . .

BRIONY: You guys coming here this weekend has meant we got out of Margaret's fish-pond party. After all the trouble with Cosmo and the bill for the wine and champers, she's only gone and enlisted his help in installing some 'interesting and unique' aquatic life into that decrepit old pond of theirs. I had no idea she was so taken with his goldfish, but I guess that's why she is always next door when she's meant to be visiting us (not that I'm complaining about that!) I often wonder if she is checking up on me. Maybe she thinks Cosmo and I are too friendly. I know she wasn't happy with me staying at his London pad during the march, and I'm not quite sure why she couldn't just pop down to the garden centre like most people, but the upshot is that the pond has had a total re-vamp and she was having a few people over to admire it this weekend. I'm just awaiting the email to request my share of the bill for her fish with some totally illogical and perplexing reason attached.

KATE: So is Cosmo guest of honour at the fish pond party– hahaha! See you tomorrow.

FRIDAY 21ST AUGUST
WHATSAPP MESSAGE
LUCY: I'm sorry it's taken me a while to reply. This whole silly business with the test drive crash has upset me rather and Tom is not being terribly supportive. I feel such a fool and everything's got out of hand and you're right; it is all my fault. Poor Algey has been so traumatised by the crash I've

had to increase his therapies, which increases the costs, and Tom says I need to get my priorities right and spend more time dealing with the children rather than Algey, which I think is rather unfair. After all, they have tennis and gym club and I'm always there to pick them up at the end of the day and tuck them in at night, so what's the problem? Tom has always been jealous of Algey. He stopped him sleeping on the bed as he said he couldn't get a good night with him there, but Algey likes company at night and hates being left downstairs, so what was I supposed to do? It's not like Tom needs me in bed with him every night to be able to sleep so I really don't see why he makes such a fuss about me sleeping in the spare bedroom with Algey. I've decided to get away from his sulking for a few days and I've booked us into a lovely hotel in the Cotswolds for a the weekend Lots of long leisurely walks and fresh air and I'm sure I'll be feeling more myself next week.

BRIONY: Christ, Lucy, sorry you've been so upset. Well, I'm sure a few days away with the kids will do you the world of good and Tom will come round after he's been left to stew on his own.

LUCY: I'm going away with Algey, not the kids! I'd hardly get any peace otherwise, would I?! Tom can keep them amused all weekend to show him just how hard it is sometimes.

BRIONY: Ahh right . . . Umm, have you heard anything else from the car showroom people or the police? It is rather on my mind . . .

LUCY: Oh, It's all sorted out with the car showroom—did I not mention? X

BRIONY: No, you did not mention everything was sorted, Lucy! I've been hitting the medicinal mojitos every bloody night through stress! Are you really sleeping in the spare room with Algey?!

LUCY: Honestly, Briony, Tom's lucky I didn't kick him out the master bedroom. He doesn't understand, Algey, he really doesn't.

BRIONY: I know you're upset, but I'm really not sure sleeping with the dog as opposed to your husband is healthy, but who you sleep with is none of my business 😉

LUCY: What do you mean by 'who I sleep with is none of your business'? Why would you say that? I told you I have had to increase Algey's therapies since the accident, and it's no more than that, Briony, I can assure you.

BRIONY: I was referring to your sleeping arrangements with the dog whilst your husband sleeps alone. It is quite unusual, Lucy. What did you think I meant?! You're not sleeping with anyone else other than Algey are you, you saucy minx?—hehe. Anyway, I'm at the beach and got to put my phone in my bag now before it explodes in this heat. Hope you and Algey have a nice weekend away!

MONDAY *24TH AUGUST*
SUBJECT: POND LIFE
Dear Margaret

Arthur and I had a lovely weekend enjoying your pond,

and once again, the gin and conversation did flow! I have to say, Richard's conversation was on the . . . fruity side, shall we say? Not quite the conversation one is used to hearing over barbecued chicken breasts and a Tom Collins. I think you need to keep the gin a little higher up and out of Richard's reach in future. Have you managed to identify the funny little frogs yet? They look far too pretty to be a native species, Margaret, and one must be terribly careful with introducing alien species into our delicately balanced eco systems. Look what happened with the cane toad; carnage! Maybe try licking them and see if you start hallucinating? We all have an ecological responsibility to protect our planet, so please don't forget that.

Your friend,
Celia

P.S. I had an answer phone message from Angela Fothergill thanking us for the return of her pashmina. She said she would have thanked you herself, but didn't have your number. I take it you would rather I didn't pass it on . . . .? I'm not sure what John and I will do about their New Year's Eve party this year. We usually always go—if only to have an excuse not to baby-sit the grandchildren. Why is it that our children seem to think once they have reproduced, it is our job to give up our social lives to look after their children, Margaret? Do you have plans for New Year's? I warn you now; it is highly likely the Fothergills will request the pleasure of your company this year also, so have your excuses at the ready . . .

WEDNESDAY 26TH AUGUST
SUBJECT: RE: POND LIFE
Dear Celia

Yes, it was such fun, wasn't it? I am glad you both enjoyed the weekend. I don't think the Scrabble board has had that much play in a long time. As for Richard . . . Arthur and I think he may be a little lonely and so have encouraged him to join an online dating agency. We both thought this a marvellous idea as this way he is able to sift through potential candidates in the comfort of his own home before he makes any decisions. Arthur did initially suggest speed dating, and although Richard is certainly pretty speedy in his wheelchair coming down the hill to us, I felt he would be at a disadvantage in the confines of a single room packed with other singletons.

You are correct in your assumption that I would rather you did not pass on my details to your friends, the Fothergills. They must be terribly thick-skinned to think I would want an invite to any party of theirs after the events at the cottage, and I would advise you to be cautious, Celia. I really don't have any plans for New Year's Eve as of yet, but am thinking a little soiree of my own might be in order. What are your thoughts on that, Celia?

Your dearest friend, Margaret

PS I am not worried about the brightly coloured frogs and I certainly have no intention of licking them, Celia. They do all sorts of weird and wonderful things these days to make normal frogs more attractive. I expect the supplier fed them brightly coloured food or something.

WEDNESDAY 26TH AUGUST
SUBJECT: RE: POND LIFE
Just a little lick, Margaret! I might try it myself next time and see what happens.

THURSDAY 27TH AUGUST
WHATSAPP GROUP MESSAGE
BRIONY: Hey Guys. How's about a BBQ at mine on Sunday before the kids go back to school?

LUCY: Yes, that would be fab. Sunday suits us. Will make salads to bring—pasta and cous cous—okay? Look forward to it. Is it okay to bring Algey?

GAYLE: Just what we need! Will bring veggie kebabs and bits and pieces.

KARA: Sunday good for us—you know I'm gluten free now?

BRIONY: No, Kara, I didn't know you were gluten free now! Swap the cous cous for quinoa, Lucy, and I'll order GF rolls.

GAYLE: How was your weekend with Kate?

BRIONY: Hmm . . . . Interesting. Call me old fashioned but is it considered acceptable to shag loudly in the family bathroom every morning whilst your host has to wait outside fielding their children away from the pornographic noises emanating from within?

GAYLE: Noooooooooo! They didn't?!

BRIONY: Yes they did. Or rather, 'yes, yes yes yes yeeeeeeeeessssssss!' they did.

LUCY: Ewww. That's so grim.

KARA: And unsanitary.

BRIONY: Breakfast was an interesting affair with shrieks of, 'Oh God baby, I'm coming, I'm coming,' still ringing in my ears.

GAYLE: 😱

BRIONY: How can anyone use a bathroom knowing scenes of utter indecency have been committed without anti-bac'ing it all down first. I do have children to consider and Zac is at that age where the first thing he does when he comes into contact with a strange substance is wipe his finger in it and try it for taste.

LUCY: Oh God . . .

KARA: Baby! 😃

THURSDAY 27TH AUGUST
SUBJECT: MONIQUE
Hi Melissa

Got your voicemail re: meeting. Lunch Sat sounds fab. Just to confirm, is this meeting with Monique herself, or a meeting to discuss when I can have a meeting with Monique?

Yes, I was at Briony's last weekend but, no, we didn't arrange to have a weekend and not invite you—stop being so paranoid! It was all very last minute as Piers had to see someone down that way so I tagged along and we ended up staying at Bri's to save on a hotel etc. I'll probably go for a hotel in future as I think she's gone a bit OCD or something. She was constantly cleaning the bathroom with pungent smelling products and was rather uptight and twitchy to boot. It seemed every morning she couldn't relax until she had bleached that bathroom to within an inch of its life! Other than that, it was a nice weekend, although, James seemed very distant. She's probably told you things aren't great between them, and I have to admit even I noticed he was always checking his phone. Maybe her OCD cleaning is a reaction to her marital problems?

See you Sat

Kate x

MONDAY 31ST AUGUST
WHATSAPP MESSAGE

KATE: Hey, Bri. Guess who I had the pleasure of meeting at the weekend? None other than the wedding planner extraordinaire, Monique! Jesus! She's a scary one! She rattled on for hours without taking a breath and informed me with frightening intensity that, 'Weddings are not just my business, darlink, they are my life. Do you understand me, darlink; my life!' I swear to you, Melissa basked in her wedding guru's glow. It's like she's joined a cult and Monique is her leader. It's taken over her life. I'm frightened, Bri. What if this happens to everyone?

BRIONY: It doesn't happen to everyone, Kate! It didn't happen to me! She won't scare me, I can tell you that much for sure. I suppose I am going to have to go up before Christmas to see her and get it over with.

KATE: You can stay with me when you come to London. You won't want to stay with the wedding obsessed mad woman—no fun to be had there. Let's make a date and you can make a weekend of it. Just try not to chuck your boots at any policemen this time, eh 😉

BRIONY: Thanks, Kate. What weekends are you free? I mean, are there any dates Piers is going to be away?

KATE: Why does Piers have to be away? Don't you like him? You were a bit odd when we stayed if you don't mind my saying, Bri. Not quite yourself.

BRIONY: Of course I like Piers. I just meant if we are having a girls' weekend it would be better if Piers wasn't around or he might feel left out. I wasn't odd at the weekend!

KATE: You were deep cleaning the bathroom for an hour every morning, Briony, and you had a face like someone had stuffed a Donald Trump butt plug up your arse.

BRIONY: Kate, it sounded like a very bad porn film was being made in my bathroom every morning, and I wasn't too happy having my kids listen to it—but I'm funny like that . . .

KATE: You mean you could hear us? Oh, Christ. Really? That's horrifying.

BRIONY: Yes, it was horrifying, Kate.

KATE: *Dying*

BRIONY: But it's good to know you haven't let Piers' 'little problem' get the better of you. In fact, from what I heard, he certainly doesn't have a problem satisfying you . . . . .

SEPTEMBER

TUESDAY 1ST SEPTEMBER

WHATSAPP MESSAGE

BRIONY: Hey, Lucy. Have you recovered from the BBQ? Starting mojitos at lunchtime is never a good idea and someone needs to remind us of that next time.

LUCY: Ya think?!?

BRIONY: Have you heard from Kara? I fear we have not heard the last of the cous cous/quinoa incident, but fgs you would have thought that if you are going gluten free you would know the difference between cous cous and quinoa by sight. And as for being made to dig the salad dressing bottle out the bin so she could check the ingredients and then expect me to make my GF version! Do I look like Nigella, ffs?I I thought her raw food stage was bad enough but this is far worse.

LUCY: I got a text from Kara saying she was bloated and gassy all night and hardly slept. It's amazing how she never used to suffer that like that after eating cous cous. But, you

231

know it won't be long before she tires of this fad and moves onto something else . . . just like the Buddhist/scientology phase. It's amazing how interchangeable these religions are if you believe Kara . . .

BRIONY: How's your chin? Did the bleeding stop eventually? Good job it happened at the end of the night otherwise you would have had that sanitary pad taped to your chin for even longer. Thankfully, James managed to bleach and scrub the bloodstains off the Cotswold stone tiles, so don't worry about that, although I guess you won't be doing 'The Worm' again for a while, eh?

LUCY: No, Briony, the bleeding didn't stop, and after using half a packet of 'Always with wings' I ended up going to casualty at 3am for stitches. The swelling and bruising is quite severe but I couldn't have pain killers due to the amount of alcohol I had consumed. Hopefully it won't scar too badly, and I can chew a little better today, so managing some food for the first time in two days. So glad your Cotswold paving slabs are okay. That must have been such a worry for you 😬

BRIONY: You could have bleed on the lawn—much easier to sort out. So, are we all still on for lunch Thursday? God, I hate the first day back after the holidays—never know what to do with myself (although the dust balls floating along the hall tell me what I should be doing). I'm happy with going to 'Aubergine,' so I guess we'll all meet there twelve-ish?

LUCY: Looking forward to Thursday. Is Aubergine the vegan, gluten, dairy, taste free place Kara has been on about?

BRIONY: Yep . . . But don't worry, if you're still having problems by then we can ask them to liquidize your lunch.

LUCY: Might taste better that way . . .

BRIONY: I didn't get a chance to ask at the weekend, but, I take it all is okay with you and Tom after your weekend away with Algey? Does that mean you will be getting the new car after all?

LUCY: Oh, yes, Tom has got over is little tiff now. It's amazing what a weekend alone with your own children can do to a man—makes them appreciate you all the more. So, yes, I am getting the new car and am so excited! It's the main reason the showroom dropped the issue of your little bump—didn't want to lose a sale. I'll treat everyone to a nice drive out to a country pub for lunch when it gets delivered next month.

BRIONY: I fear that may bring back distressing flashbacks . . .

LUCY: Did you ever find out what your mother-in-law was doing at your neighbour's on Sunday? I know we were all pissed but it really was most bizarre! Didn't you mention something about dementia a while ago? I'd get James to maybe have a word with his dad or her doctor if I were you. I'm all for women celebrating their golden years and all that but, truthfully, Bri, she was dressed rather bizarrely for a woman of any age, and why was she hiding in the laurel? What did Cosmo have to say about it all? It's all getting rather embarrassing now, isn't it? Tom's aunt started to get like that. She would pop out for the newspaper in her nightie and forget where she was going and turn up at a friend's 3 miles away. Having said that, I think she's spying on you in case you and Cosmo are getting a little too friendly whilst her darling son is away . . . .

BRIONY: You know, Margaret is behaving in a very sporadically odd manner. Most of the time she is fine (well, far from 'fine,' but her normal self if you know what I mean?) And then suddenly, she does something really very odd and out of character. I'm sure something happened with her friends when they were staying in that cottage after Sarah's party. When James jokingly asked her if they all behaved themselves or did they have mad swinging parties every night, she got very flustered and said she didn't know what he meant by that and how disappointing it was to discover people are not really who they claim to be—whatever that means?! I don't think she would even entertain the idea that Cosmo and I are too friendly, but I suppose you never know. I have said before I think she is poor Cosmo's stalker. Imagine the embarrassment of having a pensioner as an admirer, Lucy! To his credit, Cosmo is very charming about it, and hasn't complained to us at all. Although, I think that's half down to the fact he makes a few quid out of her to be honest—what with his (what must have been quite substantial) profit from the wine for the party, and the fish he arranged for her pond. It amuses me in a twisted sort of way, but, I know James is getting quite annoyed about it. He thinks Cosmo is taking advantage—ha! I say poor Cosmo deserves to get something from putting up with her cringe-worthy amorous behaviour—the woman is so disillusioned! Seriously, what does she expect to happen? For Cosmo to whisk her off for a life of luxury at his Chelsea pied-à-terre while she lives out her winter years. Snort! Winter years?! An ice age settled on that woman sometime around 1972 and we're all still awaiting the thaw. Arthur seems to be turning a blind eye to the whole situation, but, who can blame him? As long as she is not at home bugging him, why would he care if she is making an embarrassment of herself with our neighbour? I'm sure her 'crush' is a Godsend to him . . . unless it's sent her hormones into overdrive and she comes home all . . . . ..oh, god, no; that doesn't bear thinking about. Yuck Yuck, yuck, yuck, yuck yuck. Sorry, got to go and bleach the mental image of Margaret and Arthur getting all 'biblical' out of my mind . . .

LUCY: Don't make me laugh—it hurts my chin!

BRIONY: So sorry about your chin, again. I'll tell Gayle to take the photos off FB is you'd prefer?

LUCY: F*cking Facebook! I didn't even know she'd put them on FB!

LUCY: How many likes did I get?

TEXT MESSAGE RECEIVED THURSDAY 3RD SEPTEMBER 1.07PM
Pooped earlier but you out? Free tomato night? Abhor this textile business—keeps making up words?! You.Not.Answer.Phone? Marvellous. Marketing. Margaret.

TEXT MESSAGE SENT THURSDAY 3RD SEPTEMBER 1.11PM

I'm at lunch with friends, Margaret, hence why not answering mobile. Try turning your predictive text off in settings. Not sure if free tomorrow. Why?

TEXT MESSAGE RECEIVED THURSDAY 3RD SEPTEMBER 1.25PM

You.Still.No.Answer? Need CHAPERONE FOR Richard's date. Can't truss womble on internet. Will email detailing for you. Just fingering lunch. Enjoy!

THURSDAY 3RD SEPTEMBER
SUBJECT: FWD: CHAPERONE FOR RICHARD

James—I am at lunch with the girls and your mother is bothering me with nonsensical and obscene texts and now this rambling email regarding chaperoning Richard from number 52 on a date tomorrow night! (fwd below) Please deal with this for me. It's all far too absurd! And fgs show her how to turn predictive texting off, she makes even less sense than usual.

Love Bri x

^^^Fwd^^^
Dear Briony

I am sorry to have interrupted your lunch. I would have thought you would have had a huge amount of housework to catch up on after the holidays, but how nice you found time to see friends. I remember how when James and Sa-

236

rah were children, I would spend the whole week on their return to school, washing and dusting, sweeping and cleaning, trying to get the house back all shipshape. I saw a programme which claimed it's good for children to be exposed to dirt, but we must be careful about taking things too far, Briony.

As I was trying to explain in my text message, Richard has a date on Friday night, which is all very exciting, and, due to his circumstances he has decided to entertain the lady in question at home. As I am sure you are aware, all manner of terrible things can happen when one meets someone from the internet (did I mention he met her via an internet dating agency? Arthur and I encouraged him to join after it became quite obvious to us he was in need of female companionship). So, we thought it might be prudent to install a chaperone at Richard's house for the duration of the 'date' and thought you might like to do it?

Do let me know as soon as possible that you can make it—7pm would give you enough time to settle in before 'Jennifer' (I hope she's using her real name) arrives. Richard is making spaghetti bolognaise which doesn't take long to eat, so I imagine they will be all done and dusted by nine. Then we can have a quick de-briefing over a cup of tea at ours and you'll be home by eleven.

Love Margaret

THURSDAY 3RD SEPTEMBER

SUBJECT: RE: FWD CHAPERONE FOR RICHARD

Mother, Briony has forwarded this to me as she's rather concerned. Why on earth are you enlisting a chaperone for Richard's date? He is a 40 something robust and bearded man over the age of consent, is he not? Does he know he has a date? Just how far have you meddled? Are you sure he just doesn't think a new home help is stopping by?

While I'm at it, have you pulled yourself together since Sunday? What on earth were you doing hiding in the bushes wearing a swimming costume? Briony and I had friends over and you made a complete spectacle of yourself. Enough is enough, mum, and I think it's time you stopped bothering Mr Huntington Jones before he gets a restraining order out against you.

James

THURSDAY 3RD SEPTEMBER

SUBJECT: RE: FWD CHAPERONE FOR RICHARD

Dear James

I'm so sorry to have interrupted Briony's lunch. I hope that by passing on my email to you, I am not now interrupting your lunch? Do you even have time for lunch, James, because I have to say, you were looking rather malnourished when I saw you on Sunday, and you know how I worry.

However, I really don't know what you mean by 'bothering' Mr Huntington Jones. Cosmo, as he is known to me, and I are very good friends, and in case it had slipped your memory, James, he supplied the wonderful champagne and wines for your sister's birthday. What a good job it was that so many fine wines were on offer to placate your poor Sarah when your wife turned up wearing a replica dress, causing her huge embarrassment. Cosmo has also been kind enough to advise and supply a number of rare and exotic aquatic life for our newly re-instated pond. Of course, you will not have seen what a joy and beauty this is in our garden, as you never visit. I often sit in the beautiful garden and as I watch the exquisitely coloured fish and snakes, I am tinged with sadness that my grandsons are never here to enjoy this with me. Celia has her grandchildren staying with her all the time. In fact, barely a weekend goes by without a visit and she finds it hard to book a free weekend to come and visit us.

Please reassure Briony that I am not 'meddling,' and that Arthur and I only have Richard's best interests at heart. It had become quite obvious he was in need of female companionship and we merely helped him along the way. Knowing full well the pitfalls of inviting strange women into your home, I simply thought it prudent to have someone else in the house when his lady visitor calls in order to avoid 'misunderstandings'.

So, do I take it Briony is unable or unwilling to help out a disabled gentleman on this occasion? I thought as much. I find it quite incredulous that she pays for the education of

Tibetan children yet cannot help closer to home.

Don't work too hard, James, darling. Now the boys are a little older, might Briony be taking a little part-time job to occupy her extensive free-time and contribute to the household income?

Much love, Mum xxx

THURSDAY 3RD SEPTEMBER
SUBJECT: RE: FWD CHAPERONE FOR RICHARD
Snakes? Are you telling me you have non-native water snakes living in the pond?!? For God's sake mother! I'm sure that's not legal . . . or safe for that matter.

No, Briony cannot baby-sit Richard. May I ask why you cannot do the deed?

I'll be over at the weekend to look at these 'snakes.' Are you sure they're not eels? Can you tell the difference, mother? I suggest you stay away from them whatever they are until I have had a look.

James

MONDAY 7TH SEPTEMBER
SUBJECT: LONDON WEEKEND DATES
Hi Kate

What about the last weekend in Sept? Is that good for you?

Have had a mad and surreal weekend after James' mother waxed lyrical about the beautifully coloured snakes in her pond! James thought she was on medication, drunk, or was confusing snakes with eels, but thought he had better check it out to be on the safe side. Turns out they are harmless grass snakes but, hilariously, Margaret bought them from some 'exclusive' supplier Cosmo put her in touch with, and it turns out grass snakes are in fact protected and can't be traded without a licence so . . . as ignorance is no defence, turns out Margaret has committed a criminal offence. She also mentioned brightly coloured frogs, although they appear to have disappeared—either fled the pond, or, predated by the neighbour's cat, which seems a likely explanation after it was rushed to the vet with some form of unidentified poisoning . . .

So, if those dates are good for you, double-check to see if Melissa and Monique can meet us on the Saturday to get that over and done with.

MONDAY 7TH SEPTEMBER
SUBJECT: RE: LONDON WEEKEND DATES
Sounds good to me. I'll check with Melissa and make it a Piers-free weekend—he's even more mortified than me about our little faux pas at yours, so will probably be keen to stay away from your teasing.

Oh, when emailing me at work, can you put something more work related in the subject title—just in case the boss is browsing through my emails. x

WEDNESDAY 9TH SEPTEMBER

WHATSAPP MESSAGE

GAYLE: Hey Bri, I've been roped into doing this posh style meals on wheels round for a friend who couldn't find anyone to take over while she's away for a month, and I thought I'd make it a bit special for the 'clients' and give them little pots of homemade jam . . . only I don't make jam, and you do—sooooo if I bring round the mini pots I've bought, can you fill them with some of yours? Is Saturday alright as I start the round on Monday.

BRIONY: I've made jam once, Gayle. This summer was my first season and I won't be repeating it. I have loads though so yeah, no probs.

GAYLE: Merci! FYI I saw Lucy and her chin is healing nicely now and she can almost laugh without keeling over in pain.

BRIONY: Although I am glad to hear that, I should point out that although she injured herself in my garden, the injury was entirely self-inflicted and in no way am I to feel guilty for what happened.

GAYLE: You encouraged her . . .

BRIONY: When a woman of a certain age consumes too many rum-based cocktails and then proceeds to get down with the kids by trying to impress them with her break dancing moves, then she only has herself to blame. And anyway, she's lucky it was Cotswold stone as it's far softer then concrete which would most certainly have seen her off with a broken jaw!

242

BRIONY: Anyway, what's posh about meals on wheels?

GAYLE: It's posh because the client chooses what they want based on a specific diet and they can have them delivered hot and ready to eat, or a week's worth for the fridge/freezer. So I have to make sure the daily clients get their meals piping hot and the weeklies just get the right meals to put in their freezers. In fact, I'll email Kara details as they do gluten free diets—or has she moved on from that already?

BRIONY: Oh, I heard her mention something about the paleo diet or something . . .

GAYLE: You can't do paleo if you're veggie! Isn't that just eating raw meat and stuff?!

BRIONY: Dunno. Don't take much notice. Anyway, how are you going to fit that around work?

GAYLE: I'm just doing the two days I usually have off work and it's only going to take a couple of hours, so no probs. I even get a special little van to drive.

BRIONY: See you Sat. Come for lunch with the girls and Dudley if he's not busy doing 'man things.' No mojitos this time though and no breakdancing.

THURSDAY 10TH SEPTEMBER
SUBJECT: HELLO.

Dear Briony

I do hope the boys have settled into their new term at school? I was rather hoping you might have joined James and come to admire our new pond last weekend. What a shame the boys had their Mandarin lesson. I had no idea they were learning an oriental language and to do so out of school hours at weekends must mean they are terribly keen? It will benefit them so much more than the normal activities children do at weekends—after all, just how many David Beckhams and Wayne Rooneys do we need? I insist they come and recite something impressive the next time my friend, Celia, visits us. She is always telling me how special her eldest grandson is—so many out of school activities to keep his apparently brilliant mind occupied. Although if you ask me, it sounds like he's more likely got ACDC than advanced intelligence. The child doesn't sit still for a minute if Celia's anything to go by. Always asking questions, taking things apart and demanding attention. Usually I'm the first to say ACDC doesn't exist and it's all in the mother's mind and lack of parental authority, but on this occasion ACDC is the culprit!

You will be pleased to hear Richard's date went very well. As you were too busy to help us out, Arthur had the clever idea of putting our telephone number on speed dial so Richard just had to press one button of his phone to alert us of any improperness. You hear such tales of drugs and 'date rape', we really thought it best to err on the side of caution. But, no; it all went swimmingly! Never one to drop his options, Richard has informed us he has yet another date on Friday and another on Saturday, which Arthur and I found a little 'modern' but apparently it's quite acceptable with this online dating agency to meet up with a few different members before making any decisions. I don't think Richard's had so much fun in a long time! He's even been on his computer to order some new clothes as he's obviously eager to impress his dates. Quite a specialised outfitters, by all accounts, or so he tells us. 'Black Mambo' was the name on the box I took delivery of whilst he was getting his hair trimmed in the village—well it certainly sounds rather special doesn't it? Arthur and I look forward to meeting the lucky lady he finally settles on. I think we'll invite her over for drinks in the garden where Richard's efforts on the pond can be admired at the same time.

I, myself, am going on a weekend shopping trip to London very soon. I thought it was time I treated myself to a few bits and pieces before the festive season is upon us. If there is anything you need, do tell me now and I can pick them up for you whilst I am there.

Much love
Margaret

TEXT MESSAGE RECEIVED 1.43PM

George called me to ask if it's okay if he stays next weekend. He's got a business meeting in the area. He caught me off guard so I said yes—that's okay with you, isn't it, Briony?

TEXT MESSAGE SENT 1.47PM

FGS James, well, it will have to be won't it? Just as long as your sister doesn't turn up, that's all! What is the situation with the dildo in the magazine? Are we all pretending it never happened? I've not heard a peep out of her so presumed she had either gone into denial or had a breakdown. Either way, it's saved her gloating about the whole bloody magazine thing, which pleases me no end!

SUBJECT: RE: HELLO.

Dear Margaret

Yes, it was unfortunate we were unable to come with James last weekend, but we thought you might have popped in for a cup of tea when you were at Cosmo's on the Sunday. Were you discussing the snake incident with him? Have you decided what to do about the gardening company who supplied them? It must be awful to have that on your conscience. It's bad enough their natural habitat is being destroyed to make way for housing estates and bypasses, without knowing you were party to the illegal removal of a protected species for your own benefits. I suppose you could always claim you were hoping they would breed in the ideal conditions created by your garden and pond and maybe then they will spare you a custodial sentence and you'll just get community service?

So glad Richard is having success with the online dating agency. You have to be aware of unscrupulous agencies taking money and supplying appropriate matches, but I'm sure this is a reputable agency as you have researched it yourself?

As for London, I am off there myself, shortly. Are you

getting the train or is Arthur driving? It's quite a drive and you can reserve seats on the train you know, which might be best for the two of you.

James informs me that George will be coming over to see us next weekend as he is on business in the area. How is Sarah? I've not heard from her since the magazine feature. Did all her friends manage to get a copy, do you know? I've got a spare copy here if she needs it—just say the word and I can pop it in the post.

I'm not sure I understand how ACDC are to blame for Celia's son's behaviour? Surely he's too young to be into that sort of music? Did you mean ADHD? Or OCD? I used to be a fan of OMD myself, but again, I'm pretty sure they don't adversely affect the behaviour of school-age boys.

Briony

MONDAY 14TH SEPTEMBER
SUBJECT: ORIENTAL STUDIES
Dear Celia

I do hope this finds you well and you have recovered from yet another weekend looking after your dear grand-children. What a shame we couldn't speak for long on Sat-urday when I telephoned—Joshua certainly seems terribly demanding. Has John managed to repair the telephone yet? I believe I had started to tell you all about my grandsons, Sam and Zac, before we were unfortunately cut off. As I was telling you, both have developed quite a precocious talent for Oriental languages and Briony has promised me she will bring them over to demonstrate when you next visit. Is Joshua fluent in any languages, yet?

I am off to London soon for a weekend of pampering and 'retail therapy,' as the term is now! I thought I might get some festive party outfits and have decided that Arthur and I will commit to a New Year's Party—which I hope John and yourself will attend? It will give us both a good excuse to turn down the Fothergill's party and reacquaint with old friends in a far more sanitary manner than the Fothergill party, I suspect. Now, Celia, I know what you are going to say but please hear me out—shall I ask Mr Huntington Jones to supply the champagne and wine for my party? It cannot be denied that the quality was quite superb and if I give him a budget this time there will be no little surprises regarding the bill.

I am going to forgo entertainment this time, Celia, for both our sakes; if things get a little slow we can always get the scrabble board out and charades is always popular that time of year.

Hopefully Richard will have settled on a special lady friend who he might like to bring along and spare us from the 'fruity' jokes he seems to rather enjoy telling after a few Baileys. Did I tell you about the online dating agency Arthur and I encouraged him to join? He's having so much fun, Celia; the change in him is quite astounding. Arthur worries he won't be as keen to help with the garden once he's settled with a lady friend or even, dare I say, wife!

I look forward to hearing from you soon.

Namaste,
Margaret

SUBJECT: RE: ORIENTAL STUDIES
Dear Margaret

I do confess, Joshua has driven me to the brink this past weekend. I had a word with his mother, who in my opinion spoils him. He may be gifted, but he still needs boundaries! Not only did the child take apart the telephone, but also the DVD player. It was only through shear stealth that I still have my laptop intact, after I intercepted him in the pantry about to use a brulee blow torch on it. I pale to think what he thought he might do with his baby sister and the pastry fork, as we had just been playing 'Operation,' so it doesn't bare thinking about.

Now, about this party. Yes, to coming but no, to Cosmo and the wine. Just get it from the supermarket, Margaret, one of those wine warehouses or better still let's go on a booze cruise! We'll take the Volvo, leave the men at home, and find some little French B&B to stay overnight. Can't do it all in one day at our age, after all. I think sometime next month would be prudent as I imagine it will start getting busy with people stocking up for Christmas by November.

Do let me know some dates, Margaret and we can book the ferry tickets.

Au revoir
Celia

THURSDAY 17TH SEPTEMBER
WHATSAPP MESSAGE

BRIONY: How's posh meals on wheels going?

GAYLE: Not a brilliant start, to be honest, Bri. Took out an elderly gent's wing mirror trying to be eco-friendly free-wheeling the van down the hill. And another curmudgeon insists on testing the temp of his meal with a bloody thermometer before I'm allowed to leave.

BRIONY: Oh. Was thinking I might do something like that myself now I'm becoming a bored housewife, but doesn't sound like fun. I need a job or a lover to brighten up my day so . . .

GAYLE: Dangerous ground, Briony. Especially with the dashing bachelor next door!

BRIONY: Flirting isn't a divorceable offence, Gayle. However, what my husband is up to might be.

GAYLE: ???

BRIONY: Found a pair of strange socks in the wash after a business trip. They're def not his, mine or the boys 😩

GAYLE: Socks, Briony? Not knickers? Socks?!

BRIONY: Strange socks, Gayle.

GAYLE: But not knickers.

BRIONY: Where did he get strange socks from ?

GAYLE: The woman he's having an affair with, obviously

BRIONY: Thing is, not sure I even care any more. Which is why I think why shouldn't I have a little flirtation?

GAYLE: You don't mean that.

BRIONY: Don't I?

GAYLE: Look we can talk about this later. I've got to go. Just had to put down a kid's dwarf hamster which arrived in a bloody mess (anal prolapse—not nice at all but seeing it far too often in dwarf varieties) and now I've got a guinea pig with a tumour on its testicle to contend with. Meatballs are off the dinner menu for tonight!

BRIONY: Ewww

GAYLE: Is Kara still on a fad diet? I've been afraid to ask as she's mighty irritable at the moment! Apparently she had a date last weekend. Did you know? She kept that quiet I thought. I only heard through Lucy. Hope it went well—if only for the fact if she got a shag she might be in a better mood. I told her to join Tinder—actually, maybe you should join Tinder?

BRIONY: Kate showed me her Tinder the other weekend. She still has her account from before she met Piers. Dick pics a-go-go! It was pretty grim tbh, but . . .

GAYLE: Fuck, I was joking, Bri, you're happily married.

BRIONY: Married, yes. Happily, less so these days . . .

LUCY HAS BEEN ADDED TO THE GROUP

GAYLE: How did Kara's date go? How did she meet him exactly?

LUCY: Oh, hi, yeah, via this single parents' forum she 'occasionally' goes on for advice (trawls for single dads on). They exchanged emails and photos

BRIONY: Dick pics . . .

LUCY: Anyway, and they arranged to meet. As you can imagine, Kara was super excited and even wore her 'lucky knickers' out for the occasion.

GAYLE: Kara has lucky knickers?!

BRIONY: Kara is so not a lucky knickers kinda gal.

LUCY: Okay, so, she wore her clean knickers with elastic intact out for the occasion.

GAYLE: That's more like it.

LUCY: Then she gets a text from him just two hours before they are due to meet saying, 'Thought it was only fair to tell you, but I realised I forgot to mention it before, but I only have one leg'.

GAYLE: Ahh.

BRIONY: Ohhhhh.

LUCY: Now what the hell are you supposed to say about that?!? If you cancel you look like a shallow bitch, and if you go, you risk him thinking you only came as a sympathy date! And then if you don't get on in real life and don't want to see him again, is he going to think it's because of his leg?

BRIONY: It's a situation strewn with political correctness.

GAYLE: He shouldn't have mentioned it. If they'd got on it really wouldn't matter. Mentioning it was unfair and put her in a moral predicament.

LUCY: Well, invariably it didn't matter. They'd been exchanging texts for some time beforehand and she already had a photo of his erect cock on her phone, so he'd already passed the most important test 😀

BRIONY: This means single mother Kara is having more sex than 'happily married' me . . . 😬

TEXT MESSAGE RECEIVED 3.27PM
Sorry—Madrid flight delayed. Unavoidable. Apols to George. Jxxx

TEXT MESSAGE RECEIVED 3.29PM
Oh FFS James!

TEXT MESSAGE RECEIVED 3.32PM
Just give George the whiskey bottle and let him watch repeats of Top Gear and you won't even know he's there. x

FRIDAY 18TH SEPT
WHATSAPP GROUP MESSAGE
BRIONY: URGENT! I need someone to call me on the home phone in three mins.

LUCY: What's wrong? I'm watching X Factor on catchup while Tom's out. That young boy, Dan, is rather sweet isn't he? I've watched his performance five times now and boy can that kid sing.

GAYLE: He's only seventeen, Lucy! A peri-menopausal woman shouldn't be juicing up watching a boy that age.

LUCY: I'm not peri-menopausal, thank you, Gayle.

BRIONY: Hello! Someone call me!

KATE: Hey, what's going on?

BRIONY: Sarah's husband is here and it's gone too far. He tried to kiss me.

GAYLE: Fuck, Briony, I know you were feeling desperate, but I didn't think you were going to flirt with your brother in-law!

BRIONY: I wasn't! Eww, not George! No, he's pissed on whiskey and I've never known him to be like this—not with me anyway!

KATE: Christ. You minx! What are you wearing? You haven't been showing off your lacy Brazilian knicks again have you? We've all see them after a few mojitos!

BRIONY: Call my home phone and I can pretend it's James on his way home just asking if I need milk or something.

LUCY: Why isn't James at home?

BRIONY: Delayed flight from Madrid.

KATE: I'm sexting with Piers, can't call yet . . .

LUCY: Sexting while chatting here?!

KATE: Multi-tasking, Lucy.

BRIONY: FFS.

GAYLE: Airline socks!

LUCY: ??

GAYLE: Strange socks!

KATE: Cum hard, baby.

BRIONY: Kate!

LUCY: Wrong chat, Kate!

GAYLE: The strange socks were airline socks! The ones

you get on a long haul flight in business class.

LUCY: ??

BRIONY: Oh yeah!

LUCY: You're wearing airline socks??

BRIONY: I'm in flesh coloured laser cut sports knickers and they really aren't very sexy but great for avoiding VPL under yoga pants. Please call me!

GAYLE: Hmm . . . maybe he likes the gym knickers Mallory Towers look?

BRIONY: Please stop talking about my knickers and call me. I am freaked out and I've been in the loo almost twenty minutes now!

KATE: Okay. I'm done—calling now

LUCY: Ewwwww.

MONDAY 21ST SEPTEMBER
SUBJECT: WEEKEND

Hey, Briony. Are you driving up Fri night or Sat morning? We're booked in to meet Monique at her 'Wedding Emporium' on the Saturday morning at 10am and trying on replica style dresses for sizing as the actual dresses will be made by some people in Italy apparently . . . 'Why Italy,' you ask? I don't know but it sounds better than China, I guess. Once all that malarkey's over we can go shopping, have lunch and decide what we want to do that night. Hope it went okay with George after my call Fri night. What exactly went on?!

Kate

MONDAY 21ST SEPTEMBER
SUBJECT: RE: WEEKEND

Yeah, thanks for the call Fri. Went back in to the living room to find George crying like a baby! Starts telling me how cold Sarah is (like we hadn't figured that one out). How he bought a few 'marital aids' to try and spice their sex life up, because she's always been a 'pull your night-ie up after the lights go out kinda gal' (REALLY could've done without that info, thanks, George!) and how now the offending 'marital aid' had accidently ended up gracing the pages of 'Village Homes,' she was refusing him any physical contact at all. S'pose he was feeling, I don't know, lonely and needy, so the whiskey made him act in a way I've never known him to be with me before. Well, I sat right at the far end of the sofa during his drunken ramblings and thank the lord, Cosmo turned up half an hour later asking for his spare key as he'd locked himself out. George sloped off to bed and Cosmo and I downed a bottle of Shiraz as I told all! It's always the ones you least expect, hey?

MONDAY 21ST SEPTEMBER
SUBJECT: RE: WEEKEND

Cosmo saves the day . . .

So, straight up question: Could you/would you with Cosmo?? He does seem to be more of a feature in your life than your husband at present . . . who, I hope, brought you back something nice from Madrid as way of apology?

SUBJECT: RE: WEEKEND

Cosmo is a gentleman. I enjoy his company. He's charming, interesting, funny . . . but I am married . . . and I'm not flirty. Not really. When have I ever been inappropriate since being married?

SUBJECT: RE: WEEKEND

Oh I dunno, Bri. Christmas party of 2007 when you asked the hosts' friend's gynaecologist consultant husband what most of his patients wore to an appointment and what would he think if a woman was wearing Simone Perele 'midnight stars'—was she making an effort on his behalf or could he tell if she was usually a M&S tango multi pack kinda girl?

All I'm saying, is, sometimes you may possibly and unintentionally, give the wrong impression . . .

Then again, maybe Cosmo is gay after all.

SUBJECT: RE: WEEKEND

I am still trying to erase that party from my mind . . . I didn't drink for weeks afterwards and it took months of physio to sort my hip out after the lap dancing and splits.

But, yes, Kate, You're right; if Cosmo is not trying to shaft me up against the Rangemaster then he must be gay. Shame, as there is something very attractive about a man who seems to intrinsically understand the needs of a woman. Also, the man is a saint. He puts up with mad Margaret stalking him. She spends more time next door than she does here, I tell you! I think she might actually be jealous of me. I'm married to her son fgs but I seriously think she is jealous of my friendship with Cosmo. She could barely hide her irritation when she learnt he had put us up at his place in London. It's absurd. The woman is old enough to be his mother!

And no, I didn't get a lovely present form James. A packet of crackers and a mini bottle of wine he'd obviously slipped in his bag from the flight. He'd even had a swig as the seal was broken. There's a man who could learn something about women from Cosmo!

See you Sat.

THURSDAY 24TH SEPTEMBER
WHATSAPP MESSAGE
LUCY: What are you doing at the weekend? Thought I might pop over for a chat?

BRIONY: Sorry, Lucy. I'm going to London to see Kate and Melissa and the bloody wedding planner! Is everything okay?

LUCY: Don't worry, Briony. It's fine. Maybe catch up next week? Have fun in London. Can you get me some chocolate scorpions and fart jellybeans from Selfridges? Always popular stocking fillers.

SUBJECT: LONDON

Dear Briony

As you know, I am going to London for a weekend of R&R as the saying goes! It suddenly occurred to me that it is your birthday next month and so I wondered if there is anything special you might like that I can get in London? Please do let me know by today as I leave tomorrow afternoon.

You will be pleased to hear Richard has yet another date this weekend. To be truthful, Briony, Arthur and I are quite astounded at how many ladies he has arriving every weekend. I did advise him to make sure his banking details and any cash were under lock and key before they visit as you do hear such terrible stories of people having their identities stolen, and it was only last week he asked me to drive him to the post office so as he could withdraw some money—a sizeable amount of cash, in fact. Richard has asked me to get a few bits and pieces for him in London, but I am not sure I will be able to help him on this occasion as he did state I would need to go to Soho, and I'm not sure I will be venturing into that part of London. I know he is only getting excited about my New Year's Eve party and doing his bit to help, but really you can buy party poppers anywhere and don't need to go to Soho for them. I'm not sure what an Arab strap is either, but after all the problems this country has had with the Middle East, I am not sure I want to buy anything Arabian to help their economy just now.

How did you find George when he visited? I think Sarah is having some problems with him at the moment. She was rather tearful when I spoke to her last and it all seems to stem back to that blasted empty lavatory roll holder in the Village Homes spread. I think I shall buy them one of those nice ballerina holders for Christmas and then no one will know if it's got a tissue roll under it or not. I don't know why they ever went out of fashion and if Sarah had one in the first place all this upset could have been avoided. Do you think they will sell them in Harvey Nicks? You know the sort I mean, don't you; with the full skirt where you hide the tissue roll underneath? We used to have one years ago until it slipped off the cistern and into the lavatory causing a terrible blockage.

Love to the boys. and of course my special boy. Is he eating, Briony? He looked rather pale and malnourished when I saw him last? Maybe you could go on a cookery course now you have more time on your hands?

Margaret x

Thursday 24th September
WHATSAPP MESSAGE

GAYLE: I've resigned! I couldn't hack another two weeks of the meals on wheels round after this week's drama. On Monday, I was accused of stealing some mad old boy's money from the previous week! This is the same man who I chatted politely to for a good ten minutes last week as he told me some of his stories from the blitz! Ungrateful old sod! He locked his front door as I carried his meals to the kitchen and told me he wasn't letting me out until the police arrived. I had visions of me being held hostage while the cul-de-sac was evacuated and news teams cowered behind my van doing their pieces to camera for the six o'clock news. I tried to make a run for it through the back door but he blocked my way using his Zimmerframe as a barricade, so I panicked and ran for the nearest door to escape, grabbing the handle and rushing through before he could catch up with me . . . unfortunately, it was his larder and a dozen tins of mackerel fell on my head. Fearing I might now sue him he let me go.

BRIONY: Fuck, Gayle. You should be given danger money.

GAYLE: On Wednesday, no reply when I knock at door of a unit in the retirement village and just as I am about to see if I can leave the hot meal with the warden, I hear shouting, so open the door (which was unlocked—why do these people leave their doors unlocked for any old fraudster to come in?!) and Mrs Belcher (a very large lady on a low fat meal plan) is calling from upstairs. I rush to her aid and find her lying on the bathroom floor claiming she can't get up. She's unhurt but no match for me as I'm half her size and I'm not risking putting my back out for anyone. So leaving the meal on the floor outside the bathroom, I hurry to the warden's flat for help. By the time the warden and I arrive back to help Mrs Belcher, she has managed to crawl out the bathroom and is lying on her stomach scooping her grilled chicken and seasonal veg into her mouth from the floor.

BRIONY: Without a knife and fork?!

GAYLE: She was tearing that chicken breast apart with just her bare teeth, Bri.

WEDNESDAY 30TH SEPTEMBER
SUBJECT: HACKED
Margaret, I'm getting emails from Arthur, again. This time he's boasting about the benefits of 'giving his woman herbal aphrodisiacs to make her hot and horny for me all night long.'

I'm more than a little disturbed. Please get him to change his password to something much harder to hack.

Briony

OCTOBER

THURSDAY 1ST OCTOBER
SUBJECT: RE: HACKED
Dear Briony

I do apologise. I too find it terribly disturbing that there are people in this world with nothing better to do than to 'hack' innocent people's email accounts in order to send out such crude messages. We have exhausted all passwords and are struggling to come up with something new and 'un-hackable.' Do you have any suggestions, Briony? Below is a list of previously used combinations.

Arthur

arthur

Arthur1

Arthur2

Arthur3

Arthur1939

Arthur5

Arthur6

Arthur7
Arthur8
Arthur9
Arthur10

Much Love, Margaret.

PS—Have you booked that cookery course yet?

SUBJECT: RE: HACKED

Gosh, Margaret. Can't imagine how they've managed to continue hacking him with those cryptic passwords. Were you one of the code breakers during the war?

You don't bank online, do you?

SUBJECT: RE: HACKED

Dear Briony

My thoughts exactly! They must be terribly clever! Shall I inform the relevant police department, do you think?

As a matter of fact, we started online banking just last month after a charming man in Nigeria sent us an email telling us how he was the attorney of a sadly deceased gentleman who had requested to leave a sizeable sum of money to us! Further correspondence revealed that the deceased had learnt of our Christian charitable ways and had wanted to reward us while he was still alive, but tragically, just as he was about to contact us directly, he was killed in a plane crash in the Andes. His solicitor, Mr Quinton Tarantino, said that luckily for us, Mr Travolta's wishes had been put in writing before his untimely death and therefore he was able to carry out his generous intentions posthumously. Regrettably, due to some oversight by Mr Travolta, our banking details had not yet been obtained but all we had to do was forward him the account details and passwords and he would do the rest!

Isn't it wonderful to know there are still some genuinely kind and thoughtful people left in the world, Briony? We haven't yet received the funds but Mr Tarantino did say it might take some time, so not to bother checking our accounts for 28 days.

Arthur and I are looking forward to seeing you for lunch on Sunday. I thought I'd make a shepherd's pie as it's a bit of waste doing a full roast with vegetarians at the table—and not fair on you really to tempt you with all that succulent meat.

Much Love,
Margaret

FRIDAY 2ND OCTOBER
SUBJECT: URGENT FWD: RE: HACKED
James—See below for details of how your mother has apparently given Quinton Tarantino her banking details and passwords while she awaits a hefty deposit by a deceased John Travolta. I think they need their internet access taken

away before they have your inheritance siphoned away by any dodgy Nigerian 'solicitor' who emails them.

Bri

Oh, and PS—thanks for telling me we're going to lunch at theirs on Sunday! Your mother's making shepherd's pie especially for the vegetarians!?!

Friday 2nd October
SUBJECT: RE: URGENT FWD: RE: HACKED
Shit. I'll get on to it straight away.

I thought I'd sent you a message about lunch? And anyway, Briony, surely you know by now that minced animals aren't like eating real animals in my mother's eyes?!

Saturday 3rd October
SUBJECT: MONIQUE AND POINTS TO REMEMBER
Hey Bri

Good to finally see you at the weekend. I hope you've had time to take in everything Monique explained to you? I know it was a lot to take in and I know you were both pretty moved by it all judging by the teary eyes. I hope you now see why this day is going to be so important to me and why it's imperative that we all work together in making this the most special day of my life.

What did you think of my dress? Be truthful. I need honesty. I'm a little worried the look is less traditional than I would have liked but Monique is insisting I should be bold in order to make an impression.

Please remember to book the sun-bed sessions well ahead of my wedding day. As Monique explained, your complexion is very sallow and does not complement the shade of the bridesmaid dress at all. We don't want you ruining the photos which in years to come will be handed down the generations as a family heirloom.

I hope you had a nice time with Kate on Saturday night. Where did you end up going? I'm sorry I couldn't join you but I can't risk gaining weight before my big day now the measurements have been taken and the silks and lace ordered—and neither can you guys.

Melissa x

MONDAY 5TH OCTOBER
SUBJECT: FWD: RE: MONIQUE AND POINTS TO REMEMBER
Hey Kate—Look what Melissa emailed me at the weekend! 'Teary eyed!' Ha! We had tears running down our cheeks from either stifling yawns or wetting ourselves with laughter every time they disappeared out the back for Melissa to try on another dress! Sallow complexion? How dare she! I was losing the will to live by that point and my blood sugar level was non-existent after Monique wouldn't let us out the 'Wedding Emporium' to get coffee and pastries! Scared we'd make a run for freedom, no doubt! Bloody hell! What are we going to do? Melissa wants honesty but who is going to be the one to tell her she looked like Simon Le Bon

circa 1982 in her New Romantic stylie lacy fishtail wedding gown with slashes of magenta silk?! Well, Simon never wore a fishtail dress as far as I know, but you get my meaning. I was half expecting her to bring us Adam Ant replica military jackets, bolero style, to wear with our dresses; although, that would sex them up a bit, I s'pose. Sixteen year old girls wear less virginal dresses to their proms these days.

Speak soon, Bx

MONDAY 5TH OCTOBER
SUBJECT: RE: MONIQUE AND POINTS TO REMEMBER
Hi Melissa

Yes, thank you for your reminder points. I think I've had time to take it all in. Although, as you say, it was an awful lot to come to terms with over the space of just five hours. I have to be honest and tell you I'm not prepared to risk melanoma for the sake of your nuptials, and therefore will not be booking myself in to be nuked at the tanning salon anytime soon. I am, however, prepared to compromise and will agree to using a little powdered bronzer on the day so as I sparkle in the photos, if, by all accounts it looks like I am going to end up being fingered by Bunny Campione on 'Antiques Roadshow' one day. x

WHATSAPP MESSAGE

BRIONY: Hey, Lucy, did you get the flyer handed out by the PTA mafia yesterday? I presume one was in the girls' book bags as you weren't there to pick them up. How are they liking the yoga after school club, anyway? You know I don't care much for that yoga teacher after she expelled Sam for refusing to hum during the wind down. Bit of a nazi for a yoga enthusiast if you ask me.

LUCY: It wasn't Sam's refusal to join in with the humming that got him removed from the yoga group, Briony. It was the fact he would put his hands over his ears and start singing rude rhymes loudly to try and drown out the sound. Anyway, what's Virginia after now?

BRIONY: She's demanding volunteers for the fete and managed to corner me as I went in the playground. God, I don't want to do it. All those bloody paper plates full of crappy, vile looking cakes covered in whatever bacteria was on the hands of the child who made them. It takes forever to plate them all up equally and then price them, and for what?! Half a plastic cup of left over, lower end of the market, supermarket own brand mulled wine. I'm going to say I've got other commitments and I suggest you get your excuses ready now or you'll be back on the half-used nail polish and novelty jewellery stall again, and you know how that stall just attracts the kleptomaniacs like it's a serial shoplifters' convention.

LUCY: Thanks for the head up. How was lunch at the in-laws? Were you force-fed meat and shop-bought puddings?

BRIONY: Lunch at the out-laws was bizarre—well more bizarre than usual, I should say. The boys and I scraped the mash off our vegetarian-unfriendly real minced lamb shepherd's pie, which was served with veggie sausages (maybe she thinks this cancels out the lamb?!)

LUCY: Better than the bananas and rice cakes you were served at that family BBQ though.

BRIONY: Marginally. Margaret's face appears to no longer have any movement from the mouth up since her weekend trip to London, and parts of her face are visibly plumper, spurring scurrilous rumours that her R&R weekend actually consisted of some hefty botox and filler treatments.

LUCY: At her age?!

BRIONY: If that wasn't bemusing enough, I was pulled aside on the way back from the loo and asked if I had ever had, 'one of those special lady-hair treatments?' Thinking she meant she was booked into have her grey rejuvenated with a chestnut rinse at the hairdressers, I replied that my salon was a bit cutting edge for her needs, but as long as she went to a reputable salon I was sure it would be fine. It was then my sixty-five year old mother-in-law informed me in a barely decipherable whisper (it's a bugger to whisper when your facial muscles are non-compliant) 'No, I mean your 'special lady-hair.' For Margaret has had a Brazilian wax and is concerned as there is still some rawness 'down there'.

LUCY: 😱

BRIONY: The image of my mother-in-law's pink, wrinkled lady-lips was not something I wanted thrust into my mind, particularly after forcing down a small helping of congealed strawberry blancmange for dessert.

LUCY: I can't even . . .

BRIONY: Why the merry fuck does she want or need a tidy minge for at her age?!

LUCY: Muff diving, Briony.

BRIONY: At their age?!? Noooooooooo!

LUCY: Maybe Peggy sports a Hollywood? Who knows? Talking of which, Tom's going to see his parents in Cornwall for the weekend, so let's do mojitos at mine. I think Kara will be in need as she's having a hard time with this gluten withdrawal.

BRIONY: Still?!

LUCY: She turned up here yesterday morning and collapsed into a sobbing wreck on the kitchen floor as I warmed croissants. Apparently she can be found salivating at the cake counter in Waitrose most mornings. They'll be refusing her entry if she carries on like that, it unnerves the other shoppers, you know.

FRIDAY 9TH OCTOBER
SUBJECT: CHRISTMAS PREPARATIONS
Dear Briony

I expect, just like George and I, you have been thinking about Christmas for some time now. I have decided that we should have a big family affair this year and make it something really special for mum and dad, who may not be with us for much longer. Of course, the children will simply adore spending the day together, opening presents and playing games whilst we prepare the Christmas feast. I thought the best idea would be for George, the children and I to stay at mum and dad's, as obviously they have a lot more room than you and we wouldn't want everyone to be squashed, sleeping on the floor when Santa visits—he might trip over one of us! Then on Christmas morning, we will all drive over to you and James and spend the day there. I have not yet decided if we will have breakfast before we leave, or make it a special family breakfast with us all at your cottage. I think if we do the latter, we will make it more of a brunch to see us through the day and then you can prepare Christmas dinner for everyone to be served at six-ish. I'm going to run it past mum and dad before I make a firm decision.

Now, Briony, with regards to the present opening, I thought problems could arise if ours have more gifts to open then yours, and therefore, I think it best we liaise closely in this area so as all the children have the exact same number of presents to unwrap from under the tree. Size is always an issue as well, isn't it? So presents will need to be approximately the same size, again to avoid upset with the children. Obviously, you are going to need a bigger tree this year to accommodate all the extra presents.

Wrapping: I usually wrap children's gifts in foiled boy/girl appropriate patterned paper and the adults in foiled plain coloured paper with matching bows. Colours are to be traditional silver, gold, green or red. I don't subscribe to this nonsense 'modern/funky' wrapping of blue, purple or, heaven forbid, black! Bows must always match the wrap. We need to stick to this scheme or the presents will end up looking messy and uncoordinated and although I am aware you favour this 'shabby chic' style, I do think more of an effort is appropriate for Christmas, don't you agree, Briony? Tags must match the wrap and bow and be stuck on using clear tape with the tag facing down so as the writing cannot be seen until the tag is turned over. Nothing worse than being able to see the hand written message from under the tree.

Tree decorations: Traditionally, we use silver tinsel and gold baubles. Chocolates are not permitted as children have a habit of removing them before the day, leaving the tree looking sparse in certain areas. We enjoy looking at traditional candy canes and plain white twinkling lights. Too many colours look fussy, Briony, I am sure you agree.

You have wooden floors, don't you? I think it wise to purchase some appropriately tasteful festive floor cushions for the children to sit on during the present opening. The adults will sit on the sofas. I like to have one of those giant disposable Santa sacks all ready for the discarded wrapping to be placed—looks so much nicer than a bin liner and remember, photos will be being taken throughout, and no one wants a black bin liner in their shots. In fact, that reminds me—we like to take informal photographs of the children opening their presents and then an official photo with each individual gift after it's unwrapped so as the children put a copy in with their thank you letters.

We can discuss the dinner menu in a couple of weeks when you have had time to think about what your kitchen and oven is capable of when providing for twelve people. Do you have a double oven, Briony? Plate warmer? Mum wasn't sure when I phoned her. In fact, it was hard to get much information out of her at all. Dad said she's had some dentistry done whilst in London and it has caused parts of her face to freeze. All sounds quite alarming so I hope she wasn't at one of these backstreet dentists you hear about so often.

Well, I'm going to leave you to get in the Christmas spirit and I'll call you at the weekend to discuss the finer details.

Love Sarah.

PS Did I mention I'd put Barnaby and Ella's Christmas wish-lists online? You can access them now by going to the Hamleys website and putting their full names and postcode in.

FRIDAY 9TH OCTOBER
SUBJECT: FWD: CHRISTMAS PREPARATIONS
James.

Please read this email I received from your sister today and then tell me if I have died and gone to hell. This can't happen. I am not spending Christmas Day with your parents, sister and her family—oh and God knows who else as she said to cater for 12? It's simply not happening. Ever. We need to put a stop to this now. I can't even begin to express to you how sick this made me feel. Please deal with it.

SATURDAY 10TH OCTOBER

SUBJECT: BOOZE CRUISE

Dear Margaret

It was lovely to chat to you and as discussed during our conversation last night, I have attached the details of our ferry booking to Calais. As you can see, I have booked a lovely little hotel or 'l'hotel', as they say in France, 'Le Chien Rose,' which is a short train ride away in the next town from the ferry port. I was struggling rather with the thought of either of us driving around France, so decided it best that we leave the car in the hypermarket car park overnight while we go off to do our sight-seeing. If you have a look at the links with my attachment, I have cleverly sourced some film clips of a charming young man on YouTube who has recorded French tutorials for people to use. What a marvellous idea, don't you think, Margaret? He teaches all the popular phrases, so I suggest we brush up using his clips before we go.

John is looking forward to spending some time in Arthur's company whilst we are on our jaunt. I suspect the scrabble board will get some serious action, knowing those two competitive wordsmiths!

Your friend,
Celia

PS I do hope you get your teeth sorted out before we go. How unfortunate for the dentist to have suffered a stroke just as he was injecting your gums with the anaesthetic causing him to inject a nerve that controls many of your facial muscles. Very unfortunate and more than a little bizarre, Margaret. You do know people pay for something similar to alleviate fine lines and wrinkles which I believe is called 'botox'.

SUNDAY 11TH OCTOBER
SUBJECT: RE: BOOZE CRUISE
Dear Celia

How exciting! The hotel looks quite lovely and I agree it would be foolish for us to drive around France. I had always hoped that being part of the European community we might convince Europe to start driving on our side of the road—makes so much more sense after all, but alas, that's never going to happen now.

Yes, my dental accident is very unfortunate but rest assured I will be returning to London next weekend for an emergency seeing to.

I do believe Richard plans to join the 'boys' whilst we are away, and knowing Richard's love of Monopoly, I don't doubt it will turn into two days of extreme board-gaming fun! I shall have to make sure I stock up on twiglets and cheesy footballs for them.

Bests,

Margaret

PS I don't think we should be calling this a 'booze cruise' as it conjures up rather salacious images, and let's face it Celia, nothing remotely salacious is going to happen with us.

SUBJECT: SAGA LOUT'S TRIP

Dear Margaret

I forgot to ask, did you manage to do any shopping whilst in London or did the effects of your dental emergency force an early return? If you plan on returning at the end of the week, I could meet you there and we could shop for Christmas outfits and bits and bobs together! So much more fun with a friend, don't you agree?

Will Richard not be busy entertaining one of his lady friends? Or does Monopoly still take precedence over love? Have you met any of the ladies yet, Margaret? I wonder if you will be buying a hat soon? How wonderful if your efforts result in a wife for dear Richard!

Yours,
Celia

PS. I am the proud owner of a smartphone now so can email and twitter wherever I am! I was tweeting to Stephen Fry whilst at the hairdressers last week—we've become such good friends that I wouldn't be surprised if I get an invite to accompany him to the BAFTAs.

277

WEDNESDAY 14TH OCTOBER

SUBJECT: RE: SAGA LOUTS TRIP

Dear Celia

I really have no idea as to what a smartphone is or if 'tweeting' with Stephen Fry is a socially acceptable pastime for a married woman of your age, but I can only hope it's with John's approval. Nor am I sure your subject title is much more tasteful that the previous, although I can see the humour in it—just.

Unfortunately, I will have little time for shopping on Friday, so it's really not worth your bother to meet me there. We will have plenty of time for shopping in France.

As I am still only able to reply to emails from the comfort of my own home, you may have to wait longer than a few minutes for replies, but please remember Celia, I also have a home telephone and I have noticed you seem to have an aversion to that piece of twentieth century technology of late.

Bests
Margaret

TEXT MESSAGE RECEIVED THURSDAY 15TH OCTOBER 9.43AM

Sorry to bother you, Briony, it's Tom. Just wondered if you knew anything about Lucy and this Abbie woman she's gone off with. The kids are fine, but I'm feeling a little stunned at it all to be honest and didn't see it coming. I know you don't want to betray a friend's confidence, but I'm not sure really where to turn. Sorry.

278

TEXT MESSAGE SENT THURSDAY 15TH OCTOBER 9.51AM

What's going on, Tom? I hadn't seen Lucy this week at school but I've been rushing around rather a lot. I texted her to ask about something a couple of days ago and her reply said nothing about an Abbie? Do you want me to come round or are you at work? I'll ask the others if they know anything, but honestly, Tom, I didn't even know she had a friend called Abbie. I'm sure she'll be back soon. Couples have tiffs and sometimes it's good to get some breathing space and go ranting to a friend.

TEXT MESSAGE RECEIVED THURSDAY 15TH OCTOBER 9.55AM

Thanks, Briony. She's taken the blasted dog and left me with the kids who think mummy's just gone away with her friend for a few days. I've taken the week off work as couldn't face going in. I know you hear about women suddenly realising they're lesbians even though they've been married for years and have a family, but, not Lucy. She won't even get changed in front of other women at the gym, for God's sake. Where's this all come from, Briony?

TEXT MESSAGE SENT THURSDAY 15TH OCTOBER 10.01AM

Sorry? Lucy has become a lesbian? With her friend, Abbie?? Are you sure, Tom?! I'll pick the kids up for you and drop them round after school and we can have a chat. I'm sure you've got this all wrong. x

THURSDAY 15TH OCTOBER 10.07

WHATSAPP GROUP MESSAGE

BRIONY: Just got text from Tom saying Lucy's become a lesbian! I've tried to call Lucy but not answering. Do you think Tom is having paranoid delusions or something? Lucy is the last person to become a lesbian. There were no signs of lesbianism when we were test driving that bloody car the other week and who the hell is this Abbie woman?!? Tom must be losing it.

KARA: Oh, yes, Abbie. I did wonder if Lucy had said anything to you yet. I guess not. Am in supermarket so will call later.

GAYLE: She's not a lesbian. It's called sexual fluidity or something. She and Abbie were telling me all about it.

BRIONY: You know about this Abbie and Lucy?!

GAYLE: You've met Abbie, she's nice. I didn't expect her to actually leave Tom though. You won't get through to Lucy at the mo as she's in Madeira with Abbie. I'll call Tom after I've dealt with this morning's patients.

BRIONY: It's not Abbie the dog homeopath is it? She was at Lucy's Christmas party and said I had an amazing aura— do you think she was just flirting with me as well?

GAYLE: Yes, that's her. She's lovely. I recommend her to some owners who want to take a more holistic approach to long term problems with their pets. Of course she wasn't flirting with you! I'm sure from the right angle with the light falling a certain way you do have an amazing aura. But, Lucy's is quite obviously more amazing than yours 😉

THURSDAY 15TH OCTOBER

WHATSAPP MESSAGE

BRIONY: Oh, Lucy. I know you are getting these messages from your secret lesbian love nest in Madeira; Gayle told me so . . . I can't make you answer your phone but I can make you read this. Well, sort of—you know what I mean. Look, what's going on and why am I the last to find out about this?! I'm not sure what I'm more hurt about; the fact you didn't tell me you were dipping your finger into the furry cup or the fact you've never tried it on with me? Why have you never tried it on with me? I was once told by a lesbian at Uni that I was very attractive and sexy and just her type. Am I not your type? Is it because I'm not obviously sexually fluid enough? You know how much I love Gwen Stefani, I'm always going on about it. If this is the same 'Abbie' who complimented me on my aura at your Christmas party, then I have to say I am think I am much sexier than her, at least two dress sizes smaller and a full cup size bigger. (No offence Abbie if you're reading this.) You've seen me in my underwear in the changing rooms of department stores across the south of England countless times, and never has this warranted so much as an 'uncomfortable moment' between us as your eyes linger just a moment too long on my pert bottom. I'm hugely offended, Lucy, really I am.

LUCY: Oh Briony! You are sycophantic about Gwen Stefani and want her to be your BFF so stop pretending it's anything more than that! Anyway, you always said you could

281

only be a lesbian for the foreplay but then you'd need cock.

BRIONY: Did I?

LUCY: After the 2nd mojito it's always about the cock with you.

BRIONY: True . . .

LUCY: Abbie and I were giggling away at your message and you've cheered us up no end after the dreadful weather we've been having. Honestly, more rain than England in the summertime! How is Tom?

BRIONY: He doesn't know what's hit him. He says you've taken Algey? You haven't taken him to Madeira, surely? That would have taken planning, a pet passport, vaccinations and paperwork from a . . . vet . . .

LUCY: 😶

BRIONY: Ah, now I see. You've been in cahoots with Gayle all along. God, I feel soo out of the loop!

LUCY: You've been so unhappy with James lately that I didn't want to rub my new-found happiness in your face. There never seemed to be a right time to bring it up. There's you, sexually frustrated, wandering if he's having an affair or if he's just lost interest in you, and then there's me having a sexual awakening of sorts and . . .

BRIONY: Well, just to get a few points straight, it goes without saying that your sexual preference is of no odds to me—but you know that anyway. I'm far more upset that I was the last to find out about your extra marital rug munching. I just didn't even see it coming and I feel like a bad friend as you're always listening to my rantings and moanings about my life and problems with James, so God knows I know how it can happen—things go a bit stale in the bedroom . . . husband doesn't pay you enough attention . . . you start browsing a bit of soft porn on your phone during that spare half an hour between Facebook stalking old boyfriends and school pick up . . . oh yeah, we've all done it, Lucy.

LUCY: I've never wanked whilst watching lesbian porn on my phone of an afternoon, Briony.

BRIONY: Oh. Really?

LUCY: And then rushed off to pick my kids up from school!

BRIONY: Let's not be too judgey now, Lucy.

LUCY: I have called Tom but, he either sniffles so much I can't understand what he's saying or he gets really mad and starts threatening to get custody of Algey. He really knows how to hit where it hurts. Actually, Algey isn't here with us, but I told Tom he was so as he wouldn't try and find where he was back home and kidnap him. To be fair on me though, I was going to tell you about Abbie when we went for lunch during the test drive, but I needed that glass of wine for Dutch courage and then when it reacted badly with the antibiotics . . . well, we all know that day didn't turn out quite as either of us planned.

BRIONY: Hmm, okay well, let me know when you're coming back and message me if you need anything or to talk.

LUCY: Thanks Briony 😌 Are you okay though? I know you put a brave face on it, but I know the whole James thing is really upsetting you, and Gayle was saying you were asking if she thought Cosmo fancied you—don't do anything silly, Briony.

BRIONY: I don't have a gay canine aromatherapist to do anything silly with, Lucy 😉

MONDAY 19TH OCTOBER
SUBJECT: RE: CHRISTMAS
Hi Sarah

Thanks for your email re: all the Christmas plans and sorry for the delay in responding but one of my best friends has become sexually fluid and run off to Madeira with her dog's alternative therapist.

I think James called you to explain that we are going up north shortly after Christmas for a friend's wedding, therefore, with so much to do, we think it's best we have a quiet, bog standard nuclear family Christmas this year. I'm sure you'll have a lovely time with Margaret and Arthur, although, we may find time to pop over for a couple of hours sometime after Boxing Day before we head off to Yorkshire, but time is tight.

I'm so glad you mentioned the children's Christmas presents. I do feel they've got to that age where they have pretty much everything they need and therefore James and I will be sending charity token gifts to nieces and nephews again this year, just as we have done for the adult family members in previous years. I know how gratefully received they are, and of course, a goat to a poor African family goes so much farther than the latest XBox game, doesn't it? Obviously, this goes both ways and therefore Sam and Zac will be thrilled to receive a similar charity gift or donation of your choice. I know you'll agree this is a great way to avoid present overload as so often happens with the children at this time of year, and of course, with you being a Christian this will have particular significance to you—season of goodwill and all that!

It was lovely to see George while he was in the area. I do hope you two are back on track. You don't need me to tell you that marriage can be a rollercoaster at times.

All the best
Bri

WEDNESDAY 21ST OCTOBER
SUBJECT: FESTIVE PLANS
James

I've just had an email from Briony saying you can't participate in the family Christmas I had planned as you are going to a wedding sometime after Christmas? I really don't see how this affects the festivities I have organised. She claims you should have already discussed this with me—which you have not.

I'm also somewhat dismayed that you won't be getting your niece and nephew a Christmas present this year. I'm sorry, but as I have said before, I don't subscribe to this ridiculous charity Christmas rubbish—after all, charity begins at home and the last time I checked, I did not live in a third world country. Therefore, I shall still be buying my nephews a proper present for them to unwrap on the day. In previous years I have tolerated Briony's 'gifts' of malaria tablets in Sudan and chickens to Cambodia, but this year clean water for poor Zambians and warm blankets to orphaned Indonesians really do not a merry Christmas make!

Mum is currently on a little break in France with her friend, Celia, but I shall be discussing this with her when she returns this evening. I will not have Briony ruin my Christmas, James, and I will not have my children going without presents this Christmas just so some street kids in Bangladesh can go to school.

Sarah.

WEDNESDAY 21ST OCTOBER
SUBJECT: RE: FESTIVE PLANS
At the risk of sounding pious, Sarah; I think clean water and blankets would make for a very merry Christmas for a child in a developing country, but if you insist, I shall tell Briony to shelve that idea and get Barnaby and Ella something to add to their pile. Good to see you so full of Christian goodwill.

SUBJECT: RE: CHRISTMAS

Dear Briony

I have to confess, I was somewhat confused and taken aback by your email. Firstly, there is no 'rollercoaster' with regards to my marriage, so I don't know how you got this impression—although going by the amount of wine George said you alone consumed the night he was staying, I'm going to assume your memory was a little 'fogged'.

Secondly, I'm sorry you consider yourself too busy to take part in the lovely family Christmas I was organising, and I can only hope that next year you might have more time to participate, and that mum and dad stay in good health over the next year to be with us to celebrate.

Thirdly, yes, Briony; being a Christian, I am fully aware of the importance of charity and giving to the less fortunate—it was, after all, my idea to allow the village school children to use Grayson Private School's sports field for their sports day this year. After all, as Jesus said, 'charity begins at home, my son'. So therefore, please make a donation to the Grayson School charitable fund on behalf of Barnaby and Ella which helps pay towards the school skiing trips. Thank you.

Sarah

FRIDAY 23RD OCTOBER
SUBJECT: RE: CHRISTMAS
Dear Sarah

Firstly; I thought you charged a fee for the village school to use Grayson School's facilities, and as far as I am aware, money making schemes are not considered 'charity'.

Secondly; no, I won't be making a donation to a privately funded school as for reasons stated above, I don't consider them to be 'in need'.

Thirdly; admittedly, I've not read the Bible since I was seven and forced to attend Sunday School in an effort to ease my parents' conscience regarding their own lackadaisical attitude towards religion, but I'm pretty sure Jesus didn't say, 'charity begins at home. my son'. I think you may be confusing him with Arthur Daley.

Briony

PS—And fourthly; I am surprised George can remember how much wine I had drunk with the best part of a bottle of finest single malt inside him . . .

SATURDAY 24TH OCTOBER
SUBJECT: HOME SWEET HOME
Dear Celia

I do hope your drive back home was trouble free and John sobered up by the time you arrived. I'm still really rather aghast at the situation that greeted us upon our return, and still not wholly sure who to point the finger of blame at . . . although my instincts are going with Richard. I'm not sure those lady friends he invited over for scrabble with Arthur and John are a suitable sort. And then there are the never ending deliveries arriving at his door—and often ours when Richard is not in to receive them. I know Richard is seen as a wealthy man to many and I worry that these dating agency ladies are taking advantage of his kind and generous nature, Celia. I have told him we would like him to bring someone with him to my New Year's Eve party, so we shall see . . .

Since returning home, I have also had to deal with upset from Sarah regarding James and Briony's refusal to partake of a family Christmas this year. Sarah is beside herself as she had been thoughtful enough to go into great detail in attempting to arrange the day but, Briony has apparently said they don't have time for the fuss as they are travelling to Yorkshire for a wedding a few days after Christmas. Can you believe that, Celia? No time for a family Christmas! I don't think Sarah has given up yet, though, and is soldiering on trying to come to a compromise. I'm loathe to get involved as Briony can be a very difficult daughter-in-law with all her 'opinions' and such like! I don't understand why she doesn't just enjoy sitting back and letting Sarah and I take control of everything. Honestly, Celia, we do nothing but try and make her life easy by arranging everything for her and she seems to thank us by refusing to go along with whatever we have decided and have an 'opinion' or 'point of view' on the issue. Sarah only ever tries to make people's lives easier. She's even put a gift wish-list online for the children's presents this year—just as she did with her birthday—and would you believe Briony has refused to buy those poor children—her niece and nephew, no less—a gift, and is instead insisting on giving money away to strange children in Asia! Christmas is all about family, isn't it, Celia? Not children one has never met who live in mud huts and worship false gods.

Anyway, I digress. I wanted you to know the fruits of our trip are all safely stored in the garage, awaiting in anticipation of what I hope will be the New Year's Eve party of the year!

Bests, as always,
Margaret

PS—I forgot to ask—are you going to your son for Christmas or are the family coming to you, this year, Celia?

SATURDAY 24TH OCTOBER
SUBJECT: RE: HOME SWEET HOME
Dear Margaret

Our drive back was indeed traffic free and John managed to sleep the alcohol off for the most part. You know, Margaret, having had a few days to digest the scene that greeted us upon our home-coming, I am not at all sure if all was as it seemed. On hindsight, Richard's 'lady friends' were rather inappropriately dressed for a scrabble marathon in October, don't you think? And I am not at all sure I believe the story regarding the rather brazen looking redhead working for a condom manufacturer—even if that were the case, why would she carry so many boxes of the respective items on her person? I have never seen such a selection and variety that tumbled out of her bag when John accidently knocked it off the table in his hurry to show us the woodpecker that was apparently perched on the windowsill. I got the distinct impression he was trying to hurriedly usher us out the room. Do you think they were playing for money, Margaret? I'm sure I spotted quite a bundle of cash inbetween the boxes of condoms on the floor. I hope those silly men haven't got themselves involved with a gambling ring of some sort.

In answer to your question, no, we're not going to Patrick and Melanie or Susan and Eliot's this year, and the last thing I want is all the grandchildren over for Christmas when we have quite enough of them every weekend whilst their parents are gallivanting around farmers' markets and art galleries! No, this year, Margaret, John and I have booked into a lovely spa hotel in the Cotswolds for a few days of pampering. It hasn't gone down too well with the children who were looking to us for baby-sitting duties as usual, but hey ho! It's about time they learnt to cook their own Yorkshire puddings and didn't rely on their father and me, to run around after their children all day.

I'm afraid I have to say Briony sounds as if she has the right idea with these charity presents. I've been Googling whilst having a coffee in town and I've found a fantastic website that provides school books and uniforms for third world children, so I'm going to order those for the spoilt brats—God knows they have enough of everything already and I know they are all but forced to scrawl their names on those generic 'thank you' cards we receive well into the New Year; so that's that sorted as far as I'm concerned.

Anyway, I must rush as I have a nail appointment in five mins. You really should get a smartphone, Margaret. I can even eBay on it so am able to put in sniper bids at the last min.

Yours,
Celia

PS How's the face? Any more news on that clumsy dentist? I'm sure the anaesthetic should have worn off by now you know, so terribly worrying you still have no movement to your forehead and mouth area . . . I'm almost tempted to go to your dentist and ask for the same procedure as I have to admit, it's certainly taken a few years off you . . .

TUESDAY 27TH OCTOBER
SUBJECT: RE: HOME SWEET HOME
Dear Celia

I have to confess, I too was more than a little concerned as to the moral character of Richard's unsuitably attired lady friends, and so Arthur and I have formally request-ed he bring a companion to afternoon tea at the weekend where we will be able to observe her in more detail. Of course, we have no idea as yet who he will be arriving with, as he seems to have at least three who are regular visitors to his house. I will be making it quite clear in no uncertain terms that Arthur and I are on to the schemes and scams of certain woman who take advantage of men in Richard's position. James, Briony and the children will be here as well as it's Briony's birthday today but I have been too busy to take her present over so James has said they will come by on Saturday so it will be a full house for us!

Thank you again for your concern regarding my, admittedly rather freak accident with the dentist, but I am afraid there will be no comeuppance for him as he died after the stroke. Tragic, but we move on.

I can't say I do enough eBaying to warrant a smartphone so I don't think I shall bother with that for now, Celia.

Bests,
Margaret

Wednesday 28th October
WHATSAPP MESSAGE
BRIONY: Hey Kate, thanks for the sumptuous beauty box full of goodies I received yesterday. I take it you're managing the 'Spa Babe' contract now? How lucky it arrived on my birthday otherwise I might have thought you'd forgotten one of your oldest friend's birthday....

KATE: Ohhhhhhhhh I'd never forget your birthday!

Didn't you get my card? Must be stuck in the postal strike. How was your day, anyway? Glad you liked the goodies. My flat smells divine with all the stuff I've got, although Piers loathes it and claims the smell gives him a migraine.

BRIONY: There is currently no postal strike that I know of, Kate . . . . .and the last time you sent me a card was when you had the personalised online cards account and I got a birthday card in June with 'not to be opened until October 27th' on the envelope.

KATE: Better early than late! Were you spoilt? Did James pull it out the bag for once and surprise you?

BRIONY: It was what I pulled out the fucking bag that killed it! James took the day off work and I planned to spend the day shagging to within an inch of my life while the boys were at school. Christ knows I'm owed a good seeing to. However, my libido took a nosedive when I unwrapped his present to discover he had purchased a slanket for me . . .

KATE: WTF is a slanket?

BRIONY: A bloody all in one fleecy body bag with arms for God's sake!

KATE: Christ on a bike, Bri. That is shitacious!

BRIONY: Surely a marriage is deemed officially over when a woman's husband buys their still under forty-year-old wife such a passion killer as a slanket! God, I'm depressed. James promised Margaret we'd pop over on Saturday as she's been too busy to bring me my present apparently—although I know for a fact she was here last week because her car was parked around the corner near the lane, oddly enough. James said she must have gone for a walk in the woods near there. I still think she's stalking poor Cosmo. I know she went to London just the other weekend when he was and she'd only been there a couple of weeks previously. I think James is going to have to say something to her. We can't have his OAP mother stalking our charming, eligible bachelor neighbour; it's gone on long enough and what with the botox and Brazilian I really think she's having some sort of post-menopausal crisis?! I still shudder when I think about the Brazilian. This time last year I swear the woman wouldn't have even believed women paid beauticians to tidy up their lady-gardens and now she's a fully paid up member of the stubbly runway club.

KATE: Euck! Although I still think she's stalking you as she thinks you're up to something with Cosmo

BRIONY: Chance would be fine thing.

KATE: Would it? Would you?!

BRIONY: He is very charismatic and very charming . . . A little flirtation might make James jealous.

KATE: Fuck, Bri . . . just tread carefully. I know you are pissed off and upset with the way James is but you don't want to do anything you might regret.

BRIONY: Hmm . . . .Oh, did I tell you Lucy has become sexually fluid with her dog's aromatherapist?

KATE: Sex fluid?! Eugh!

BRIONY: Sexually fluid. Like a lesbian but not a lesbian because she might go back to men again one day.

KATE: So what we used to call bi-sexual back in the old days? No you didn't tell me about Lucy! Wow! Wonder why she never tried anything with me. I mean, I know we're not close friends, but I've met her a few times over the past few years when I've been down staying with you in Dorset, so you would have thought if anyone was going to ignite that lesbian lust spark it would be me. I appeal to woman, you see. It's that strong powerful aura I emit wrapped up in a soft feminine exterior.

BRIONY: And modest with it.

KATE: Good luck with Margaret. Maybe she's forgone the birthday voucher for something special this year? Didn't she get you a giant pepper mill and some gravy granules one year as had serious concerns that your gravy wasn't good enough for her darling son?!? She can't beat that, surely?!

TEXT MESSAGE RECEIVED SATURDAY 31ST OCTOBER 10.27AM
Only have ham in, no cheese for vagatarians. Honey roasted so doesn't taste like ham, really. Will that be okay? Margaret x

TEXT MESSAGE SENT SATURDAY 31ST OCTOBER 10.35AM
Not really okay, Margaret, no. I'll stop at shop for cheese on route. And I think you'll find the term is 'sexually fluid' these days—vagatarian so 90s.

NOVEMBER

MONDAY 2ND NOVEMBER
WHATSAPP MESSAGE

BRIONY: Well, Margaret exceeded herself on the birthday front this year, when in front of everyone including my children and Margaret and Arthur's wheelchair-bound neighbour and his dominatrix 'girlfriend,' I unwrapped a g-string made from nothing but little sweeties threaded on elastic, a sponge cake mix and some flowery post-it notes. I'm still working out how they relate to each other. Apparently, Margaret thought the sweetie knickers, 'fun,' whilst James almost spat his tea out and Richard nodded approvingly. The boys ate them on the drive home, which in itself I am not sure was an entirely wise decision and I have visions of this coming out in therapy in years to come. Also, I know how Sam likes to shock with his tales of 'life at home,' so I fully expect to read about this latest instalment in his school workbook at the next parents evening. It will go down well after previous stories including of daddy bludgeoning a fish to death with an umbrella (fishing trip—umbrella was all James had to hand as he wasn't expecting to catch anything!). On the plus side, his teacher says he has a very vivid imagination and a descriptive writing style quite advanced for his age. I think that's a polite way of saying she thinks we let him watch 18 cert films whilst we re-enact violent video games all day.

KATE: Dominatrix girlfriend? You mean she was just wearing too much eyeliner and black heels? You're so judgemental.

BRIONY: No, she's def a dom. She slipped James a card after cornering him on his way back from the loo. 'Dita Adore,' who specialises in submission fantasies and gentle bondage in the comfort of your own home.' How convenient! There's nothing more annoying when you get that urge to be dressed up in gimp gear, licking the bathroom floor whilst a stiletto clad dom walks up and down your back, and then realising it's too cold to go out and the car's low on petrol.

KATE: Dial-A-Dom :o)))

BRIONY: Obviously, Margaret and Arthur are oblivious to the fact they have set their neighbour up with a professional purveyor of S&M.

KATE: You should have saved the sweetie knickers to tempt James that evening

BRIONY: Nothing can tempt him out of his study. I happened to accidently check the browsing history last week . . .

KATE: Funny, as I'm always 'accidently' checking Piers'

text messages 😉 What did you find?

BRIONY: Hmm . . . .I don't know . . . a bit odd.

KATE: What Bri??

BRIONY: Lots of browsing nightlife in Hong Kong—restaurants, bars, clubs ffs . . .

KATE: So he's just looking for where to go when he's over there? That's okay isn't it?

BRIONY: James always claims he never has time to socialise when away on business, Kate. It's a boring dinner with clients and back to the hotel where he always makes quite a big issue of the fact he's working. It pisses me off as he will always be irritated by my messages and never skypes anymore. If he doesn't have time to communicate with his wife or sons, wtf is he doing looking for the best places to go for the nightlife?

KATE: Hmmm.

BRIONY: And rental properties. He's been looking at rental properties.

KATE: But he stays in hotels?

BRIONY: 1 bed rental properties. Who is he looking for a 1 bed rental for?

KATE: OMG he's going to leave you and move to HK?!

BRIONY: Actually, I thought he might just have a mistress out there, which was bad enough, but now you've got him leaving me for her.

KATE: You need to talk to him, Bri.

BRIONY: 🙁

WEDNESDAY 4TH NOVEMBER

SUBJECT: HORACE

Dear All

Abbie and I are thrilled to announce the arrival of Horace Sentongo, our sponsor child from Uganda! Horace weighs in at a whopping seven years old and lists his favourite things as helping his brother collect water and grinding cassava for flour. Through our sponsorship of Horace, we are able to send him to school, make sure he has necessary medicines and generally help the well-being of his village. Sadly, we are not able to change his name.

Please find attached a couple of photos of Horace. (The man wielding the machete in one hand with his other around Horace's shoulders in the second pic is his father, so do not be alarmed.)

Love, Lucy & Abbie xx

PS If anyone knows what cassava is, please could they let us know. X

FRIDAY 6TH NOVEMBER

SUBJECT: OUR MOTHER

Dear James

As you will be aware I have tried a number of times to call you but I am always re-directed to your voicemail and you are yet to return my calls.

As you will not yet be aware, our mother has left our father and is currently residing with me. I am absolutely beside myself, James, and could really do with some support from you, my brother. George and I lead very busy lives and I currently have no time to look after mother, who, appears to be having some sort of what I can only describe as, late and extreme mid-life crisis. I don't know what to do with her and I have the school Christmas fayre and nativities to organise, not to mention the Village Players rely on me quite heavily at this time of year. Dad seems to think she's just having a bit of a tizzy after finding out she inadvertently encouraged Richard from number 52 to sign up with an escort agency. Apparently, Richard brought around a couple of escorts to the house when mum and Celia were away in France for a couple of days. Dad swears blind they were all just playing scrabble tournaments but mum's had some trouble 'down below' and claims the trouble came from dad. Oh, dear God, I can't believe I am writing this about our own mother!

I think under the circumstances, it would be best if you or Briony came to pick mum up at the earliest convenience. I appreciate that collecting her by tonight might be a bit of a stretch, so, we'll just have to leave her at the house while we go to the Church fireworks display. We can't miss it. It's a very important event for us all and we don't have a spare ticket for mum, I'm afraid. Then we have the Forsythes coming round for lunch on Sunday, and I really can't have mum here then. It was bad enough explaining away the transvestites at my birthday, but I really can't have her babbling on about dad and ladies of ill repute. I will be given a very wide berth at the carol concert and there is a chance I wouldn't be re-elected at the village parish council, so please confirm you can get her tomorrow and if you send Briony please ask her to do her shopping on the return journey—I know how she has a habit of stopping off in Truro and losing track of time. It would be best for everyone if mum was gone by lunchtime at latest.

Much Love
Sarah x

PS—Were you aware our mother has been frittering away our inheritance on cosmetic procedures? I had to stop her going out in the village after Mrs Grasby saw her in the post office, noticed her inanimate features, and asked me if she's come to stay to recover from her stroke. If this is Briony and her misplaced, insensitive comments that's caused this I'm going to be furious. I remember how paranoid she made me that summer she asked if I was 'smuggling tobacco in my tankini bottoms'. Please remind your wife that not all we woman feel the need to indulge in extreme pubic pruning.

Friday 6th November
SUBJECT: FWD: MUM
Bri—see email below from Sarah. Do you want to reply to this or shall I? Not sure what to make of it to be honest, but got no intention of driving to Devon at Sarah's insistence.

James x

FRIDAY 6TH NOVEMBER
SUBJECT: RE: FWD: MUM

Oh Christ, James. Are you sure Sarah is not just exaggerating and she's just popped down for a little break and to see the spoil the brats some more? I'm not going to collect her; she's a grown woman and perfectly able to drive herself home when she's ready.

I can't believe she's still going on about the tankini incident. Ffs she looked like she had half a packet of Golden Virginia sticking out there.

I'll reply and say we're busy. We've got everyone coming over for the bonfire and hot chocolate tomorrow night anyway—which reminds me, I'd better pop over to see Cosmo and warn him there might be fireworks tonight. Literally– Boom Boom!

FRIDAY 6TH NOVEMBER
SUBJECT: RE: FWD: MUM

Sorry Sarah but James v busy so fwd to me. No can do this weekend I'm afraid. Got a lot on with friends and stuff. James says he'll pop round to see Arthur though if he gets the chance to see what he's got to say. Shouldn't worry too much. I expect she just fancied a break in your lovely house and to see her delightful grandchildren for a weekend and admire your unique loo roll holders.

Sorry you're still touchy about your tankini/burst mattress faux pas, but pubic topiary isn't an extreme sport, Sarah—ask your mother who I believe is a new recruit to

303

the virtues of a tidy snatch.

Have fun at the church thing. I had no idea Christians celebrated sixteenth century foiled terrorist plots so enthusiastically.

Love Bri

Saturday 7th November
SUBJECT: RE: MUM
Briony. I'm afraid I do think you are being very selfish. I insist you come and get mother this weekend. I simply can't cope. My life is very full and I have a reputation in the village which must be upheld. If you really are unable to collect her I shall have to phone social services to deal with it, and I really would rather avoid that. It would portray you in rather a bad light if mum had to be taken into a care home as her son and daughter-in-law refused to take care of her.

I can assure you the only topiary my parents indulge in involves gardening shears and box hedging. There is no need for crudity.

Sarah

Friday 6th November
SUBJECT: RE: MUM
I'm afraid that as far as I know, there is no government body who will take an elderly woman away from her daughter's

home simply because having her stay doesn't fit in with said daughter's social arrangements.

Nothing crude about it, Sarah. Your mother has had her minge waxed to within an inch of its life. It caused quite a rash and some septic spots from ingrown hairs, apparently. Maybe pop her along to the village doctor on Monday to get it checked out.

Have a great weekend!

Briony x

SATURDAY 7TH NOVEMBER
SUBJECT: UPSETTING NEWS
Dear Celia

I am staying with Sarah for a few days whilst I let Arthur stew in his own juices. I'm afraid our concerns regarding Richard's 'lady friends' have proved to be not altogether without foundation, and to add insult to injury, I have discovered Arthur was aware of these facts some time ago. Celia, I do hope you are sitting down whilst I convey my findings and if you are reading this email in the hairdressers, I do hope the pungent aroma of hair colorant and perming solution stops you from fainting.

Celia; Richard has not been entertaining an array of respectable single lady friends through the dating agency with a view to finding a potential long-term companion, but has instead been indulging in perverted practices with women of ill repute. I am both embarrassed and ashamed

305

to inform you that the dating agency Arthur and I encouraged Richard to use, is in fact, what is known as an 'escort' agency. A place where women can be picked online to come to the homes of men where they are paid to indulge in whatever obscene practice the man desires. It was these women who were in my home playing scrabble and Monopoly tournaments with our husbands, Celia! Paying these women to play board games for goodness sake! Mrs Bridges and her daughter would have been happy to join in a game for nothing more than a nice cup of tea and an iced bun—and they would have been wearing far more suitable clothing to boot! I am afraid that is not all I have to tell you, Celia. I can hardly bring myself to say this but I fear that after over forty-five years of marriage, an irritation in my nether regions is hinting to me that my husband may have been indulging in more than just triple word scores whilst you and I were on our French jaunt.

To make matters worse, I have to say, Celia, that I am not being made to feel altogether as welcome as a mother and grandmother should be made to feel when she visits her daughter and family. I don't know what has got into Sarah, but, I was not taken along with the rest of the family to the Church bonfire event last night and have been told it would be appreciated if I stay in my room tonight whilst they entertain guests. I overheard Sarah arguing with George about having to drive me home as apparently James and Briony have refused to come and collect me! Well, although I don't want to be pushed from pillar to post and have no intentions of going home just yet, it's not nice to know my son is happy to let me stay here where I am unwanted and banished to my room.

I should have come to stay with you, Celia. Maybe I will see if there is a train that can take me to you on Monday.

Your friend
Margaret

SUNDAY 8TH NOVEMBER
SUBJECT: RE: UPSETTING NEWS
Dear Margaret

I am so sorry to hear you are feeling this way. Although I am sure Sarah is thrilled to have you stay unexpectedly, I have always thought she does seem to have a very busy schedule. I remember when we were young mothers and housewives, all that was expected of us was to take care of the children and keep the house spick and span. It seems these days that so much more is expected of women and I'm really not so sure that's a good thing. I have to confess, I always found motherhood a bit of a breeze—although, admittedly, I did spend most of my children's pre-school years on Valium, which certainly took the edge off. It's a shame you can't buy mild narcotics along with teething rings in Mothercare. It would solve a multitude of problems, of that I am sure.

Now, Margaret. You know, that as my oldest and dearest friend, my home is always open to you. However, I have to admit I am not sure how wise staying away from home for too long under the current circumstances is. I was reading in Women's Weekly just the other day how a lady's husband moved his mistress into the marital home while she was just at the chiropodists having her corns filed. Goodness knows what was going on whilst you were at the dentist in London, Margaret.

I received news last week that Eliot and Susan are expecting another baby. With the youngest being just 18 months, I wouldn't be surprised if this one was conceived whilst I was looking after the others and they were meant to be visiting some farmers market or art gallery! I had to tell them in no uncertain terms that they are going to have to look at getting professional paid help with the children as I'm simply too busy to be looking after all these children in my spare time. If it's not them it's Patrick and Melanie dumping theirs on me under the guise of 'spending quality time with granny.' Well, Margaret, I've also told them that my idea of quality time doesn't involve changing nappies, mushing up organic yams and pretending to be interested in the shenanigans of some mind numbingly idiotic children's television show. Susan is now upset at my lack of enthusiasm at the impending arrival. Well, at least if she's not talking to me I've got my weekends free for the foreseeable.

Do give my advice serious consideration and don't put off going back home, Margaret. We really wouldn't want Richard leading Arthur further astray now, would we?

Your friend,
Celia

P.S. Is this irritation in your nether region an actual irritation or were you speaking metaphorically, Margaret?

TEXT MESSAGE SENT TUESDAY 10TH NOVEMBER 11.27AM
Bri, how do you fancy coming with me to the Buddhist centre on Thursday? It might be good for your karma after the demo incident . . . K x

TEXT MESSAGE RECEIVED TUESDAY 10TH NOVEMBER 11.35AM
Sorry, Kara, busy. Besides, I befriended the Buddha on Facebook and now the Dalai Lama keeps spamming me.

THURSDAY 12TH NOVEMBER
SUBJECT: DIETARY REQUIREMENTS
Hey bridesmaids! Just wanted to run a couple of things past you . . .

Monique and I are rather surprised at the fussiness of many of guests. Out of politeness the invites contained a small section where guests could give any information regarding special dietary requirements. Of course, I expected one or two like-minded vegetarians, but, I have been inundated with people claiming they can have no food which has been within a mile of a nut, whilst others are claiming to be coeliacs and in need of gluten-free meals. We have a whole family of lactose intolerants, and even more are requesting only organic meat and no GM foods! To be quite frank, I wish I had not bothered now and I'll bet you they wouldn't have complained at the meal put in front of them on the day. Do you think it would be acceptable to ask the coeliacs and lactose intolerants to bring their own food in a Tupperware box which the caterers would very kindly re-heat and serve to them on a plate with all the other guests? Apparently those with nut allergies will have to sign some-thing on arrival as although the meal will be nut free, the hotel has to cover itself against legal action should a nut spore happen to waft past at the wrong moment. Uncle Edgar is a doctor anyway so I'll just make sure he doesn't get too tipsy until after the meal and then he can be on hand to revive anyone in need.

Also, just wanted to check when my hen weekend was? I know you've been doing a good job of keeping it very quiet to surprise me but I am going to need some details as I've got a very busy few weeks ahead and I need to make sure I have the right clothes and passport all up to date of course.

Thanks girls!
Melissa x

Thursday 12th November
WHATSAPP MESSAGE
BRIONY: Hen weekend?!? Shiiiiiiiiiiiiiiiiiiiittt!

KATE: Have you got any ideas? I hadn't even given this a thought!

BRIONY: I assumed she would just tell us we were all go-ing out for a meal and drinks one weekend and you and I would just turn up.

KATE: I know. Had no idea we were expected to arrange this! I wouldn't even know who to invite. Briony: WTF are we going to do, Kate?!

KATE: Leave it with me. I'll book a spa weekend or something. You get a list of friends off Melissa to invite.

THURSDAY 12TH NOVEMBER
SUBJECT: RE: DIETARY REQUIREMENTS
Food: Melissa, I really don't think you can ask people to bring their left over Christmas food to eat at your wedding.

Re: Hen weekend—funnily enough, Kate and I had been covertly trying to organise this for weeks now! Can you just email me the contact details of your closest friends so we can make sure they are all able to come.

MONDAY 16TH NOVEMBER
WHATSAPP MESSAGE
KATE: So I've managed to book a spa in Cornwall for the last weekend in Nov (27th—29th).

BRIONY: Cornwall? In November? I think Melissa is thinking a weekend in Paris or Barcelona or something?

KATE: Cornwall is virtually another country anyway. I've emailed everyone on the list you sent me so just waiting for them to confirm. Didn't recognise many names actually so must be uni and work friends of hers?

BRIONY: Does it have all facilities on-site?

KATE: Not sure. It says it's not far from the town so will be a short walk to the restaurants and bars either way.

BRIONY: Cool.

KATE: How are things with James? Did you speak to him about the stuff you found he's been looking at?

BRIONY: How can I? I'd have to say I was looking at the internet history on the PC in his study. If he was leading a double life with some woman in Hong Kong, surely I'd notice money disappearing out the account?

KATE: He could have another bank account. And using money from that account for the drug addiction as well.

BRIONY: Yeah, you're right. Why didn't I think of that. While I think he's away on business in SE Asia, he's quite obviously snorting mieow mieow with his mistress at their HK lovenest.

KATE: Just saying . . .

BRIONY: You're right though, something must be going on. He's quite obviously lost all interest in me. He never leaves his phone lying around, even takes it to the bathroom

KATE: So he's cracking one out in the bog. Christ, he can't control himself, Briony!

BRIONY: You're really not making me feel any better . . .

Monday 16th November

SUBJECT: YOUR HEN WEEKEND ITINERARY!

Hi Melissa

As I am sure you are eager to hear the plans, we won't keep you in suspense any longer.

So, we are booked to arrive on Friday night 27th Nov

at the Thai Sensual Spa in a beautiful little place in Cornwall (the dark haired one from Bananarama lives near there with Andrew Ridgley and uses it all the time, so I've heard!) We are booked to have a delicious dinner in the restaurant that evening and the next day we have a full day of spa therapies—hot stones, massage, facials, whatever we want. Of course, a scrumptious lunch included and then that evening we thought it would be nice to set off and sample some local cuisine and a few drinks from the lovely quaint town nearby. After a mouth-watering breakfast on the Sunday, we thought it might be nice to have a morning to mooch around the local town and maybe buy some local craft or art type stuff and have lunch before we all set off, relaxed and refreshed, for home.

Kate thought it would be best for you to take your car as hers is always a bit dodgy on long trips and can you transfer the cost of the weekend (£275) into her account or give her a cheque when you pick her up next weekend. She said it's probably best to leave early to avoid traffic so can you book the afternoon off work and pick her up no later than 3pm?

Everyone's looking forward to it—and I promise not an 'L' plate, fairy wings or condom packet it sight!

Bri x

SUBJECT: RE: YOUR HEN WEEKEND ITINERARY?

So I won't be needing my passport then? Never mind. So who exactly is everyone? How many are joining us? Fiona has a people carrier (you'd need one with all those kids!) so might be better if she drives and she can pick up Rosie and Issy on the way. We'll need quite a few changes of driver with that long journey! I don't mean to sound ungrateful but would it not have been easier to get the Eurostar to Paris?

Anyway, I'll make sure I book the afternoon off work.

Melissa x

Wednesday 18th November
SUBJECT: RE: YOUR HEN WEEKEND ITINERARY?

Oh, Paris is soo last decade, Melissa. In fact, Paris is to hen weekends what Amsterdam is to stags; tacky, predictable and crass. Cornwall is going to be great and with the mild Cornish climate you'll feel like we are in some sub-tropical paradise for the weekend. We'll even get the chance to pick up a few last minute Christmas presents I expect.

Friday 20th November
WHATSAPP GROUP MESSAGE

LUCY: Hey guys, Abbie, Tom and I would like to invite you all to Christmas drinks and nibbles on the 5th December. Nothing too formal; just bring a bottle and we'll do the rest. Book your baby-sitters for an 8pm start and see you all here.

BRIONY: Sounds very cosy!

LUCY: Ohh, things have moved on, Bri! You are so out of the loop! We've all reached an arrangement for the sake of the children.

GAYLE: How very . . . modern

KARA: And will Channel 4 be making a documentary on you and your 'arrangement'?

LUCY: Nothing remotely salacious. Sorry to disappoint you all.

SUNDAY 22ND NOVEMBER
SUBJECT: APOLOGIES
Dear Celia

I am so sorry I missed your telephone call last week, I had a man over cleaning my oven and I thought it rude to abandon him when he was elbow deep in the past year's roasted grease and grime. If I am totally honest, I am rather loathe to leave tradesmen of any sort alone since I watched a programme on 'cowboy workmen' where a plumber did something wholly unsavoury in the bathroom sink whilst the owner was making him a cup of tea in the kitchen. It certainly brought a new meaning to the phrase, 'having a passion for your job'. As you will be aware, I have left several messages on your answer-phone, all of which have been left unreturned. Surely you are not still having problems with your phone connection. Being rather fond of my brain in its un-fried state, I prefer not to engage in long conversation on my mobile phone, so hence, I have resorted to emailing you from my old fashioned computer in the study. I simply can't even begin to imagine where you will be reading this on your 'brightphone.'

This weekend has seen me busy writing out my Christmas cards and round robins in anticipation of getting them in the post for the first of December. We have so many old friends and I do like to update everyone on the year's triumphs and to give the postal service half a chance of actually delivering the cards before the New Year. I always find it helps to be prompt with the posting and maybe that is a tip of which you might make a note, as I recall last year we didn't receive your card until 3rd Jan where I felt it was pointless to put it on display so close to twelfth night.

I do look forward to receiving everyone else's news at this time of year, although I admit it saddens me somewhat to realise that no one ever seems to have had a year quite as full and successful as we always seem to. Still, that's what the spirit of Christmas is all about isn't it; thinking about those less fortunate than oneself?

Christmas Day itself appears to be still rather 'up in the air' since Briony started to be difficult regarding having everyone over to the cottage. Sarah is insisting that her brood will all come to us for Christmas Eve, stay the night and then we shall go over to James and Briony just for Christmas lunch. I am not entirely sure Briony has agreed to this, but Sarah is not one to give up once she's decid-

316

ed on something, so I'm sure all will be confirmed soon enough.

As for Arthur and me, it seems my little break away did him the world of good and he appears to have seen the error of his ways and will not be inviting women of ill repute to Scrabble matches in the foreseeable future. I have invited Richard over for tea and scones this afternoon, where I intend to speak to him regarding my disappointment at the situation which has unfolded. Although, I accept his personal life is his business, I do feel rather betrayed that my welcoming and good nature has been taken advantage of. Forgiving as I am though, I have decided to introduce him to Gloria Sweetman's daughter who sadly divorced her husband last year after he spent too much time tending his dahlias at the allotment. Verity is a lovely lady whom I feel Richard would get on with extremely well. So, who knows, Celia, maybe we will get him married off next year after all!

I do hope all is well with you.

Your friend,
Margaret.

SUNDAY 22ND NOVEMBER
SUBJECT: APOLOGY ACCEPTED
Dear Margaret

I do apologise myself for not returning your calls after you returned my call. I too have been busy cleaning my own oven. I was quite unaware one could call in a man to do it for you—my goodness, just how far the feminist movement has come since we all burnt our bras! (or, is it a step back for feminism if we need to employ a man for a job a woman is perfectly able to do herself?)

Thank you so much for your gentle reminder to get my Christmas cards written and in the post early this year. I intend to start them just as soon as all the grandchildren have been taken back to their own homes and left me in peace. This week I believe Eliot and Susan have gone to some Scandinavian superstore to look for furniture and accessories for the new baby's nursery. It must be an awfully super superstore for them to need to leave the children with me for what will be nine whole hours by the time they estimate they will be back. You don't know how lucky you are to have a son and daughter-in-law who actually prefer to spend time with their children as opposed to wandering farmers' markets, superstores and brunching in brasseries every weekend, whilst I am left in charge of their snotty nosed, dribbly brood!

John is in the garage sulking as he rather thought he was in for a 'promise' last night after I accidentally put on a silky nightie, when in fact I was just a bit tipsy after too much sherry watching that lovely Jonathan Ross on television and couldn't find my pyjamas. This morning I noticed some seams looked rather pulled on it, so I think John has been wearing it when I do my Good Samaritan hospital visits. I wouldn't mind but he never puts it in the wash after wearing and I'm a stickler for hygiene, Margaret.

How lovely that Sarah is coming to you for Christmas. John and I have told the children we are toying with becoming Jehovah Witnesses, so as to put them off trying to burden us. We've said we will still buy the grandchildren gifts but, we just won't be partaking of the festivities on the day so no point coming to us. Although we will get a tree as it's not Christmas without a tree now, is it?

We are certainly looking forward to the New Year's Eve party, although, I have heard no end of comments from our spawn insinuating how selfish we are, and do we know how much baby -sitters charge for that night of the year and what's the point when they have to be back before midnight anyway and why are people our age even bothering going to a New Year's Eve Party ourselves? I did remind Susan she shouldn't be drinking in her condition anyway and got some smart answer about how organic red wine was actually beneficial to the growing baby, to which I replied, that was lucky then, because I drank half a bottle of sherry a night when I was expecting Eliot, and it was all organic in those days anyway . . . as were the cigarettes.

I do hope all goes well with Richard and Verity this afternoon. Do keep me posted.

Bests,
Celia

SUBJECT: RE: APOLOGY ACCEPTED

Dear Celia

I do think you are a woman of extraordinary patience and understanding. I confess, I do not think I would be so accepting of Arthur soiling my nightdress. Although, having retained my pre-baby figure into my Autumn years, I am really not sure he would even get it over his shoulders, and to be honest, Celia, it is not a thought I like to dwell on.

Afternoon tea with Richard and Verity went very well indeed. As is understandable, Verity is still rather bruised from her failed marriage, and did rather interrogate Richard on his hobbies and interests for fear of getting involved with another man who preferred to tend to the needs of his freesias than those of his wife's. I think Richard put her mind at rest though, telling her his hobbies were in no way related to horticulture and he was much more inclined to more sociable hobbies involving other people. So that was reassuring. I think.

I've invited Verity to our New Year's Eve party anyway, so maybe a little champagne and the air of excitement being on the cusp of a new year brings, will lead to romance!

I have to sign off now, Celia, for I am on baby-sitting duties this weekend. I believe Briony is deserting her post at the family home, yet again, to go off on some weekend with friends, and James has asked me to come and look after the boys on the Saturday as he needs to go off somewhere to attend to some business. I hope Briony realises just how lucky she is to have a husband who is prepared to work weekends in order to fund her social life. I can't imagine being able to abandon my husband and children and just go off like that in our day, can you, Celia? Indeed, I think you are right and that this feminist movement has gone too far. I wonder if her friends are feminists? I shall have to ask James. Although, I doubt Briony would be burning any bras. I've seen the exotic array of under-garments on her washing line and they certainly looked far too expensive to be burnt. No doubt another reason poor James has to work weekends.

So anyway, I am off into town to buy some bits and pieces to keep the boys amused and well fed on Saturday. There will be no avocado, tuna and sprouted seed salads with superfood smoothies on my watch! Growing boys need protein and plenty of it!

Bests,
Margaret.

THURSDAY 26TH NOVEMBER
WHATSAPP MESSAGE
GAYLE: Would you think it odd if James put a vibrating cock ring on your child's teddy and left it on your pillow?

BRIONY: I'd think it more odd that my child had a teddy with a cock, Gayle, actually.

GAYLE: It was on teddy's leg, Briony. Obviously.

BRIONY: Oh, well, that's alright then.

WHATSAPP MESSAGE

KATE: We're on our way. Melissa driving like a pensioner in slow motion as per. We'll never get out of London at this rate.

BRIONY: I'll leave in a couple of hours. Who else is in the car and who's making their own way down? I didn't see anything about wifi at the spa and the 4G coverage doesn't look great.

KATE: Umm, just Issy who used to go to Uni with Melissa. I've not met her before but she seems nice enough.

BRIONY: Oh. Okay. Does Melissa know no one else is coming? I think she envisaged a slightly larger party, Kate?!

KATE: I haven't told her yet. I'm working up to it. She's assumed others are meeting us there ... 🙁

SUNDAY 29TH NOVEMBER
SUBJECT: DRAINED.

Dear Celia

I thought I would just drop you a line and let you know how my day with the boys went. I have to confess, although much fun was had by all, I can see why you are tiring of having yours every weekend. Of course, Sam and Zac are delightful children, but being boys they never sit still, they ask constant questions and have a very short attention span.

322

I had booked tickets for us all at the museum to hear a talk on the Tudors by a local historian, Ralph Meldrew, which I thought the boys would find fascinating. They were particularly interested in the practise of beheading traitors and boiling people alive, and asked many a thought-provokaying question to our speaker. I think poor Mr Meldrew was quite unprepared for such probing questions; especially those concerning bodily functions at the moment of death, which it seems, Sam was already particularly knowledgeable, enlightening the audience with his own rather descriptive accounts of medieval torture and execution. I think most were quite impressed with his extensive vocabulary and amusingly macabre tone, and only a few of the weaker stomached members had to leave the room. It was, however, unfortunate that the boys chose to demonstrate the practice of being hung, drawn and quartered on a doll belonging to the museum curator's grand-daughter. Although I appreciate having one's doll disembowelled and amputated might be distressing, I did emphasise to the curator that I thought the more serious matter here was that there was a health and safety issue involved, when children that age are able to get into locked display cabinets and obtain nineteenth century paper knives which can be sharpened on stones in the geology section to such a degree that they are capable of tearing apart a plastic doll. I'm not sure he was entirely sympathetic with my concerns, but, all in all, I think it was a very successful and educational trip.

I treated the boys to lunch whilst we were out, which

seemed to have a restorative effect on their already, not altogether, un-waning energies; quite, overwhelmingly so, in fact. By the time they had run around a freezing cold park for two boisterous hours, they claimed to be hungry and thirsty again! Feeding them was not cheap, I can tell you! I can see why Briony takes a picnic and only gives them tap water now. The cost of those Loopy Froot drinks alone is astronomical and I am not sure a drink which stains clothes blue and lime green to such an effect that stain remover and bleach cannot remove, is entirely healthy for children.

I see on the news today that much of Devon and Cornwall has snow already, and quite a heavy fall by all accounts. Sarah phoned to say she doubted the children would make it into school tomorrow unless there was a sudden thaw. Apparently, they have not had it as bad as other places, but, Sarah won't drive the Range Rover in adverse weather, and to walk the mile to school on icy pavements would be lethal. She did ask if I could go down and help out as she has so much to do which will be made harder with the children home from school and she has a bit of a cold coming on, but unfortunately the trains and coaches are all cancelled past Honiton.

Bests,
Margaret

PS I did try and phone but no one's answering. Again.

SUBJECT: RE: DRAINED

Goodness me, Margaret, you must be exhausted! Have the boys been tested for ADHD or one of those other modern-day afflictions? I know I'm 'forbidden' from giving mine anything other than water, milk or pure organic juice to drink, as according to Susan, there's something in certain drinks that makes children go a bit crazy. Maybe the Loopy Froots were too much for them? Mothers these days are so fussy about anything that goes into their children's mouths. Gone are the days when a can of cola and a packet of crisps was considered a balanced meal—more's the pity! These days it's all got to be organic and hand-reared, massaged and happy meat, seasonal, local vegetables or nothing. These mothers have made a rod for their own backs. I cheat by keeping the packaging from an old packet of organic farmer's market sausages and just keep re-wrapping supermarket basic sausages in it. Same goes for eggs—battery hen eggs in organic box; children don't know the difference, and I am a pensioner after all, Margaret!

Sorry about not answering the phone. I am here of course, as I always am on a Sunday, but it's impossible to have a conversation surrounded by these children, so I'm trying to block out the anarchy by browsing 'on fleek' eyebrows and raw foodists on Instagram. Funnily enough, none of the raw foodists have on fleek eyebrows and no-one with on fleek brows appears to favour raw food. Everyone seems to have a 'bae' though. So that's nice.

We simply must catch up next week—although I am out most days and as you don't like calling on my mobile it's going to be hard to catch me in—such is the life of a social butterfly such as myself!

Bests
Celia #pensioner #crossdressinghusband #fruitcakeaffecionado

MONDAY 30TH NOVEMBER
WHATSAPP MESSAGE

BRIONY: Hey guys. Can anyone pick the boys up from school and have them until me or James can collect them from you? Stranded in the spa from hell with all this snow.

GAYLE: Spa from hell? Don't worry, we'll sort something out between us.

KARA: Yep. I can have them, Bri, no worries. Why is spa hell?! We thought you must be enjoying it as haven't heard a peep out of you!

BRIONY: No wifi, No 4G, using basic signal hanging out a window.

LUCY: Don't worry, we can help with the boys until you get back. I've called James and arranged everything with him so he knows where to pick the boys up each night.

BRIONY: Thanks. I hope to be back in a day or two otherwise I may do a Jack Nicholson on Melissa's friend, Issy.

LUCY: You mean you are going to drink too much and seduce her with your leering charm?!

BRIONY: No, Lucy. I mean Jack Nicholson in 'The Shining'. I'm going to chase her around the hotel brandishing an axe if she continues to whine and moan about every little thing and baby talk to people.

LUCY: Baby talk??

BRIONY: She speaks to everyone—staff included—like I imagine she speaks to her precious five-year-old daughter, who, going by the amount we have had to hear about her this weekend, is the most spoiled, overly pandered, precious little madam ever conceived. You know, according to Issy, darling Amelia talked at six months, but not the standard 'Dada' like most babies but fully formed words. She walked at nine months having totally skipped crawling and cruising to just get up one day and strut across the large kitchen extension (designed by that guy on TV, no less. We've all seen the photos on her phone). Darling, gifted, Amelia never suffered the normal tantrums of a toddler, oh no. According to Issy, Amelia would look aghast at her screaming peers during baby yoga sessions and smile sympathetically at the stressed mothers! Amelia is truly a precious gift to behold and as Issy and her husband, Benedict, want to be able to give their gifted spawn all their attention and don't think it's fair to make a child 'share' a parent's love with a sibling, Issy had her tubes lasered., and we've been shown the microscopic keyhole surgery scar to prove it.

KARA: Fuck. Me.

BRIONY: Oh that was nothing, I feared her episiotomy

scar would be getting an airing after the silent birthing story we were all told.

LUCY: My episiotomy didn't really leave behind a scar . . .

GAYLE: Of course it did, you just can't see it, Lucy.

BRIONY: Apparently, Issy believes women who have more than one child are selfish, and, in The World According to Issey, all women truly long for a daughter. I only had a second child because I would have been desperately trying to conceive a girl.

KARA: She really doesn't know you does she?

BRIONY: I told her I truly cannot bear pink and lilac frilly and sparkly shit, and noticed she packed away the framed photo of Amelia wearing her pink sequinned princess dress which she's placed by her bed, pretty soon after that.

LUCY: Omg. And the spa? Surely that's been a bit okay?

BRIONY: Middle of nowhere—and I mean nowhere. Food in a prison would be tastier and more filling, and no chance of popping out to the nearest town for a decent meal and a few cheery cocktails as the nearest 'town' is seven miles away and consists with no public transport or local cabs here, and anyway, choice there is limited to one seafood restaurant that only opens May-September!

GAYLE: Dare I ask if Melissa enjoyed her hen weekend?

BRIONY: Melissa can't complain. Well, she is, obviously, but she bloody well shouldn't be.

KARA: Yeah, who even does hen weekends any more? People our age have families and lives and mortgages. We can't just swan off to spas in the middle of nowhere to blow the best part of five hundred quid on hot stone therapy and a colonic just because a friend has decided she does finally want to get married before her ovaries shrivel up once and for all.

BRIONY: Exactly. Unfortunately, on the Saturday morning, Melissa decided to start off with a detoxifying facial to kick things off and had quite a severe allergic reaction to the 'natural' plant extracts in the mask which caused her face to puff up, and skin to take on the appearance of a radish. She's spent the rest of the time with her face dabbed with Calamine lotion wearing large sunglasses and she can't drink any alcohol while taking the antihistamine and steroid tablets the doctor gave her to help bring down the swelling.

GAYLE: Omg, did she have to go to hospital or was there a doctor in the nearest town?

BRIONY: No, she saw the 'doctor' at the spa hotel, who does the more cosmetic/medical procedures.

LUCY: Sounds dodgy!

BRIONY: Kate said his certificates displayed on the wall outside his office looked like they had been printed straight off the internet. And for a doctor who supposedly gained his medical degree in Manchester, he didn't actually appear to speak a word of English. In fact, his nurse translated everything that was said, and badly at that, as at one point Melissa was asked to go behind the curtain and remove her underwear for an examination!

GAYLE: Remove her knickers?!

BRIONY: It took a while before Kate managed to make it clear to the doctor via his nurse, that it was only Melissa's face that was swollen. Apparently, there had been some confusion regarding her swollen, 'lips' . . .

KARA: 😱

LUCY: 👀

GAYLE: 😬

DECEMBER

SUBJECT: SEASONAL FELICITATIONS!

Dear All

As the festive season is finally upon us I thought I would take this opportunity to update you all with the past year's events—and what a year it has been!

Arthur and I continue to live in our family home, although we have pondered downsizing within the next year, as with five bedrooms, the cleaner, Mrs Dewberry, who celebrated her 79th birthday this year, has asked for a pay rise. This came as quite a shock to Arthur and I who thought she enjoyed coming to the house to watch the birds during her tea breaks and considered the little something we paid her as a bonus for doing something she enjoyed.

Our dear daughter Sarah, who has always been so very house-proud, and with such a fantastic natural flair for interior design, had her stunning home featured in the pages of an esteemed national publication, 'Village Homes'. We were all delighted with the feature and I have taken the liberty of attaching scanned images of the feature for those whom I was unable to send a copy personally. Sarah's children, Barnaby and Ella, continue to thrive at their highly regarded private school, which, I'm not sure I have mentioned before, but has been shortlisted by William and Kate for baby George. Sarah continues to keep herself busy with her charitable works, and the whole family enjoy skiing twice a year.

Our son, James, has finally been able to reap some rewards for all his hard work and move his family out of the inner city to a country property where they are fortunate to have the most delightful neighbour, Mr Cosmo Huntington Jones, who, amongst his many and varied business interests, is a wine merchant and owns a vineyard in France. Mr Huntington Jones has been kind enough to educate my palate on wines of the world, and supplied the wine and champagne for Sarah's birthday celebration—which was a venerable success and featured a famous and world renowned dance group, organised by myself. I am told that the party is still the talk of the village almost six months later!

Arthur and I wish you all a very merry Christmas and a very happy new year, and hope you all enjoy the digital photos of our wonderful grandchildren, and garden pond, which we had brought back to life with a plethora of exotic aquatic pond life this summer.

Margaret and Arthur (Denley)

SUBJECT: RE: SEASONAL FELICITATIONS!

Margaret! Have you gone quite senile or been having a tipple of the festive sherry already? We are in regular contact with each other and I was even a participant in one of your round robin stories—although your unique interpretation of the event did leave me to query if we were in fact at the same party.

For your information, I shall be posting my cards and round robins out this afternoon using the postal service, as I was lead to believe you would be doing?

I would put this blip down to menopausal memory loss, but we both know that horse bolted long ago.

Your friend
Celia

SUBJECT: RE: SEASONAL FELICITATIONS!

Oh, Celia! Did I not mention? I decided to forgo the dreaded postal service this year and send out my festive felicitations by socially, economically, and environmentally friendly email. Of course, those without the technology will not be forgotten and will be mailed with a 2nd class stamp post haste—although with the strikes I am unable to guarantee any 'haste' on the part of the postal service. I thought you, of all people, who carries the latest in 'brightphone' technology in her handbag, would highly approve of my technologically designed festive felicitation this year.

I look forward to receiving your effort in due course, although, with the backlog of mail at the sorting offices, I doubt it will be for some considerable time yet.

Your friend,
Margaret

TUESDAY 1ST DECEMBER
SUBJECT: RE: SEASONAL FELICITATIONS!

Dear Margaret

It is a 'smartphone,' not a 'bright phone'. I do believe I have corrected you on this more than once now, and I do rather find that keeping up with the new technology keeps my brain active and sharp. Maybe you could hint to Arthur that a smartphone would go down well wrapped under the tree this Christmas? I think your model of mobile is considered vintage, by today's standards. With a smartphone we could send each other photographs and enjoy Scrabble tournaments and all sorts!

Yours,
Celia

PS—You could also join my Facebook group where I have actually already posted my festive greetings along with a number of photo albums. I've had an awful lot of likes and everyone is making very lovely comments. You're missing out Margaret, email is so noughties—it's all social media and apps these days, and you'd never keep up if you had to log-on via the desktop every day.

WEDNESDAY 2ND DECEMBER
SUBJECT: CHRISTMAS PLANS
Dear James

I do hope this email finds you well. It feels like some considerable time since we actually spoke to each other properly, and I do think email is not the best source of communication between a brother and sister when matters of the heart are to be discussed. But, as you fail to reply to my voicemail messages and requests to phone me at your earliest convenience, I am forced, yet again, to attempt communication with you via email.

As we are both well aware, Briony, for matters only known to herself, appears to be doing her best to sabotage what I hoped would be a wonderful last family Christmas gathering for our parents. I shall tell you now, James, that having spent the past month or so attempting to accept your wife's stubborn and precious ways, I have decided I am not prepared to forgo what could well be our parents last opportunity to have their beloved children and grandchildren around them during what is, after all, supposedly, the 'season of goodwill.' I do appreciate that Briony can be a very difficult woman, and you find it easier to sit back and let her walk all over you rather then stand up for yourself and your family, but on this occasion, I simply must insist you take the initiative and take matters into your own hands.

I have, as always, done my best to compromise on the situation, and therefore I have reviewed my plans to best accommodate your wife's concerns. George, the children and I will drive to Dorset on Christmas Eve and stay the night with mum and dad. We will breakfast there and open presents before driving over to you with our gifts for a second round of present opening. I will bring a turkey crown, Christmas pudding and mum's Christmas cake. If Briony could see her way to providing the potatoes and vegetables that would be greatly appreciated. She could even use those pre prepared packs I have seen in supermarkets to save time and stress. I, myself, do not find preparing vegetables stressful, but, it takes all sorts, I suppose, and I think Briony is one of those 'sorts'. We will leave by early evening to return to mum and dad's for another night, before departing back to Devon on Boxing Day. Obviously, I have had to let down Jemima and Ivan who were so looking forward to joining us all in Dorset for a family Christmas.

If you could see your way to replying and letting me know these plans suit you, I would be most grateful.

Best Regards
Sarah

WEDNESDAY 2ND DECEMBER
SUBJECT: FWD: CHRISTMAS PLANS

Some light entertainment for you whilst you're stuck in snowy 'sub-tropical' Cornwall.

James x

WEDNESDAY 2ND DECEMBER
SUBJECT: RE: FWD: CHRISTMAS PLANS

Who the hell are Jemima and Ivan and why did they want to spend a 'family' Christmas with us anyway?! I've never heard of them, have you?

She's not going to give up, is she? Why does she go on about it being a last chance? Are your parents ill? Well, of course, Margaret's definitely been acting rather odd lately, but neither appears to be on death's door, are they? Leave it and let me reply tonight. I hate it when she emails you surreptitiously making insinuations about me. Does she really think you are not going to show me the email? Anyway, I like winding her up. It's one of the few pleasures I have left in life.

Actually, I just got your email while I stopped off at the services. Didn't bother calling you before I attempted an escape from spa hell as wasn't sure how far I'd manage to get, but as luck would have it, once I'd skated (literally) along the empty country lanes which were just slippery with compacted snow from the tractors, but perfectly passable, the main road has been fine—so far. Should be home for dinner, so I'll pick the boys up from Lucy's.

See you soon! Have you missed me?

PS—Your father's email has been hacked again. Got loads of emails from him telling me all about his latest money making scheme—selling salt to the Congo . . . !? It was a relief we appear to have moved on from penile dysfunction, and the benefits of fruit-flavoured vaginal lubricant.

WEDNESDAY 2ND DECEMBER
SUBJECT: RE: FWD: CHRISTMAS PLANS
Of course I've missed you. The boys are sick of pasta, I'm sick of pizza, and the dishwasher needs emptying.

James

THURSDAY 3RD DECEMBER
SUBJECT: RE: FWD: CHRISTMAS PLANS
Dear Sarah

Firstly, I would like to say that my husband and I do no appreciate snide comments directed at me in emails. I am neither 'stubborn'. nor 'difficult'. for failing to drop everything in order to fit in with your own plans for Christmas. This may come as a huge shock to you, Sarah, but the world does not revolve around you, and other people do have lives of their own and manage to function perfectly well without the need for you arrange social engagements for them.

Secondly, James and I do not have a clue who 'Jemima

338

and Ivan' are, or why they were so keen to spend a 'family' Christmas with us—and even less so as to why we would want to cater for and give up our bed for them (as was apparently suggested to Margaret by yourself due to Ivan needing an en-suite bathroom?!) on Christmas night.

Lastly, (for now at least, as hard as it is for you to believe, I too have a very full and busy life and do not have time for this nonsense) I emphasise to you that in our household, Christmas is a relaxed affair and therefore my children will not be taking part in organised photo shoots for the purpose of 'thank you' cards. In fact, James and I like to celebrate the birth of baby Jesus by staying in our pyjamas all day, but on this occasion we have agreed to compromise and will be appropriately attired by lunchtime—minus shoes of course as the polished wood floors would suffer.

I hope this is all to your satisfaction, and that we can all have a pleasant first and last family Christmas together. With the emphasis on 'last.'

Briony

P.S. It was lovely to get your mother's annual 'Round Robin' in email form this year, detailing the past year with such creative licence. I thought the attached scanned pics of your Village Homes magazine shoot was an interesting touch. She is obviously very proud of your achievement and no doubt her numerous friends on the email Christmas card list will be thrilled to be able to view all those glorious photos of your house from the comfort of their computer screens. They're even able to zoom in on objects to get a better look at all your interesting 'nick-nacks'. and I am sure your unique fertility symbol loo roll holder will arouse great interest.

Thursday 3rd December

WHATSAPP GROUP MESSAGE

BRIONY: Can any of you make coffee/lunch tomorrow and a spot of the dreaded Christmas shopping.

KARA: Yep, I was going to get some last min stocking fillers anyway. Meet at mine after school run.

BRIONY: Great. Oh, and does anyone have anything vaguely resembling a squirrel costume that I can borrow?

GAYLE: I'm in. Hate shopping alone. I have a brown fake fur shrug and woolly grey tights if that's any help?

LUCY: Abbie and I are up for that. We've still got to get Tom something. We'll meet you later though—say 11ish— as have a counselling session first thing. Will text when we get to town to see where you are. Got a pink tutu. Angelina Ballerina wears one. Is that any help?

BRIONY: Angelina Ballerina is a mouse, not a squirrel, Lucy. Besides it's for Zac who's a squirrel in the school nativity and I don't think he'd appreciate wearing a pink tutu or a faux fur shrug.

KARA: Do they even have squirrels in Bethlehem? And anyway, even if they did it wouldn't be in a stable in December.

GAYLE: Counselling, Lucy?

340

LUCY: Couples counselling. For three of us. Just don't ask.

SATURDAY 5TH DECEMBER
SUBJECT: WEDDING PLANS
Dear (lucky-still-to-be) bridesmaids

You'll be pleased to hear the facial swelling has subsided completely now, and I am just left with slight raw patches of skin on my face and neck. My doctor has assured me she is confident it will have all healed up by Christmas and I hope she's right, or otherwise the wedding will have to be postponed. After all, I can't possibly be expected to appear in my wedding photos looking like I've had a botched facial acid peel.

I was hoping we could meet up before Christmas for the final fittings and just to go over the ceremony—a sort of dress rehearsal. Next weekend would be best or I can do Wednesday if weekend is too much of a juggle? The hairdressers are all booked for the day itself and as a special treat I've booked us all in to have nail extensions that morning as well.

Melissa x

SATURDAY 5TH DECEMBER
SUBJECT: RE: WEDDING PLANS
Sorry, Melissa. I've absolutely no time for trips to London before Christmas—going to have to wing it on the day. Pretty sure Kate and I can follow you down the aisle with-

out a practice run and I'm sure the dresses will fit fine, so
don't worry—after all, everyone will be looking at you, not
us!

Glad your face is better. Take it you won't be having
a facial before the wedding now? Don't worry about my
nails, I really don't want extensions.

How are your mum and dad? Did your mother decide
on an outfit yet? If not, she can borrow the sparkly number I'm wearing for Christmas drinks at the ménage à trois
tonight.

SUNDAY 6TH DECEMBER
SUBJECT: RE: WEDDING PLANS
Bri, you have to have the nails! We need them to look nice
for the photos. Can you really not pop up to London for a
day at least? What if the dress doesn't fit and needs alter-
ing? And it's more than just following me down the aisle.
You've never been a bridesmaid before, so you have no idea
of exactly what is required of you.

Mum is psychotic and dad is bearing the brunt of it. She
got some outfit from a local boutique in the end. Owner
told her it was from a very limited edition French collection so she's taken to telling everyone it was designed especially for her; a one off.

What's all this ménage a trois business? Are you going
to an orgy tonight? Growing pampas grass in the garden
now are we?

SUNDAY 6TH DECEMBER
SUBJECT: RE: WEDDING PLANS
No orgy—drinks at Tom, Lucy and Abbie's tonight. I'm far too self-conscious to participate in an orgy! I'd be more worried about who was getting a view of my arse in an unflattering position than actually enjoying any of it.

Melissa, no-one is going to notice my nails unless you've invited some nail fetishist to the wedding?

And I'll have you know I have been a bridesmaid before. My Aunt's wedding when I was three. I peed myself in the aisle and her train dragged through it on the way out of the church, so she stank of wee for the reception. I'm better at holding my bladder these days. Just . . .

MONDAY 7TH DECEMBER 2.17PM
WHATSAPP MESSAGE
GAYLE: Bri, can you pick the kids up for me and keep them at yours? In A&E after dog scooter accident.

BRIONY: Of course. What happened?! Are you badly hurt?

GAYLE: No. Just cuts and bruises luckily. Neighbours are away and I promised to walk their hound. Cleverly decided to tie him to the kid's scooter as feeling lazy and thought I could scoot down the hill with him running alongside. Bloody fox ran across road—middle of day ffs!—hound sees fox and natural instinct kicks in so I'm flying down the hill on the scooter at what feels like 50mph as hound attempts to leap over low garden wall taking scooter with it. Dog fine. Scooter not so.

BRIONY: Ouch! But, surely, not worth waiting hours in A&E for cuts and bruises though?

GAYLE: No! Not here for me. When hound leapt over wall, flying scooter took man in his garden out, smashing against his shin and knocking him into wheelbarrow backwards. Nasty. Felt I had to take him to A&E as obviously he couldn't drive himself, might have concussion. Just hope I don't get sued . . .

TUESDAY 8TH DECEMBER
SUBJECT: RE: CHRISTMAS PLANS
Dear Briony

Thank you so much for your . . . direct reply. It appears you have taken offence where none was meant and may even have jumped to conclusions, which have in turn, caused your somewhat 'prickly' reply. I do hope you will be altogether more welcoming when we arrive on Christmas Day, as let us not forget, it is the season of goodwill—whether you are a Christian or not. After all, Briony, no one is forcing you to celebrate the birth of Christ—you are choosing to do so—and therefore please respect our beliefs for the duration and no more digs at little baby Jesus.

Festive Regards
Sarah

P.S. How can you have forgotten Ivan and Jemima? You met at my wedding and by all accounts you got on very well with them, so I thought you might actually enjoy seeing them again. I apologise for trying to bring joy and happiness to your home this Christmastide. I know they were very much looking forward to seeing you and James again.

WEDNESDAY 9TH DECEMBER

SUBJECT: RE: CHRISTMAS PLANS

Dear Sarah

How silly of me. Of course I remember Ivan and Jemima from your wedding 17 YEARS AGO when I was half-cut on vodka for most of the day in a vain attempt to numb the pain of having to sit around for seven hours listening to sickeningly twee self-penned vows, sycophantic speeches dotted with 'jokes' which appeared to have come from Christmas crackers circa 1977, and a meal that dragged on for so long, I actually lost weight between courses. How could I ever forget 'eyeful' Ivan—as we nicknamed him for leeringly attempting to look down my dress every time I moved. In fact, I sincerely doubt that if you asked him what colour hair I had, he would have a clue, yet, could accurately describe my tits in astoundingly fine detail.

Heathen Regards
Briony

P.S. We don't celebrate the birth of baby Jesus in this household. Christmas is a time to rejoice in the blessing that is the nine months interest free credit card. Hallelujah!

SUBJECT: RE: CHRISTMAS PLANS

Briony. At least we HAD vows and speeches and a seven course reception. At least we shared our day with our friends and families—unlike some people who selfishly chose to elope to Thailand and announce their nuptials on the back of a postcard from Koh Samui. My mother will go to her grave heavy of heart knowing she missed out on her only son's most special day.

Sarah

SUBJECT: RE: CHRISTMAS PLANS

Au contraire, Sarah! I think you will find your mother was actually rather relieved she didn't have to pay out for another set of fine china dinnerware, sterling silver canteen or other ostentatious wedding presents that are put away in a cupboard and only dusted off once a year for 'special' events.

Talking of once a year special events, I really can't ignore it any more. Just why DID you display your Randy Rabbit vibrator in the bathroom for the Village Homes photo shoot? And more importantly, would you recommend that, or is the Silver Stallion as a more, err . . . satisfying buy?

Much love
Briony x

WHATSAPP MESSAGE

GAYLE: What time tomorrow? Is Abbie coming as well? Did Lucy confide any more about the counselling?

BRIONY: Not sure Abbie is coming now. Lucy's been very guarded over the counselling thing. She obviously isn't ready to talk about it with any of us yet. No idea where this is all going to go—I mean had you told me last Christmas one of my best friends would start a lesbian affair with her dog's aromatherapist and then moved her girlfriend into the marital home . . . well . . .

GAYLE: Hmm . . . What's going on with your sis-in-law? Did you put them off Christmas at yours?

BRIONY: No. More's the pity. She left a voicemail message on James' mobile sobbing that I've gone too far this time. I really don't know what all the fuss is about as I simply enquired as to why she had a Randy Rabbit on show for the photo shoot? It's what everybody has been wondering, after all. Some people are just sooooo touchy 😕

GAYLE: Lol! Aren't they just! Hahaha. What vibe did you get from drinks last Sat? Maybe it was me just being over sensitive to the situation, but it wasn't the most comfortable of evenings for me.

BRIONY: Oh God, I agree! I was knocking back the mojitos for that very reason—as was Lucy. I guess it's just not a very comfortable situation when one of your hosts gets so plastered she starts lap dancing for her lover in front of her guests and husband. Kara didn't know where to look, being sat right next to Abbie in deep conversation about acupuncture for pets when suddenly Lucy starts gyrating and grinding and straddling Abbie!

GAYLE: Fuck, yeah, and by the looks Abbie was giving Tom, she seemed more concerned for his feelings than Lucy was.

BRIONY: Extraordinary!

GAYLE: Ordinarily extraordinary, but for our lives these days it's becoming the norm. Anyway, see you tomorrow. Is Kara still gluten free?

BRIONY: No. I caught her licking a croissant last week and she admitted it wasn't the first time.

FRIDAY 11TH DECEMBER
WHATSAPP MESSAGE

KATE: Well, thank you very much, Briony! Too busy to 'pop' up to London are you? Well, that's lumbered me with having no choice but to go to the dress rehearsal myself, as apparently, I have to be your stand in for the alterations. I did point out I am a more buxom babe than your waif-like self, but allowances will be made, says wedding guru extraordinaire, Monique (who, I noticed appears to have been a little lax with the moustache waxing of late and is sporting the start of what could be a very impressive lip tickler.) I'm going to miss a great party (the sex toy company Xmas bash) and all to spend hours in that freaky wedding emporium of Monique's. We're not even allowed drinks or nibbles as we have to be clear headed and no finger marks on the gowns—huh!

BRIONY: Count yourself lucky. I'm currently at lunch with Lucy, who, although having moved her girlfriend into the house she shares with her husband, is now in a jealous, suspicious rage that he is having an affair, as she noticed hand prints on the French doors one sunny morning?!?

KATE: How do hand prints denote a marital affair? And anyway, I'm not sure she is allowed to be jealous if she had already moved her lover in.

BRIONY: One set of handprints, large and high up + one smaller pair lower down + slight unidentified smearing somewhere in the middle = husband banging mistress from behind and up against the French doors. Logical? No! We've spent an hour trying to convince her of other more plausible explanations to no avail, and now I would like to actually order Death By Chocolate before I expire of frustration and am late picking the boys up again.

MONDAY 14TH DECEMBER
WHATSAPP MESSAGE

BRIONY: Are we all going to the school nativity on Wed?

GAYLE: Of course! Why would I want to miss out on watching my daughter, the 'lead' Christmas tree, in a cold, overcrowded church on a freezing, dark Wednesday evening when I could be sat at home watching TV and drinking mulled wine by the open fire?

KARA: Who's taking a hip flask?

LUCY: Does anyone have a spare ticket? We were only

allocated two and obviously Tom wants to come as well.

GAYLE: They were strict on tickets this year as too many people brought grandparents, aunts and third cousins twice removed, which caused the issue with overcrowding. Apparently, it's a fire hazard to have the aisle blocked up with people, so this year they are filming it for those who don't get a ticket. However, due to paedo hysteria, only those with an up to date CRB check can purchase copies of the DVD.

BRIONY: Umm, I think Tom should have the ticket, Lucy!

LUCY: Why? Christ we live in such a fucked up, bigoted world. Is it because Abbie and I are gay and God won't approve and everyone will tut at us and give disapproving glares at being so disrespectful to God and the church and to Jesus and all because people can't accept that two people loving each other is not sinister or distasteful IT IS SIMPLY LOVE!!

BRIONY: Umm, no, Lucy . . . because Tom is their father . . . 🙁

LUCY: Oh. I see your point.

KARA: Calm down, calm down! I've got a spare ticket. Just no lap-dancing in the pews during the boring bits ;o)

TUESDAY 15TH DECEMBER
SUBJECT: SCHOOL NATIVITY
Dear Briony

I just wanted to check what time the school nativity starts tomorrow? Shall I meet you at the church or come to your lovely cottage first?

I am so glad everyone has come to a mutually convenient arrangement for Christmas Day. We are so looking forward to spending the day together this year, and I am sure much fun will be had by all! Such a shame Ivan and Jemima had to be left out—they are terribly disappointed and were so looking forward to seeing you both again.

Love
Margaret xx

SUBJECT: RE: SCHOOL NATIVITY
Hi Margaret

Sorry, I thought James had mentioned that only parents can come to the nativity from now on, as last year's overcrowding problems were a health and safety risk. The school has hired a professional to film the play though, so you can buy a DVD for a fiver I think and all proceeds go to the PTA.

Yes, it is such a shame about Ivan and Jemima isn't it? Maybe we'll invite them over for a weekend in the New Year? We'll have a lot of catching up to do after seventeen years of no contact . . .

Briony

Tuesday 15th December

SUBJECT: RE: SCHOOL NATIVITY

Dear Briony

What utter nonsense! God would not allow there to be a health and safety risk in his church! I suspect this is just an excuse for that school of theirs to make money from DVD sales. This would never happen at Barnaby and Ella's school. I can assure you, all are welcome to their school nativity.

What sort of films has this 'professional' made in the past? How do we know he won't make copies and distribute them to unsavoury types across the world? I was just reading in the newspaper about this being virtually endemic nowadays. Really, it is such a worry, Briony. Do you think if you went back to work the boys might benefit from a private education?

Love Margaret

Tuesday 15th December

SUBJECT: RE: SCHOOL NATIVITY

Of course everyone is welcome at Barnaby and Ella's school nativity, Margaret—they built their own 'church' using parental contributions just for these events. I didn't actually know you went to Barnaby and Ella's nativity? Did Arthur go too? Was Barnaby given a part this year? I know Sarah was frightfully vocal about his lack of leading role last year, although, to be fair, a shepherd is a main character, and the poor angel he slam dunked off the stage the year before did have to spend Christmas day in hospital recovering from her injuries. He's a bit of a loose cannon when it comes to school productions isn't he?

For your information, the videographer is a parent who has his own company specialising in filming weddings and special events so I'm pretty confident the play won't be being offered under cover of darkness to any 'unsavoury types'. Please stop reading the Daily Mail, Margaret.

I'll order you a copy of the DVD then, shall I?

TUESDAY 15TH DECEMBER
SUBJECT: RE: SCHOOL NATIVITY
Dear Briony

Well, no. We've never actually been to one of Barnaby and Ella's nativities. It's a long way to go for one night. But we would be more than welcome if we ever did want to go. And the school provides festive refreshments absolutely free of charge. Not like the boys' state school who were asking for fifty pence for a hot chocolate and biscuit when I went to that coffee morning they hosted!

Love,
Margaret

SUBJECT: RE: SCHOOL NATIVITY

Margaret, that was a charity coffee morning to raise funds for the international disaster relief fund. The tea and biscuits you consumed probably paid for a whole family to eat for a month. And anyway, I'm not sure one can claim refreshments are 'free' when you are paying thirty thousand pounds a year for their combined education.

I'll be sure to get you a DVD. We could all watch it on Christmas Day. I know Sarah will thoroughly enjoy that.

SUBJECT: HOLA!

Dear Margaret

I do hope this email finds you well and enjoying the festive preparations.

John and I decided to go away for Christmas this year since the children didn't take our news of becoming Jehovah Witnesses terribly well, and insisted upon descending upon us for a family Christmas, regardless of our new found beliefs. You'd think at their age they might have had enough of Christmas with their parents, but as long as we are there to dump the children on so as they can go off to the pub and leave the cooking all to me, they will carry on coming. I had half a mind just to not get anything in, in the hope they'd all have to slope off and try and find a corner shop open to buy provisions for the day. However, John saw a terribly good deal on the internet and we booked it there and then!

We will be flying out on the 23rd and back on the 30th—just in time to drive down to you and Arthur for the New Year's Eve party. Now, I know this means I have left very little time to help you prepare for the gathering, but as you know, too many cooks do tend to burn the vol-au-vents, so I shall leave the majority of the preparations to you. After all, it will give you something to do between Christmas and then—which can drag rather if you don't have family around. Well, the opposite in my case, but you actually enjoy your grandchildren, don't you, Margaret? I do sometimes think I am cursed with such gifted grandchildren. How wonderful it would be to have less intellectually exhausting ones and enjoy their innocent childlike ways. Count your blessings, Margaret!

I will phone you before we leave, to go through the party arrangements.

Yours
Celia

Friday 18th December
SUBJECT: RE: HOLA?
Oh Celia! What a lot of nonsense. You won't get a turkey dinner with all the trimmings in Spain! What will you do? Do you think somewhere might do you a turkey paella with stuffing balls on the side? I'd take my own Paxo if I

were you—better to be safe than sorry.

Bests
Margaret

PS. I think you are confusing 'gifted' with 'precocious,' Celia.

TEXT MESSAGE SENT SATURDAY 19TH DECEMBER 05.11AM
James darling, Briony will be making proper gravy won't she? Mum x

TEXT MESSAGE SENT SATURDAY 19TH DECEMBER 06.33AM
James? Did you get my message? I don't want to phone in case you're not up yet, but I do need to know. Mum x

TEXT MESSAGE SENT SATURDAY 19TH DECEMBER 06.57AM
James?

TEXT MESSAGE SENT SATURDAY 19TH DECEMBER 07.23AM
Are you getting my messages James? I need to know about the gravy. I can't be doing with Briony's fish gravy. It really won't go with the turkey.

TEXT MESSAGE SENT SATURDAY 19TH DECEMBER 07.41AM
Okay I'm going to have to phone you now, James. I hope you're up.

WHATSAPP MESSAGE

GAYLE: My two have just gone fucking feral as the shopping was delivered by a driver in elf costume with sidekick Christmas fairy—seriously, what are the supermarkets trying to do to us?! And they subbed 'Chef's Best' mince pies for mince pie flavoured boiled sweets?!? Wtf?!?

BRIONY: Sadists.

KARA: I call it Hellmas

BRIONY: I used an app to create a Christmas card with a photo of my bum in tight jeans with the greeting, 'Happy ChristmArse!' Was tempted to send it to Sarah.

GAYLE: Is that the same app you used last year to create the one of you in your knickers with 'Happy ChristMuff' emblazoned across your snatch?

BRIONY: Yes, Gayle, it is.

GAYLE: The one you emailed to James who 'accidentally' fwd it to his colleagues?

BRIONY: Yes, Gayle, it is. And thank you for reminding me about that little incident.

LUCY: Why isn't Santa Trak working? Where the bloody hell is Santa? Has the website changed??

KARA: Maybe he forgot to switch on his GPS, Lucy . . .

BRIONY: Actually, mine is working. He's in Eastern Russia, if that helps?

LUCY: BUT WHY ISNT MY SANTA TRAK WORKING?!?!

LUCY: Oh, it's okay. Working now . . . as you were . . .

BRIONY: Gayle, is reindeer food poisonous to hedgehogs . . . ?

GAYLE: Depends what's in the reindeer food . . . ?

BRIONY: I don't know. I bought it from a Big Issue seller wearing a red carrier bag in lieu of a Santa hat—thought he showed initiative. It's lumpy and glittery. And it smells . . . odd.

GAYLE: Hedgehogs are hibernating, Briony.

KARA: WHY WONT THEY JUST GO TO SLEEEEEEEEEP?!?!?!?!? I am tired and I want to go to sleep! Next year, Santa is depositing stockings downstairs.

LUCY: OMG I feel your pain. Wish I'd never polished off the rest of the Baileys after the prosecco. At least Tom used to stay up to do the stockings with me. He'll be too plastered by the time he gets in from the pub. Bastard.

BRIONY: Christ, I haven't been to the pub on Christmas Eve since I was . . . well, since before the boys. Who did he go with? The pub will just be full of childless *young* people, surely?!

LUCY: He went with Abbie

BRIONY: Oh . . . *raises eyebrow in concerned yet perturbed manner*

LUCY: Hence why she is now in bed asleep and stinking of whiskey and why I've been drinking prosecco and Baileys on my lonesome. I can't bear to think about the state Tom will be in when he eventually gets back—it's like having two teenagers at home with me as well as the kids 😕

FRIDAY 25TH DECEMBER 3.15PM

BRIONY: They've brought a Tupperware container of bloody gravy! They ACTUALLY DID THAT! And that's not all. Oh no! Supermarket value quiches, pork pies, scotch eggs and vol-au-vents, for later 'in case there's not enough Christmas lunch to go round'. I'm pouring cheeky shots of rum into the red wine.

LUCY: Oh, you've got is easy! Tom's mother brought her own homemade leek and potato soup—you know, the one that has the consistency of, and tastes like wallpaper paste. Hung over Abbie vommed all over Algey, and Phoebe informed Grandma it was because, 'Abbie is a rug muncher so she probably has a hairball like Puddy once had'.

BRIONY: Haha! OMG! Comedy gold. On pre-dinner walk in woods now. James and I hiding and drinking sherry from hip flask after marching along like soldiers on speed in vain bid to get away from Sarah's tales of Ella being the star of the nativity and the best Mary the school has *ever* seen. I've already proudly recited our school nativity taking particular pleasure in the bit where Sam used his shepherd's staff to start sword fighting with another shepherd and almost impaled Joseph in the process.

LUCY: Pheebs now just asked Grandma if she likes to drink from a furry cup, like Abbie. Going to KILL Tom. It's him who they've heard all this from.

BRIONY: Hiding in bathroom. Quite pissed. Fricking Denley crones filled oven with turkey and cheap meat crap, no room for seabass which neither of them bothered to tell me had been removed from the oven to make way for the supper quiches. The 'supper quiches'?!?!? It's 5.30 and we've not had pudding yet. What time are they bloody going to leave if they plan on having cold quiche for supper?! Margaret tried to use opportunity to force feed scotch eggs to the boys insisting they were 'virtually vegetarian anyway'. Much frostiness between Sarah and George—not sure what's up there. Margaret keeps going into back garden and peering over towards Cosmo's—very odd. Claims she thought she heard a noise and might be burglars. She's done this about five times now. I swear the woman's going senile or is having paranoid delusions.

BRIONY: And now bloody Sarah's brought up the porn again . . .

KARA: Porn??? Again?!?!?

BRIONY: Barnaby and Ella came across a discarded copy of some 'Lads' Mag' in the woods—you know, soap stars in bikinis with orange tans and Scouse brows. That's hardened porn to a God-fearing Christian like Sarah and the children are going to need counselling, apparently. Cue James, drunk on single malt and high on the fumes of designer aftershave, who asked, 'But Sarah, what about the massive dildo you had proudly photographed in your bathroom for that magazine—that's on display in all its glossy glory on coffee tables around the country for innocent children to see . . . ' You could have cut the atmosphere with an ice pick . . .

KARA: I love drunk James.

GAYLE: Hope everyone had a great day. I've been up to my elbows in dog intestines and tampons—makes a change from tinsel I suppose. You'd think with all the Christmas food around a dog would prefer that to a box of tampons, but not so Mrs Bingham's hound.

BRIONY: Finally been left in peace by the out-laws who packed up cold quiches and left-over pork pies and drove off into the night. Never have I been so glad of whiskey and dildos.

SATURDAY 26TH DECEMBER
SUBJECT: FELIZ NAVIDAD!
Dear Margaret

I do hope today finds you well, and relaxing after the glut of yesterday's celebrations. John and I enjoyed a peaceful family-free day in a local beachfront tavern. I'm afraid to say we did rather over indulge, but as it was seafood platters and sangria, it felt so much healthier than the stodge of the traditional British cuisine.

If you do happen to hear from the children, please don't let on that I've been in touch. I did tell them I would have no signal in Spain. But how wonderful for us to be able to share some of our sunny, hot and bright Yuletide celebrations with you in damp Britain. I do hope my email warms your heart and toes, during what the English news channel are telling us, is one of the coldest and wettest Christmases for 25 years! Hopefully it will have passed by the time John and I return. One acclimatises to warmer weather so quickly and I'm not sure we could re-adjust to the bitter winter you appear to be having over there. I do hope the adverse conditions do not affect our party food and drink, although I am sure your local supermarket will be open so you and Arthur can always pop there for everything if needs be. You do have winter tyres on the car this year, don't you, Margaret?

Muchos Amorous, Celia x

Tuesday 29th December
SUBJECT: RE: FELIZ NAVIDAD!
Dear Celia

I apologise for the delay in replying to your Spanish email, but, as you know, not having a phone such as yours renders me at the mercy of a bog standard computer, to reply to correspondence.

I'm afraid the big day itself was a bit of an anti-climax for Arthur and myself. Sarah and George had a little tiff over something or other, so the atmosphere was not as festive as it could have been. When we arrived at James and Briony's, I have a sneaking suspicion Briony had already indulged in an alcoholic beverage or two. Sarah and I thought it best to help out and so took it upon ourselves to fill the oven (luckily, we had the foresight to bring a few choice bits and pieces including my own gravy—and that saved the day believe you and me, Celia—how poor James has survived on a diet lacking meat for so long is beyond me, it's a divorceable offence, I'm sure! Unfortunately, after our traditional Christmas pre-dinner walk, in a countryside littered with pornography which apparently only made Briony and James snigger (lewd magazines, Celia, the sort that are probably illegal in many countries) Briony, in her even 'merrier' state forgot to put the fish in the oven (fish, Celia! For Christmas! I ask you, did the infant baby Jesus eat fish with a tomato salsa to celebrate his birthday?! I think not!) In a desperate bid to give those poor malnourished boys nutrition, I attempted to remove the egg part from the scotch eggs we had brought, and pick out the bacon from the quiche Lorraine. But of course, that didn't go down too well with her ladyship, and, do you know, we were asked to remove our footwear, Celia? She didn't want damp shoes and boots on her wooden and stone floors. Honestly, if there were ever a floor suitable for damp boots it's a stone floor!

I have to say that girl is very ungrateful. I sensed a distinct underwhelming atmosphere when she opened up my gift to her—a lovely cruet set with Mary as salt and Joseph as pepper. I'm not sure I will give her the matching baby Jesus in his manger sugar bowl for her birthday now. It was so lovely as well, his halo is the lid; so clever.

Regarding the weather, I think you will find it's more our friends in the north who are suffering with the cold, but they are used to it, up there. I don't have any snow tyres and if the delivery man cannot get to us then I would imagine neither can our guests, in which case we would have to cancel the gathering. So fingers crossed it doesn't come to that—after all, we have all that wine from our little jaunt to France, and at the prices we paid, I'm not convinced it's of the quality that ages well, Celia. Though we need not mention that to anyone . . .

Enjoy the rest of your sunny break.

Fondests
Margaret.

TUES 29TH DEC
WHATSAPP MESSAGE

BRIONY: Great post Christmas soirée last night, Gayle, but why did you get me so drunk the night before we had to drive to Yorkshire?! Christ, Gayle, I'm dying. James in foul mood as he's had to stop three times already and one of those was on the hard shoulder of the motorway where I had to vom by the carcass of a road-kill badger.

GAYLE: Eugh tell me about it. I've called in sick. I think it was the drama that made everyone drink more. Awkward wasn't the word for it. Count yourself lucky you are away for a few days and don't have to be around the vitriolic wreck that is Lucy now she's discovered it was Tom and Abbie's handprints on the French doors.

BRIONY: Yeah. Now the uncomfortable looks during the lap dance all make sense. Kind off. Blardy hell. But who in their right mind has sex standing up against French doors?! I still don't get it!

GAYLE: No, we know you don't get it, Briony. But I think trying to get Tom and Abbie to demonstrate the position as the drama was unfolding didn't really help matters . . .

BRIONY: Oh. Did I? I don't remember that!

GAYLE: Don't worry, everyone else does. It was just before you started twiddling Kara's nipples with your toes. . . . and I think someone probably recorded that on their phone for good measure. Have fun at the wedding. Maybe lay off the mojitos, eh? 😉

WED 30TH DEC
WHATSAPP MESSAGE

MELISSA: Where are you?!? You're meant to be here! My mother is driving me mad! She keeps staring at anyone from Dan's family or friends who try to speak to her with a blank expression and asking for a translator. You'd think she's never watched an episode of Emmerdale in her life.

BRIONY: I'm right here, three tables away, eating my poached egg and staring incredulously at the table with the woman who loudly bemoans the need for an interpreter every time the waitress speaks to her. Why is she wearing that hat, Melissa. And please do not draw attention to me. I need coffee and lots of it before I face your mother today.

MELISSA: MEET ME OUTSIDE NOW! And if you value your sanity, do not let my mother see you. And where is Kate?

WHATSAPP MESSAGE 10.31AM

BRIONY: Kate. Why are you not answering your phone?

Melissa's mother is upsetting the locals and her father is numbing the pain with a hip flask permanently glued to his lips. The hotel won't tell me what room you are in due to 'data protection'!!! What time did you arrive last night anyway? I was feeling the effects of Gayle's post-Christmas drinks soirée and had to retire early.

BRIONY: KATE! Answer your bloody phone! I can see you've read this message!

KATE: Sorry, Briony, was a little busy. Will meet you in the lounge in half an hour. Can't chat now.

WHATSAPP MESSAGE 11.03AM

BRIONY: Kara, how's Luce? Is she very cut up? Crying lots? Is she still staying at yours? Are the kids with Tom? Where's Abbie gone? What a mess, eh?

KARA: Yes, Lucy's still with me. I'm not sure 'cut up' is quite how to describe her. The devil incarnate would be a better description. No tears. Just lots of saliva as she hisses and spits profanities regarding Abbie's betrayal. The twins have learnt lots of new swear words. Who says school holidays aren't educational?

BRIONY: Oh. I expect that's a good thing though. Tears never solved anything after all. Have Tom or Abbie been in touch?

KARA: No, Briony, I don't think it is a good thing. When I said 'devil incarnate'. I really did mean it. Beelzebub is living in my spare room. I had to confiscate her phone as feared the texts she was sending to them could be used in

366

evidence. I asked Gayle for a mild animal tranquilizer, just something to take the edge off, but she refused and suggested I make a doctor's apt.

BRIONY: Who is Lucy's doctor? Maybe it would be good to make an apt and get her something?

KARA: No, Briony, I wanted the animal tranquilizer for myself, not Lucy. If Satan were a woman with severe PMT, it would still be marginally more pleasant than having Lucy here at the moment. But anyway, how is Yorkshire? All frosty dales, romantic pubs and hearty grub?

BRIONY: Err, no. Only arrived yesterday and went to bed early as suffering after Gayle's soirée. Bloody Kate arrived late last night and ended up pulling some local! She turned up an hour ago in the hotel lounge all rosy cheeked and glinty eyed. No idea who the chap was but by the way she's walking he gave her quite a work out. Snigger 😉

TEXT MESSAGE SENT WEDNESDAY 30TH DECEMBER 8.35PM

Hola, Margaret! Landed safely back in Blighty! Plan to drive down to you early tomorrow. Looks like the South will escape the snow but its forecast to be quite a fall for the Midlands and Yorkshire. Do we have any guests coming from that way, Margaret? I doubt they'll make it if it's as bad as predicted.

TEXT MESSAGE SENT WEDNESDAY 30TH DECEMBER 8.50PM

Good evening, Celia. No one coming from that far afield I'm afraid, but James and the family are up there somewhere for a wedding, so that will be romantic for the bride and groom to have snow in their photos.

TEXT MESSAGE SENT WEDNESDAY 30TH DECEMBER 9.03PM

Where are you, James?! Kate's disappeared and I'm left with the Melissa's Clan. Melissa and her mother are sipping tonic water with faces like constipated pugs and her father is drowning his sorrows at the bar.

TEXT MESSAGE SENT THURSDAY 31ST DECEMBER 8.07AM

Buenos Dias, Margaret! Looks like the snow blanketed out most of Yorkshire but gave us a wide berth. Should be at yours by lunchtime, so I'll be able to help you with the baking and setting up once I've had my little nap.

TEXT MESSAGE SENT THURSDAY 31ST DECEMBER 10.39AM

Celia, please remember you are back in England now and therefore speak English.. Have you made good progress so far? Not expecting too many tonight, but so much to prepare. Will be a nice little gathering and catch up for us all. Richard is bringing a friend at late notice, so I'll make sure I put a couple of extra mini quiches in the oven later.

TEXT MESSAGE SENT THURSDAY 31ST DECEMBER 11.45AM

We've hit traffic, Margaret. Best you start preps without me—will keep you updated!

WHATSAPP MESSAGE 11.47AM

KARA: Just seen news—snow over most of Yorkshire—did you get a sprinkling? Looks like I'll be seeing the new year in with she-devil Lucy and a few glasses of red tonight. I might water down the red and hide her phone again though as fear what she'll do if she gets too drunk. Nothing worse than drunk texting to inflame a situation!

BRIONY: A sprinkling? A sprinkling? No Kara, we didn't get 'a sprinkling'. we got a bloody great shed load of the stuff dumped overnight. I was woken at 6am by a shrieking banshee aka Melissa who, having looked out her window to be met with the sight of a white landscape, started having a cardiac arrest in the knowledge it was highly unlikely we'd be able to get into the next town for our hair and nail appointments. I'm living in the hotel from The Shining and Melissa is Jack . . .

KARA: Oh, blimey (understatement, but my new year's resolution is to swear less). No fake nails and over lacquered hair for a wedding. Bet you're secretly thrilled 😉

BRIONY: Nope. Wrong, again Kara. I'm not thrilled. Primarily due to the fact we now have to do each other and as I was voted 'person least likely to be walloped by the bride', I have therefore spent all morning perfecting my hairdressing skills on her. As you will be aware, being the mother of boys, I have had no need to practise my hairstyling since I was seven and got given a Girls World plastic doll head for Christmas. Even then, I used to have to turn the whole doll's head upside down and hold it between my knees to do a ponytail. I have the dexterity of a dyspraxic boxer. Needless to say, Melissa was not impressed when asked to put her head, upside down between my knees in order for me to attempt the chignon she thought she was getting. Possibly a good thing, as the way I was feeling by then, I may have been sorely tempted to crush her freaking bridezilla head between my knees and put an end to this misery for all of us.

KARA: A night in with psychotic Lucy's not looking too bad then . . . Will all the guests be able to get there? Who was Kate's dirty shag? Did you find out?

BRIONY: Most of the guests are either staying in the hotel, live in the village, have tractors to bring them to the church or know a man who can. It's the catering that's problem number two. The caterers and waiting staff were coming from a town 25 miles away. They had to order an outside catering as the hotel is a) not known for its haute cuisine, specialising in chicken in the basket and other 70s classic 'bar snax' and b) doesn't have the staff during the winter when they are usually carrying out a refurb ready for the next season. James and Mr Cornish are attempting to negotiate something with the manager as I text . . . And no, Kate is keeping schtum on the growler prowler.

KARA: At least there is booze, Briony! What time is the ceremony?

BRIONY: The keg pipes are blocked leaving just bottled beer at a premium price and expensive wines (claims the manager who I suspect is seeing this as an opportunity to rip off we 'soft southerners'). At least Kate appears to have emerged herself in the local hospitality—to the extreme. Ceremony at 2pm. It's going to be a long day and for some reason James appears very distracted again. He was like this all Christmas. Always checking his phone. It's his ho in HK I just know it is. Kate was right. I'm going to confront him once we get this bollocks over with.

KARA: Maybe he's bored and playing Angry Birds?!

BRIONY: He's not playing Angry Birds. He gives me shifty yet distant looks after checking it. Like he wants to say something but can't. He's been like this for months remember and I've put it down to various things—work, the house, his mother's possible dementia.

KARA: I think you are getting over sensitive because it's a wedding and people always get over sensitive at weddings—especially people who have been married a long time because it reminds them of when they were young and in love and had no responsibilities. And stuff.

BRIONY: Melissa is neither young nor without responsibilities. And we never had a big wedding so nothing to reminisce on. Anyway, he's been like this on and off for months. He's holding something back from me. I can feel it. He's distracted, the sex is virtually non-existent and he's never been that bothered about Cosmo's attention towards me. I could easily have had an affair with Cosmo and James wouldn't have noticed. I still could in fact.

KARA: You can't have an affair with Cosmo just because

your husband is playing Angry Birds on his phone all the time.

BRIONY: Fuck I've got to go. Mrs Cornish is worrying the manager again and Melissa is threatening to confiscate my phone.

TEXT MESSAGE SENT THURSDAY 31ST DECEMBER 2.45PM

Traffic eased off. Can't imagine where these people are all going to on New Years' Eve? Certainly not our little gathering by the sounds of it. Did you not get any more RSVPs over Christmas, Margaret? I mentioned it to a fair few people I've recently got back in contact with and gave your address to RSVP to. You know how some people are so slack at replying and then find themselves at a loose end come the 31st and decided to come anyway. You never know. Anyway, we've stopped for lunch (John needed to relieve himself and get sustenance for the rest of the journey) so don't worry about laying on lunch when we arrive.

THURSDAY 31ST DECEMBER

WHATSAPP MESSAGE

KARA: She's pregnant!!! That's what all the excessive emotional outpouring has been about! She's bloody pregnant!

BRIONY: OMG! Lucy's pregnant?! Well, that's put the cat amongst the pigeons. Think sleeping with your husband after moving your lesbian lover into the family home is called having your cake and eating it! You need to keep her off the booze now, Kara, for the baby's sake. God, I'm so bored now. Waiting ages between courses—think they are being delivered from local take-aways as have had pizza, Indian and Chinese so far. At least the bubbly's flowing. God knows I need it. Sat here at head bloody table watching my philandering husband message his Asian babe in HK. OMG what if she's pregnant and that's why he's looking to rent a house for them?

KARA: Not Lucy! ABBIE!! Abbie is pregnant!

BRIONY: Abbie is pregnant?! How did they manage that? Was it a turkey baster job? Who's the donor?!

KARA: FFS Briony! Abbie is pregnant by TOM! No turkey baster required.

BRIONY: Blimey.

KARA: Blimey? Our friend's lesbian lover is pregnant by her lover's estranged husband and you choose now to become all chaste in the language department?

BRIONY: Fucking hellfire!!!!!!!!!!!!!!!!!!!!!

KARA: That's more like it.

BRIONY: No. Fucking hellfire, I've just found out who Kate's local shag was.

KARA: Unless it's her gay lover's estranged husband then it's not going to trump my news.

BRIONY: Dan's dad!

KARA: Blimey.

BRIONY: Going by the look on her face, she's only just realised this for herself.

KARA: ???

BRIONY: Dan's parents are divorced. Brought up by stepfather. Bio dad (Dave)—Kate's local shag—lives in Spain.

Invited to wedding but not placed at top table for obvious reasons. He just got up to do an impromptu speech from his table, Kate started blushing and looking all coy, I thought, bloody hell, why's she gone all funny next to me? Dave (dad) mentions 'the son who is never far from his thoughts even though they might be far away in miles', and Kate spat her wine out all over the lychees and brandy cream. Melissa looking very unimpressed.

TEXT MESSAGE SENT THURSDAY 31ST DECEMBER 7.47PM
Mum, don't call me as we're hosting NY supper and I have to pretend all is well, but mum, it's not all well at all. I can't quite explain at the mo but I need to get away for a few days. Can you come and look after the children for me asap. Thinking of flying to Paris to clear my head. I can bring them to stay with you if easier, but to be honest, I can fly to Paris from Exeter so bit inconvenient to have to take kids all way to Dorset. Sarah Xxx

TEXT MESSAGE SENT THURSDAY 31ST DECEMBER 8.09PM
Mum? Need reply as trying to book online whilst soufflés in oven.

TEXT MESSAGE SENT THURSDAY 31ST DECEMBER 10.37PM

Mum? What is going on?! I'm having a trauma here you know! I'm in turmoil. Called house and no reply? I've booked a flight to Paris now anyway so will speak to you tomorrow when you get here.

THURSDAY 31ST DECEMBER
WHATSAPP MESSAGE 11.01PM

KARA: Tom and Abbie are now hassling me wanting to come and speak to Lucy TOGETHER! Why am I dealing with this on my own BRIONY?!? This has to be the worst NYE ever—and believe me, I've had a few!

BRIONY: Soz Kara, but bit pished. Bog drama with Dan and best man. Speak tomorrow.

KARA: I hate you. I'm sober and baby-sitting a grown woman when I should be half-cut by now. Another NYE with bloody Jools Holland for me, and the knowledge that from midnight I'll receive a surge of not remotely amusing auto-correct fails as obligatory Happy New Year texts from friends in various states of drunkenness . . .

JANUARY

TEXT MESSAGE SENT FRIDAY 1ST JANUARY 12.01AM
Hoppy Newt Year Bobbity Bear with love always your
Magsy Bear xxx

TEXT MESSAGE SENT FRIDAY 1ST JANUARY 10.31AM
Mother? Were you on the sherry last night?

TUESDAY 5TH JANUARY
WHATSAPP MESSAGE
  BRIONY: Hey Kate, sorry we didn't get to see you before we
left on Sunday but I was loathe to knock on your door with
the noises that were coming from inside . . . I take it Dan's dad
had his flight back to Spain delayed due to the weather . . . ?
  KATE: Please stop referring to him as Dan's dad.
  BRIONY: Sorry. Ageing lothario 😃
  KATE: He's not that old, Briony. Anyway, have you heard
anything from Melissa? Is she still mad as hell with me?
  BRIONY: Well, it was quite a unique situation to find one-

self in, wasn't it? Watching your best mate and bridesmaid 'getting off' with your new husband's father on the dance floor in front of all his family, and yes, I'm pretty sure his sister did mean all those things she said about you over the mic to the wedding party when she announced the buffet supper was ready. But you really didn't need to take a bow as everyone turned to look at you.

KATE: I was very, very drunk, Briony.

BRIONY: Oh yes, but you can't blame the antihistamines for your over-friendly vagina this time, can you, Kate?

KATE: I can for the sake of my reputation.

BRIONY: However, I do think events of the early hours have somewhat overtaken your faux pas by some considerable length, so at the risk of sounding heartless as to your concerns regarding your reputation being sullied by Dan's sister's outburst, I do think all that will now be yesterday's news since Dan was caught getting a blow job off his best man.

KATE: Apparently they've been close since childhood.

BRIONY: Not that close since childhood I hope!

KATE: And we didn't even need the honey trap or hitman! But poor Melissa.

BRIONY: Melissa has gone on honeymoon with laser-tube-tied Issy, which in my opinion could tip her over the edge. Mrs Cornish is busy sorting out an annulment on Melissa's behalf and suing for damages(?!). I swear she is secretly thrilled at the attention this has brought her as her own friends gather around to support the poor mother-of-the-bride.

KATE: I can't believe we had to endure all those months of bridezilla only for it to end like this. And the lost weekend at the spa from hell.

BRIONY: Enough of your woes—I've got enough of my own. It would appear that James' sister has left her husband, so Margaret is currently in Devon looking after her kids again.

KATE: Really?!? What's dirty George been up to then?

BRIONY: Oh, no, George is not the one at fault! Sarah, the paragon of the perfect wife, mother, and daughter, has been shagging the Grayson School caretaker—SNORT!

KATE: Sarah?!? No way. She's the most frigid female you could ever meet.

BRIONY: I know. Always struck me as a 'pull your nightie up when the lights go out and get it over with quickly' kinda gal.

KATE: But the caretaker?

BRIONY: Yep. So now we now know why Sarah was so 'deeply' involved with all the school events and the true reason the village school kids were permitted use of the Grayson School sports field. The caretaker's kids go to the village school so Sarah used her position as school governor to sway the board on that one. George told James he suspected something was amiss when he saw the Randy Rabbit vibrator in glorious technicolour in the glossy pages of Village Homes Magazine. He had bought a few marital aids in the hope of warming up the apparently frigid Sarah, but she had responded with utter disgust that he would think she would lower herself to use such ungodly and uncouth devices. Therefore, assuming that Sarah had thrown out the offending items, it came as quite a surprise to see the gold vibrator standing shiny and proud, glinting in the sunlight for all to see in 'Village Homes.' Initially he thought she was erm, 'warming herself up' (an image I will now need a lobotomy to erase from my mind) but then rumours started of Cliff the caretaker indulging in a bit of extra marital with one of the mum's in the sports equipment shed and the Head put in CCTV (can't have those sorts of shenanigans going on in a private school as they'd have Daily Fail reporters sniffing around in no time). Imagine Sarah's surprise when she got a call from the Head just after Christmas suggesting that under the circumstances she resign from her role as governor. Cliff the caretaker's wife is pally with the head of admin at the school so got to hear of her husband's misdemeanour whereby she confronted Sarah at the house, with George present, the day before New Year's Eve. Oh, how I would have LOVED to have seen that!

KATE: OMFG! Absolute gold.

BRIONY: So, Margaret is in Devon as Sarah has hot-footed it to Paris to escape the village glare. Of course, that probably suits Margaret as the clear up operation on hers and Arthur's house is still in full swing.

KATE: Clear up? Had too many sherries and vol-au-vents on NYE did they?

BRIONY: Oh, did I not mention the house got gate-crashed by hundreds of drunken teens on NYE after her friend Celia put the party details on Facebook as an 'open event'?

KATE: Jaysus! Hahahaha!

BRIONY: I think they had intended it to be a reunion of sorts for a few old friends Celia had recently got in contact with again through FB. On the plus side, the police and neighbours are not pressing charges for the damage as long as Margaret and Arthur pay for and sort out the damage to residents' properties themselves. You know, James got the funniest text from Margaret on NYE—she must have been quite worse for wear—wishing James a happy New Year calling him 'Bobitty Bear,' although James says he doesn't recall that ever being a nickname from childhood.

KATE: I remember you said you think she's losing the plot a little . . .

BRIONY: Yeah, she needs to see a doctor as I'm sure it's all part of the dementia?

KATE: So how's Lucy? Kara was bombarding you with texts that night.

BRIONY: Fortunately, Lucy is now back in the marital home with her children. Unfortunately, however, her husband and pregnant (ex) lesbian lover, Abbie, are living with Abbie's parents, 'until they find something more permanent'. Abbie's parents, however, are thrilled, as they thought they would never get grandchildren from their (not so) gay only child—so at least someone's happy!

KATE: And what about you and James? I did notice he seemed quite stressed in Yorkshire—always checking his phone 👄

BRIONY: I'm going to suggest couple's counselling, Kate, to be honest. New year new start and all that. Got to be proactive about it all as I can't go through another year like this.

KATE: Wow. Well, it's good you've both acknowledged your relationship needs a little help

BRIONY: Oh, I haven't actually discussed this with James yet . . .

KATE: Ahhh . . .

BRIONY: And I've also made another decision.

KATE: You're not going to have another baby?

BRIONY: Are you insane? My vagina would never recover. No, now the boys are settled at school and that bit older, I've decided to get back into PR. I'm going to set up as a freelance. It can't have changed that much since we worked together BC?!

KATE: We never worked at BC. We worked at BD PR but never BC PR.

BRIONY: Before Children, Kate! Cosmo has even said he'd like to hire me to take over the PR for his wine business, so I already have my first client.

KATE: I didn't think you would EVER go back to PR! How is that going to work with Cosmo? Does he still have a soft spot for you because that could lead to trouble 😉

BRIONY: Maybe it will give James a kick up the arse seeing me back as a professional, working alongside successful men who might. Maybe I've lost my allure as far as he is concerned as I'm 'just' a wife and mother.

KATE: Talk to him soon, Bri. And ask him straight up about the internet porn addiction. Actually check his phone first to get proof and then ask him to see if he lies.

BRIONY: He deletes the history (I've checked). Porn addiction makes complete sense now.

KATE: I remember the mojito sodden evening spent Googling naked pics of Jonathan Rhys Meyers amongst other delights, and you cleared your history after that night!

BRIONY: That's not the same thing at all, Kate. That was genuine research.

FRIDAY 8TH JANUARY
SUBJECT: STARTING THE NEW YEAR AFRESH
Dear Celia

I write to you from Devon having been requested to look after the children urgently by Sarah who has had to rush off to Paris for some R&R. I suspect it was the stress of organising Christmas with little help from a rather truculent Briony which has caused this.

I do hope your journey back home was uneventful. After all, we've had enough 'events' to last us quite a while, I think? Arthur tells me the residents association are being relatively amenable after learning the advertising of our party was not our doing, but a misguided friend's. I would implore you to make use of your grandchildren and have some 'social media' lessons, as the constable told me it's called. I knew that smarty-pants phone of yours would lead to no good, Celia. However, as no charges are being pressed, we shall speak no more of this trifle and hopefully Arthur and Richard will have everything back spick and span by the time I return tonight. Speaking of Richard—I'm really not sure where he got the idea that the party was fancy dress? And what an odd fancy dress outfit it was! All that tight shiny rubber and the mask! Was he dressed as Batman, do you think, Celia? I can't imagine it was an easy outfit to get himself in or out of in his incapacitated condition.

I have heard from James that Briony has announced her intention to return to work after her 'career break'. Well, we shall see how that pans out. She hasn't worked since she had that silly job in London, before she and James moved back down to Dorset, and I'm not even sure you could call that a proper job, anyway. As far as I could gather she just swanned around drinking champagne at art gallery openings and the like. I'm not sure there is much call for that in our neck of the woods, and I shall make it quite clear I will not be used as an unpaid child-minder to the boys—I do have a life of my own and can't be expected to drop everything to drive over to look after the children just because she has some 'event' to attend. It's not as if they need the money, she's doing this to be bloody minded, Celia, you mark my words!

Fondests,
Margaret

SUNDAY 10TH JANUARY

WHATSAPP MESSAGE

GAYLE: Sorry, Bri, got to cancel lunch today—girls up vomming in the night. Next week perhaps?

BRIONY: No probs. Rather tired after being awoken in the night by what I thought were mating foxes. Turns out Cosmo had a lady friend over, according to James who went in the garden to scare the foxes away and realised it was cries of passion coming from his open window! Eek!

GAYLE: Eughh—grim! Jealous? Does this mean Cosmo has given up on you?

BRIONY: You know what Gayle, yes I did feel a bit put out, not least because I'm the sexually frustrated wife of an internet porn addict, and I thought when Cosmo said he'd hire me to handle the PR for his wine company the extra time I was spending with him might have rattled James into showing me a bit more attention. If he knows Cosmo has a girlfriend then he'll be less inclined to jealousy, dammit.

GAYLE: You need to talk to James, Bri. All this internet porn addiction thing is only speculation.

BRIONY: I had planned to this morning but he was acting rather smug which commenting about the 'howler' Cosmo was entertaining. Twunt. I can't stand him when he's being like that so thought I'd better leave the big chat for now.

GAYLE: Yes, go in even minded and level headed, Briony and don't go accusing him of anything as that will get his defences up. And forget about using Cosmo to make your husband jealous—that's not the way to go about it.

BRIONY: I am also quite intrigued as to who this girl Cosmo is seeing is—some young, airhead totty from London who he's brought down for the weekend I expect. I'm tempted to pop over in a bit with some excuse or other just so as I can have a nose . . .

GAYLE: Oh go on! You know you want to! Go hunting that vixen and report back with events to keep me amused whilst I douse the house in Dettol.

11.09am

BRIONY: OMFG! The fox/vixen!! I need a stiff drink NOW!

GAYLE: What's wrong?! Is she a Z list celeb? Tabloid totty? OMG don't tell me she was a he and charming Cosmo is in fact gay? Actually, that makes perfect sense as he's far too charming and well-dressed for a straight man.

BRIONY: Oh, rest assured, Gayle, James is certainly not gloating!

GAYLE: ??

BRIONY: The 'vixen' is neither young, nor Cosmo gay.

GAYLE: Stop drip feeding!

BRIONY: It's bloody Margaret! Margaret! I popped over on the pretence of discussing some PR strategies with Cosmo and there she was, bold as brass (yes, I'm aware I sound like my mother now).

GAYLE: Margaret? As in Margaret his mother?!

BRIONY: I think James thought someone had died by the dumbstruck look upon my pallid face as I stumbled back into the house with Margaret in hot pursuit. She's here now 'explaining' everything to James—who has the bewildered and disgusted expression a five-year-old might have after just being told the tooth fairy is the bastard love child of the Easter bunny and Santa.

GAYLE: Sweet baby Jesus! Cosmo has been shagging Margaret!

BRIONY: When I think back to all the times she was hanging around looking shifty and we thought she had the onset of dementia . . . and the sudden interest in lady-garden maintenance in her 60s. Eugh! Eugh! Eugh! Eugh! Eugh! Oh god, now it all makes sense . . .

GAYLE: And yet no sense at all . . .

BRIONY: Got to go—I need a front row seat for this.

3.52.pm

BRIONY: Okay, so, Margaret and Cosmo have departed for London. James spoke to his father, who, it has to be said, has taken the news in his stride to the point of appearing not at all bothered. I think he must be enjoying the break from her . . . ?!? I suppose you can't blame him.

GAYLE: I suppose this puts your chat to James on the backburner . . . again.

BRIONY: Of course. Any excuse not to sit down and talk to me . . .

THURSDAY 14TH JANUARY

WHATSAPP MESSAGE

BRIONY: James, I know you are not in a meeting. I know when that bloody secretary is lying to me. Call me immediately and please enlighten me as to why I have just signed for the delivery of one business class ticket to Hong Kong next month . . .

JAMES: Ah. Yes. Okay. I think we need to talk, Briony.

SUNDAY 17TH JANUARY

WHATSAPP GROUP MESSAGE

LUCY: So what exactly is going on, Briony?

KARA: And why didn't he discuss this with you before now?

KATE: He's a man, Kara, remember.

KARA: True.

GAYLE: Twunt

BRIONY: It's not that bad now I've had time to think about it.

LUCY: The company have been looking at setting up an office in the Far East for some time? And you didn't know about this?

BRIONY: Yes. Hong Kong to be exact. And as a founding director, it was going to fall on James to oversee this, so obviously, this has been a hugely stressful few months for him and he's been busy burning the candle at both ends in talks with real estate agents in HK negotiating office space in the best locations, marketing companies etc etc in order to pull this off.

KARA: And he didn't think to discuss this with you?!

LUCY: Stop defending him, Briony. It's a shitty thing to do. He should have discussed this with you.

KATE: You've been stressed to fuck yourself, remember, thinking your marriage was over. You thought he was a crack addict!

BRIONY: YOU thought he was a crack addict, Kate!

KATE: You thought he was a porn addict, Briony!

BRIONY: Only because you convinced me of that, Kate!

LUCY: ANYWAY! What are you going to do??

BRIONY: We've been talking about it a lot over the past two days now as he's flying out next month to meet some people he's been communicating with over the last few months (Mindy Chan being the lady who has been skyping with him—yes, attractive but also happily married with a young son). He knows he's been a dick not to have discussed this with me from the start.

KARA: So is this why he's been burning the midnight oil and holed up in his study with the door firmly shut?

BRIONY: Yeah. Well, but he said had I known I would have got either too excited at a possible move to exotic climes, or too pissed off having been so excited to move to Birch Cottage knowing another move might be on the cards.

KATE: Yep, that's fucked up man logic alright!

BRIONY: Anyway, I'm not going to disrupt the boys from their friends and god knows I'm not risking losing their places at secondary school now we're in this great catchment.

GAYLE: So after all this stress and secrecy he's not even going?

BRIONY: Actually, we've decided that James will be going to Hong Kong for a few months as planned.

KARA: Without you?

BRIONY: I'm used to him working away on business and he'll be back every few weeks.

LUCY: Wow . . .

BRIONY: But also, I'm not prepared to put my career on hold any longer, and I need to start taking back control of my life, so the freelance PR is still go, although I may need to re-think having Cosmo as my first client since he's bopping my mother-in-law . . .

GAYLE: Oh, I don't know. Keep it in the family and all that 😊

KATE: Arf!

KARA: Well, this isn't going to help your lack of sex life, Bri.

KATE: Rubbish! Cyber sex, dick pics and sexting will add a new element to it. Dave and I are at it all the time.

LUCY: Dave? I thought it was Piers?

KATE: No, Piers and I broke up. Things have got serious really quickly with Dave and I.

MELISSA: So you're sexting my father-in-law, Kate. Marvellous.

LUCY: Ohhhhh.

KATE: Don't speak to your potential step-mother like that, Melissa.

BRIONY: Aren't you annulled yet, Melissa?

MELISSA: Evidently not.

BRIONY: Well, yes, anyway, we'll have to indulge in a bit of cyber sex—time zone permitting of course.

KARA: I think cyber-sex is already passé, Bri. But def go for dick pics and sexting. Actually, maybe ask your mother-in-law what sexual practices are en-vogue now—after all, it would appear she's been having a more active and frenetic sex life than all of us this past year!

BRIONY: Yes, thank you, Kara. Thank you very much for reminding me . . .

Anyway, enough of this idle chatter, I have a PR business to set up . . .

ACKNOWLEDGEMENTS

Although the characters, scenarios and places are fictional, this book could never have been possible if it were not for the generosity of friends who trusted me to use creative licence with their own true stories and anecdotes.

Special thanks to: Frances, G-Gurl, Jane, Jo, Karon and Zoe for all the support, and fragile ego bolstering.

To Sarah Darby for turning my discombobulated thoughts and ideas into a fantabulous book cover; for her quirky chapter header illustrations and for guiding me through the whole process with immense patience!

And extra special thanks to Emma Staples for being my emotional fluffer.

ABOUT THE AUTHOR

Having spent her formative years getting up to mischief and seeking adventures around the world, Purbeck Wintour now lives in Dorset with her two sons, where she works as a PR consultant and writer. Her debut novel, *The Ordinarily Extraordinary Life of Briony*; written to unleash the humour of the infuriatingly frustrating scenarios of her own, and friends' lives, became a Kindle top three bestseller.

In her free time, Purbeck can be found cycling around forests pretending to be in pop videos, and walking along beaches, seeking inspiration for turning the ordinary into the extraordinary, whilst writing her next novel . . .

TO BE CONTINUED . . .

Briony Denley returns for more ordinarily extraordinary adventures in 2017 . . .

Things just got even more extraordinary for Briony Denley . . .

When not entirely unforeseen events take an unexpected turn, Briony's life once again becomes a plethora of chaos, mayhem and madness, in the much-anticipated sequel to *The Ordinarily Extraordinary Life of Briony*.

Having set up her own boutique PR agency and taken on the chain-smoking, OCD suffering, yet irrepressibly enthusiastic, Flora, as her P.A., Briony sets about raising the profile of local lothario horticulturist, 'Gardening Bob,' who has delusions of usurping Monty Don as the upper-crust housewives' favourite.

If juggling work and home life with two hormone-ridden sons wasn't hectic enough, Briony's pal, Kate, seeks comfort after her father elopes to Thailand; Lucy finds herself left holding the babies after her ex-lesbian lover, Abbie, inconveniently suffers a mid-life crisis, and there's some very odd new neighbours to welcome to Little Mistford . . .

Facebook.com/PurbeckWintour

@PurbeckWintour

@PurbeckWintour

www.purbeckwintour.com